SOLOMON'S TREASURE

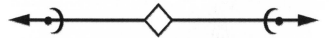

THE PRIEST'S SECRET

Book 2 of the TOMB, the TEMPLE, the TREASURE
Ben Hammott

The PRIEST'S SECRET is the sequel to BEGINNINGS

SOLOMON'S TREASURE BOOK 2
THE PRIEST'S SECRET
Book 2 of the TOMB, the TEMPLE, the TREASURE
Ben Hammott

Copyright 2019 ©Ben Hammott
2019 Revised Edition
All rights reserved
ISBN: 9781720008057

Author can be contacted at: **benhammott@gmail.com**
www.benhammottbooks.com

Note from Author

The story you are about to read continues from Solomon's Treasure - Beginnings - Book 1 of the Tomb, the Temple, the Treasure, and includes the novelization of some of the Myths and Legends associated with the tiny hilltop village of Rennes-le-Chateau and the surrounding countryside. Most of the locations mentioned in this book are real locations, including the caves. The rest is from the author's imagination.

CHAPTER 1

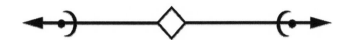

France

WHEN BEN INCREASED the wipers to maximum speed, it did little to improve his vision through the rain pounding the windscreen. The headlights highlighting every drop caught in the car's bright lights were another hindrance. At least the heater, whirring away noisily on full blast, prevented the glass he peered through from misting. His eyes scanned the roadside for the turning, which according to his instructions he gripped in one hand, should be around here somewhere. Suddenly, out of the gloom, the headlights swept over a wooden sign with two words in black, faded paint, CHATEAU DEUX TOURS, (Castle Two Towers). It was the location he sought. Failing to assess the danger of the maneuver he was about to perform, Ben braked and aimed the car at the entrance. The tires struggled to find traction on the rain-slick tarmac and skidded. Ben cursed and quickly brought the car back under control, but not before nearly demolishing the house-sign in the process, which now stood at a skew-whiff angle. Ben continued along the gravel track.

The branches of the tall trees growing both sides of the long driveway met overhead and gave the effect of driving through a leafy tunnel. Sheltered from the rain by the thick foliage of overhanging branches, Ben switched the wipers to a slower setting. When he emerged from under the tree canopy into a clearing centered on a large fountain, he slowed the car and gazed at the large house alluded to by the property's entrance sign. Though small by French Château standards, it was still an impressive three-story stone dwelling dotted with Gothic arched windows. Years of ivy growth almost covered the front of the house, its tendrils ever searching for new footholds in the soft mortar joints between the large stone blocks would, if not checked, eventually, grow to smother the whole house. The creeping plant already stretched to the top of one of the two imposing round towers set at each corner of the front façade of the house, which Ben assumed was the reason for its name.

As he drove closer, Ben noticed the woodwork not concealed by ivy had once been painted green, but now much had peeled off in large flakes and revealed the bare wood it had initially been applied to protect. The water in the circular fountain gushed from the mouths of three strange fish positioned back to back in the center. The streams ejected from their mouths formed three wet arcs that splashed into the large oyster-shaped bowl of its base. The steady streams of water, occasionally blown off course by wind gusts, glinted and sparkled in the car's headlamp beams as Ben circled around and parked next to the house.

After switching off the headlights, Ben gazed at the only source of light piercing the darkness, the dim glow from a yellow bulb filtering through the grimy porch windows.

Ben killed the engine, retrieved his coat from the rear seat and slipped it on. Protected from the rain, he climbed out and stretched his limbs; glad to be free from the confined space after the long drive from the airport. He beeped the car locked and approached the porch.

As he passed the fountain, Ben noticed, like the woodwork on the house, it had also suffered from prolonged neglect. The water was green with algae that stained the stone wherever it made contact, and its damp scent tainted the air.

Ben halted at the porch and peered through the grimy glass at a large, arched wooden door of Gothic design; it looked as solid as the day it was built two hundred years before. A turn of the rusty handle revealed the door was firmly locked. A search for a knocker or bell to announce his presence, unveiled one all but hidden under the encroaching ivy, perhaps an indication visitors were a rarity to this address. A tug on the antique bell pull, which to Ben's surprise still worked, resulted in a faint jingling of the attached bell from within the depths of the house. Faint footsteps grew gradually louder as their owner approached the other side of the door.

While he waited, Ben thought back to the emails that had brought him here, to stand in the rain at the door of what can only be described as a spooky house, somewhere in France, many hundreds of miles from his home, about to meet a total stranger. Their only contact had been through emails, the subject of which was the content of Ben's website, which informed anyone interested enough to seek it out, about the possible ancient tomb he'd discovered. Ben had posted pictures of it, as well as other information concerned with the Rennes-le-Château Mystery. It was after visiting his website that the man he was about to meet had decided to contact him. Ben had only received his first email yesterday.

Hello Ben, I have seen the Tomb photographs on your website, and it would be unwise for you to reveal the location of this tomb you've found.

Ben wasn't surprised by the message, he'd received similar. It was probably another crank seeking attention. However, as he made a point of replying to all emails, he wrote: "Why, and who are you?"

My name is not important, but the world is not ready.

Ben smiled, definitely a crank, but he decided to probe further.

"Ready for what?"

What's in the tomb!

"So you think you know what is in the tomb?"

Yes! It must not be revealed at this time because it will cause too much harm.

"What do you think is in the tomb that's so important? Why can't it be revealed and who will it harm?"

I cannot say, but it's more important than you could ever imagine.

"Please enlighten me."

I cannot!

"Then you've given me no reason not to reveal the location in due course. I've received other emails similar to yours, from people saying they either know where the tomb is or what or whose body is inside, but none of them ever do."

I'm not like them! I am not someone seeking attention or attempting to get you to reveal the location to me.

Ben grew bored. "If you're not going to give me any more information, I see no reason to carry on this conversation. Goodbye."

Ben stared at the screen waiting for a reply. None was forthcoming. It seemed his assertions had been correct. He glanced at the wall clock; it was time for dinner. He was sure he had some sausages in the fridge and went to find out.

When Ben returned to his computer an hour later, he saw the flashing email icon on his computer screen. He opened the email; it was from the crank again.

Okay, Ben, I feel I have no other choice but to reveal more to you if you are to take me seriously.

Ben smiled as he read on.

My grandfather was the Abbé, Rivière, whom I am sure you know, was the priest that heard Saunière's deathbed confession.

Ben stopped smiling.

So shocked was my grandfather by what Saunière had told him that it tormented his soul. Though he could never reveal what was said under the secrecy of the confession he felt, nevertheless, that it was too important not to be passed on, so he wrote it down. I am now in possession of what he wrote and believe me it is, in parts, shocking.

Now he had definitely caught Ben's attention.

I would be willing to show you this because I think this may be the only way to convince you that the Tomb's location must remain a secret. I have attached a file that will, I hope, prove I am genuine.

Ben re-read the message. If this person did have a copy of Saunière's deathbed confession, apart from being extremely interesting, it could prove an invaluable addition for his book. Intrigued, and a little excited, Ben downloaded the attached file and opened it. It was a photograph of an open suitcase; inside were many papers. The notebook that lay on top was what held Ben's attention. He zoomed in to read the name on its cover. Inscribed in gold embossed script was the name of the priest who had taken Saunière's confession. He stared at the book. It could easily be a forgery or something put together in Photoshop. However, if it were genuine, the information it contained could be invaluable for his research. Perhaps it would reveal exactly what Saunière had been up to. The only way to be sure would be to physically examine it.

Ben clicked on the reply button and typed: "I'm intrigued, though I'll need to see it for myself before I'm entirely convinced. Can we meet? Where are you, which country?"

The stranger's reply was instant.

Yes, we can meet, but with one condition; you tell no one of this or our meeting. This is for your safety as well as mine. I live in France.

Ben replied: "I agree. Send me your address, and I'll fly out tomorrow if that's convenient? What's your name?"

The man promptly replied with his name, and address and Ben had booked an afternoon flight for the following day.

CHAPTER 2

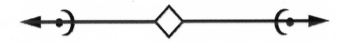

Jon Creed

THE SOUND OF the door bolt drawn back returned Ben to the present. He wondered what Jon Creed would look like. Having never heard his voice, he had no clear picture in mind. However, after seeing where the man lived Ben hoped Creed didn't have bolts through his neck or two elongated front teeth. The door opened slightly, and someone peered out from the shadowy interior. It did nothing to lessen Ben's nervousness.

"Who's there?" The man's voice was thick with a heavy French accent.

"It's me." Ben replied, but immediately realized what a stupid reply it was and quickly added, "Ben, Ben Harper. I have a meeting with Jon Creed."

The door opened wider. A man stepped into the dim, yellow glow of the porch and stared at him.

"Passport," the man demanded, as he gazed past Ben and around the driveway.

Just as chatty as his emails. Ben held his passport against the dirty glass. The man studied the photo and Ben's face to compare the two. Satisfied with the match, he unlocked the porch door and held it open.

"Hello." Ben politely held out his hand in greeting but found it ignored.

"Inside," ordered the Frenchman.

Ben found himself half pushed through the front door while the man shut and locked the porch door before stepping hastily into the house. The sounds of the closing door and heavy bolts sliding into place echoed around the dark hallway.

Though glad to be out of the rain and cold, Ben felt little comfort. His nervousness at being in a foreign country in a house with a strange man locking his only visible means of escape, a place that no one knew where he was, increased rapidly. *Why do I always get myself into these situations?*

It was true. Throughout his life, Ben had often ignored the danger signals his senses warned him of. Acting in haste, he'd become embroiled in many nightmarish situations that on occasion made him fear for his life; he hoped this wouldn't be another.

After the entrance door had been securely locked, the man headed along the hall to a door where a sliver of light escaped from the gap at the bottom.

Light spilled into the hallway when the man opened the door. "Come inside," he called out.

Said the spider to the fly. Ben glanced at the bolted front door. Maybe he'd made a mistake in coming here and should make his escape while he still could.

"Come on, Ben, what are you waiting for?" asked the man, confused as to why his guest remained in the hall.

Having lost his chance, Ben sighed and walked towards the man who so far hadn't reassured him he wasn't dealing with an oddball. He entered the room, and the man closed the door behind him.

To Ben's surprise, the room was warm, cozy and bright. Flames crackled in a large stone fireplace. Antique furniture and ornaments adorned the wood-paneled room. Ben was startled by the man's hand that touched him on the shoulder.

"Sorry about all the cloak and dagger stuff, but I have to be careful." He held out his hand and smiled. "I'm the crank you've come to meet, Jon Creed." Ben clasped the Frenchman's hand. "Welcome to my home, Ben."

Ben ended the handshake "Thanks, Jon."

"Call me Creed, everyone else does." He pointed to an armchair. "Please, sit while I fix us both a drink...and Ben, you don't have to look so worried. I'm not really a crank, you're safe here."

That's easy for to him to say, Ben thought, it's a *pity his actions so far are in direct contrast with his words.* He sat down on a comfortable armchair positioned against the wall; no one was going to sneak up behind him.

"What's your poison, Ben?" Creed asked, with a smile.

He's doing it on purpose. "Vodka, if you have it?"

"Sorry, no vodka, only wine or whiskey."

"Whiskey will be fine, with a little water."

Creed poured the drinks and Ben took it gratefully. Creed sat on the matching couch opposite. Fighting the thought the whiskey might be drugged, Ben took a sip. Though not a great whiskey drinker, after his trip to Rosslyn and meeting Malloch, he'd begun to get the taste for the strong drink.

"Have you arranged anywhere to stay yet?" Creed asked.

"No, I came straight here."

"Because you were eager to read the notebook," Creed guessed correctly. "You can stay here. I've made up a room just in case."

Ben was reluctant to stay in a strange house with an even stranger man. "I don't want to put you to any trouble."

Creed must have noticed Ben's lack of enthusiasm. "It's no trouble, I assure you. It's already done. Also, the door can be locked from the inside. Besides, we have much to discuss and more time to do it in if you remain here."

Ben inwardly sighed. "Thank you."

"Now, before we go on, I think I'd better explain my side of the story, perhaps then you'll be able to relax and begin to trust me. By telling you what I'm about to, I'm putting my trust in you, a man I know practically nothing about. I've known about the Tomb less time than you have, I only found out six months ago when my father was murdered; he was beaten to death.

"Murdered! By whom?" If this were Creed's idea of relaxing him, he'd failed miserably.

"The police never found out who was responsible, or the motive. Though it's obvious to me, he was killed for the Tomb's location, but the local gendarmes know nothing about this. Even though nothing was taken, they still attributed the murder to a botched robbery."

"Aren't you worried *they* will come after you?"

Creed shrugged, "I'm certain they'll try, but I'm not an old man like my father and won't be so easy to kill. Besides, I've taken precautions."

"Such as?"

"Please don't concern yourself, Ben. You need not worry about me or your own safety while you're here."

But Ben was concerned. "What about when I leave?"

"If you've followed my instructions and kept our meeting secret, you'll be in no more danger than you were before you arrived."

Though Creed spoke excellent English, the words he used had the habit of unsettling Ben.

"Anyway, to continue with my story, with my father's death I inherited my grandfather's papers and also instructions from my father as to what to do with them. He also left strict orders to keep them and the tomb secret. However, at first, I wasn't entirely convinced the tomb existed, or if it did, that it contained what my father believed was inside."

"What changed your mind?"

"You!"

"Me? How?"

"I came across your website showing the interior of the Tomb. Imagine my shock at seeing almost exactly what was described in my family's documents. It proved to me that the tomb was real. I was then horrified to see you were writing a book that would reveal its location."

"That's only because there's hardly anything left. The priest Saunière seems to have taken the best stuff; I'm not going to risk prison by digging into the tomb for a few trinkets and some old bones. I can understand the importance of the tomb historically. After all, how many Templar tombs, if that's what it is, have been found? But for someone to go as far as murder to find out where it is, I find that hard to believe."

"I don't want to ruin the surprise for you but, although it does involve the Knights Templar, it's not a Templar knight who's interred there."

"Then who?" Ben took another sip of whiskey.

"When you've read my grandfather's notebook you will understand. As you can see, all of this has been thrust upon me. Before my father's death, I'd no idea he was the guardian of a great secret."

"But how did your father's killer find out if it was a secret?"

A sad expression formed on Creed's face. "My father made a grave mistake. When he first found out about my grandfather's secret, he took the journal to show a good friend of his in Paris. They'd arranged to meet at his house to discuss the contents of the notebook."

Creed recounted the full story.

Pascal had barely enough time to jump aboard and slam the door shut before the train began to pull out of the station. He looked back at the entrance. The two men who had followed him dashed onto the platform. The stationmaster, who tried to block their way and demanded they produced their boarding tickets, was pushed roughly aside and he tumbled to the ground. The handful of already collected tickets fell from his hand and blown about playfully by the wind. The stationmaster glared angrily after the two men who sprinted along the platform after the train.

Much to the annoyance of its owner, one of the men dashing along the platform tripped over his suitcase and fell to the ground. His momentum carried him over the edge and onto the track the train had departed a moment earlier.

The remaining pursuer drew level with the door of the end carriage and glared at his quarry he sensed watching him from within the train's dim interior. He reached out as the train increased its speed. His fingertips brushed the handle when it was pulled from his reach. Realizing his efforts were in vain, the man slowed to a halt and with a final glance after the departing train, turned and walked back to where his partner climbed back onto the platform.

Without a word and ignoring the ravings of the angry ticket collector, the two men left the station.

Pascal let out a relieved sigh. He turned away from the door and walked along the carriage, peering through the windows of the small compartments until he found one almost empty. He entered and nodded to the only other person occupying the stuffy cubicle, receiving a weak, courteous nod in reply before the man returned his attention to his newspaper. Pascal chose a position by the window and sat down; finally, he was able to relax.

Finding the compartment warm, Pascal removed his hat and coat and placed them on top of the briefcase on the seat beside him. He was well aware the men were after the contents of the case. He shouldn't have removed the journal from its place of safety, but after learning of the secret he'd inherited from his father, Pascal wasn't sure what to do with it. The burden of the revelation contained in the journal's pages had weighed heavy on his shoulders and led him to seek advice. Unaware others suspected the journal existed and would go to any lengths to gain possession, he had contacted his good friend Antoine Bassult, professor of archaeology at the Paris Museum. A man he held in high regard and someone Pascal knew could be trusted. But the chance to share it with someone, to discuss what should be done, had made Pascal careless, a mistake he would never make again.

Pascal stared out at the landscape rushing by and thought back to how different it might have turned out if when he suspected he was being followed, he hadn't taken the precaution of slipping into the bushes that grew in the garden of Antoine's house.

A short time ago...

Pascal waited until the footsteps he'd heard following him since he left the station passed him by before peeking out from behind the bushes where he'd concealed himself. The man he believed was following him walked down the street, crossed to the other side and entered one of the houses. Pascal smiled at his foolishness. He was about to step out when a raised voice caused him to turn and look at the window of Antoine's house. He froze at what he saw, the shadow of a man, a gun clearly visible in his hand, silhouetted on the thin curtain drawn across the window.

Cautiously, Pascal moved closer and peered through a thin gap between the curtains. His friend Antoine was tied to a chair; the look of fear clearly etched on his face. The armed man walked to-and-fro past his prisoner and gestured menacingly with the weapon as he talked.

"If you don't do as…"

Antoine caught sight of his friend's face in the curtain gap and shouted. "Run! Run for your life…"

A slap around the face with the pistol silenced his outburst. The gunman rushed to the window and threw back the curtains, bathing Pascal in light. The two men stared at each other. The smile that formed on the man's thin lips wasn't conveyed to his dark eyes staring straight into Pascal's; they radiated menace.

Pascal sensed this man was someone to be feared. Awash with guilt at leaving Antoine in the hands of such a man, he fled.

The man rushed from the room and out onto the street. He glanced at Pascal fleeing with his coat flapping behind him, one hand held his hat on his head as he ran and the briefcase; the object of the man's gaze, held down at his side. The man rushed across the street and waved to a car concealed in the shadows down a side turning. The cigarette flicked out of the driver's side window left a trail of red hot ash when it struck the ground and rolled to a standstill. The sound of the car's engine starting on the first turn of the key broke the silence. The two men inside were revealed when the car pulled into the streetlights.

The gunman bent down and spoke through the car's open window when it stopped alongside him. "Our man is escaping, get after him," he ordered. He pointed at the taxi Pascal hailed at the end of the road. "Don't lose him. I must have that journal."

The driver glanced at the man climbing into the taxi. "What about Pascal?"

"I don't care a fuck about him, just bring me that suitcase."

The car accelerated and roared along the road. The gunman watched them go. With a squeal of tires, the car turned left at the T-junction in pursuit of the taxi. Confident they would be successful he returned to the house, closed the front door and entered the room where his prisoner was confined. He let out a scream of frustration. The rope used to bind Antoine was on the floor beside the now empty chair.

When a rustling brought Pascal back to the present, he observed the man opposite fold his newspaper, place it on the seat beside him and close his eyes. Pascal turned back to the scenery rushing by. Before long, lulled by the steady motion of the train, his fellow passenger drifted asleep; his intermittent snoring filled the compartment. Pascal glanced at his watch. An hour to go before he'd have to change trains. He stared out of the window and tried unsuccessfully to ignore the man's snoring.

Dread etched Pascal's features when he recognized that one of the cars driving along the road— which at times ran parallel with the train track— was the one that had chased his taxi. Though too far away to make out the details of its two occupants, there was no mistaking the vehicle. Having failed to catch him before he boarded the train, the men must be heading for the next station to intercept him. The car pulled ahead of the train and became lost from sight behind a steep nettle covered bank.

Frantic with worry, Pascal glanced down at the ground speeding by in a blur of motion; the train traveled too fast for him to risk jumping off. He was trapped. He desperately tried to think of an escape plan. A closer examination of the sleeping man revealed him to be of a similar build. Pascal believed the men couldn't have caught a good look at him, so it was doubtful they'd recognize him, except perhaps by his clothes. The briefcase, or more importantly, the journal inside, was what they were after. As far as he knew they weren't planning to hurt him, not if they got their hands on the briefcase, or thought they had.

Carefully, so as not to wake the sleeping man, he swapped his fawn hat and coat for the man's black attire. The man's briefcase, though a similar color and size, was not an exact match, but as it was on his lap, Pascal couldn't risk swapping it in case he awoke. Again, Pascal doubted the men would recognize the difference. He quietly left the carriage and walked to the front of the train, where he found a seat in an almost full compartment.

Ten minutes later, the train slowed when it pulled into the next station. Pascal lowered the hat over his eyes and looked out at the two men waiting on the platform. As soon as they'd passed by the window of his compartment, Pascal entered the hallway. The train lurched to a halt. He waited while some of the passengers disembarked and hiding amongst a group of businessmen, exited the train and made his way across the platform. The two men studied everyone that alighted. Satisfied their quarry was still on the train, they waited until the last possible moment before they climbed aboard just as it began to pull away.

Though Pascal's plan had worked, he hoped he hadn't put the sleeping man in danger. He believed the men would snatch the briefcase and warn the man to silence until they reached the next station and returned for their car.

Pascal showed his train ticket to the inspector and slipped out of the station. Parked askew across the road from the entrance was the thugs' car. He casually walked over, peered inside and smiled. The men had been in such a hurry to intercept the train they'd left the key in the ignition. Pascal climbed into the driver's seat and drove away from the station. This time he'd been lucky. He would be sure never to make the same mistake again.

The two boys scrambled over the sun-bleached wooden fence erected to stop people wandering onto the train line at the bottom of the embankment. Michel and André slid down the grassy bank and stopped a few feet from the twin set of tracks that carried trains far across the country. They both stared into the dark mouth of the tunnel a short distance away, where in five minutes the eastbound train would exit. They each pulled a coin from their pockets and smiled at each other. Tomorrow at school they would be the envy of class when they showed off the coins flattened by a speeding train. It would be far more impressive than the smelly chicken foot Thomas had brought into school earlier today, even if it did make the girls scream when he pulled one of the tendons to make its toes move. What they were doing had a sense of danger. Anyone could go to the butcher's and ask for an old chicken foot.

Michel, twelve years old and born the same year as André, was slightly older by four months. He stepped across the first rail, knelt and placed his coin on the far track, while André placed his on the one nearest to him.

André placed a hand on the top of the smooth metal track worn by the passage of hundreds of trains transporting people across France. "I can feel it vibrating."

Michel copied him. "I wonder how far away it is."

André shrugged. "It must be quite close, I suppose. Can you hear it?"

Michel nodded. "It's getting louder." He lifted his head and glanced at the tunnel. "It will soon be here."

As if to emphasize Michel's words, the coins rattled on the tracks.

André climbed to his feet. "We'd better move out of the way."

Michel stepped back across the track as André scrambled up the bank and started climbing up after him, but stopped on hearing a chinking noise behind him. He turned his head and stared down at the rails. André's coin was still where he'd placed it, but his own was nowhere in sight. *It must have vibrated off.* He jumped back down and leaped across the nearest rail. His haste caused him to land awkwardly, and his foot slipped on the loose stones packed between the wooden sleepers. He lost his balance and fell; his head struck the metal track.

André had witnessed his friend fall, and when Michel made no attempt to get up, he rushed down the bank and knelt beside him. Blood oozed from a cut on Michel's head and dripped on the metal track it rested on. Unsure what to do, André frantically shook his friend in an attempt to wake him. The train would arrive at any moment.

"Michel! Michel! Please wake up, the train's coming," he screamed anxiously.

The tracks increased vibrations indicated the train was almost upon them. He grabbed Michel under the arms and straining with the effort, dragged his limp form over to the embankment as the train entered the far end of the tunnel.

Michel awoke, looked at André and then glanced at the tracks. "Where's my coin?" He tried to stand but winced with the pain throbbing in his head.

"Stay there," ordered André. "I'll get it." He jumped across the track and scrambled amongst the stones for Michel's lost coin.

Michel glanced into the tunnel. The train was already halfway through. "Leave it, André. There's no time."

André smiled when he plucked the coin from amongst the stones and triumphantly held it up. He glanced at the train when it blasted from the tunnel. He quickly placed it on the rail and snatched away his hand as the metal wheels whooshed past with a terrific roar, drowning out Michel's shout of alarm; he was sure his friend had been struck.

The train clattered past for what seemed like ages to Michel, but in reality, was only a few seconds. When it had finally passed, he saw his friend lying unmoving on the ground. Then slowly, André lifted his head and smiled back at his friend.

Michel let out a sigh of relief.

Suddenly, André screamed and stared at something on the ground beside him. Michel climbed to his feet to discover the cause of André's distress; the body of a man with a knife sticking from his throat. A trickle of blood ran from the fatal wound and dripped onto the stones, staining them red. Michel rushed over to André and helped him to his feet. They retrieved their now flattened coins, scrambled up the embankment and back over the fence. Without stopping they ran straight to the local police station and told them about their gruesome discovery.

The children at school the following day were duly impressed, and Thomas's rapidly decaying chicken foot was soon forgotten and discarded in a waste bin. It wasn't Michel and André's flattened coins that held everyone's attention—they would save them for another day—it was the gruesome descriptions that grew more horrific with every telling of the dead body they had seen.

Though a comprehensive investigation was carried out into the murder, the killer's identity was never discovered. The last person to see him alive, apart from his killer, was the ticket inspector, who had to wake the passenger up to punch his ticket. When interviewed, the ticket inspector remembered the man was complaining that someone had stolen…no, not stolen, swapped his hat and coat. He really hadn't taken much notice as people were always losing stuff on trains.

The only clue the police had to go on, which led them to believe robbery was the motive, was the object found clutched in the dead man's hand; a handle torn from a briefcase that couldn't be found. Unbeknownst to the attackers, the reason the man wouldn't let them take the case had nothing to do with a journal. It was due to something he had purchased on his trip away; a set of crayons, a coloring book, and a small doll, presents he had promised for his four-year-old daughter's birthday the following day.

When Pascal learned of the murder, he was struck with remorse. He tracked down the dead man's wife and sent her a check for one hundred thousand pounds from a company bank account he'd set up in England. The included letter he had penned, explained the money was from a private life insurance payout her husband had arranged. Though this did nothing to lessen the guilt that plagued him, Pascal hoped it would help the family manage in the difficult times ahead. He swore he would never put another innocent soul in danger.

Creed paused and sipped his whiskey.

"After that incident my grandfather went to great lengths to conceal the trail leading to him, even faking his own death and changing the family name to Creed. According to my father's papers, there was a persistent rumor my grandfather knew Saunière's secret from his confession and may have written it down. A secret society called Rex Deus, which I'm sure you've heard of..."

Ben nodded. "...Yes, from a book I read a while ago, *Rex Deus: The True Mystery of Rennes-Le-Château and the Dynasty of Jesus*, in which the authors developed the hypothesis that a Jesus and Mary Magdalene Bloodline was part of a shadow dynasty descended from twenty-four high priests of the Temple in Jerusalem, collectively known as *Rex Deus* – the *Kings of God.*"

"Well, Ben, you know more than me, but whatever their origins, it seems they've waited hundreds of years for something to come into their possession. It's likely that whatever this object is, it's in the tomb you found, or at least they believe it to be. I did some investigating and found out a few years ago the Rex Deus had a new leader. He is, by all accounts, a man ruthless in his endeavors to get his hands on any information that will lead him to the secret they had sought for so long. I expect when they found out about the tomb from your website, they took steps to discover its location. It's likely you have been watched and perhaps still are. It's a certainty they'll not let you reveal its location while the object of their quest remains inside." Creed looked at Ben. "Now I've told you everything, it's time for you to decide what to do, stay or leave?" Creed drained his glass and stood. "Do you want a refill?"

Ben drained his glass and held it out. After what he'd just heard, he needed one. As Creed refreshed the drinks, Ben digested this new information. It confirmed the rumors and his past experiences that there were many shady characters involved in the Rennes-Le-Château mystery. The many unexplained deaths and unsolved murders over the years of people involved in the enigma were well documented and mentioned in many books about Rennes-Le-Château. Some even believed Saunière's death wasn't the result of natural causes. The involvement of secret societies in these deaths thus far had only been hinted at. The Society of the Rose Croix—not to be confused with the Rosicrucian order, said to have been founded in late medieval Germany by Christian Rosenkreuz—Rex Deus, the Masons, the Knights Templar and, perhaps the most well-known, thanks to the highly successful Da Vinci Code book and film, the Priory of Sion.

Ben knew from his encounter with Abe and Isaac, members of the Order of Black Eagles, how fanatical these so-called secret organizations can become. The news that others were also after what he'd found and would murder to obtain it caused him concern. Though the stakes had definitely risen with what Creed had revealed, he was reassured by the man's relaxed manner. After all, Creed was well aware of the danger he was in; his father was killed because of it, and yet, it seemed to cause him little concern.

As far as Ben could see he had two choices left open to him, leave now with nothing, or stay and perhaps find out all the answers to the questions he had searched so long for. *But what to do about the tomb?* If he did decide to keep it a secret, what was he to tell everyone who had already seen it on his website?

The book was also nearing its release date. Ben could, of course, put it on hold while he carried out more research, which wasn't a lie. If it came to it, he could expose it as a hoax, but that would ruin what little reputation he had. Even if he did leave now, there would be no guarantee he would be safe. These Rex Deus fanatics could easily come after him wherever he was. He then remembered the furtive manner in which Creed had greeted him at the door, perhaps evidence Creed believed he was already under surveillance, or why all the cloak and dagger antics. Maybe, unaware of the situation, he might have been followed here as he wasn't aware of the danger. At that time he had no reason to. He decided to stay and see how it panned out. If he left now, he would always wonder what might have been.

Creed handed Ben the replenished glass of whiskey.

"Thank you for your honesty, Creed. You need not have mentioned the Rex Deus and the threat they represent, knowing that it may have frightened me off, but you did, and I appreciate that. If I did leave, I'm not sure that would place me in any safer position than here with you. At least you're aware of what and who we are up against. Together we stand more of a chance to see this through to the end, whatever outcome fate holds in store for us."

"I agree," said Creed.

"However, before I make a decision on keeping the tomb a secret, I will need to read Rivière's journal."

"I would expect nothing less."

Ben began to relax for the first time since he had entered the house. Whether it was due to the fine whiskey coursing through his bloodstream, Creed's friendly manner, or both, he wasn't sure. He was a good judge of character and had learned over the years to trust his judgment. His senses told him the aura of trust and friendship emanating from Creed was genuine. Furthermore, he was beginning to like the Frenchman, and it would make a pleasant change to work with someone. He could have done with help when he faced the murderous twins at Rosslyn.

"If you do decide to keep the tomb's location a secret, we will have another decision to make. What to do with it. My father had dabbled with the idea of moving the artifacts inside to a safer place, in case someone like you, or worst Rex Deus or another interested party, discovered it."

Ben was skeptical. If it were that easy to get inside, he would have entered the tomb himself. "Even if access is possible, what location is any safer then where the artifacts have been for hundreds of years?"

"If we decide to go down that path we can discuss the details later after you have reached a decision."

"I assume, from reading your grandfathers journal, you're aware of the tomb's location?"

Creed took something from his jacket pocket and handed it to Ben. It was a photograph. The subject of which Ben instantly recognized; the entrance of the cave that hid the tomb's location.

"You don't have to confirm it is the location; that can wait until you're ready to trust me. I imagine you must be feeling disappointed you're not the only one who knows, but unlike you, who had to solve Saunière's church clues to find the tomb, I only had to read my grandfather's notebook. I still find it quite amazing that you managed to locate it, as I have discovered my family has gone to great lengths to prevent this."

Ben handed back the photo. "In what way?"

Creed placed his glass on the coffee table and crossed to the large oak cupboard standing in one corner of the room. As he passed the roaring fire, he threw the photo into the flames. It shriveled and burnt, and within seconds it was grey, flaky ash. Creed took a small cardboard box out from the cupboard, carried it back to the table and placed it in front of Ben before sitting back down.

Ben stared at the plain cardboard box. There were no markings to hint at its contents.

"Have a look inside. I'm certain you will find its contents...fascinating." Creed smiled.

Intrigued, Ben put down his drink, shifted forward in the seat and lifted up the box flaps. Surprise spread across his face on spying the object he instantly recognized. He lifted the delicate object out and turned it in his hands. Ben locked eyes with a demon. He hardly believed he held the original face of the Asmodeus demon figure that stood inside the entrance of Saunière's church. It had been smashed and stolen many years ago after someone had hacked it off. One of its glass eyes was missing, the scrape marks around the socket tell-tale signs it had been gouged out by someone who believed it to be a precious stone.

"You did this?" Ben asked in amazement. He never thought it possible he would ever gaze upon the original face of Saunière's demon other than from a photograph.

Creed held up his hands in defense and shook his head. "Not me, my father. It was done to protect the secret, or so he thought. He had tried to decipher the clues so he could remove them and thus prevent others from finding the tomb. When he failed, he took more drastic actions. He also laid many false trails, and yet you still found what he thought could not be found. Later you must tell me how, but first, there are more surprises in the box."

After placing the face carefully on the table, Ben peered into the chest. A small black box was poked down the side of something wrapped in cloth. He lifted out the box and removed the lid. He briefly stared at the ring inside before removing it and turning it over in his fingers. He stared at the capital 'A' set inside a circle inside a pentagram.

"I have no idea why the ring is with the other stuff, but it has to be important for my father to have included it," Creed said. "Perhaps it once belonged to Saunière."

Ben shook his head. "It's too satanic for a ring a priest would have worn. I vaguely recognize the symbols, but can't recall what they mean. I'm thinking of Asmodeus, though I don't know why?"

"Keep it," Creed offered. "Perhaps you can research it later as I'd be interested in finding out its importance."

"Thanks." Ben returned the ring to its small box before slipping it into his pocket.

Ben returned his attention to the cardboard box and lifted out the cloth wrapped object. After carefully removing the fabric for the second time in as many minutes, Ben was surprised by what he saw, a small glass vial containing what looked like a piece of paper.

Ben looked at Creed astounded. "Is this the glass vial Saunière found in his church, the one hidden by Antoine Bigou, a previous priest of Rennes-le-Château?"

Creed nodded. "It contains the parchments that first led Saunière to his discovery."

"But I thought the parchments associated with the Rennes-Le-Château mystery were forgeries?"

"Though the ones you refer to contain some snippets of truth, they have been drastically changed to conceal their true meaning. You are holding the originals," replied Creed. "Would you like another drink?"

"I had better not. I want to keep a clear head for when I read the journal." Ben turned the vial over in his hands as Creed replenished his own drink. "Can I look at the parchment?"

"By all means," Creed consented, as he resumed his seat. "Just handle them with care. I have copies you can examine more fully, but I thought you would appreciate seeing the originals."

Ben did. He carefully removed the two small yellowed parchments from their container. After placing the glass vial on the table, he gingerly unrolled the delicate documents until the writing was revealed. Staring in wonder at the words on the thin, crisp vellum, immediately noticing they were vastly different from the ones in circulation that many of those interested in the Rennes-le-Château mystery were aware of. He glanced up at Creed. "They're different?"

"Of course, they were changed before my father let Plantard have them."

"Was Plantard aware of the changes?"

"No, not that he would have cared. Look at the publicity they brought him and his pathetic little cause. Related to the Merovingian line, my arse. We were though, amazed at how well the deception turned out."

"But people have spent years studying them, all for nothing."

"I wouldn't say it was for nothing. They have been the source of countless books and brought notoriety to many as well as much needed wealth and publicity to the village. When you know what's in the tomb, you'll understand why such precautions were deemed necessary."

"But where did you get the originals? Did your grandfather get them from Saunière?"

Creed shook his head. "No, they were hidden in the church."

Ben looked at him in surprise. "Where in the church?"

"The vial was hidden by Saunière in the wall to the right of the altar."

"Of course!" Ben exclaimed, picturing the location in the church he had seen many times. "At the spot indicated by the sightline of the Mary Magdalene figure in the altar bas-relief, until recently the rough repair could still be seen. So it was your grandfather that dug into the wall thinking something was buried there."

"Correct, and there was, that vial in your hands. I will show you the true decipherment later."

Ben examined the diagram on the back of one of the parchments; it was unmistakably the church and graveyard before Saunière set about his renovations. He noticed the position of the original altar marked with what is now known as the Knights flagstone in front. Another cross inside a square indicted another location in the church with Latin words underneath, "Tomb of our

Lords," he translated aloud. "This must be the entrance to the church crypt."

"Correct," answered Creed. "That's what started Saunière on his road to discovery. He found something in the crypt that eventually led him to find the tomb you later discovered and the hoard of treasure that was amongst the objects inside."

Ben looked up confused. "I always assumed the parchments led him straight to the tomb?"

Creed smiled. "No, though Saunière managed to decipher them he never worked out their true meaning."

"But they do lead to the tomb?"

"No, I don't think they do. Maybe they lead to another cache of treasure yet to be found. As you probably know there are countless rumors of many hoards of treasure buried around Rennes-le-Château; perhaps some still awaits to be discovered."

"I assume you have not deciphered them either."

"No, though like my family and Saunière before them I have tried. To tell you the truth, that's another of the reasons I contacted you. Your flair for following clues is obvious. If anyone stands a chance of deciphering the true meaning of these parchments, it must be you."

"I'm flattered by your confidence, and of course I'd be willing to give it a try, but what happens if I'm successful, is that to remain a secret also?"

"It's difficult to say at this time until we discover what's there. If you decide to keep the location of the tomb a secret, maybe I will give the parchments to you and then whatever you find will be yours to do with as you wish. At the present time, I am only interested in protecting what lies in the tomb."

"And if I find nothing?"

"I'm not asking you to make a decision now, read the journal, perhaps it will help you decide. As far as I can see, you have nothing to lose and everything to gain."

Ben pondered the dilemma. "There's also the matter of other possible treasure locations alluded to by the clues Saunière left in his church, the artifacts and treasure he in all likelihood took from the tomb and hid."

"Well, I can help you there. You need not waste your time searching anymore as they have either been found or looted by my family using the journal or by other researchers and treasure hunters over the years who managed, like you, to solve some of Saunière's clues."

"That explains why every location, except for the tomb, I found so far has been empty?"

Creed nodded apologetically, "Sorry."

"What happened to the stuff your family found?"

"Some was sold to make my family, and now me, quite well off to help protect the secret. Anything of historical importance was anonymously donated to museums around the world. You must have heard of some of them, the golden figures of Solomon and the great golden crucifix for instance."

"Yes, the figures consisted of a solid gold small scale model thought to be the original Temple of Solomon and a similar sized solid gold model of the Ark of the Covenant. The crucifix was, if I remember correctly, almost a meter tall, also of solid gold, with a highly detailed figure of Christ. They were as you mentioned, donated by a mysterious unknown benefactor on the condition they were put on public view and were to be exhibited around the world, so everyone had a chance to view them. I saw them in London, wonderful works of art."

"Of course, many other smaller pieces were sent unconditionally and did not grab the attention of the world's press quite as much."

"Well, Creed, you've taken me completely by surprise and given me much to think about."

Creed glanced at the wall clock. "It's late. Sleep on it and tomorrow we can talk again to decide on our next step." He stood and walked over to a suitcase on the table, took out his grandfather's journal and handed it to Ben.

"A little bedtime reading. Hopefully, your mind will be clearer in the morning."

Ben was eager to start flicking through its pages at once, but he restrained himself. "Thanks. I doubt I'll be getting much sleep tonight."

"Come on, let's fetch your things from the car and I'll show you to your room."

Clutching the journal, Ben followed Creed out of the room. He was now glad that he hadn't bolted earlier. He was about to find out more information about the Rennes-le-Château mystery in the next few days than he had in all his previous years of research. He had no idea what the immediate future held, but with the offer of the parchments, which in all probability should lead to a remarkable discovery, on the table, the next few days should turn out to be very exciting indeed.

Ben collected his holdall from the car and climbed the stairs to his room.

An hour later, refreshed from a long soak in the deep, cast-iron rolled-top bath in his en-suite bathroom and wearing nothing but a dressing gown, Ben entered the bedroom to be greeted by a flash of lightning briefly bathing the room in light. The crash of thunder that quickly followed caused the large Gothic window to rattle in its frame. The fire burning in the ornately decorated hearth, cast an orange glow to give the room a cozy atmosphere. He peered out the window to glimpse individual raindrops highlighted by the occasional flash of lightning, caught as if frozen to hang in the air for the briefest of moments until the darkness returned. The cozy feeling of being in a warm, snug room while outside, bad weather raged, washed over him.

He sat on the bed, sinking into the soft, thick mattress. The bed was old and the pattern expertly carved onto the head and footboard exactly matched the wood paneling that covered the walls, hinting that it might be the same age as the house and constructed by the same carpenter. He ran his hand over the intricate geometric carvings on the large wooden headboard mirrored by the smaller footboard; the shiny highly polished wood mimicked a mirror to reflect the flicking firelight.

A glance around the room revealed all the furniture matched, from the two small bedside tables standing either side of the bed to the huge wardrobe that took up most of one wall; its cavernous space wasted on his few clothes hanging inside. It looked like the type that might have a secret door in the back leading to some mysterious land, like in *The Lion the Witch and the Wardrobe*. With the way events had been shaping up lately, he wasn't going to check in case it did. A matching chest of drawers, in scale with the large wardrobe, meant he only had to use a small part of one of the deep drawers for the few items he had with him. An antique armchair covered in a tapestry design had been positioned by the fireplace. Next to the chair stood a low table on which Creed had placed a small decanter of whiskey and a crystal tumbler.

Ben reached across the bed for the journal he had placed there earlier, carried it over to the fireplace, slouched into the armchair and poured himself a drink from the decanter. He took a large sip of the smooth liquid, enjoying the sensation of it warming his throat.

He opened the journal to the inscription on the first page. The handwriting of the priest Rivière was neat and readable. Ben translated as he read.

Though I have heard many deathbed confessions during my many years in the church, none have affected me as much as my friend's l'Abbé Saunière. I will never forget those words from a fellow priest that put my soul in torment, who I am unable to forgive or alas call a friend anymore. He has taken away everything I held dear, my faith, my Lord, My God. Though Saunière's confession has ruined my life, I feel the secret he confided in me is of too great importance to be lost with my dying breath. I write faithfully here those words etched on my soul. Maybe in the future, Saunière will be proved wrong, or times will change, and the shocking secret I now divulge will be shocking no more.

If you read these words, may God rest your soul.

Ben took another sip of whiskey as he turned the page eager to find out what Saunière had confided to Rivière that shocked him so.

It was a stormy night, not unusual for the time of year, June. Saunière remembered thinking at the time he hoped the villagers would be more welcoming than the weather.

A flash of lightning lit up the page, causing Ben to glance at the window when it again rattled with the force of the loud crack of thunder that filled the room. He turned back to the book and continued reading...

Couiza, France – June 1st, 1885

The narrow road that ran through the small town of Couiza was typical for France in the 1800s. Lined with houses whose shuttered windows gave the impression of it being deserted. The only signs of life to shatter this illusion came from the dim orange light escaping through the small arched windows of the old stone inn and the muffled voices drifting out from inside. The owners of the voices were just shapes of color through the grimy windows.

The sounds became louder when the door suddenly opened, flooding the street with a yellow rectangle of light with the stretched shadow of a lone figure cast at its center. The shadow's owner stepped into the street and let the old weathered door swing shut behind him and banged against the frame to which it, surprisingly, still fitted snugly. Dressed all in black, the only splash of color came from the light brown bag held in his left hand. Fashioned from leather, the scuff marks covering its surface were evidence of its well-traveled use. In an effort to prevent the gusting wind from whipping it away, he pressed the wide-brimmed hat that shadowed his face down farther onto his head. After tugging the collar of his long robe tighter around his neck in an attempt to ward off the chill wind, he strode purposefully along the deserted street. The joyful sounds of people drinking and having fun inside the inn became fainter with every step.

The man turned onto a simple dirt track and walked between the two ruts worn into the ground by the wheels of the many horse-drawn wagons that had traversed to and from the village situated out of sight high above the town. The track immediately began to slope up gently, as yet giving no indication of how steep it would become closer to his destination.

Swapping the bag that contained all his worldly possessions into his other hand, the man began his journey along the track that snaked up the hill. Any warmth he had gathered from the cozy log fire in the inn was quickly chased away by the cold seeping through his long, black robe. Before he had traveled very far, the first few drops of rain began to fall. He glanced up at the large black cloud directly above him, which seemed to be following his progress up the hill. Then, suddenly, the heavens opened to let forth a deluge of rain that beat like a drum on the stiff brim of his hat.

The track soon became awash with soil-stained water running in twin rivulets along the wagon ruts. Scarcely seconds later, the horse-churned surface turned to mud. Keeping to the higher center, he trudged through its slippery surface. The thick mud sucked at his feet to make the steep journey even more arduous. His clothes, soaked with the pouring rain, soon became sodden and heavy, but he had no choice but to carry on if he wished to reach his destination before the person he had arranged to meet retired to his bed and left him without shelter for the night.

About halfway up, he felt the need to empty his bladder of the cheap bottle of wine he had enjoyed earlier. He took refuge under one of the few trees that grew alongside the track. Protected briefly from the rain by the tree's thick canopy, he placed his bag on a rock to keep it out of the flow of muddy water and hoisted up the front of his long, and now mud-stained, robe while he urinated. He watched as it mixed with the fast flowing torrent of muddy water in the small overflowing drainage ditch that ran alongside the track.

He directed his gaze down the hill and focused on the dim lights of the inn he had vacated a short while ago. Smoke from its chimney, whipped into a mad dance by the wind, reminded him of the cozy fire flaming at its base. He could almost feel its warmth as he had when he sat beside it to eat his meal and drink the wine he had purchased with a few of the meager francs he owned. He regretted momentarily that he hadn't stayed longer in the warmth. Perhaps then he could have waited in the dry until the rain had passed. However, a glance up at the dark clouds now blanketing the sky from horizon to horizon hinted that yet might be a while. He had a feeling the rain would linger for the rest of the night at least.

A shiver brought him back to reality. Finishing his toilet, he picked up his bag and again stepped into the deluge falling from the heavens. He tried to ignore the cold water running in rivulets down his back, now soaking his clothes from the inside, as he carried on up the hill. Within the hour, cold, wet and tired, he finally reached the entrance of the tiny village that was to be his new home. He paused to stare at the seemingly deserted houses before him. His thoughts then dwelled on the reason he was here. His new appointment in this small remote hilltop village was, he knew, a punishment for his outspoken views back in Narbonne. He could only imagine the Bishop's pleasure at finding such a place to banish him.

Carcassonne, France.
The Bishops Palace - a few weeks earlier.

The Bishop, his hands clasped behind his back, gazed out the large ornate window as the rain beat against its expensive decorative colored panels of stained glass. A smile briefly appeared on his normally stern lips at the misfortune of a young priest sprinting across the courtyard. Eager to seek shelter from the rain the unfortunate priest tripped and fell onto the wet grass. The armful of papers he carried shot out of his grasp to be lifted up and blown by the wind and soaked by the rain. The Bishop's smile faded when he turned. The long shadow he cast across his desk fell on his nervous clerk sitting on a hard wooden chair. He knew the chair was uncomfortable because he had chosen it specifically for that purpose. "Well?" he said accusingly. "It was your idea to promote him to professor at the seminary of Narbonne."

The clerk squirmed in the uncomfortable seat as he desperately tried to think of some way to instigate himself into the Bishop's good favor again. That damn priest Saunière was the cause of his predicament. A short while ago during the State elections, to the astonishment of everyone, Bérenger Saunière began openly campaigning for the people to cast their votes against the Republican Party. He even told some of the women in his parish to withhold any sexual activities from their husbands unless they voted against the Republicans. This from a man who had barely begun his career in the church. Unfortunately, for the newly ordained priest, the Republicans were successful in their campaign and won the elections. Saunière would soon come to regret his actions. Obviously angry with the priest who had actively encouraged the electorate to vote against them, they went out of their way to seek retribution. Saunière was promptly denounced to the authorities of the region for inciting public disorder and trying to influence the electoral system.

"But Your Eminence," pleaded the squirming priest, "I had no idea he would start causing trouble. His career in the priesthood, though short so far, had, until this incident, been exemplary. How could I know he would start preaching anti-Republican comments?"

The Bishop waved his hand to dismiss his excuses. He knew it wasn't wholly the clerk's fault. He had also been in favor of the appointment. However, it did well to make those under him squirm every now and then to remind them of their position. "Yes! Yes! So you keep saying," he said irritably. He leaned forward to rest his hands on the large oak desk and stared at the clerk. "The question is, what are we to do with him now? I want him put someplace where he cannot cause me any more problems or embarrassment."

"I have been thinking along the same lines, Your Eminence," replied the clerk eagerly. "I have found an ideal position for the troublesome priest. I have the paperwork here." The clerk passed the papers he'd been clutching to his Bishop. "It just needs your approval and signature."

"What is this place like?" inquired the Bishop, glancing at the papers.

"It's in the middle of nowhere and with a very insignificant population," replied the nervous clerk.

Plucking an expensive silver pen from its ivory holder on the desk, the Bishop dipped its nib in the matching pot of ink and signed the papers. As he handed them back, he kept hold when the clerk tried to take them. "You had better be right. Understand this, if I hear of him stirring up any more trouble it will be you who will also be punished." He released the papers.

The clerk, not wishing to risk the wrath of his superior again, had searched long and hard for some remote location to place the priest who had put him in this position. Finally, he had found such a posting in a village he had never heard of. After making inquiries, it had turned out to be perfect. "I am confident we will hear no more from him," he stated with certainty. "After all, what possible trouble could he cause in such a remote village with such a small population?"

The Bishop was inclined to agree. It did seem ideal. Unlike his clerk, he knew of the village; he could vaguely remember visiting it once although he could no longer remember the reason. What he did remember was the torturous journey up the steep, rough track. One he had no wish ever to repeat.

"You had better be right! Now go. I want him out of the way as soon as possible."

"It will be done, Your Eminence," replied the clerk, grateful the matter had been sorted and hopefully before long, forgotten.

The Bishop turned back to face the window, dismissing the clerk with his action. There was no sign of the priest who had tripped a few moments earlier, but a few papers he had been unable to snatch back from the winds playful grasp continued to be blown around the large courtyard. He heard the door close when the clerk left.

Hopefully, that will have sorted that little problem and I will hear no more from this bothersome headstrong priest, thought the Bishop, not realizing what train of fateful destiny they had just placed this virtually unknown priest upon. Not only would their paths cross again, but there would be repercussions. In the years to come even the ears of the Vatican would hear of the priest, Bérenger Saunière, and the tiny hilltop village he had been banished to.

Saunière crossed to a wooden post all but hidden by an overgrown bush and pulled it aside to reveal a weathered sign announcing the name of the village that was to be his home for the foreseeable future. He remembered well the satisfied smile on the Bishop's clerk's face when he delivered the news of his new posting. Born only a few kilometers away in Montazels, he knew of the village. But if they thought they had silenced him, they were very much mistaken.

He stared at the words painted long ago. The faded black lettering verified what he already knew. He had almost prayed that somehow he had taken a wrong turn or climbed the wrong hill, but it wasn't to be. Although it had been many years since his last visit, when he had only been a boy, the sign was confirmation he had arrived. He let the branches spring back into place as he stepped away to enter his new home, the small hilltop village of Rennes-le-Château.

He walked alongside the weathered and worn ancient buildings on either side of the track that was the main street. He then passed by the ruins of the once proud château that gave the village its name. In times gone by it had belonged to the Hautpoul family, who had ties to the Knights Templar.

A short walk later he reached his destination. Nestled amongst some old store buildings and a stable was his new church. As he approached, he observed the boarded-up windows that prevented him from seeing if any glass still remained in the openings. He raised his face to the heavens and opened his mouth to drink in droplets of rain. He wiped the water from his face with a hand and scanned the rest of the sad-looking building. Dedicated to Mary Magdalene, the small church, like most of the buildings in the village, had suffered from the ravages of time and neglect. Unlike the houses he had passed where some evidence of repair and upkeep had been undertaken, no such signs were evident on the ignored church.

Saunière approached the entrance with no illusions that the interior would be in a better state. He paused at the door that had long ago warped to a different shape than the frame it had once fitted so snugly, explaining why it stood ajar. He gripped its rusty iron handle and pushed it open. Forced to carry out the job they had been fashioned for, the equally rusty hinges squealed in protest.

He entered the ancient church and pushed the groaning door shut as much as it was possible in its present state. Immediately, the smell of damp invaded his nostrils. He shivered, observing it was colder in the church than outside and due to the many holes in the roof, not much drier.

The ancient Holy water stoup just inside the door had a steady drip of water falling into it from the leaky roof that caused it to overflow. Though he doubted any blessed water remained in the bowl, he dipped in a finger and made the sign of the cross. He headed down the nave, knelt before the altar and said a small, silent prayer.

Afterward, he stood to examine the sorry-looking altar. A stone slab rested upon two ancient stone pillars, one unadorned and one covered in carvings that seemed pagan in design. The altar, like the rest of the church, had seen better days. Withered flowers in a simple glass vase had been placed on its weathered top.

He rested his leather bag on a pew not being rained upon, removed his soaked hat and placed it on top. After brushing his fingers through his damp hair, he climbed the few steps up to the pulpit. The whole wooden construction creaked and wobbled with his every step, threatening to collapse beneath him. On reaching the top safely, he gazed around his church from this slightly elevated position.

"Welcome to your prison, Bérenger Saunière," he spoke aloud and listened to the words echo around the small dark church.

He gazed up at the small windows. The church had been built when glass itself was a treasure. This ensured the interior would never be flooded with light even on the sunniest of days and seemed destined to forever remain shrouded in gloom. Some of the windows had been damaged by the strong winds prevalent in the area; others had suffered from the ravages of time. The few windows that had survived more-or-less intact were boarded up for protection. Only one window, buckled by the strong winds and with much of its glass missing, (some of the smashed remains still lay on the church floor where they had fallen,) remained uncovered to allow a small amount of light to penetrate the dimness of the church. It did little to banish the darkness.

Saunière turned toward the sound of squealing hinges, a signal someone had arrived. Shrouded in shadow, his black priest's clothing made him all but invisible as he watched the small figure enter. The lone person, well wrapped up against the wind and rain, walked toward the altar. Unlike his journey down the nave, this person avoided stepping in the puddles that littered their passage to it by sidestepping some and jumping over others. The figure halted before the altar to make the sign of the cross before throwing back the hood of a cloak to let free a mass of long dark hair. It was a young woman, the church too dark to see her age. He continued to observe as she took a small bunch of fresh flowers out from under her cloak. Their bright colors seemed out of place in the depressing grey atmosphere shrouding the church.

Saunière smiled. "So you are the one who brings some color to my gloomy church."

The girl, startled by the voice suddenly breaking the silence, gasped in fright and dropped the flowers.

The pulpit creaked loudly when Saunière climbed down. He walked over to join the young girl before the altar. "Please, don't be afraid," he said reassuringly. He picked up the dropped flowers. "I am your new priest."

He held out the colorful blooms to her, but the nervous girl just stared back at him, a frightened look on her face. Now he was closer, he could see how pretty and innocent she was and thought she was about eighteen years old. He knew what a sight he must look drenched from head to foot, his shoes and clothes splattered in mud. His hair, damp with rain, had become plastered to his head and face. No wonder she was nervous. "Please excuse my appearance. I have just walked up the hill and, as you know, it's not exactly hiking weather today."

The girl continued to stare at him, not attempting to speak or take the flowers from his outstretched hand. Saunière turned to the altar to replace the dead flowers with the fresh ones but turned back when he heard the sound of footsteps. He watched the girl flee from the church, her feet splashing in the puddles she had so carefully avoided previously. Saunière smiled.

He dropped the dead flowers on the ground and, seeing there was no water in the vase, he picked it up and knelt to scoop some from a puddle on the church floor. He noticed some of the water he had disturbed overflowed the worn slab and seeped in between the joint. Saunière cocked an ear. He thought he could hear it splashing. There must be a cavity beneath, but before he could ponder it further someone else entered. He looked up to see a man walking towards him. It seems the girl had wasted no time in reporting his presence.

"Hello, you must be father Saunière, our new priest? I am Monsieur Dénarnaud." He smiled and offered his hand. "My family and I are only visiting friends in the village, but I was asked to look out for you as the mayor hasn't yet returned. He is probably waiting for the rain to stop before he climbs the hill."

Saunière stood and shook his hand "Hello Monsieur Dénarnaud. Yes, that would be the sensible thing to do, but alas, I was already halfway up when the heavens opened."

"Please, call me Alfred, and don't worry we'll soon have you dried off."

"Thank you, Alfred. You share the same name as my brother. I was beginning to think the village was deserted."

"No Father, not quite, though there are few enough. Tonight the weather has chased everyone indoors."

Realizing he was still holding the vase, Saunière returned it to the altar and placed the fresh flowers inside.

"So that's what Marie was doing in here," said Alfred.

"I think I may have frightened her."

"Don't worry yourself, Father, my daughter has led a sheltered life and strangers are a rarity here. Not many can face the climb up the hill, and there's nothing in the village to encourage many to make the journey if they don't live here. But first things first, I was meant to take you to see the mayor when you arrived, but as he's still not returned, and seeing the state of you, I think we'll leave that until morning. Let's get you somewhere dry and warm so you can change out of those wet clothes."

Saunière picked up his hat and bag "Thank you, I would like to get settled in the presbytery."

"Presbytery? No, Father, have you not been told? The presbytery is a ruin; no one can live there in its present condition. You are lodging with Antoinette Marce. She has a room she rents out. All has been arranged. Come, I will take you to her."

Cold, wet, tired, and now with no home to call his own, Saunière followed Alfred out of the church in silence. Maybe upsetting his superiors hadn't been such a sensible thing to do after all.

A clap of thunder returned Ben to the present.

He took another sip of the fine whiskey and flipped through the journal, pausing on anything interesting he found. Almost two hours later, he closed the book, stretched out and yawned. It was time to get some sleep. He placed the journal on the table, drained the last of the whiskey from his glass, walked over to the bed and slipped under the covers. He was asleep five minutes after turning off the light.

The forms of two men in a black car could just be made out through its condensation covered windows; a result of their hours of confinement inside. Doyle wiped a clear streak with a hand and peered at the house when the light in the window he had been staring at went out.

"It seems that he's finally gone to bed."

David opened his eyes and glanced at the darkened house. "About bloody time," he complained, more than a little bored from sitting in the car for the past few hours. "Now we can piss off back to the hotel."

"We were told to remain here all night in case they go out," argued Doyle, lighting another of his low-tar cigarettes.

"Fuck that, I'm off. Look at the weather, numbskull, where the fuck would they go?"

"I'm only repeating what we were told. It sounded like an order to me."

"It's all right for *him* tucked up nice and warm in his bed. We're the ones freezing our arses off. I only agreed to come to France because I thought it would be fun. I wouldn't have bothered if I'd known we'd be stuck out in the arse end of nowhere. For Christ's sake, we are nearer to Spain than Paris. What a fucking dump."

Silas had been reluctant to allow Garret to follow Harper due to his anger towards him for killing his friend, Ryan. Though Silas would have liked nothing better than to see Harper dead, by Garret's hands or another, he had his orders. Unlike David, he wasn't about to disobey them. David had worked for him a couple of times before; he was a lazy bastard, but the only person available at such short notice.

"Yeah, I know what you mean. This is my last packet of Silk Cut, and they don't sell them around here. But all things aside, maybe we should wait a while longer."

"If you want to stay, then stay. I 'ain't stopping you, but I'm driving this car back to our hotel where I plan to drink the mini bar dry before falling asleep in a nice warm, dry bed. The choice is yours."

Doyle glanced out of the window at the rain lashing the glass. It displayed no signs of abating; it actually seemed to be getting worse. Perhaps David was right. Loyalty to his boss was one thing, but standing for hours in the rain, cold and soaking wet was pushing his devotion a bit too far. If David was leaving with the car, then he had no choice but to go with him. If it blew up in their faces, he could always blame David. "Yeah, maybe you're right, they're not going anywhere in this weather. We can be back by six in the morning. At least we'll get a few hours of sleep."

David started the car and switched on the blower to demist the windows. "You might be back at six, but I won't be here until eight."

"Whatever." Doyle sighed. "Let's go, that mini bar sounds awfully inviting since you mentioned it."

"Hallelujah. Finally, something we agree on."

David steered the car slowly out of the driveway entrance opposite the house they'd been watching and didn't switch the headlights on until he was driving off along the road.

A figure, shrouded in darkness between the trees lining the drive, stepped out onto the road and watched the car recede into the distance. Now free of the protective shelter of leafy branches, the rain drummed incessantly on the hood of his black, waterproof PVC coat. He wondered whom the men worked for.

A flash of lightning highlighted the man for a second; its bright light briefly glinting off the gun held in Creed's hand. He had thought about killing the two men there and then, but knew they would have already reported his location. If they disappeared others would be sent to replace them and this time they would be more alert to danger. No, he would bide his time, for now. He guessed they must have followed Ben from England. It was evidence of the man's lack of experience in such matters. He would need to learn fast or suffer the consequences.

However, with the danger past, for now, Creed slipped the gun into his pocket. As he turned back towards the house, he spied the house sign at a drunken angle and the skid mark in the gravel. He shook his head and walked back along the driveway.

CHAPTER 3

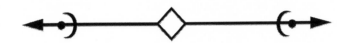

REX DEUS

R ABBI SOLOMON PACED back and forth at the head of the long table while he waited impatiently for the others to finish debating the information he had revealed to them: that they were not the only ones interested in what Harper had discovered. Another concerned party watched the house in France where Harper had recently arrived. They didn't yet know who he'd gone there to meet, but he was sure that information would soon be forthcoming. He had suggested they err on the side of caution and watch the watchers until they knew exactly who they were and the threat they posed to their quest to retrieve what was rightfully theirs. Some of them had disagreed with his decision, instead preferring to dispose of them immediately before they lost what they'd waited to gain possession of for so long.

Solomon glanced around at the Rabbis arguing the merits and pitfalls of the two courses of action open to them. Irritated by their incessant squabbling, he slammed a fist on the table to silence them. It had the desired effect; all ceased speaking and turned to stare at him.

"Brethren," he said, forcing himself to remain calm. "What we have to take into consideration is we are not the powerful Order we once were. Yes, we have men we can hire to do those deeds none of us are able or willing to do, but it's always a risk they will fail as they lack our commitment. To show our hand now by killing off those in our way could backfire with catastrophic results. Even if the men observing Harper are successfully disposed of, we will have alerted their employers to our presence. We like to call ourselves a Secret Order, but are we really? If an unfortunate bout of events brings about our demise, then we have failed all those before us. Again, I state that we should watch and wait until we can find out more. We must also devise an achievable plan to dispose of anyone who threatens to thwart our mission. I believe, at this moment in time, this is our best and safest course of action." He glanced around at the faces while they again digested his words and resumed his seat.

Rabbi Abiram stood to address those present. "In principle, I agree with Solomon's proposal; however, I would like to stress the point that at the first sign we might lose that which is finally so close, we act with swift and deadly force." He sat to nods of agreement from all those seated around the table.

Solomon gave him a nod of thanks as he stood. "Are we all in agreement?"

All indicated they were.

"Good, then I will make the arrangements. Now that matter has been settled, I call this meeting to an end."

The Rabbis left the room until only his two trusted companions remained. He would not risk using hired thugs to carry out the task ahead. It was too important to trust to others. He would take care of the matter personally. He informed his fellow conspirators of his plan.

CHAPTER 4

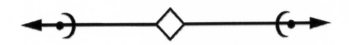

Murder

AWAKENED BY A knocking on the bedroom door, Ben groggily wiped the sleep from his eyes. It was only after he had glanced around the room did he remember where he was.

"Breakfast in half an hour," called Creed's voice from the other side of the door.

"Okay," Ben replied, sleepily.

"I'll leave your coffee on the table out here by the door."

"Thanks."

A coffee cup rattled, and Creed's footsteps faded into the distance.

Ben climbed out of bed, unlocked the door and retrieved the cup. He preferred tea, very rarely drinking coffee unless it was a frothy cappuccino. The coffee was as black as midnight and smelt awfully strong.

At least it will wake me up. Ben took a sip and grimaced. It was far too strong for his taste; he doubted he would sleep for a week if he drunk the extremely bitter brew. It also lacked any milk or sugar, which was drastic news for his sweet tooth. He went to the bathroom and tipped the vile drink down the sink.

After a quick shower to wake him up, Ben dressed and went downstairs, taking the empty coffee cup and journal with him. The aroma of fried bacon filled the hallway. When he entered the kitchen, he saw Creed busy at the stove where bacon sizzled away in one frying pan and a couple of eggs in another. Two sausages and fried tomatoes occupied each of the two plates next to the stove.

"Good morning, Creed. I didn't know the French had a fry up for breakfast."

Creed looked around and laughed. "Morning, Ben. We don't, we normally eat something far healthier. I cook English breakfast especially for you, to make you feel at home." He indicated a steaming coffee pot on the table set for two. "Please help yourself to coffee."

Ben grimaced and ignored the strong brew.

"Did you sleep well?"

"Like the proverbial log, when I eventually got to bed, that is. I stayed up late reading your grandfather's journal."

Noticing that Creed had set another one on the table, Ben placed the cup he had brought down in the sink. He sat down and saw Creed staring at him.

"Well?" said Creed. "What are your thoughts?"

"I've not read it all, but I did flick through and read some of the more interesting parts. As you said last night, the journal is in parts a shocking read. It's no wonder your grandfather was so upset by what Saunière revealed to him, especially the Gélis incident. It's said by those waiting outside the room during Saunière's deathbed confession, which included Marie Dénarnaud, who witnessed Rivière rush from the room visibly traumatized by Saunière's confession. We know from those who lived in the tiny village of Coustaussa that Gélis wasn't well liked and a miser. If he had discovered Saunière's secret, perhaps his greed turned Gélis to blackmail."

Ben had previously read the police report and autopsy, which was very grisly reading. After reading Saunière's account of his involvement in the priest's demise, he had wondered what events had taken place to bring about the drastic action that led to such a horrific outcome...

France – 1891 – Location near Rennes-Le-Château

Breathing heavily from the long trek through the rough and hilly countryside, l'Abbé Gélis parted the branches of the bush behind which he had concealed himself and observed the lone, black-clad figure descend the steep, shrub-covered slope and disappear. Gélis moved forward into a position where he could peer over the edge and saw Saunière scramble behind a large bush growing against the side of the rocky outcrop ten meters away. Though he couldn't see it from his position, Gélis guessed Saunière had entered an opening in the rock, perhaps a cave entrance hidden by the large bush. He moved to a suitable place where his large bulk would be concealed but gave him a good view of the spot where Saunière had vanished and waited for him to reappear. When Saunière had gone, he would go and find out precisely what secret the mysterious priest had discovered.

Gélis was about to drift off to sleep when Saunière appeared a little over two hours later. Gélis rubbed the tiredness from his eyes and observed Saunière's climb up the steep slope. Whatever was in the wicker basket slung on his back weighed enough to hamper his progress. Gélis pondered the contents of the basket that had been empty previously and concealed himself farther behind the bush when Saunière paused and glanced around. His eyes briefly lingered on his hiding place before beginning his long walk back to the village of Rennes-le-Château.

Like most who knew Saunière, Gélis wondered at the source of his sudden wealth shortly after carrying out some minor renovations to his church. When his grand building scheme had begun, the rumors he had found a vast treasure had spread. With the Knights Templar once having a strong presence in the area, many believed Saunière had discovered their long lost treasure. Gélis wasn't so sure, though he knew whatever Saunière was profiting from he deserved more than the small pittance he currently received for his silence. He would have more, or he would make sure Saunière suffered the consequences. First though, he had to find the source, the reason for his presence here today. He had spied on the priest for days, waiting for him to lead him to it. He was now certain today his efforts would be rewarded.

Gélis climbed to his knees and stared in the direction Saunière had taken but saw no sign of him. Confident the man had gone, he slipped down the steep slope and scrambled through the thick undergrowth until he arrived at the bush behind which Saunière had previously disappeared. He pulled back a branch and stared at the dark opening of a cave entrance. To not alert Saunière someone other than he had entered, he squeezed his bulk behind the bush, watchful not to break any branches. He stood in the entrance and peered into its dark interior, but due to the bush blocking most of the sunlight it was too dark to see more than a short distance. He wondered what Saunière had used as a light source. A glance around the entrance revealed a pile of dirt-soiled clothes, a candle holder with a three-inch stub of candle, and a box of matches placed on a rock. He picked up both, lit the candle and entered the cave to discover Saunière's secret.

When he emerged thirty minutes later, his clothes were stained with red earth and his expression a mixture of fear and excitement. Dragging his stout body through the small tunnel hadn't been pleasant, but the reward made the discomfort worthwhile. It had led to a chamber that Saunière had almost completely ransacked of valuables. What remained were the objects too large or too dangerous for the priest to steal and sell. The most shocking of all stood in the center of the chamber. Though once covered by a shroud, time had turned it to tatters, exposing an ancient corpse. It was a tomb. Gélis had nervously moved closer to see if there were any clues to the corpse's identity. It wasn't the sight of the dead that caused him concern—he saw many in his profession—it was the foreboding atmosphere inside the tomb he found hard to explain. He thought back to what he had seen.

A chilling cold draft entered through the tunnel behind him, threatening to extinguish the unsteady yellow flame of the candle gripped tightly in his shaking hand, his only real sanctuary in the oppressing darkness of the tomb. Although his senses attempted to persuade him to leave immediately, the sight of the ancient corpse had struck a balance between his fear and curiosity to make him linger a while longer.

He stared down at the face, surprised that even though the tightly stretched skin had deformed the features, he could still perceive the face of a woman. Long black hair hung down onto the rose marble slab she had, it seemed, been laid reverently upon. An impression swept over him that she was once quite beautiful. He stepped back, shocked at the image that had popped suddenly into his head. It was as if he had seen the woman when she was alive.

He directed the candle over the large chunk of marble that was slightly longer than the body and briefly wondering how it had been transported to this place. He noticed a dark area almost hidden by a draped piece of tattered shroud. He lifted the cloth. Beneath was a dark hollow space. The marble wasn't solid; it was a sarcophagus! Saunière must have slid the top aside slightly to see what lay within. He directed the candlelight into the dark opening and stared at the neck of the corpse; the head was missing and had been replaced by one of glass. He stared at the head in puzzlement. He slid the top aside to increase the gap so he could view more of the preserved body. What he saw made him stumble away in shock. He fell, almost dropping the candle when he struck the ground. He lay there for a few moments staring at the sarcophagus. *It could not be so.*

He glanced up at the body resting on its top and guessed her identity and the reason why she was here. He climbed to his feet and rushed from the chamber too shocked to grab any of the gold coins or jewelry spilling from one of the decayed wooden chests.

He would never return.

Though he found it difficult to believe what he'd just seen, Gélis sensed it was true. For better or worse, he now knew Saunière's secret. He arrived back at the entrance and dropped the candle to the floor. Then, making no attempt to hide his presence, he shoved his large body through the bush, snapping two branches that snagged on his robe in the process. The climb back up the steep slope was difficult. He only succeeded by using the tough shrubs growing there to pull himself up to the top. Exhausted and sweating profusely from the exertion, he flopped down onto his back as soon as he reached level ground. While he lay there recovering, he considered what he'd just witnessed and what his next move should be. He had two options, and though both had their risks, both could prove profitable.

Unaware that the choice he was about to make would bring about his demise, Gélis decided to try option one first. If that didn't prove financially rewarding, he would move onto the second.

Saunière had spent the past few months emptying the tomb of its valuable contents, some of which he had stashed in secret locations nearer to his village so he could dip into them when his funds grew low. On his last visit to the tomb, he discovered signs that someone had been there. To safeguard the secret, he had removed some of the remaining objects and backfilled the tunnel.

He had confided in his brother, Alfred, about the treasure in the tomb, but not its location or the bodies inside. With Alfred's help, many of the objects from the tomb were sold to a man they'd found in Toulouse. They didn't receive market value, but considering the circumstances of how they were obtained, it was as much as they could expect. It had been this man who had put Alfred in contact with the two men Saunière was about to meet in Coustaussa. Although he had concerns about what he was about to put into motion, because of recent circumstances, it was a step he had no choice but to take or risk losing everything.

It hadn't been long before the visitor to the tomb had made himself known. Gélis had been blackmailing him for a few months now, but lately, his demands had increased and so had his threats of exposure if Saunière didn't double the payments. This would come in the form of a letter Gélis had written, detailing what Saunière had discovered and its location. If he sent it to Rome, as Gélis had threatened to do, once the secret was disclosed to the Vatican, they would assuredly take steps to ensure it was never revealed. Saunière was under no illusions that one of those steps would bring about his death. Hence Gélis's actions had forced him to hire two men to ensure the letter would never be sent and the priest would never try anything like this again.

While he waited in the shadows of the ancient Château ruins cast by the half-moon, Saunière glanced down at the small village. The shuttered windows of the houses and deserted streets gave the impression it was abandoned. The only sign of life was hinted at by a single light piercing the darkness from a presbytery window. Gélis was awake and awaiting his visitor.

Saunière turned toward the sounds of approaching footsteps. It was the two men he recognized from Alfred's descriptions. He observed them for a few moments before stepping forward to greet them. When he had finished explaining their mission, he glanced at the two men. Their causal expressions were evidence that a crime of this nature wasn't a stranger to them.

"You understand what you have to do?" he confirmed. "Gélis is not to be harmed. Your unexpected presence alone should be enough to frighten him, so he doesn't attempt anything like this again and to reveal the whereabouts of the letter."

The two men ensured him they understood.

"But what if he won't tell us, can we hit him a bit until he does?"

Saunière stared at the man, wondering what level his *a bit* entailed. "Only if there's no other recourse, but don' be too rough. As I explained, I expect he will talk readily enough after the shock of seeing you two at his door. He's expecting me to visit him tonight and you'll need to give a password before he grants you access. It is *Viva Angelina*."

One of the men took a packet of cigarette papers from his pocket and used a pencil to scrawl the password onto one of them. "Viva Angelina," he repeated.

Saunière, being of a collective nature and interested in such things—he had an extensive collection of books and postcards—noticed the cigarette papers were a Russian brand, *Le Tsar*.

"When you have the letter, meet me back here so I can pay you and get the letter and then you must leave the area immediately." Saunière pointed down at the quiet village below. "The house with the light in the window is the presbytery. Knock softly on the door, give the password and Gélis will let you in."

Gélis was in the cellar when someone knocked on the front door. He smiled greedily. It was Saunière with his monthly payment. He finished stashing the gold coins, a previous payment from Saunière, in an old length of pipe and placed it amongst the pile of firewood. He grabbed the lamp and climbed the cellar steps. Caution momentarily held his greed in check, and he paused at the door. "Who is it?"

"Viva Angelina," was the muffled reply.

Satisfied with the password, Gélis drew back the two bolts, turned the key in the lock and opened the door to his murderers. It had hardly opened a crack when it slammed into him and knocked him to the ground. He struck his head on the stairs when he landed. A look of fear spread across his face when two men entered. He reached for his stout wooden cane to defend off the intruders but was stopped when one of the men stamped on his chest, smashing his pocket watch in the process. The time, now frozen on the timepiece, would indicate the time of the intruders' entry: 12.15 AM.

While one man closed and locked the door, the other man kicked him and ordered him to his feet. Gélis stood shakily and was roughly ushered into the kitchen where he was forced to sit in an armchair.

Gélis looked fearfully at the two men who he believed were robbers after the gold coins he had stashed in various places around the house. "What do you want?"

One of the men placed a hand on each arm of the chair and leaned forward until his face almost touched the priest's. "We want the letter," he snarled, forcing the priest to breathe in his tobacco-stained breath.

It then dawned on Gélis who had sent them, Saunière! He feigned ignorance. "What letter?"

The man smiled cruelly. "Good, I was hoping I would get the chance to play." He backed away from the chair and glanced around the room. He spied a suitable object for his intentions and snatched up the nearby fire tongs. Without warning, he lashed out, striking Gélis on the arm and eliciting a groan of pain from the helpless priest.

"Please, I have no idea what letter you…"

The man struck him a savage blow around the head. The tongs split skin.

Dazed by the painful blow, Gélis screeched in pain.

"Be careful, hit him too hard and you'll kill him," warned the other man.

The interrogator glanced back at his accomplice. "Go see if you can find the letter."

The man left the kitchen.

Three more blows rained down on Gélis's head. All were designed to bring pain and suffering, but hold death at bay, for now.

"I'll ask you one more time, where's the fucking letter?"

Gélis glanced around the room. Now they were alone it might be his only chance to escape. He gazed up at the man standing menacingly over him. "Saunière sent you."

"That's none of your concern, but telling me the whereabouts of the letter is." He raised the tongs to strike again.

"Stop, please stop! I'll tell you."

A look of disappointment spread across the man's face. "So soon?"

Gélis indicated behind him with a nod of his head. "Above the fireplace, there's a loose brick. The letter's hidden behind it."

The man's eyes searched the fireplace until they spied a small gap around one of the bricks. He walked over, laid the tongs on the hearth, gripped the block and wiggled it as he pulled it out. In the small space behind was a piece of folded paper. He pulled it out and examined the writing. Though he couldn't read very well, he recognized it as a list of some kind and not the letter he was hired to find. He was about to confront the priest when something slammed into him. As he tumbled to the floor, he glimpsed the priest rush as fast as his rotund frame would allow, for the door. He'd been tricked. The man threw the brick.

Briefly, Gélis experienced hope. He was almost at the door leading to the hallway. If he hurried, he could dash along the hall, unlock the front door, run onto the street and raise the alarm before he was caught. His optimism was dashed when the brick struck the back of his head. He gripped both sides of the door frame to steady himself. Though dazed, he heard the faint rush of footsteps. The second intruder appeared at the bottom of the stairs and stood between him and the front door, blocking his dash for freedom. The priest backed into the room when the man approached.

The first blow knocked him to his knees, the second to the floor. The third and fourth were unnecessary.

"Stop it you fool. You'll kill him," said the second man.

The man gripping the raised axe stepped back. "He attacked me."

The second man knelt and examined the priest. There was a lot of blood. He stood. "He's not dead yet, but it won't be long coming."

The thug lowered the axe. "Did you find the letter?"

The second man shook his head. "No." He glanced down at the priest. "Did he tell you anything?"

"Not anything helpful." He also looked at the dying priest. "If I weren't going to hell before this, I am now," he smirked.

"He's in no condition to tell us anything now, and we can't linger here after this. If we get caught, it's a murder charge. Let's go tell the other priest what happened."

They left the kitchen.

"You think we'll still get paid?"

"The first man raised the axe he still held. "Oh, I'm sure of it."

They quietly slipped unseen out of the house and along the street towards the ruins.

A short while later, carnage greeted Saunière when he entered the presbytery. Sickened by the gruesome sight, he stared down at Gélis' body for a few moments. He knelt, careful to avoid the blood pooling on the floor around the dying man. A quick examination revealed Gélis was still alive, but only just. He placed a wooden shoe under his shoulder to prevent him from drowning in his own blood.

Gélis opened his eyes and looked at him. "I guess your secret's safe, now."

"You should not have done what you did my friend. I didn't want your death."

"And yet here I am, dying because of you."

"It's something I will always deeply regret. Where is the letter?"

Gélis smiled. "You will have to ask Jesus," he replied cryptically. "You will go to Hell for your actions here tonight."

Saunière knew the dying priest was right. "That's as may be, but to ensure you do not, if you agree, I will administer extreme unction."

"You've left me no choice, do it."

Gélis died a few minutes later.

After Saunière had laid Gélis out formally, he said a prayer and then searched the house. He eventually found the letter wedged behind a painting of the crucifixion, explaining the dying priest's cryptic words.

He left the house and slipped into the night.

It was on the 1st November 1897, the day following All Saints Day when news of the grisly murder shook the small village of Coustaussa situated across the valley from Rennes-le-Château.

Saunière was one of the priests that attended the funeral.

The guilt he felt from his involvement in the death of Gélis would weigh heavily on his conscience until his dying day.

"I find it unbelievable that Saunière, though he didn't undertake the actual killing, was directly responsible for the horrific murder of a fellow priest, who was also his friend, just to keep his secret safe," replied Creed, dishing up the cooked breakfast.

"During my investigations into the mystery I came across the rumor that Saunière may have been responsible for Gélis's death, but to see it in black and white from his own lips, so to speak, is still a shock."

Creed placed the plate of food in front of Ben. "An English breakfast for an Englishman."

Ben stared hungrily at the food. "Thank you. It's just what I need." He waited until Creed sat opposite and they ate in silence for a while, enjoying the meal.

When he had finished eating, Creed poured himself a coffee and offered it to Ben, "So, what do you think about what Saunière described in the Tomb?"

Ben quickly shook his head. "No thanks, I don't really drink coffee. I don't suppose you have tea, I normally bring my own when I travel abroad, but I left in such a hurry that I forgot to pack any."

Creed searched the cupboards and found some Earl Grey tea bags that he held up. "Will these do?"

Ben nodded. "Just about, they're a bit weak. Can you stick a couple in a cup of hot water?"

After Creed had made the tea, he sat back down at the table and sipped his strong coffee. "So, back to the tomb."

Ben looked at Creed. "If anyone should believe what Saunière said is in the tomb, it should be me as you wouldn't believe some of the things I've found on my travels, but...I'm not entirely convinced. If it's true, then I can understand why your grandfather and maybe even your father wanted it kept a secret, but why do you? You don't seem a particularly religious man. Why not just reveal it? Let the authorities excavate the tomb and then you wouldn't be in any danger from the Rex Deus or any other fanatical organizations. Times have changed. Religion, to many, is not as important as it used to be and I'm sure the Catholic Church will weather this revelation as they have done other setbacks many times previously."

"You are an atheist, yes?"

Ben shrugged. "I'm not really sure what I am. I believe there probably was a man called Jesus, who preached a good story of harmonious righteous living, even that this man was persecuted and crucified, but something that he staged to be at a time so he would only be on the cross for a short while. But I don't believe he was the son of God or that God exists. Like most people, I would like death not to be the end, but it won't be the Heaven or Hell described in the bible. Perhaps our consciousness lives on in some shape or form, or maybe not. I'll only know for certain when I'm dead."

"Interesting thoughts. I'm also not of a religious persuasion. But we have to imagine how those who have spent their whole lives believing in something would react if they suddenly found out it has all been a lie?" Creed clicked his fingers. "Your belief; taken away just like that!"

Ben finished eating and thought about the question. "I think if what I believed in was a lie, I would rather know the truth."

"I knew you would find it hard to understand. I'm not sure what would happen if this secret became public knowledge, but if it destroyed the Catholic Church, perhaps thousands will die as a result. Apart from the fighting between religious groups proclaiming their religion is the one true faith to fill the void left by the Church's collapse, there's also the possibility that many people might be so distraught they will choose death rather than live without their faith. In a worst-case scenario, it could bring about an epidemic of suicides. Could you live with that on your conscience, Ben, honestly?"

"Of course not, but you're only guessing what might happen, it doesn't mean it will. I'm not so sure it will be as bad as you think; this is the 21st century after all."

"Let's just say I'm not prepared to take the risk, but it seems you are."

The two men stared at each other.

Ben shrugged his shoulders. "This could all be irrelevant. We don't know for certain what's in the tomb. We only have Saunière's word for that. He could be mistaken or lying."

"Why would he confess his guilt and involvement with Gélis's death, and then tell such a lie on his deathbed during his last chance at salvation. It doesn't make sense."

"And everything else does? I find it easier to believe Saunière was mistaken. Just because the body has the marks of crucifixion, it doesn't mean it's Jesus. Many thousands were crucified during the Roman occupation of Jerusalem. Perhaps the Templars found the body of a crucified man and used it to persuade the Pope to grant them the favors and privileges that we know he did."

Creed pointed a fork at Ben. "You say thousands were crucified, but how many bodies showing marks of crucifixion have been discovered?"

"I see your point. I only know of one and that, if my memory serves me well, was just a large nail through a foot. However, even if there are the remains of a crucified man in the Tomb, there's still no possible way you could prove that anybody bearing the marks of the crucifixion is actually the Jesus mentioned in the Bible. Something the Vatican is sure to proclaim if the body was ever revealed. They'll find a way to work around it and survive as they have in the past."

"Okay. Let's not argue...I see only one solution."

"And that is?"

"I think we both need to see exactly what's in the Tomb."

Ben looked at Creed skeptically. "And how do you propose we achieve that?"

"We will have to enter the Tomb of course. Come on, you must have thought about it? My father did, and so have I."

"Of course I've thought about it, but there's no way in, I've searched the area. We might have to dig up half the hillside to find an entrance."

"Not necessarily. According to my father, his research led him to believe the Templars, through their network of spies, discovered the French king was constructing plans to arrest them. Forewarned, they decided on a plan to hide their most sacred possessions. Believing it would only be for a brief time and too risky to move them by ship in case they ended up at the bottom of the ocean, they elected to hide them on land. They found a perfect place near Rennes-le-Château, a suitable cave or tunnel, perhaps enlarging it for their purpose. Given the location of the tomb, I would imagine the original entrance was next to the river; perhaps partially or fully submerged. They could have dammed the river, temporally changing its course, excavated a tunnel leading into the side of the hill until they reached a natural cavern, as the tomb chamber seems to be from your film and photographs, which they then used to store their most precious objects. After they had placed everything inside, they backfilled the tunnel with earth and rocks, destroyed the dam and the river flowed again to hide the entrance. I assume they dug the tunnel at a rising angle so the water wouldn't enter the cavern."

"I agree it's a likely scenario," Ben said. "As Saunière makes no mention of damming a river, which we know is still there, he must have found another way in and, from the journal, we know his entrance was inside the cave above the tomb."

"Exactly, he must have dug a tunnel, and that's how we'll enter the Tomb, the same way Saunière did if we can find his entrance."

"It won't be easy. The cave covers a wide area, and I saw no hint of any entrance while I was there and believe me, I had a good look." Ben suddenly remembered something. "I could be wrong, but I think Saunière may have left us a clue in his church to point to the location of his tunnel entrance."

"That would be great if he has, what's the clue?"

"It will be easier to show you as it's in the altar bas-relief in Saunière's Mary Magdalene church. We must go to Rennes-le-Château so I can check if I'm right and you can see it for yourself."

"Now you have me worried. If Saunière left clues to find his tunnel, others might also find them."

"As far as I'm aware they haven't so far. I've only just realized because I read parts of the journal and I know the actual location." Ben glanced at the wall clock. "We have about an hour until the church opens."

"Okay, we'd better get a move on as I want to call into the bank on the way to put the journal back into safe keeping. I wanted you to see and read it, so you knew it was genuine and hopefully persuade you to do what's right."

"I appreciate the gesture."

Within ten minutes they were ready to leave. To save time searching for a parking space, they drove in Ben's hired car so he could wait outside the bank while Creed went inside. They arrived at Rennes-le-Château with a few minutes to spare.

After a wait of a couple of minutes, the jangling of keys signaled the approach of the museum's curator. A stern-faced woman appeared and used a large iron key to unlock the church door. She stepped inside its gloomy interior, switched on the lights and stood sentry just inside the entrance.

Ben and Creed went inside the church and like all who entered, were greeted by the sight of the demon — not the woman standing by the door — the Asmodeus statue. Although after a brief comparison of the two, the demon's face seemed more welcoming than the woman's — standing guard lest they attempted to vandalize the church as others had done in the past. Ben hoped Creed felt guilty.

Ben knew from past visits that if she were true to form, after assessing them to ensure they weren't about to damage anything, she would return to the museum office. They walked around the church, acting like the hundreds of tourists that visited each year. A few minutes later, she left.

Ben nipped outside and was back within a few seconds. "She's in the museum shop unpacking some boxes of books, so she'll be busy for a while."

They walked the length of the black and white checkered tiled floor leading to the altar, stepped over the low wrought iron gate and knelt to examine the bas-relief on the altar front. It portrayed Mary Magdalene kneeling in a cave with the opening behind her. Out through the entrance were some buildings, perhaps ruins, atop a hill, and a mountain. A small sapling, fashioned into a living cross, grew out of the cave floor and an open book and a skull were next to Mary.

Ben pointed to Mary's hands. "Look at her fingers, what do you see?"

Creed leaned closer. "Well, her fingers are entwined."

"Correct, or even crossed! Now look at the book, what do you see?"

"It's open and has some unreadable words on the pages and at the top two crosses."

Ben pointed to Mary Magdalene's face. "Now look at her eyes, where is she looking?"

"Apart from that patch of new plaster on the wall you mean?" replied Creed, as he examined the picture. "She looks directly at the wooden cross sprouting from the cave floor."

Ben ran a finger over the cross at the point from Mary's sightline. "To be more precise, she stares at the top of the cross."

Creed shrugged. "So there are many references to the cross in this scene. It's a religious picture after all?"

"But this is the only decoration in the church Saunière thought important enough to paint himself. If it was important to him, then it's as equally important to us as the priest did nothing without a purpose. There are so many crosses in the picture because I now believe he wanted to draw our attention to them. What is a cross if you turn it slightly?" Ben made a cross shape with two fingers and then turned them.

Creed stared at Ben's fingers, suddenly realizing what he was getting at. "An X!"

"Exactly! And on a treasure map, an X always marks the spot where you must dig. It's standard iconography." Ben pointed at the cross in the picture. "This cross is our X." He ran a finger down the length of the living cross and stopped at its base where it disappeared into the ground. "I believe this is where we'll find the entrance to Saunière's tunnel. It's all here in this picture; the open book is a symbol meaning that a secret is revealed here. The skull, also a symbol, tells us a body will be found, and as it's a skull, the body has been there a long time, probably a skeleton. And look where it's been placed in the picture, at the base of the cross. The rock forming the cave entrance here matches, more or less exactly, the rocks forming the entrance to the mountain cave." Ben stood as Creed continued to stare at the details in the picture.

After a few moments, Creed looked at Ben and smiled. "You really are good at this sort of thing."

Ben returned the smile. "Yes, I really am."

"You have me convinced, but it seems so obvious."

"Yes, but like I said before, only when you have found the cave does it all become obvious. Though I have no idea whether this X clue leads to Saunière's entrance to the tomb, I'm certain it leads to something hidden under the cave floor. As I said, the rocks forming the entrance to the cave, or grotto, above the tomb match exactly the entrance of the cave seen behind Mary Magdalene here, so using them as a reference it'll be easy to find the X position. There are clues all around us if you know how to read them." Ben was about to explain further when footsteps entered the church. They turned to see the woman curator glaring at them with her arms folded. She raised one arm to point at the exit. A group of German tourists wandered in, chattering excitedly. They briefly glanced at the two men climbing over the wrought iron gate before they turned their attention to studying the church decorations.

As they had finished what they came here to see, Ben and Creed exited the church, closely followed by the severe-faced curator. Creed suddenly grabbed Ben's arm and dragged him into the presbytery courtyard.

"What the…"

"Shush! We have company," Creed whispered urgently, as he peered around the side of the wall.

Ben felt eyes upon him. He turned. The curator, who had returned to the museum shop, stared at them through the large glass window. She probably wondered what mischief they were about to get up to now.

Creed looked over his shoulder at Ben. "Go buy two tickets for the museum, I'll explain in a minute, but hurry."

Ben glanced at the po-faced woman staring at them. *Thanks, Creed.* He entered the shop and purchased two tickets. The woman inside didn't say one word. She just glared. When he returned outside, Creed still peered around the stone wall. "I got them."

Creed glanced at the tickets in Ben's hand. "Follow me," he ordered and headed for the museum entrance.

Ben followed Creed through the open doorway and up the stairs. They rushed past exhibits connected to the mystery, which included one of the original pillars that once supported the original stone altar, and the knights stone that Saunière had found face down in his church until they arrived in the garden. A man at the controls of a mini-excavator was busy demolishing a building in the corner that had once been a café bistro. Ben had eaten breakfast and dinner there once when he had stayed in the Villa Bethania—one of Saunière's extravagant constructions—when it had been a hotel and before it became an integral part of the museum. The workman's tools were in an old wheelbarrow that had a length of orange tape tied to one handle, the other end fixed to the rail of the fence opposite, to cordon off the area where he worked.

Ben followed Creed into the room under the curved walkway where once a film on continuous loop informed visitors about the mystery that had brought them here, but now it was empty, except for a man varnishing a display case that would eventually house more exhibits in the museum. The man glanced briefly at the intruders with disinterest and carried on with his work.

Creed's eyes scanned the room. He ignored the landscape vistas out through the arched windows dynamited into the wall by one of the domain's previous owners; he looked for an escape route, but seeing none, he rushed back out into the garden. They raced up the steps onto the curved battlements that led to the Magdala Tower to the left, and to the right, a replica of the tower made in glass, the Orangery.

Creed peered over the edge. It was a long drop to the ground. No escape that way. "Go inside the tower, I'll be back in a minute." Creed sprinted across the garden without further explanation.

Willing to follow Creed's lead, for now, Ben entered the Magdala Tower that was once home to Saunière's collection of books, stamps, and postcards, and waited for him to return. He gazed through one of the windows, shivering involuntarily at the sight of the cobwebs around its frame; where there were cobwebs, there were spiders. Though he didn't see any eight-legged fiends, he did see Creed grab something from the workman's wheelbarrow and run back toward the tower. *What's he up to now?* A movement caught his eye. Two men dressed in dark suits exited the museum and watched Creed rush along the terrace and into the tower.

Ben glanced at the rope Creed held. "Those two men saw you come in here."

Creed glanced out at the two men staring at the tower. "Good, now all they have to do is follow us inside."

A worried frown creased Ben's forehead as he observed the two men. "Are they Rex Deus?"

Creed shrugged. "I'm not sure, but they were watching my house last night and must have again this morning and followed us here. They are learning as normally I spot them easily."

"Why are we running from them? Surely they won't do anything in such a public place."

"You're probably right, but I don't want to take the risk with you here. Anyway, we'll have to give them the slip before we go to the Tomb."

Ben again glanced at the rope Creed held. "I assume you have a plan to accomplish this?"

Creed smiled. "I do. But first, we have to wait for them to come into the tower. In the meantime perhaps you can tell me how you found the tomb cave using Saunière's clues."

"It's easy really. In the altar bas-relief, did you notice the unusual formations out through the entrance of the grotto Mary Magdalene kneels in? They look like 'J' and 'M,' perhaps Jesus and Mary's initials."

"Yes, I noticed them."

"I believe they could also be 'T' and 'M' to stand for this tower, the Tour Magdala. The second part of the clue is the grotto Mary kneels in. All I did was draw a line on a map of the area from this tower; from the small side tower that contains twenty-two steps to be exact. July 22nd is Mary Magdalene's feast day when she is celebrated and remembered. I extended the line through the grotto Saunière built in his garden, which once held a statue of Mary

Magdalene, and into the landscape. The line ran through a rock formation on a nearby hill, and to another rock formation shaped liked two Ms. It's clearly visible on a map of the area."

"Mary Magdalene," said Creed with interest.

"Believing this couldn't be a coincidence, and Saunière was pointing to something important, I went to this rock formation below the two Ms rock and found a cave — or grotto- hidden behind a bush. It matches the image of a priest standing beside a bush in the large Fleury tableau above the confessional. That's how I found the cave, which I've named the *M Cave*. A search and some digging revealed the small shaft I lowered a video camera down to film the hidden tomb below.

Creed was impressed. That's amazing and seems so simple when it's explained like that, yet no one else seems to have deciphered the clues to find it."

Ben shrugged. "Maybe it's too simple, and researchers dismiss it." He looked out at the two men. They hadn't moved from their position by the Villa Bethania. "Maybe they won't come in here, they seem to be waiting for us to come out."

"They'll come," stated Creed, with certainty.

But David and Doyle made no attempt to approach the tower. They were probably content to wait them out as the only exit was back through the museum and they had that covered.

While they all waited for each other to make a move, the German tourists continuing their tour of Saunière's domain, entered the garden and eventually arrived at the Tour Magdala. They stared at Ben and Creed as they crossed the small square room and climbed the narrow, winding stairs onto the battlements. After ten minutes spent admiring, photographing and filming the panoramic views, they descended the staircase and, in single file, exited the tower. Ben and Creed watched their progress through the garden and into the Villa Bethania.

One of the men glanced at his watch and said something to his partner as they looked over at the tower, no doubt wondering what they were doing in there for so long. Finally, they came to a decision and headed for the tower.

"Creed, they're coming."

Creed peered out of the window and smiled. "Good, now it's time to put my plan into action. Come with me." Ben followed

Creed up the narrow stairs to the flat roof. "Keep low, so they don't see you," Creed advised when they reached the metal door that led onto the top of the tower. Crouching below the level of the crenels, Creed laid the rope on the roof and pushed the door closed, its rusty hinges squealed loudly. "Give me a hand with the ladder."

Together they picked up the long, rusty metal ladder, used for access to the tall round tower that rose up in one corner and overlooked the side of the hill the village was built on. When Creed placed his end against the door, Ben realized part of the Frenchman's plan and wedged his end against the opposite side of the tower. Creed tested the door. Firmly jammed shut by the ladder, it didn't budge.

Voices drifted up to them when the two men paused at the entrance to the tower below. Ben and Creed remained silent and tried to eavesdrop on what was being said, but they spoke too quietly. Creed peered cautiously over the top and watched the men entered the tower. He quickly looped the rope around one of the crenels and let both ends drop to the ground. "Climb down after me," he whispered.

Creed climbed onto the top of the wall and slid down the rope onto the walkway. Ben followed him down. Creed peered around the side of the open door into the tower. The two men were looking up the spiral steps.

"They must be on the roof as there's nowhere else to go," said David.

"Maybe they jumped off," suggested Doyle.

"Don't be so damned stupid." David then thought about it. "Come on, we had better take a look."

When they stepped onto the stairs, Creed slipped quietly inside, rushed across the room and slammed the thick, wooden staircase door shut and slid the two heavy bolts into place. The shouts of surprise from the men now trapped in the stairwell could be heard from the other side of the thick door. The curve and narrowness of the stairway and the strong bolts holding it closed prevented them from kicking it open.

Creed walked out onto the walkway, closed the tower's main door and slipped the padlock into place. He pulled on the rope, which uncurled from around the crenel and dropped to the ground.

"Plan accomplished," Creed stated as he coiled the rope.

Ben smiled. "You're good at this."

Creed smiled back. "Yes, I am. See what a good team we make?"

They both laughed.

"Let's get out of here. We have much work to do."

On the way back to the museum and the exit, Creed deposited the rope he had borrowed back into the workman's wheelbarrow. The workman, sitting down eating his lunch, shot Creed a confused stare.

CHAPTER 5

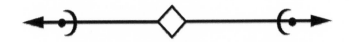

X Marks the Spot

THE WINDING DIRT track, rutted and covered in potholes, was not the best surface condition for the small rental car to traverse. The wheels threw up stones that ricocheted loudly off the bottom of the vehicle. Over-hanging branches whipped and scraped at the paintwork and in places the car bottomed and scrapped on the rough track. Ben grimaced with every bang, clink, and scrape and imagined a trail of car parts left in its wake. The previous day's rain had collected into too many muddy puddles to avoid them all and splashed dirty water over the paintwork and windscreen, which the wipers duly smeared over the glass.

Ben pressed the brakes hard, bringing the car to a skidding halt. They both peered through the dirty screen at the deep ruts made by the much larger foresters' vehicles that generally used the track.

"There's no way this car will get past that," Ben stated.

Creed agreed. "It's not far now, we'll continue on foot."

Ben reversed and parked the car on a patch of wild grass off to one side of the track. He climbed out and gazed forlornly at the mud-splattered vehicle; it looked like it had been in a rally through a swamp. He pulled off a small branch that had lodged in the bumper. "Bang goes my insurance deposit."

Creed laughed. "Don't worry; it'll look as good as new when it's cleaned."

Ben gazed at the car doubtfully; he didn't share Creed's confidence. After they had collected their rucksacks from the boot, he beeped the vehicle locked, and followed Creed along the track. Though they avoided treading in the deepest sections of mud, in places it covered the tracks' width so couldn't be avoided. After walking for twenty minutes, they arrived at the M Cave entrance. Ben noticed the bush was a lot bushier than on his last visit, concealing the opening even more from casual passers-by. This was good as the track had recently become part of a wide-ranging group of trekking routes that covered the hills, valleys, and mountains.

After checking no one was about, Ben and Creed climbed up the rocky cliff, squeezed behind the bush that hid the entrance and slipped inside the cave. Ben held Creed back with an outstretched arm and examined the dirt strewn cave floor for footprints, a sign that someone had been here. It had become a habit for him to wipe the cave floor with a branch every time he left not only to cover his tracks but also to alert him if someone else had visited the cave. He stared at the single set of footprints, evidence someone had.

Creed saw the object of Ben's concern. "It's okay, they're mine." He planted his foot next to one of the prints to leave an imprint; they matched precisely.

Relieved, Ben gazed around the cave dimly lit by the light penetrating through the thick undergrowth covering the entrance. Creed took the powerful lamp from his rucksack and switched it on, flooding the cave with its bright light. Ben crossed to the back of the cave and took from his pocket the large postcard he'd hurriedly purchased from the Rennes-le-Château bookshop before they'd left the village earlier. He was still amazed at how well the cave in the altar matched the rocks forming the entrance. He stepped forward a few paces, knelt down at the spot he thought was indicated by the living cross in the picture and drew a cross in the soft earth with a finger.

"X marks the spot," said Creed.

Ben slipped the small rucksack from his shoulder, pulled out a fold-up spade and began digging while Creed kept watch at the entrance for any hikers who might wander along the trail below.

After digging down half a meter, Ben struck rock. He widened the hole until he revealed more of the bedrock. The area he'd excavated was solid except for one place one side of it. He pointed at the edge of the rock. "Take a look at this, Creed, chisel marks!"

"Saunière?" questioned Creek.

Ben nodded. "I assume so. I'll widen the hole farther to see how big it is." Ten minutes more digging revealed a roughly shaped area almost a meter square chiseled from the rock.

"That has to be the start of Saunière's tunnel, exactly where the cross in the altar pinpointed it," said Ben triumphantly.

Creed grinned. "Well done."

"We have no choice now, we have to excavate the tunnel," Ben said, excited at the prospect of entering the tomb that had for so long been out of his reach. "It will be hard work, but we have to find out what's really in the tomb." Ben looked at Creed, knowing he would agree; he couldn't do it alone. "We need to discover if Saunière was telling the truth. As you said, entering the tomb would prove it one way or the other."

Creed glanced at the hole and then at Ben. "I need no convincing. We follow in Saunière's footsteps and enter the tomb. It's only a matter of time before someone else like you solves the clues and finds the tomb. If we do find out Saunière was telling the truth, then we can safeguard the secret by moving the stuff to a safer place, if not, then it doesn't matter, you can do what you want with it."

Ben held out a hand. "It's a deal." They shook hands. "To err on the side of caution, let's refill the hole until we can return with some better equipment."

As they pushed the earth back into place,

Creed glanced around the cave. "I think when we do return we'd better stay here. It's dry, and there's plenty of room for a couple of sleeping bags. Traveling back and forth each day will only attract attention. Also, there are the two men to consider. Having to give them the slip every day could prove difficult. I have a four-wheel drive we can use, so we can drive right up to the cave entrance to unload all the stuff we'll need, but I'll have to find somewhere to hide it while we excavate."

"I agree," said Ben. "Those men we locked in the tower must have been let out by now and are probably waiting at your house for our return?"

"They might have escaped from the tower, but it's going to take them some time to get four tires fixed. While you were buying the postcard, I slashed the tires on their car."

Ben admired Frenchman's quick thinking. "Brilliant!"

"If we hurry we might be able to get to my place, load up with the stuff we need and be back before they return. Normally I wouldn't take the risk, but everything we need is at the house. If they're waiting for us, I'll just have to think of another plan to shake them off."

Remembering how easily Creed had foiled them before, Ben had every confidence that he could do again.

They walked back to the car and drove to Creed's home. Both were relieved to see no sign of the black car or the two men. Creed led Ben into a large detached building that he assumed was once a stable. Creed walked over to the back wall and pulled back a tarpaulin to reveal everything they would need to dig a tunnel and more. Ben stared at the stack of items; shovels, forks, hammers, chisels, even wooden props, and planks of wood to support the tunnel as they dug; all cut to size. There was a pile of lamps and a box of spare batteries. Also buckets, rope, a gas-powered cooking stove, tins of food, saucepans, and cooking implements, a bag of plastic plates, spoons, knives, and forks. Toilet paper, bottles of water, sleeping bags, in fact, everything they could possibly need for the work ahead.

Creed smiled at the astonished look on Ben's face. "Surprised?"

"That's an understatement. Why is all this stuff here?"

"To use as a last resort. I didn't know if you would answer my emails or if you would decide to go ahead and publish the Tomb's location. I was prepared to dig a tunnel myself, though I had no idea where to start of course. I put it all on hold when you agreed to meet me."

Ben was astonished. "If you'd gone ahead and cleared the tomb, it would have been empty when I published my book. When the authorities excavated, they would have found nothing. I would have been ridiculed."

Creed grinned. "But now everything has changed, we're in this together whatever happens. You'll still have a book to write, it just won't be the story you first envisioned."

"I suppose you're right."

"Of course I am. Now let's get this stuff loaded before those two thugs turn up again. I don't expect they'll be in the best of moods when they do finally arrive."

Spurred on by the thought of re-encountering the two men, they soon had all the stuff loaded on Creed's 4x4. Ben drove his hire car into the building and Creed locked the large door.

They thought if all went well, it would take them about five or six days to dig through to the Tomb chamber, but they allowed enough food and water for nine. When Creed steered the Landrover out of his drive, the black car drove at speed towards them.

"Creed, they're back."

Creed had seen them. He pressed down on the accelerator. The powerful three-liter engine shot the Landrover forward and passed the men coming from the opposite direction before they had time to react.

Ben saw them glare at him as they shot by. "They don't look very happy."

"Now there's a surprise. Don't worry, I have an idea."

"What are you going to do?"

"Something I planned on in case this situation arose. Make sure your seatbelt's fastened tight, it's going to be a bumpy ride."

Placing his trust in the Frenchman, Ben checked his seatbelt was secured.

Creed glanced in the rear-view mirror. The black car skidded an impressive U-turn, accelerated fast and soon closed the gap. "Here they come."

Ben turned to gaze back as the car pulled up behind them and matched their speed. The traffic prevented Creed from increasing his speed or overtaking, but he wasn't unduly concerned. Ten minutes later he saw the signpost he'd been waiting for and turned off the main route onto the road that led to the small village of Rennes-les-Bains.

Ben stared at the towering Mount Cardou rising on his left. According to the authors Richard Andrews and Paul Schellenberger, in their book, *The Tomb of God*, hidden under tons of rock on this mountain is a secret burial, in fact, the Tomb of God.

Content to follow, the black car made no attempt to overtake, but continued to match Creed's speed and remained a short distance behind.

Creed led them straight through the village, past the local campsite and swung sharp left onto a small bridge spanning the shallow river and onto a narrow, twisting country lane with trees lining both sides. The black car continued its pursuit.

Without any warning, Creed turned the steering wheel hard to the left. The car skewed to the side as it sought purchase on the stony track. Creed changed down a gear and pressed hard on the accelerator. The rear wheels spun, flipping up two arcs of dirt and stones. When the tires found traction, the Landrover shot forward.

"This is where it gets bumpy so hang on," Creed warned.

Ben thought Creed seemed to actually be enjoying himself. When the wheels hit a large bump, Ben was thrown to one side. He grabbed the handle above the door to steady himself.

David, caught unaware by the sudden change of direction, over-shot the turning. The car skidded to a halt, leaving two lines of burnt rubber on the tarmac. He crunched it into reverse, shot backward and after breaking hard slammed it into first gear and drove onto the track after the fleeing Landrover. The black car's lower ground clearance scraped bottom on the dirt mounds, sometimes taking the tops off, with the speed of the vehicle the being the only thing that carried it over.

The dirt track became gradually bumpier and pitted with mud-filled potholes and ruts. The rougher it got, the faster Creed seemed to go. This caused the car following to increase its speed to keep up. Ben was thrown around all over the place. He could only imagine how uncomfortable it was for those men following in their ill-suited saloon car.

After rounding a sharp bend, the track dropped into a steep slope and then rose up again. Ben gazed at the large puddle of water collected at the bottom and knew the submerged road would be nothing but mud.

Creed didn't hesitate. He sped down the hill and straight through the deep puddle. Two fountains of muddy water sprayed out from under the wheels either side. The vehicle struggled to find a grip in the thick mud and skidded towards the steep drop on their left. Creed turned into the skid until the four-wheel drive found traction and carried them through onto solid ground.

David tried his hardest to see through the mud splattered windscreen, but the useless wipers smeared the mud and dirty water the Landrover threw in his path over the glass. He felt the car dip as he sped down the steep slope. The depth pool of water at the bottom only became apparent when the Landrover entered the puddle to spray his car with a fresh supply of thick muddy water. When the wipers had cleared the screen enough for him to see through the smeared glass, he glimpsed the large puddle and knew the car would never get through. He slammed on his brakes. The wheels locked and skidded. David released his foot from the brake pedal and pressed on the gas pedal; hoping speed would carry them through. The car entered the puddle, and the two men thought they were going to make it, but halfway across the wheels lost traction and spun in the thick mud. The car slowly skewed towards the long drop into the valley below. Luckily the car's slide halted when one of its front wheels dropped over the edge and grounded the vehicle on the front axle. David glanced down at the steep drop and the rocks below and then glared at the Landrover pulling to a stop at the top of the hill. He cursed its passengers. He slipped the car into reverse and pressed the accelerator. He sighed when the wheels spun freely. He lifted his foot off the throttle; they were going nowhere fast. As the car settled into the mud, the water washing over the engine sizzled on the hot metal. Steam rose into the air as the engine coughed and died.

Creed turned in his seat to join Ben looking back at the black car.

"Plan accomplished," said Creed smugly. "They won't be getting out of there any time soon."

Creed pressed the horn and waved.

The two men glared back through the mud-smeared windscreen and Doyle wound down his window and gave them the finger.

Creed put the Landrover in gear, drove off and they were soon on the track to the M-Cave far from the stranded black car and the two angry men.

David seethed with anger. He regretted ever setting foot on French soil. It was far from the relaxing outing he had imagined when Silas had first mentioned it.

"So…what's next?"

David turned his head and looked at Doyle. "One of us has to go and find someone to tow us out of this swamp. Obviously, when I say one of us, I mean you."

Doyle was about to argue, but the angry look on David's face convinced him that wouldn't be his wisest option. "But I have no idea where we are or what direction to go in for help," he complained.

"We passed what seemed to be a farm a while back, they might have a four-wheel drive or a tractor to tow us out."

"But that's about five kilometers away."

David shook his head. "More like ten, so you'd better get moving. I don't want to sit here all day."

Grumbling under his breath, Doyle opened the car door and stared at the muddy water he would have to step through to reach solid ground.

David grinned. "Looks like you'll get your feet wet."

Doyle placed one foot in the water and shivered. "It's fucking freezing."

"So is the draft flooding through that open door, get out and shut the damn thing."

Doyle glared at his partner before placing his other foot in the water and climbed out. The thick mud sucked at his feet when he stepped away from the car and slammed the door shut. When he took another step, he had to tug hard to pull his foot from the mud's grasp. Suddenly, his foot came free, but the clinging mud kept hold of his shoe. He toppled and fell to his knees in the muddy water.

David had been watching Doyle in the wing mirror, and he grinned when Doyle tripped and continued smirking as Doyle groped in the mud for his missing shoe.

Doyle pulled his shoe from the sucking mud and scrambled onto dry land. He emptied the thick muddy water from it and slipped it onto his muddy foot. He glared at David sitting in the car and cursed the man's laziness. He turned away and began his walk up the steep track. His feet squelched with every step. He had a long uncomfortable walk ahead of him.

Creed pulled the car to a stop directly below the M-Cave and together they quickly unloaded the car and carried everything up into the cave. Thirty minutes later, while Ben organized the gear in the cave, Creed drove his car back along the track to a turn-off they'd spied earlier. It sloped down to the river, and by the look of the weeds, brambles, and wildflowers growing over its surface it hadn't been used for years. He was confident car would remain undetected for the duration of their excavation.

By the time Creed returned, Ben had everything stored out of the way along the back of the cave. He had also set up the gas ring and put some water on ready for Creed's coffee and his tea. After leaving the two men stranded, Creed had driven to a shop so Ben could purchase tea bags, milk, sugar, butter, cookies, fresh bread and a packet of six chocolate bars.

Soon, they were both sitting against the side of the cave sipping their warm drinks. It had been an eventful day, and it wasn't over yet.

"Do you think they've managed to get their car out of the mud yet?" asked Ben, adding a smile.

Creed shook his head. "I think that is most unlikely. They'll have to find someone to tow them out, probably need a tractor to do that. Unluckily for them, no one lives near there so they'll have a long walk to find help."

Ben smiled. "Good."

After they finished their drinks, they started digging and soon uncovered Saunière's tunnel entrance again. Ben loosened the earth with a small pickaxe and Creed shoveled it out, throwing it to one side where it wouldn't be in their way. After they had dug down about a meter, they hit solid rock. They cleared away the soil and found the rock was only on three sides. The fourth was filled with earth and headed for the back of the cave. They continued digging in that direction, slowly forming a tunnel that led into the hillside.

The first meter led through rock, which needed no supporting, but after that, it went through soil, which did. To prevent the roof and sides caving in, they used the timber they had brought with them to shore up the shaft. The size of the wood governed the size of the tunnel; slightly less than a meter square. Any large rocks they came across were carried out and stacked at the cave entrance to form a wall, which gave them another place to pile the excavated earth. Before long, they had to use buckets to move the dirt as they dug farther into the hill.

When they tipped the soil out, they compacted it by stamping on it to try and reduce the space it took up. Both men wanted to avoid having to carry the dirt out of the cave as not only would this be time-consuming, it might be seen by someone.

When it grew dark outside, they lit a couple of lanterns, the brightness at first making them squint after their adjustment to the gloomy cave. Worried that the light would be seen, Ben went outside to check. He stood on the track below and looked up at the light escaping from the cave, which would become brighter as the night grew darker. Though it was unlikely anyone would be on the mountain so late, if someone did pass below the cave, the light would stand out like a beacon to signal their presence.

Ben returned to the cave and with some difficulty managed to fix a blanket over the entrance. When he checked outside, he was pleased to see the thick material blocked any light from escaping.

They had been digging for five hours, and the strenuous work that was a stranger to them both had made them tired and hungry. They decided to take a break and have something to eat. Ben searched through the stores and chose a large tin of stew. It had, according to the description on the tin, delicious chunks of prime beef and succulent vegetables, which included carrots, swede, peas, and potatoes. Ben opened the can and stared at the congealed mass of fatty gravy with lumps of the ingredients described on the tin poking above the surface; it bore little resemblance to the enticing image on the label.

"Don't look so worried, it'll taste okay," reassured Creed when he noticed the look of doubt on his friend's face.

"I've yet to be convinced." Ben stood the tin in a large saucepan half-full of water boiling away on the gas ring and stirred the contents occasionally while Creed buttered some slices of French bread. While he waited for the stew to heat through, Ben glanced at the remaining tins of stew left in the box and hoped that miraculously its contents would taste as appetizing as the mouthwatering picture on the label.

When the stew was ready, Ben dished it out onto two, deep paper plates. Ben tasted a spoonful and was surprised to find that Creed had been right, it was quite tasty. They both eagerly ate until the large tin was empty.

"Do you fancy some wine to wash it down?" asked Creed.

Ben nodded as his mouth was too full of stew to speak. Creed opened a bottle and poured some into two plastic cups. Ben finished his meal and placed the disposable plates, cutlery and the empty can into a black plastic bag.

"That was surprisingly nice, and filling," Ben said as he leaned against the side of the cave wall to rest while sipping the wine.

They both looked at the tunnel, deep in their own thoughts. Ben wondered how far it went before it opened into the tomb below. So far it showed no sign of angling down as he'd expected it would but reasoned so far they'd only dug a short passage. No doubt, when they dug farther, the direction will change.

Creed stood and stretched out in an attempt to relieve his aching muscles. Revived by the meal, Ben drank the remainder of his wine and climbed to his feet and they continued digging.

The width of the tunnel only allowed one of them to excavate at a time, so they took turns. While Creed dug and filled the buckets, Ben emptied them. Every half a meter they paused to shore it up and swap positions. Although the work was hard and working conditions uncomfortable, Ben found hacking away at the soil strangely therapeutic. When he struck the tunnel face with the blade of the shovel to loosen the wall of earth, it clanged on a rock, as it had done many times before. The rock was at the top of the tunnel so Ben dug underneath it so it could be removed. It turned out to be quite large compared to the others, about half a meter in diameter, though only a few centimeters thick, so he thought it should be easy enough to move. Before long he had it cleared, and though it was no longer supported by the earth underneath, it remained in place. He placed the spade on the ground to leave both hands free, gripped the rock as best he could in the cramped space and pulled. After some effort, it came loose. Before he had time to react, a torrent of earth covered his head and shoulders. Unable to breathe when his mouth and nose were smothered by the suffocating earth, Ben began to panic. He tried to move backward, but the earth pressing down on his chest was too heavy. He was trapped and dying. His only hope was Creed.

Unaware of the danger Ben faced, Creed tipped the bucket of earth onto the pile and set to the ritual of stamping it down. When he was done, he grabbed a bottle of water and took a long gulp before replacing the lid. He picked up the empty bucket, crossed to the tunnel and bent down to pass it to Ben. Shock spread across his face when he saw Ben's legs sticking out from underneath a pile of earth that had collapsed on top of him.

"Ben!" He shouted. He jumped into the hole, crawled along the tunnel, grabbed hold of his ankles and pulled with all his strength. Slowly, Ben slid out from under the cave-in. Creed quickly cleared the soil from his mouth and nose. He had blacked out but was still breathing, as Creed saw from his rising and falling chest. He slapped him gently on his cheeks in an attempt to revive him. Ben slowly came to. His eyes focused on Creed's worried face. He turned his head and spat out the mouthful of dirt he'd nearly swallowed when he'd gasped for breath.

"Can't a man get any sleep around here?" he said, smiling weakly.

"I could always put you back," Creek replied, relieved his friend was okay. He helped Ben to sit up. "Are you okay?"

"I think so, thanks to you."

"Don't mention it. I would've left you there, but you were blocking the tunnel."

Ben laughed painfully. His chest felt like someone had jumped on it. He glanced back at the cave in. "Is there much damage?"

"Just some extra earth to move is all," replied Creed, "but that can wait until tomorrow. I think we've done enough for today. We should get some rest."

Ben readily agreed and climbed out of the hole.

Still shaken, Ben sat against the wall. His chest ached from the weight of the soil pressing on it. He watched Creed lay out the thick sleeping bags as he thought about the lucky escape he'd just had. *If Creed had not been here, I would've died.*

"Thanks again, Creed. I owe you."

"You would do the same for me."

Ben stared over at the hole. "Let's hope that won't be necessary."

CHAPTER 6

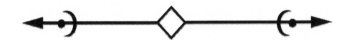

Hunter and Hunted

THE LARGE MALE wild boar, oblivious to the lethal weapon aimed at him by the man concealed in the bushes close by, sniffed the air with his blunt snout. The scent trail of the female it had followed was much stronger here and an indication she might be near. As it moved nearer to the source, it suddenly bounded off into the bushes.

Philippe cursed as he fired the crossbow bolt at the fleeing boar. He had spent weeks hunting down the large beast he'd only glimpsed once before. It was a legend amongst local hunters. Some had also glimpsed it, others said it didn't exist and was something they had imagined. Tonight he'd set out to prove them wrong and had almost succeeded until the boar was frightened off by someone shouting out a name, *Ben*.

The hunter knew the urine he had taken from the bladder of the female boar he'd killed almost a week ago would lead the male to him. The bait had worked. Another few seconds and he would've had a perfect shot. He, too, had heard the man's voice that had frightened away his prey and brought a swift end to his hunt. He walked over to where he'd last seen the boar and stared at the patch of darkness on the ground. He knelt, dabbed a finger in it and looked at his red-stained finger; blood. He had injured the beast. He glanced over to where it had disappeared. Its large size already established it as a formidable opponent, but now wounded it would be in pain and angry. He pitied anyone who got in its way. He would return tomorrow to follow the blood trail to its lair.

He crossed to the edge of the drop and looked down. Though too dark to see much, faint voices indicated there were at least two people somewhere below. Puzzled as to where they were and what they were up to, Philippe went to find out.

Ben stood with a grimace from his aching chest and shoulders. "I'm nipping out for a piss."

He pulled back the blanket curtain, stepped out and gazed up at the star-speckled sky while he emptied his bladder over the side of the cliff. It was a cold, clear night full of stars that shone brightly amidst the sea of blackness. It never ceased to amaze Ben how much clearer and closer the stars seemed here without any light pollution to shroud them.

Creed came out and stood beside him as he too urinated. Dark grey clouds loomed over the moon ominously as they both stared up at the night sky. Ben smiled at the sight they would have made to anyone watching.

They finished and returned to the cave, the light within briefly escaping when they shifted the blanket aside to enter, momentarily illuminating the face of the man hiding in the shadows close to where they'd been standing.

Philippe, a seasoned hunter, was an expert at moving silently through the undergrowth. He had followed the sound of the voices and had been listening to them outside the cave for some time, even peering through the curtain he had moved aside slightly to see what those inside were doing. With no time to climb down when Ben unexpectedly emerged from the cave, he had quickly slipped over the side to conceal himself in the shadows of the shrub-covered rock. He had to endure the splashes of urine on his face and clothes so as not to reveal his presence. When the two men had returned to the cave, he remained still for a few moments longer, listening until he'd heard enough. Philippe quietly climbed back up onto the ancient mule trail above the cave, now rarely used by anyone except the occasional hunter or wild boar since the building of the modern roads; it was once part of the network of mule trails forming the main routes in and out of the area, reaching as far as Spain. Now forgotten and unused they were all but overgrown, but the hunter knew the trails well; he'd been using them since he was a young boy when his father taught him how to hunt. Silently he set off along the path and disappeared into the night.

Ben and Creed sat in their sleeping bags while they finished off the bottle of wine opened earlier. Ben, deep in thought, glanced around the cave lit by a single battery powered lantern. Its light cast a plethora of shadows across the cave roof and walls. His gaze lingered on the dark tunnel opening that had nearly become his grave.

Creed noticed him looking. "Will you be able to go back in tomorrow?"

Ben thought for a moment, though shook up by the experience he wasn't going to let it stop him from entering the tomb. "I'll be fine. We'll just have to be more careful."

"Do you have any idea why it caved in?"

"It happened when I removed a rock from the roof of the tunnel. I had dug farther than normal to clear the dirt around it, and earth poured in when I removed it."

"Do you think it was deliberate, a trap?"

Ben shrugged. "It's possible. By all accounts, Saunière was a resourceful guy. Maybe he set it as a precaution in case Gélis or someone else tried to reach the tomb."

"But why would Saunière leave clues to the tomb in his church and then leave traps to protect it. Where's the sense in that?"

"Don't forget, Saunière refilled this tunnel before he built the church...therefore," replied Ben, summarising a possible conclusion, "perhaps, before he decided to leave clues to its whereabouts, he had set the trap as a safeguard in case someone tried to gain access before he finally decided what to do with what remained inside. Maybe he planned to come back sometime in the future."

"Whatever the reason, a trap or not, as you suggested, we'll have to proceed with extra caution from now on. I propose we get some rest, we've got a lot to do tomorrow." Creed switched off the light, shrouding the cave in darkness.

As Philippe made his way along the old trail, he thought about how much the information about the two men might be worth. They were obviously treasure hunters, just two of the many who had visited the area over the past years. All believed they'd solved the clues supposedly left by that damn fool of a priest, Saunière, to the hidden source of his wealth.

Philippe too, when he'd been younger and naive, though he wouldn't admit it, had once wasted much of his time in the fruitless search, but no more, he was certain it was just a myth. Whatever Saunière may have found, he now believed it was long gone. Though the two men in the cave seemed to be taking it more seriously than most, he had no doubt they would also have a fruitless search. They could dig up the whole hill and would still find nothing. But just because the two men wouldn't profit from their digging, there was no reason he shouldn't. He knew of someone who had recently moved to the area and who kept a very close eye on all that happened in and around Rennes-le-Château. The rumor was that he would pay well for such information. His only concern was the lateness of the night. The man was probably asleep.

Philippe stepped off the rough ground onto the flat tarmac of the modern road. He looked both ways as he tried to reach a decision as to what he should do. Turning left would lead him back home to his house in Couiza, where his wife lay snuggled up in bed, or right to Arques, where the man lived. If he waited until morning the men might have given up and scarpered, or, if miracles did happen, find what they were searching for and leave. Both scenarios left him with nothing. His greed got the better of him. He hid his crossbow in the bushes to collect on his return and turned towards Arques. He would rather risk the man's anger than risk losing any money he could have received for the information. Being shouted at he could live with, being poor was a lot harder.

A short while later, he arrived at the gate barring the driveway that led to the house of the man he'd come to see. Philippe peered through the railings at the light shining from one of the upstairs windows, an indication someone was still awake. He searched for a way to open the gate or make his presence known. He found a bell push and pressed the button. While he waited, he glanced around and noticed the camera staring down at him from the end of a high pole set in the grounds of the house.

Philippe was startled by a man's tinny voice from the small speaker fixed to the gatepost.

"What do you want?"

He leaned nearer the speaker. "Hello, I have some information."

"What sort of information?" inquired the voice.

"Information about some treasure hunters," Philippe replied, nervously.

The man inside the house stared at the monochrome screen of the security monitor set atop the chest of drawers in his bedroom. He had similar monitors all around the house connected to the many cameras strategically positioned around the grounds. All were motion sensitive. He was naked and still damp from his recent shower, the tattoo of a rose with a cross at its center clearly visible over his heart. He'd been about to retire when he had been alerted to the man's presence even before he had reached the gate and pressed the bell. He stared at the man on the monitor, who was obviously nervous and posed no threat. He pressed a button on the front of the monitor. The gate swung open as he spoke into the microphone built into the unit.

Philippe was wondering why the man was taking so long to reply when he was again startled by the speaker's voice.

"Come to the front door."

Again, Philippe jumped when the gate latch buzzed loudly, and the electrically operated gate swung open.

He stepped onto the driveway and approached the large house, turning to glance at the gate when it clanged shut. It was only a short distance and he soon arrived at the front door that was already open. Another camera stared down at him from above the door. Hesitantly, Philippe stepped into the house. The hall was in darkness except for light spilling from the open door of a room just inside. "Hello," he called out.

"In here. Close the front door," ordered the man, his voice emanated from the lit room.

Philippe did as instructed and entered the room. He squinted at the bright light aimed at him from across the room and raised a hand to shield his eyes. He could just make out the shape of a man behind it, a movement and then the desk lamp's angle was altered to relieve his discomfort. Philippe lowered his arm and peered at the person sitting behind the desk. Though he could see an outline, he could make out no details of the man's face but noticed he wore a bathrobe and slippers. Philippe stepped toward the desk but froze mid-step when the man spoke.

"Stay there."

Philippe stepped back.

"I will ask some questions which you will answer. You will give clear, precise answers. Do you understand?"

Philippe nodded.

"Your name?"

"Philippe Comberre."

"Okay, Philippe, who are these treasure hunters?"

"I don't know them personally, but I heard them talking, their names are Creed and Ben."

A few moments went by before the man spoke again.

"Where are they?"

"In a cave in the Bezis valley. By a tributary of the River Sals. It's not easy to describe in words exactly where they are, but I can draw you a map."

"Sit down at the table behind you with your back to me. You are to remain facing the wall and not turn around, is that clear?"

Again Philippe nodded. Heeding the man's instructions, he sat at the table positioned beside the door with his back facing the room. He heard a drawer open and the rustle of paper but failed to hear the man's soft footsteps on the plush carpet, only realizing he had crossed the room when he startled him by leaning over his shoulder to place the paper and a pencil on the table before him. He smelt the taint of garlic on the man's breath. The highly polished surface of the mahogany table reflected the man's face. He was unable to stop himself from staring at it; the thin face and bald head, the eyes no more than dark shadows, but he could just make out the whiteness and the pupil at their center. Philippe watched as the eyes in the reflected image moved to stare directly into his own reflected face. He quickly averted his eyes and concentrated on drawing the map, missing the cruel smile that appeared on the thin-faced man's lips.

With the man's continued presence behind him, Philippe soon finished the map. After explaining the roads and local landmarks, Philippe traced his finger over the line representing the foresters' track.

"Just here." He said nervously, pointing to the X he'd marked on the rough sketch. "Here is the cave, just around this bend in the track. That's where they are."

Philippe sensed the man examining the map; this time he avoided looking at his reflection. Suddenly the map was snatched from the table. Philippe just had time to glimpse the ring on the man's finger, a blood-red rose on a black background.

Philippe heard the rustle of paper when the man returned behind his desk.

"What are they doing inside this cave?"

"Digging."

"Do you know what they are digging for?"

"Not exactly, but it's something to do with the priest, Saunière, probably looking for his treasure."

"How do you know this?" Enquired the man; a note of interest apparent in his voice.

"I heard them mention his name."

"But they didn't say exactly what they are looking for?"

"No."

"Is there anything else you can tell me about them?"

"Only that whatever they are digging for they don't expect to find it straight away as they have many provisions, also a small cooking stove. They might be staying there overnight as they have sleeping bags, but I don't know how long they've been there."

"You saw all this...how?"

"I was out hunting boar when I heard voices, so I followed them and peeked through the blanket they'd covered the cave entrance with. They didn't see me."

The man remained silent while he thought over the news. "You have done well, Philippe. Though I believe they are wasting their time, Saunière's treasure is nothing more than a myth, but we need to keep an eye on these treasure hunters."

"I agree, that's why I thought it best that I bring this information to you, in case it was important."

"You did the right thing."

A few moments later Philippe jolted in surprise when the man laid a hand on his shoulder and dropped something onto the desk in front of him.

"Something to show my appreciation."

Philippe looked at the money and then slid his hand across the table to clasp it in a sweaty palm.

"I have been generous, Philippe, because I feel I can trust you to keep this matter a secret."

Philippe nodded. "I will tell no one, Monsieur, of that you can be assured."

"I knew you would not let me down." He leaned closer and spoke into Philippe's ear while squeezing his shoulder tightly. "If I do hear you have spoken of this to anyone else, I will cut out your tongue and feed it to my dog."

Philippe grimaced, more from the man's threat than the pain caused to his shoulder. By the tone of the man's voice, he was sure he meant it.

"Speak of what, Monsieur? My memory is not what it used to be, I have forgotten already. By the time I'm out of your gate, I will have forgotten I have ever been here."

The man released his grip. "That is excellent. Sometimes forgetfulness is a virtue, no? Now go."

Philippe did not need telling twice. He quickly left.

The man crossed the room and switched on the security monitor sat on his desk, casting a grey light into the room. He watched Philippe walk quickly along the drive and opened the gate as he approached. Philippe hurried through without a backward glance. With the press of a button the gate closed. The man turned off the desk lamp, lit a cigarette and took a long drag. He exhaled the smoke in a single long breath.

He opened a drawer, took out a plain brown folder and laid it on the desk. After flipping it open, he picked up the photograph inside and stared at the man in the picture as he took another long drag of the cigarette.

"Well, Monsieur Harper, you have finally led me to your tomb."

He laid the photo down, walked over to a tall cupboard and pulled open the door. He ran a finger along racks of hanging files until he found the one he wanted, and carried it back to his desk. He opened the file and stared at the face of Jon Creed. A smile played on his lips.

"Your father may have thwarted me once, Creed, but you will not."

He picked up the phone and dialed a number. It rang once. "Yes."

"It's time," he said.

"Are you sure?" questioned the voice on the other end.

"I wouldn't be ringing if I wasn't. Harper and Creed have joined forces and are digging towards the tomb as we speak."

"How long do we have?"

"It's difficult to know for certain, but perhaps a few days at most."

"This is incredibly good news."

"I will put things in motion this end, and you will be contacted shortly with further details." He ended the call.

He took another drag on the cigarette and blew a smoke ring at the two photos on the desk. "At last, after all these years, our patience has been rewarded." He smiled cruelly.

CHAPTER 7

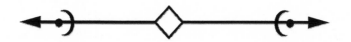

Unexpected Visitors

THOUGH BEN AWOKE to rays of sunlight filtering through the makeshift curtain into the cave, it wasn't this that dragged him out of his restful sleep; the aroma of strong coffee was guilty of this offense. Ben sat up. Creed knelt on the cave floor boiling a pan of water on the small gas ring.

Creed glanced over and smiled. "Good morning, Ben. I thought you were going to sleep all day."

"Morning Creed, I must have been more tired than I thought. I'm not used to all this hard work." He stretched out his chest and arms in an attempt to bring some relief to his aching muscles. "What's the time?"

"Just after eight, water's boiled if you want some tea."

"Thanks. That would be great." Ben climbed out of his sleeping bag and pulled on his clothes, dirt-stained from the previous day's toil. He had a clean set, but it was pointless wearing them until they'd finished the excavation. He nipped outside to urinate and on his return made himself a cup of tea. While Creed ate a breakfast of cold meat, cheese, and French bread, Ben had a Kit-Kat and drunk his tea.

"Is that all you're going to eat?" Creed questioned.

"It gives me a much needed morning energy boost. I'll eat something more substantial later." Ben glanced at the hole.

Creed saw the worried look appear briefly on Ben's face. He stood and picked up a spade. "I'll take the first shift in the tunnel."

"Fine with me," the thought of the collapsed tunnel was still fresh in Ben's mind.

Creed climbed into the hole and working together they soon cleared away the cave-in. As Creed dragged out the rock whose removal had caused the accident and lifted it onto the edge of the hole, he noticed something unusual. "Hey, Ben, come and look at this."

Ben recognized the excitement in Creed's voice and eagerly joined him to discover the reason. He looked at something on the slab Creed pointed at; the crudely fashioned skull and crossbones scratched onto its surface. Underneath were carved two letters, B.S.

"Bérenger Saunière, the priest's initials," stated Ben, now also excited by the discovery. "If we had any doubts the priest had not dug this tunnel before, there can be none now."

Creed nodded. "I agree. Its evidence he was responsible."

"So it was a trap!" Ben exclaimed.

Creed glanced at the skull and crossbones motif. "Seems likely," he agreed. "Give me a hand to move it."

Together they propped the large stone against the cave wall.

Shortly after Creed had re-entered the tunnel, he called for Ben to join him.

Ben crawled into the tunnel.

"That slab was blocking something." Creed pointed at the hole in the tunnel roof. "It's still blocked a little way in, but it must lead up to the surface. When Saunière backfilled the tunnel, he jammed this slab up against the roof to cover the opening and then filled it with soil from above."

Ben squirmed alongside Creed so he could peer into the shaft. Two meters up the narrow rocky hole, a plug of earth had been compacted by time in the small space. "We'll need to block the opening as it could collapse at any moment." Ben moved back along the tunnel. "I'll pass some wood along to you."

Ben passed Creed some pieces of wood and Creed used them to block the opening as the slab had done. Any earth that fell would be stopped by the planks. As he fitted the last upright support in place, hammering it with the shovel until it was wedged tight against the wood and the tunnel floor, earth in the shaft fell to land with a loud thud on the wood directly above his head.

Ben froze at the sound and stared along the tunnel. A small amount of dirt fell through the small gaps between the planks, but though the wood creaked, it held back the weight of the soil.

Creed gave a sigh of relief and smiled back at Ben. "Finished it just in time."

"Let's swap places," said Ben. "I'll have a go at digging now."

"Are you sure?"

"Yeah, it's not a problem."

Ben tried to ignore the tons of earth pressing down on the boards above him as he again began lengthening Saunière's tunnel. Though the soil did not always fill the passage completely, Saunière had done a satisfactory job of blocking it. Ben marveled at the hard work and effort for just one man and wondered why he had gone to so much trouble to fill the full length of the tunnel when he could have just filled the end few meters. *What was it that Saunière felt so important to conceal so thoroughly?*

1891 BEZIS VALLEY – TOMB CAVE

Saunière climbed down the steep slope and the rocky outcrop until he stood in front of the bush concealing the cave entrance. He paused to stare at the broken branches, evidence someone had discovered his secret. He was about to enter to find out what the unwelcome visitor had been up to when he noticed something glinting in the sunlight. He reached for the small silver chain snagged on a lower branch and dangled it in front of his eyes. He recognized it immediately. He had seen it hanging around the neck of a priest many times; Gélis had been here. The only way he could have discovered the cave was if he had followed him. He gripped the chain tightly. He was well aware of the man's miser's thirst for wealth and was sure a demand for payment would soon follow. The revelation would force him to conceal the secret earlier than planned. He slipped behind the bush and entered the cave.

After changing out of his priest's robes and pulling on his work attire, Saunière crawled along the tunnel and entered the chamber. He was surprised that everything seemed to be in place and Gélis had taken nothing. He crossed to the marble sarcophagus. The top had been slid open farther than he'd left it. Gélis had seen inside. He pulled the lid back into place and laid the new shroud he'd had made over the female corpse and smoothed it out, so the red Knights Templar cross was crease free. He stood back to admire his handiwork. It was, as far as he could tell, a fair replacement for the original tattered shroud that covered the body when he first gained entry to the tomb. He gazed around the chamber he had ransacked of any precious items he could easily dispose of. He would have taken more, but some of the objects were too precious or holy to be melted down or sold to the contact he and Alfred had found in Toulouse. For now, they would remain here with their keepers. His gaze turned to the shrouded body and sarcophagus once more. How he wished the body inside had been that of a knight. He sighed. What is done is done. "Alea iacta est!" (The die has been cast.) There can be no going back now. He would take the secret to his grave. He hadn't even told Maria. It was a burden that must weigh on his shoulders alone.

He moved to the entrance, crawled through the gap where he had removed blocks from the stone-wall the Knights Templar had constructed to protect the tomb so many hundreds of years ago and knelt beside the pile of rocks he had placed there and proceeded to block the hole with the stones. When he put the last stone in place, he briefly wondered who would be the next person to discover this secret. He knew he would probably never return.

He spent the next two days transporting the earth he had spent so many days excavating back into the tunnel. When he had a sufficient amount, he lay on his back and used his feet to compress it into the full height of the passage. He repeated this many times until at last the arduous task was completed. He spread the extra displaced soil over the cave floor until he was satisfied no trace of the tunnel entrance remained. He stripped off his dirty clothes, and after dressing in his black priest attire, he placed the dirty clothes and his tools into the wicker basket he had used to transport the treasure and left.

Three hours later Ben and Creed had dug another three meters into the hillside, but there was still no sign that the tunnel sloped down. Ben rammed the shovel into the earth ahead of him, jarring his arms when it struck something solid. Believing it to be another rock, he scraped the soil away and found he had come to a dead end, ahead was solid rock. "Creed, come and have a look at this," he called back along the tunnel.

Creed emptied the bucket of earth and then joined Ben in the tunnel. He watched as Ben struck the rock with the spade to show him the problem.

"It's solid."

Creed shone his head torch over the rock and pointed to something. "What's that?"

Ben followed his pointing finger and cleaned the dirt away from the indicated spot. Something had been scratched into the rock, another message; an arrow pointing down and underneath two initials, B.S. Again, Saunière pointed the way.

"Saunière's telling us to dig down here, which is good news as I was beginning to wonder if we were digging in the wrong place. Maybe a false passage Saunière set up as another safeguard for the tomb's contents, but not now. His second message proves we're heading in the right direction."

"Let's stop for a rest and then I'll take over."

Ben readily agreed. "I could do with stretching my aching limbs. All this digging is playing hell with my back."

They crawled out of the tunnel and into the cave. While Creed made them both cheese sandwiches, Ben boiled water for tea and coffee and they sat down to eat.

David had waited four hours for the disgruntled and muddy Doyle to walk to the nearest farm and return with the farmer and his tractor, who, on discovering their predicament, had demanded two hundred Euros to tow them out. It had taken all of David's self-control to refrain from shooting the greedy French bastard as he handed over the cash. Twenty minutes later, the car was back on solid ground. Angry at being stranded, they had spent the remainder of the day attempting to follow the trail of the Landrover, but to no avail.

The following morning they began their search again when they had received a call telling them exactly where Creed and Harper could be found.

Unwilling to risk becoming stuck again or warn the two men of their approach, David had parked the car halfway down the mountain. A long walk along the foresters' ever-rising track that twisted through the thick forest covered slopes would bring them straight to the cave. The views from this height were exceptional. The landscape stretched for many kilometers, and when they entered the gorge, the rocky cliffs towering either side were breathtaking. This was lost on them though, with their thoughts firmly planted on finding their quarry, David and Doyle had ignored the far-reaching and rocky tree covered vistas.

The gentle sound of the river rushing down the valley filled the air, a calming backdrop for all except the two men walking on the stony track alongside its hard level surface hiding the passage of any vehicles that had traveled along it.

Doyle sniffed the air. "Smells like coffee."

David put a finger to his lips to warn him to silence; he had smelt it also. He drew his gun from its shoulder holster and continued silently forward. Doyle followed with his weapon also drawn and ready.

On hearing some faint talking, David paused and put his hand out to halt his partner. He stared up at where the two voices drifted down to him it seemed, out of the very hillside. He pointed at the rocky outcrop above with his gun and whispered, "The voices are coming from up there. It must be the cave the Boss mentioned."

Doyle looked up but shrugged when he saw only rock and bushes.

When David climbed up the rocky outcrop, he noticed the blanket that had been masked from sight below by the dense foliage. The sound of voices, clearer now, came from the other side. He put his fingers to his lips to warn Doyle to be quiet and motioned for him to climb up. He waited until Doyle stood beside him, and with his gun held at the ready, he gripped the edge of the blanket and ripped it down.

Though both enjoyed the respite from the repetitive toil, Ben and Creed were excited to be nearing the tomb.

"Do you think we have much farther to go?"

"Who can tell, but from reading your grandfather's journal, it looks as if Saunière spent a couple of weeks digging the tunnel, but we have no idea if he dug every day or for how long. He also worked alone and had to force a tunnel through the earth, we only have to clear out his backfill, and there are two of us. We seem to be making good progress, and we are about to start digging down, so the tomb can't be far away. Perhaps a couple of days, or hopefully less, and we'll reach it."

Suddenly, bright sunlight flooded into the cave as the blanket that had been blocking it out was ripped down. Shocked, Ben stared at the shape of the two figures standing at the entrance, their features masked by the bright sunlight streaming past them.

Creed reacted swiftly and dived for his rucksack and the weapon inside. The shot that rang out was deafening within the confines of the small cave. The bullet ricocheted off rock inches above Creed's head.

"As much as I want you to grab the weapon you no doubt have stashed in your bag, Creed, for now, my orders are for you to remain alive. But, give me a good enough reason and I assure you I will take great pleasure in disobeying that order. The choice is yours." David stepped farther into the cave.

Creed stared at the man who had spoken, recognizing him as the driver of the black car, and then at the gun he held trained on him. He wondered how they'd found the cave. He moved his hand slowly away from the bag and sat beside Ben.

Creed picked up his coffee and casually took a sip. "So, gentlemen, and I use the term most lightly, what can we do for you?"

David walked over and pressed the gun against Creed's forehead. "For starters, you can shut yer smart mouth because I'm a hairsbreadth away from putting a bullet in that garlic riddled brain of yours. We had to walk fucking miles through mud to find someone to tow the car."

"Well I did, you just sat in the car sleeping," moaned Doyle. He still hadn't forgiven David for the hellish walk he had forced him to undertake.

David turned to glare at his partner and forced himself to remain calm. He kept his gun trained on Creed when he took a couple of steps away. He glanced around the cave and noticed the piles of earth.

"What are you two doing here?"

Ben and Creed said nothing.

David's gaze fell on the hole in the floor. "Doyle, go and check that hole out."

Doyle walked over and bent down to look into the hole. "They've dug a tunnel."

David glared at Creed. "Where does it lead?"

Creed remained silent.

David kicked him. "The next one will be aimed at your head. Where does it lead?"

Creed said nothing.

"Nowhere yet," Ben answered, hoping to save Creed another kicking.

David looked at Ben. "Why are you digging it?"

"We're searching for something."

"That much is fucking obvious, what are you searching for?"

"Don't tell them," ordered Creed, risking another kicking.

David aimed the gun at his head. "One more word from you and it'll be your last." He turned his attention back to Ben but kept his gun trained on Creed. "I'll ask you once again, what are you looking for?"

Ben shrugged. "We're not sure. We're following clues that Saunière left in his church."

"And they led you here?" David asked. A hint of interest had crept into his voice. He knew a little about the priest and his rumored treasure.

Ben nodded. "But we found nothing in the cave so, thinking it might be buried, we decided to dig for it, but we've hit solid rock. We were just about to give up as we must have misread the clues or we're in the right place, but someone else found it first."

David stared at Ben trying to work out if he told the truth. "Doyle, go and check out the tunnel."

Doyle sighed. "Why me? I have my last set of clean clothes on," he moaned.

"Oh for fuck's sake, stop complaining and just fucking do it."

Forever the dogsbody, Doyle removed his jacket and crawled into the tunnel. A few minutes later he poked his head out of the hole, his clothes stained with red earth from crawling through the tunnel. He climbed out and unsuccessfully tried to brush the dirt off.

David shook his head impatiently. "Well...what did you find?"

"Like he said, the tunnel stops at a dead end, they've reached solid rock."

David looked at Ben. "It seems you told the truth."

"But..." continued Doyle, "I found something scratched on the rock; an arrow pointing down. Underneath were two letters, 'B' and 'S.'"

David glared at Doyle. "Is that everything now?"

Doyle nodded. "You can always crawl inside and check for yerself."

David ignored the snide comment and lashed out with his foot, landing a blow to Ben's stomach. "Don't you fucking lie to me again, Harper. The arrow means you must dig down, so it seems you may be onto something after all. What do the letters B.S mean?"

"They stand for *bull shit*, you moron," said Creed.

David lunged and pressed the gun roughly against Creed's head. "I'm warning you, Creed, one more word out of place and I swear I'll pull this fucking trigger."

"So what's next," asked Doyle, trying to calm David before he killed someone.

"I know what I'd like to do." He pushed Creed's head roughly with the barrel of the gun and stepped away.

"Wait here while I ring the boss and find out what he wants us to do. Keep these two covered and don't fuck it up."

Doyle nodded and trained his gun on Ben and Creed while David went outside.

He returned a few moments later and looked at Ben and Creed. "Bad news I'm afraid, I ain't going to kill you, well not yet anyway. You're to continue digging the tunnel. If you refuse, the bad news becomes good news because I'll shoot you and someone else will do the digging."

Doyle groaned. He knew just who that someone would be.

"The choice is yours. Personally, I hope you refuse so I can shoot you both for the trouble you've caused me the last couple of days. So what's it going to be, a shovel or a bullet? Dig or die?"

Ben looked at Creed and shrugged. They both knew they had no other choice. "We'll dig."

"Now that is a shame. Go on then, get to it."

Ben and Creed entered the tunnel and crawled along to its end. A glance back revealed David watching them from the entrance.

"I can't see any digging," he called out, waving his gun threateningly at them.

Ben picked up the shovel and started digging into the tunnel floor. "So, how do we get out of this situation?" he whispered.

"We wait for an opportunity to get the drop on them," was Creed's whispered reply.

"And if an opportunity doesn't arise?"

"It will. The trick is to recognize it when it does and act quickly."

"Be careful, Creed, we don't want to get ourselves killed."

"If we don't escape from this situation that moron will kill us anyway. Don't worry, I'll think of something."

"Oy! Stop the fucking whispering and dig," David shouted, still watching them from the tunnel entrance.

Having no choice other than to obey, Ben and Creed carried on digging and waited for an opportunity to turn the tables on the two men. While he dug, Ben's mind wandered back to Creed's grandfather's journal, remembering what had first led Saunière to find the tomb.

CHAPTER 8

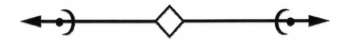

Saunière's Confession

May 27th, 1887– Rennes-Le-Château – The Priest Rivière

There can be in no doubt that Saunière had led a very interesting life, I remember how fascinated I was when Saunière told me about the steps leading to his discovery.

'The incident took place after the stone depicting the knights on horseback was lifted and beneath I found a single skull. I dismissed Ellie Bot and his workman and later returned to dig farther in secret. The church was shrouded in gloom with the only light came from the moonlight penetrating weakly through the single window not boarded up. I locked the church door, which now shut properly thanks to the carpentry skills of Ellie Bot, and lit the two lanterns I had placed inside the church earlier. I positioned the lamps beside the rectangle hole left by the removal of the knight's stone and dug away earth heavy with water until I struck stone. When I had cleared away the muddy earth, I discovered a large gravestone. The few words that had been chiseled into the surface over the top of its original inscription, that someone had taken time to all but remove, could just be made out faintly, but the newer inscription stood out starkly, the grooves of the words being filled with dark moist soil, REGALIS CRYPTA - Royal Crypt. The gravestone was old, but what Royal could possibly be buried here? I knew Rhedae was what some thought was the ancient name of the village. If any bodies of the Royals' were interred here then perhaps they were the Royals of Rhedae. Their *treasure, or a portion of it, might have been buried with them. I was certain with the mention of a Royal Crypt that something of great value lay hidden beneath the gravestone. However, the slab was too heavy for me to lift by hand, so using some lengths of timber and a mason's pry bar I managed to lift and slide the slab to one side, revealing a dark opening underneath. The smell of ancient decay that wafted out was an indication it was as the inscription suggested; a crypt.'*

Like many living in the area at the time, I had heard the rumors that Saunière had found a crypt under the church, but he had always refused to confirm this. His late night excavations, like many of his unusual activities, had been the source of much speculation. Looking at Saunière as he remembered, I knew by the expression on his face it was only his body lying ill in his bed, his mind had left him to travel back in time, back to the church and the crypt to relive the moment.

'Though cold in the church, the air that rose out of the hole was colder still. I shivered as a chill swept through my bones. I shone one of the lamps into the opening. The light revealed stone steps, green with dampness, leading down into darkness. Eager to discover what lay below, I placed a foot on the top step and slowly started my descent.

The smell of dampness and decay was strong in the small chamber I found below. The air, trapped down here for so long, was musty and stale and so cold every breath I exhaled was visible in the chilled air. Though I wasn't sure what to expect, when I held up the lantern, the disappointingly small crypt highlighted was not it. Water seeped through the church floor and dripped from the vaulted ceiling to form small puddles on the cobblestone floor. Four decaying coffins occupied the four alcoves set into the damp, slime-covered walls. I was disappointed to see no obvious signs of treasure.

I approached the nearest alcove to examine the decaying casket that had become so weak it had collapsed to reveal the yellowed bones of its occupant. The skull had rolled onto the floor where its eyeless sockets seemed to be watching me. The damp atmosphere had spawned fluffy spores of wet rot to breed in abundance, covering what little wood of the coffin remained. Sending out creeping fingers of mold, it had crept over the fleshless bones and spread over the damp brickwork, reaching and covering some of the inscription carved into the stone lintel above the alcove. Raising the lamp higher, I saw parts of the occupant's name, Baron and Blanchefort. Underneath this, the year of his death was visible, 1752.

I moved along to the next alcove. Here there remained no evidence of a casket, only a covering of furry spores. If the body had been buried in one, like the burial clothes it once wore; all had become food for mold and decay. With no skin or muscle left to hold the carcass together, all that remained were a heap of bones. But what really caught my attention was what was missing, the skull.

I looked on the floor to see if it had fallen from the alcove like the previous one, but it was nowhere to be seen. I turned my attention to the inscription above, but it had been removed; all that remained were the chisel marks that had struck it from the stone. This puzzled me. I then remembered the skull I had found buried under the carved flagstone, I wondered if it had come from down here, from this skeleton. But if so, why?

I shone the lamp over the bones and noticed something lying beside them. The long, rusty stain on the brickwork and the remaining rust cankered hilt was all that remained of the sword placed next to the body so long ago.

The third coffin was much more interesting. The inscription above it informed me it belonged to Marie Darles Dame d'Hautpoul De Blanchefort. The inscription further informed me that she had died on January 17th, 1781 aged 67. She must have been the last person interred down here. Her coffin was in far better condition than the previous two. Although some of the wood had rotted away, enough remained to keep its shape. I reached out to touch the lead lining of the rotting casket showing through. As far as I could tell, it remained sealed, so there was a good chance that whatever was inside would have withstood the ravages of time.

Having brought no tools down with me, I climbed the stairs and grabbed the pry bar from the church floor. I placed the lantern on the alcove shelf and gripped the foot end of the coffin to slide it forward so I could rest it on the floor to make it easier to remove the lid. It was heavier than I had anticipated. The slime on the alcove shelf caused the coffin to slide. Unable to hold back the unbalanced weight the casket slid to the floor with a crash. The remaining bits of wooden shell broke away, some of it so rotten it crumbled to dust. The lead casket burst open to reveal the mummified body contained within. A waft of ancient corpse mixed with stale air enveloped me, taking away my breath and causing me to gag. I stepped away to recover and stared at the grisly remains of the dead body thrown half out of *its box like a gruesome rag doll. Taut dry skin stretched over her skull and hands. Brown shoulder length hair draped the face. The once white burial gown, though yellowed with age, still looked in fair condition. Splashes of color could still be seen on the small-embroidered flowers across her chest and around the end of the sleeves. I then noticed something glinting and knelt to brush aside the wispy hair from around her neck to reveal the glint of gold. I smiled as I pulled back the collar to see a small gold chain, a necklace. Through the material of the dress, I noticed an unusual shaped lump hinting at the object fixed to the chain. I dragged the object out and stared at the ugly piece of jewelry crudely shaped like a spider. Crafted from gold was the only thing in its favor. I let it drop back around the corpse's neck while I searched the rest of the corpse, but found nothing more.*

Disappointed by the lack of treasure, I placed all of my hopes on the final coffin. There was no inscription carved into the lintel. I lifted its lid to discover it was a rotten shell that fell to pieces with my touch. I jumped back when it collapsed into a heap of decomposed wood to reveal the dirty brown skeleton inside. I searched the remains for anything of value but again found nothing.

I glanced around the crypt. Perhaps if there was any treasure down here, it was hidden in a secret room or cavity. I searched the walls for any sign of a loose piece of masonry or a bricked-up opening. I even tapped the walls with the metal pry bar and listened for any hint of a hollow space behind. After an hour of unsuccessful searching, I gave up. There was no treasure.

As I prepared to leave, the lamplight glinted off the spider necklace still around Marie d'Hautpoul's neck. I stared at it and then at the face of the corpse that now seemed to be smiling at me, mocking my fruitless search for wealth. I grabbed hold of the necklace and snatched it from around her throat. I turned to leave, but when I reached the bottom of the stairway, I stopped and glanced back at the corpse. A pang of guilt washed over me. I walked back over to the corpse, reverently placed it back in the lead coffin and sealed the lid back in place as best I could. It was too heavy to lift back onto the alcove so I had no choice but to leave it on the floor. With one last look around the cold musty crypt, I climbed the stone steps to leave the dead in peace once more.'

Returning to the present, Saunière had turned to look at me. He told me he had been confused why someone would go to the trouble of inscribing the gravestone to mark it as a royal crypt when all it contained were those that as far as he could tell were not Royals.

I had shrugged my shoulders. I had become fascinated by his story and was more than a little intrigued to see where it was leading. I encouraged him to continue, and after a few words, he had drifted back in time again.

'Disappointed as I was that night, the following day I was back on the trail of the treasure. Marie had pointed me in the right direction. Fed up with living at Antoinette Marce's and paying the high stipend she demanded for the room, I had Ellie Bot carry out some repairs to the presbytery so I could live there. It was not very comfortable but it was good to have my own space again. I sat in the kitchen looking at the ugly spider necklace when Marie entered. She had, as was usual, brought me a hot meal. As soon as she saw the necklace, she recognized it.

"It's just like the one on the gravestone," said Maria, nonchalantly, as she placed the plate of rabbit stew on the table in front of me.

I stared at her. "What did you say, Marie?"

She took the necklace and examined at it before handing it back.

"It's the same as the one carved on a gravestone in the cemetery."

"Are you certain?"

Marie shrugged. "I think so. It certainly seems the same. You must have walked past it many times."

"You must show it to me." I stood and headed for the door.

"Sit down and eat, Father. There's no rush. It has been there for many years and will wait until after you have eaten."

I glanced at the meal. It smelt delicious and I was hungry. Marie was right, it would still be there after I had eaten. "You are right as usual Marie. First I will eat and then we visit the graveyard."

As was her custom, she sat down at the table to keep me company while I ate. Picking up the necklace, she looked at it again. "Where did you get this?"

I stared at Maria wondering if I should tell her.

"Can you keep a secret?"

Marie nodded excitedly. She had become infatuated with me as I had with her, a secret shared could only bring us closer together. I told her everything, what I had found buried under the church floor and in the crypt. *To my surprise, Marie was not shocked and from that day onwards she was always by my side. She knew all my secrets, well nearly all; there were some things she was better off not knowing. She never revealed them to anyone.*

After I had finished my meal, she took me to the graveyard...

"There it is," said Marie, pointing at an old gravestone.

I stared at the slab of stone by the wall of my church just inside the entrance to the graveyard. She was right, I had passed it many times without giving it a second glance. But in my defense, through many years of neglect, the weeds had encroached over the grave. I pulled aside the tall weeds and examined the spider carving situated at the base of the stone. It was identical to the necklace. It too, crudely depicted. I read the inscription on the tomb, finding it unusual. The date of her death was incorrect and the inscription seemed to be labeling her a whore. Something was wrong. Also, she is buried in the crypt so why was there a gravestone marking her grave here?

I let the weeds fall back into place and turned to Marie who had leaned forward to read the inscription. Her face was close to mine, almost touching. I stared into her eyes and then leaned closer. She became breathless and did not resist when our lips found each other's. It was not a kiss of passion. That would come later; it was a kiss of two people in love for the very first time. A love that would endure for many years to come and would only end when both were finally laid to rest.

We parted our brief embrace.

Marie smiled sheepishly. Her cheeks flushed. It had been her first kiss.

"Well done, Marie, you were right. Somehow the necklace and this tombstone are connected. I have a strong feeling it is a clue."

"A clue? A clue to what?"

"I am not sure, but we must return when it is dark so we will not be seen and do some secret digging. I think we are on the verge of an amazing discovery."

"It's all so exciting," she uttered, as she followed me out of the cemetery and back to the cottage.

That night we made love.'

Saunière had paused, turned to me and asked if I was shocked by his affair with Marie.

I told him that I was not. He had hardly kept his relationship with the girl a secret. Like most people who knew them, it was only too apparent Marie was much more than just his housekeeper.

He told me he knew Marie will miss him when he is gone. As well as his lover, she had also been a dear friend and faithful companion. They loved each other dearly. That they shall be parted by his death was his only regret. Otherwise, he should die a happy man.

He was silent for a few moments before continuing, *"Marie would do anything for me, even grave robbing."*

'Having removed the gravestone, I set to work digging and before long my spade struck something. At first, I thought it must be a coffin, but after brushing away the soil I saw that whatever it was it was encased in lead, just like Marie d'Hautpoul's body in the crypt. I dug around it to find the edges. It was too small to be a coffin, even that of an infant. Eventually, I had freed it enough to lift out. Because of the lead, it was heavy for its size. After placing it to one side I dug deeper to see if anything else was hidden but found nothing more. After filling the grave back in and replacing the gravestone, I picked up the chest and joined Marie at the churchyard entrance.

"What have you found?" asked Maria, seeing something stuffed under my arm.

"A chest. Let's go home and find out what is inside."

We excitedly made our way back to the cottage.

I lost no time in opening it. I used a knife to lift up the edges of the lead lid until I could remove it. The top of an ornately carved wooden chest was revealed. The lead had protected the chest and prevented it from rotting away in the damp earth. After pulling the lead away from the wooden box where the weight of the earth had crushed it, I was able to lift out the small chest. We both examined the carvings decorating the box. It looked old. The chest had three scenes from the bible carved on it. The front panel was of the last supper. The back panel depicted Jesus being taken down from the cross. I sensed something was wrong with the image but was unable to discern what. The carving on the lid was the strangest of all, it showed an empty tomb. The two smaller end panels were the same, each decorated with the symbol of the Knights Templars, a red, cross pattee. The red of these crosses the only color on the chest. The box had no lock but a simple brass clasp, which I released and before opening it I looked at Marie.

"What wonders shall we find hidden inside do you think?"

"I have no idea. Open it and we shall find out," she replied excitedly. Marie had never done anything like this before and she was enjoying every single minute.

I ran my fingers over the carvings and then onto Marie's hand. I stared into her eyes. "This chest has probably been buried for centuries. Everyone who has ever touched it is dead. We are almost certainly the only two people alive who know of its existence. Who knows what treasure or secrets are hidden inside, but whatever we find it will be ours. We are together now Marie, our fates are entwined. I love you now and I will love you always."

A tear of happiness rolled down her cheek. The man before her had just made her the happiest woman alive. She leaned forward to kiss me gently. "I love you too so very much. I will always be yours whatever happens and where ever fate takes us."

We kissed again and embraced, holding each other for a while, enjoying the moment. Finally, we parted.

"Now, I suppose we had better see what's inside."

Marie nodded eagerly.

We both gazed in anticipation at the chest when I raised the lid.

The first things we saw were two rolled parchments. I lifted them out, noticing they had survived the ravages of time surprisingly well. Beneath the scrolls was a small amount of treasure: gold and silver coins and a few pieces of jewelry. I lifted out a necklace that seemed Visigoth in design and placed it around Marie's neck. She was thrilled with the gift and rewarded me with a kiss.

Though pleased with the treasure in the box, I knew it would contribute little to the grand scheme I wished to carry out in my church. I unrolled one of the parchments and after examining it for a moment I smiled and knew everything would be okay.

"What is it," Marie asked.

"A treasure map, my darling. But not just any treasure, one, which if the legends are true, could be very vast indeed."

"Whose treasure is it?" Marie asked excitedly, grabbing my arm.

"The lost treasure of the Knights Templar!"

CHAPTER 9

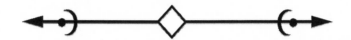

5M, Rocks – Tomb

AFTER DIGGING DOWN a farther two meters, Creed hit a large stone slab. He cleared away the dirt to look for another sign from Saunière and discovered an arrow pointing in the direction to dig next. As well as his initials there was something else scratched onto the surface, a message, *5M, ROCKS – TOMB.*

He turned on hearing Ben crawl along the tunnel, the empty bucket scraped on the sides of the passage and banged on the wooden supports. Creed informed him of the new discovery.

Ben leaned into the hole and stared at the message chiseled crudely into the rock's surface and spoke aloud its meaning was. "After five meters we will reach rocks and behind them is the tomb. The rocks must be the ones he mentioned in his confession that he used to block the tomb entrance. And look, the arrow is pointing back to the cave entrance, towards the hole I filmed through." He could hardly contain the excitement in his voice. "We're nearly there."

They both turned when Doyle dropped into the entrance hole and glared at them menacingly.

"I can't hear any digging. What's the problem?"

"No problem," Creed answered.

"Then dig," Doyle ordered.

Creed flipped the slab over to hide the inscription. Now they knew how far they had to go, they worked slower, certain that as soon as they reached the tomb, they would become redundant. Of no further use, they would probably be killed. Also the longer it took them, the more chance they would have of overpowering their captors.

They were kept hard at work until they were exhausted and even David could see they needed a break. He called them out of the tunnel and told them to rest. Ben was ordered to cook enough food for them all, so he heated two cans of stew. When it was ready, they ate in silence.

"I need to take a leak," stated Creed, after he had finished eating.

David nodded to Doyle. "Take him outside, but keep an eye on him."

Creed crossed to the blanket Doyle had replaced over the entrance.

"I need to go as well," said Ben, spying an opportunity. If he were allowed out with Creed, it would be two against one. They might be able to overpower Doyle. He began to stand.

David pointed his gun at Ben. "Sit the fuck down. You really think I'm that stupid? You can go when your boyfriend gets back."

Ben sat. It had been worth a try. "I need a smoke, they're in my rucksack."

David glanced at the rucksack Ben pointed at and nodded his permission. They had already been searched for weapons. His eyes followed Ben as he carefully reached for his cigarettes and lighter, slipped one from out from the packet and lit it with a lighter.

David scrutinized the lighter. "Is that gold?"

Ben was about to lie but thought better of it. "It is."

David held out a hand. "Gimme."

Ben threw it to David and watched him examine it.

"It's heavy and no doubt expensive, even just for its gold value," stated David.

Ben held out his hand to retrieve his lighter. "It was a present."

He sighed when David slipped it into his pocket and smiled. He blew smoke at David, but he didn't seem to mind. Unfortunately, death by passive smoking took too long to be a viable solution; he would have to think of a quicker method.

Creed soon returned, and when they'd both been toilet, Creed and Ben were ordered to sleep. They climbed into their sleeping bags. Though they tried to stay awake, hoping to catch the men unawares if they nodded off, exhausted by the long day's work it wasn't long they were both asleep.

David left Doyle to guard the two sleeping men while he went to fetch the car. Having walked the track earlier, he reckoned he could drive the car all the way to the cave. Except for a couple of places where it was deeper, causing the vehicle to slide, the day's hot sun had dried up the few patches of mud, The ride up had been easy, and within an hour he was back.

So they could both get some rest, they took turns guarding the men. David sent Doyle to the car to get some sleep, telling him to relieve him in four hours.

The next day, the routine started again. After breakfast, Ben and Creed were set to work in the tunnel. After digging for a couple of hours, Ben was tipping a bucket of soil on the huge pile that had accumulated in the cave when David's mobile phone rang.

"Hello Boss," David answered, after reading the caller ID.

I wonder if he has his number filed under Boss. Ben pondered, arriving at the conclusion he probably had. He took his time emptying the bucket so he could listen in on the call.

"Okay…Yes, everything's fine…No they're still digging…I don't know…Okay." David tapped Ben on the shoulder with his gun. "How much longer before you reach the tomb?"

Ben shrugged. "How could I possibly know that?"

"Take a fucking guess."

"Two days, three, maybe a week, I don't know."

David raised the gun as if to strike Ben around the head. "Get back in the tunnel and work harder." He placed the phone back to his ear. "Harper reckons about two days…Okay." He hung up and turned to Ben as he was about to climb into the hole. "You both need to dig faster. The boss will be here later to check on your progress."

"What's his name, I take it Boss is just an alias?"

"Very fucking funny, you'll find out when he gets here."

"What's going to happen to us when we reach the tomb?"

"That's not my decision, but I wouldn't make any long term plans." David smiled. "Now back to work and tell Frenchie to get a move on and no more slacking."

Ben jumped into the entrance, crawled along the tunnel and dropped into the hole at the end and informed Creed about the phone call and the imminent arrival of the thugs' boss.

"We can't let them get their hands on the stuff in the tomb," Creed stated.

"I know, but what can we do, they have guns."

"And they aren't making any mistakes, well not so far, and soon there'll be three of them if their boss stays, making it even harder to get the drop on them."

David shouted into the tunnel. "I can't hear any digging, don't make me come in there."

Ben swapped places with Creed.

"We have no choice other than to carry on and hope something turns up." Ben hacked at the dirt with the spade. "It's doubtful, but there may even be another way out through the tomb. The original entrance perhaps, though it would mean more digging."

"I hadn't thought of that." Creed put the bucket in position so Ben could fill it.

After digging a couple of more meters, they ran out of timber supports. David refused to go and fetch a fresh supply and ordered Ben to remove some they'd already used earlier in the tunnel. To not put too much strain on the boards, Ben took out every third one, which meant that as the wood was twenty centimeters wide there were two boards then a twenty centimeters gap then another two boards then a gap and so on. It seemed to work because the roof didn't cave in.

As the tunnel progressed, digging suddenly became easier as the earth wasn't so compacted, they only had to touch it, and it crumbled. They soon found out why, the roof of the tunnel was now solid rock, with no weight pressing down on the soil, it had remained relatively loose after Saunière had backfilled his excavation.

Though they dug faster, they didn't alter the amount of earth they took out of the tunnel. The excess they removed was spread over the tunnel floor.

Four hours later, they measured from the position of the 5M marked stone to the end of the tunnel. They had dug three meters, which left only two more before they reached the tomb. They continued digging until they came across the rocks mentioned in Saunière's message scratched on the slab. After clearing away the loose earth, they saw the rocks had been piled up to build a wall across the tunnel.

Ben stared at the rock wall. "We've only dug about three and a half meters from the slab, not the five meters it indicated."

"Maybe it's another of Saunière's traps?" Creed suggested.

"Let's proceed with caution." Ben began removing the rocks and found another layer behind.

"It looks like we might have a couple of meters of rocks to remove."

"Then we'll have to remove them, those bits of stone are all that stands between us and the tomb. Some I can take out, the rest can be placed along the edges of the tunnel."

"Good thinking."

To keep up the pretense of digging, a bucket of earth scraped off the floor was taken out every few minutes.

Ben soon had enough rocks removed to see that it was only two layers deep. As soon as Creed returned he told him the good news.

Creed peered at the wall. "What's on the other side?"

"Pass that lamp behind you, and I'll take a look."

Ben pushed a few rocks into the space the other side of the wall and held up the brighter light.

"What do you see?" Creed asked, excitedly.

"Not much. The tunnel continues a short distance and then turns, but it looks clear. Ben handed the lamp to Creed, "I'll remove enough rocks for us to squeeze through, but you had better take another bucket of soil up to prevent them from becoming suspicious."

Creed quickly filled the bucket with soil. As he turned to leave, he glanced back at Ben. "Don't go in until I get back."

"I won't, we'll go in together."

Dragging the bucket of soil alongside him, Creed scrambled along the tunnel. When he returned, Ben had made a gap big enough to crawl through. Excited at what they were about to see, they scrambled through the hole.

To the right, the tunnel was blocked by a cave in. To the left, it led around a corner. The larger tunnel was almost high enough for them to stand up straight. Ben held up the light. The first thing he saw was Latin words chiseled into the tunnel wall.

Creed emerged from the smaller tunnel and stood next to Ben. "What does it say?"

Ben Translated. "*Be gone I conceal the secrets of God.*" Ben ran his fingers over the neatly carved writing. "This must be the original tunnel entrance dug by the Knights Templar."

Creed moved his light around the tunnel. "The original entrance must be in that direction, toward the river."

Ben gazed at the collapsed heap of earth and rocks reaching from floor to ceiling. "You notice how the floor slopes down? It must go below the level of the river outside."

"It looks impossible to move quickly, which means the only way out is back through the tunnel."

"Come on, let's go find out what is really in the tomb."

Creed followed Ben along the tunnel where it led off to the right. As they approached, Ben could tell the opening was too straight and square to occur naturally, it was made by the hand of man. He paused at the opening blocked by a wall constructed from stone blocks. He recognized the wall; he'd seen its other side when he'd filmed it with the video camera he'd lowered throw a small shaft in the top of the tomb chamber.

In the bottom left of the wall was a pile of stones. "That's how Saunière gained entry," Ben explained. "He removed just enough of the blocks so he could fit through."

It only took them a few moments to remove the rocks and then, just as Saunière had done many years before, they entered the Tomb.

THE TOMB

CHAPTER 10

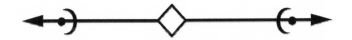

TOMB DISCOVERY - 1891

SAUNIÈRE RAN HIS hands over the old wall built by the Knights Templar in 1307, shortly before most of their Order was arrested. Not many had survived the determination of the French King, Philip IV, to see an end to the Templars privileged reign. He wondered what he'd find on the other side. He grabbed a hammer and a chisel and set to removing a few of the blocks. He grabbed the candle and crawled through the hole he had made in the lower left corner. Once through he stood upright and held the light aloft. Its flickering flame glinted off many wondrous objects. Even their covering of dust failed to hide their beauty or their worth.

Saunière felt a sense of awe and excitement as his eyes wandered over the incredible treasure, unable to decide what object to linger on. He stepped forward and lifted the lid of the nearest chest. Inside he saw garments. He assumed they were probably worn in one of the Templar secret ceremonies. He rummaged beneath the clothes to find a large cross. He pulled it out and held the candle beside it. The light glinted off its gold surface, and the many jewels along its length sparkled. He knew this one object alone would pay for any alterations he cared to make to his neglected church. He closed the lid of the chest and laid the cross on top. His eyes came to rest on the object in the center of the room covered by a tattered shroud.

He moved closer to investigate.

The candlelight highlighted the body the old shroud had once covered. After removing a ragged piece from the corpse's head, he held the candle closer and peered at the ancient face and its feminine features.

"It's a woman!"

He wondered what made her so special to have been so revered by the Knights Templar they placed here with their other precious possessions. He glanced at the pile of scrolls on the far side of the chamber. Perhaps they will reveal her identity.

He turned his attention to the block of marble she had been placed upon. He recognized the pinkish-red Rose marble mined from the local old Templar quarry a few kilometers away. Further inspection revealed a joint running the length of the marble near the top. It was not solid as he had first assumed. He placed the candle on a nearby chest, he rested his hands on the edge of the marble and, careful to not disturb the body on top, he pushed. A grinding sound filled the chamber when the top slid over to reveal a dark void. He grabbed the candle and shone it inside.

The flame picked out a second body. Saunière was unable to tell if it was male or female as the head was missing. It had been replaced with one of glass. He remembered reading the Templars were accused of worshipping a head. He gazed at the headless corpse and wondered if its absent head was the one they had worshipped, if so, who was interred here?

The documents found in the grave chest revealed no indication of the identity of the tomb's occupant. In fact, they had barely mentioned it was a tomb at all. They did state that what he would find here is a great and dangerous secret. On first entering the chamber he had thought this great secret alluded to the treasure, but now he wasn't so sure.

He moved the candle down the length of the body and paused on the hands folded over its chest. They were male hands. He noticed something on the wrists, a blemish on the taut skin. He reached in and lifted one of the hands, surprised at how easily it moved. The skin wasn't as cold as it usually should be. As a priest, he often had contact with the dead, though never one as ancient as the body before him.

He turned the wrist over. The blemish was on both sides. An examination of the other wrist revealed identical marks. He then stepped back in shock when he realized what had made them. His breathing increased as he stared into the darkness of the marble coffin, unable to believe what he knew to be true. To make sure, he forced himself to approach the coffin again. He moved to the feet end and subconsciously held his breath when he shone the candlelight at the man's feet. He stared at the marks where the Romans had driven a nail through. There could be no mistake, this man had been crucified.

"It can't be," he argued, unwilling or unable to believe the man before him was Jesus Christ. "His body rose to Heaven."

He turned away, grabbed an armful of gold items and the cross and left the chamber.

CHAPTER 11

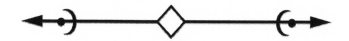

The Tomb

STANDING SIDE BY side at the entrance, Ben and Creed held up their lamps. The small cavern, apart from the light from Ben's video camera, was flooded with light for the first time since Saunière last set foot inside. Ben was amazed to be finally standing in the tomb he'd seen so many times on the video footage. He directed the light onto the cavern roof and saw the end of the shaft he had filmed through.

He returned his attention to objects littering the tomb. It felt strange to be seeing them from a different angle, and though the same, they looked different. The other thing that surprised Ben was their size; they seemed huge compared to the video footage.

He looked around at the objects he was so familiar with; the covered body in the center, and to his right, was a chest with a dust-covered book and a candlestick on top. On the ground to the left and slightly behind the chest, was a large cauldron shaped metal bowl full of objects, which he'd glimpsed in the second video film footage he'd taken, but couldn't tell what they were as rocks that had fallen from the cave roof had landed on top. Many trinkets lay scattered on the ground behind the chest as if they had been rummaged through and the best pieces taken by Saunière. To Ben's left stood the mysterious object covered by the cloth decorated with the Star of David. Ben was eager to see what it concealed. Next to this and at the foot of the body, leaning against the cavern wall, stood a large wooden cross that was a twin of the one leaning against the wall opposite him. Both showed signs of decay. On the floor, at the head of the body, was a metal chest. To the left of the cross at the back of the cave were some old wooden chests, now rotten and weak, they were losing the battle to keep their contents contained. One had split open and even though dusty, the gold coins and jewelry that had spilled out still glinted in the lamplight.

"I had better take another bucket of dirt out before they wonder what we're doing," said Creed, forcing his gaze away from the many artifacts.

"Good idea," Ben agreed, "but it's my turn, I'll go."

Creed put his hand on Ben's shoulder. "No Ben, you stay and enjoy your tomb. I'm sure you're eager to explore."

Creed crawled back through the tomb entrance, along the passage, and into the tunnel.

"What the fuck are you two doing down there?" David's voice echoed through the tunnel.

Ben smiled at Creed's quick reply.

"Digging, why don't you come and give us a hand?"

"Less of the smart mouth, Frenchie, and hurry up. I don't want you two slacking."

Creed shouted a reply as he filled the bucket with rocks and earth. "I'm coming, I'm coming. It's not easy working down here; the tunnel could collapse at any moment. We have to be careful."

"You can be careful just as long as you're quick about being careful," David replied.

Ben smiled and turned his attention back to the tomb. To the right of the far cross were the parchments he'd seen many times before and had often wondered what secrets they contained. Soon he would find out.

At the base of the cross lay a couple of jugs, one was earthenware and the other, dull and stained, might be copper, brass or bronze. If it had been gold, he was sure Saunière would have taken it, though he had left the chest of gold coins. Ben briefly wondered why he'd not taken everything. Behind the cross was a round pot, but he couldn't see what was inside. Ben looked at the object that had confused him. From above he had been unable to fathom what it was, a bowl, a helmet, or maybe even a glass globe, but from this angle, he could see exactly what it was placed next to the head of the body, a simple round container. He had often wondered if it was the Holy Grail, but as he now knew where that was; what was the significance of the bowl? Obviously, it held some importance to have been placed in such a position. Staring at the bowl, Ben almost laughed when he realized exactly why it had been put there. His eyes sought out the source of the drip that had just splashed into the bowl. It had come from the stub of a stalactite protruding from the ceiling, wet and glassy, formed from years of mineral-rich water seeping through the rock above. Saunière must have placed the bowl there to catch the drips and prevent the water from damaging the body. Over the years the bowl had filled giving it that glassy appearance to reflect the light from the video camera. It explained why it was the only object in the tomb not covered in dust.

He looked down at the floor strewn with debris and then shone the lamp up to examine the cavern roof, fearing it may be unsafe, especially with all the extra weight of rocks and earth from the tunnel they had placed on it. Ben knew by the shaft he had filmed the tomb through that the rock between the floor of the entrance cave and the roof of the tomb was almost three meters thick, so he guessed it should be strong enough.

He returned his attention to the cave floor and knelt down to move some of the debris, he'd seen something. He stared at the uncovered footprints; left behind by the priest of Rennes-Le-Château, Bérenger Saunière, over one hundred years ago.

Ben heard a noise coming from the tunnel and turned.

Creed entered. "Is everything okay?"

"Yeah, I told David we are hitting a lot of rocks which made digging difficult, so we should be okay for ten or twenty minutes before we have to take the next lot out."

"Good, that gives us a bit of time to explore. Let's take a look at the body to finally find out if it's who Saunière thought it was entombed here."

Creed nodded his agreement.

Ben pointed at the ground. "Saunière's footprints."

Creed looked at them and smiled. "Amazing."

They approached the cloth-covered body, just as Saunière must have done all those years ago, and stared at the dusty Templar cross, now much clearer than in the video footage. Ben stared at the head and the features of the face where the cloth had molded into it over the years. This face was the reason why he didn't believe Saunière. He knew where the head of Jesus was, in his house in England, safely stored in its airtight container. Whoever lay hidden under this cloth still had its head. He thought it was probably an important Templar knight.

"Go on, Ben, you do the honors," said Creed.

Ben gripped the top edge of the shroud Saunière had placed over the body to replace the tattered one and, wondering whose body they would find; he gently started to pull back the cloth.

David stared along the tunnel and then turned to Doyle. "They're up to something. I can't hear a bloody thing. Whatever they are doing they aren't digging, and they should've brought out another bucket of soil by now."

"They did say there were a lot of rocks, making it harder to dig," offered Doyle.

David was suspicious. He peered along the dimly lit tunnel. He didn't like confined spaces and wasn't keen to enter the narrow passage, but he would if he had too. He dropped into the hole and listened. He glanced up at Doyle. "I still can't hear a fucking thing."

Doyle shrugged.

David removed his jacket. "Come on, let's go and see what they're up to."

Doyle had no fear of small spaces, but he was concerned about getting his clothes dirty again. Aware it would be useless to argue, he reluctantly followed David through the tunnel.

With his gun at the ready, David cautiously peered over the edge of the pit where the shaft dropped down. There was no sign of the two men. He leaned farther into the hole and peered along the lower tunnel.

"I was right," whispered David. "They're up to something. I can hear faint voices. I think they've reached the tomb. Keep quiet and follow me."

Ben was just about to reveal the corpses' head when he froze.

David's order echoed around the cavern. "Remain exactly where you are."

Ben released his hold on the cloth and turned. David and Doyle crawled into the cavern and aimed their guns at them. The two men glanced around the tomb. They ignored the body as their eyes came to rest on the broken chest of gold coins.

"You didn't think it important enough to tell us you had reached the tomb?" said David, menacingly.

"We did all the work, why shouldn't we be the first to have a look? It's not as if we can steal any, not with you two guarding the entrance," Creed argued in their defense.

Surprisingly, David agreed. "Yeah, I can accept that, but it's not as if you're going to live long enough to enjoy your discovery."

"What happens now?" Ben asked, believing they had now outlived their usefulness.

David glanced worriedly up at the roof when a small piece of rock fell to the ground. "Luckily for you two, that's not up to me."

Ben had noticed David's worried glance at the ceiling and seized the chance to increase the man's fear. "It's all the weight on the cave floor above, where we tipped the spoils from the tunnel."

Creed picked up on Ben's plan. "Yeah, it could collapse at any time." He smiled when David took a step nearer to the exit.

"I'm going to phone the boss. I can't get a signal in here. Doyle, keep your eye on these two and if they try anything, shoot them." David shot the ceiling another nervous glance.

Everyone has a weakness, thought Creed and David's might have given them an opportunity to even the odds.

"Okay, will do," Doyle assured him with a grin, happy about his partner's discomfort.

David crawled back into the tunnel and was gone. Creed looked at Doyle, weighing him up. Now it was two against one. It might be their only chance.

Doyle noticed the body and pointed at it with his gun. "Who's the stiff?"

Creed gave Ben a slight nod and a wink. "Tell him."

"You wouldn't believe me if I told you," Ben said, drawing Doyle's attention away from Creed.

"Try me," Doyle replied.

"You've heard of the Bible I take it."

"Of course I fucking have. Believe it or not, I used to go to Sunday school."

Ben chose not to believe. "So you'll know that in the Bible there was this man called Jesus who was crucified on the cross, but before he died he was taken down and his body spirited away by Mary Magdalene who then came to France."

Doyle looked at the covered body. "You're kidding? Not the crucified bit, but that Jesus didn't die on the cross and came to France."

Ben shook his head. "No, I'm not kidding. You are standing only a few feet away from Jesus Christ, the Son of God."

Doyle shook his head. "You're shitting me. Why would his body be down here?"

"It's a long story, but I'm telling the truth."

"So this is what that priest found, is it?"

Ben nodded. "Among other things, yes."

Doyle shook his head. "No, I don't believe it. Wasn't his body meant to have ascended to heaven or something?"

"So the Bible tells us. We didn't believe it either until we laid eyes on him."

Noticing that Creed had moved, Doyle pointed the gun at him. "Back over there, Frenchie," he ordered, motioning with the weapon.

"Take a peek, and then you'll know I speak the truth," Ben suggested, in an attempt to turn the thug's attention back away from Creed.

Doyle stared at the body as if considering the suggestion. "Okay, but you do it. Lift the cloth so I can see the body."

Ben moved to the head of the corpse.

Creed never took his eyes off the gunman while he waited for an advantage if it arose.

"I'll have to move the bowl of water or I won't be able to uncover the body enough for you to see it."

Doyle glanced at the bowl on top of a corner of the shroud and nodded his permission.

To draw the man's gaze as far away from Creed as possible, Ben walked around to the far side of the body and halted by the bowl. As he gripped the bronze container, Doyle stepped a couple of paces nearer. Hoping Creed was ready, Ben lifted the bowl and threw its contents in Doyle's face.

Though the shock of the cold water momentarily blinded Doyle, he instinctively pulled the trigger of the gun aimed in Ben's direction. The gunshot was deafening in the confined space. Ben dropped the bowl, his hands stinging from the impact of the bullet ricocheting off the metal container.

Creed reacted before the bowl hit the floor. He'd already noticed a weapon he could use if the chance arose, a weapon that probably had in past times already done its fair share of killing; an ancient sword leaning against the wall, hidden in the shadows only an arm's length away. He lunged at it, grabbed the weapon and moved toward Doyle intending to strike him a hard blow around the head with the sword's heavy pommel.

Ben saw Creed grab the sword and move towards Doyle, he also saw him stumble on the rocks littering the floor.

Doyle sensed danger. He ignored Ben and turned to see Creed off balance, a large sword raised in the air ready to strike him. He aimed the gun at Creed's chest and squeezed the trigger.

Creed had seen the gun turn in his direction. Doyle was too close to miss. He closed his eyes as the deafening gunshot echoed around the tomb and waited for pain and death to arrive, but it never came. Surprised, he opened his eyes. Ben struggled with Doyle. Ben had grabbed the gun a fraction of a second before the trigger was pulled. The bullet had embedded itself into the wall of the tomb. Creed quickly swung the sword pommel at the back of Doyle's head. The gunman let out a groan, went limp and fell unconscious to the floor where lay as still as the nearby corpse.

Breathing heavily from adrenaline and his struggle with the gunman, Ben smiled weakly at Creed. "Now we are even."

Creed picked up Doyle's gun. "Thanks, I was certain I was a dead man."

Ben looked at Doyle crumpled on the floor, soaked from the water he had thrown. "Is he dead?"

Creed checked. "No, out cold. He's going to have one hell of a headache when he comes round."

"And a temper to match I should think, let's hope we're not around when he does."

"Let's find something to tie him up with and then wait for the other one to come and investigate. David must have heard the gunshots." Creed held up Doyle's gun. "At least we're armed now."

A glance around the room revealed nothing suitable for binding their prisoner.

"We'll have to use his laces," said Creed. He looked at Doyle's shoes. "Shit! He's wearing slip-ons. Give me a hand. We'll use his trousers."

Ben knelt beside Doyle's feet, and while Creed unfastened the unconscious man's trousers, Ben slipped off the man's shoes. He grabbed hold of the trouser legs, and when Creed lifted Doyle up off the floor slightly, he slid them down their owner's legs."

"Well, well, well, isn't this cozy."

CHAPTER 12

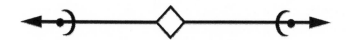

A Man Crucified

C **REED DROPPED DOYLE**, raised the gun and spun toward the voice. He yelped in pain from a blow to his knuckles from the weapon held by the man that had spoken. It bounced across the floor out of reach.

The man pressed the barrel hard against Creed's temple. "Now, I suggest we all calm down before someone gets killed, and by someone, I obviously mean one of you two. You'll not find me as easy to overpower as that useless turd on the ground. No doubt another of Silas's cheap lackey's." He lashed out with his foot. The kick struck Doyle hard on the shoulder. Doyle moaned but remained unconscious.

Ben stared at the man, not daring to move. This was evidently the man David had phoned.

The man stared at Creed's face. "It's difficult to see much of a resemblance between you and your father, but then," he smiled cruelly, "your face isn't covered in bruises."

Creed tensed. "So you're the bastard who killed my father."

The man smiled unapologetically. "Guilty as charged. Long have we suspected your grandfather had written down Saunière's confession and would have passed it onto your father before his death. We were keen to have the journal because we believed this information would be very advantageous to our cause. Though we had knowledge of the tomb, we had no idea of its location. For many long years, we had eyes on him in the hope one day he would lead us here to the Tomb, but it was not to be. We, or to be exact, *I* became impatient..."

"...So you kidnapped him," Creed interrupted.

"Not me personally, but yes, I gave that order. Though I did elect to question him myself..."

"...By question, you mean torture!"

"If you like, Creed, yes, torture did play its part. He left me no other choice. Not that it did any good as his secret died with him."

"You killed him for nothing you murdering bastard," Creed spat angrily.

"Steady," he warned, pressing the gun harder against Creed's temple, forcing his head back. There is a bullet..." he paused to look at the barrel, "...about twenty centimeters away from your brain. I'm sure you wouldn't like me to drastically reduce its distance. If you behave, you will live a little longer. Maybe I'll even let you go now I'm finally in possession of that which we have sought all these years. My final decision concerning this matter is still being processed. I am presently in a good mood, but I warn you, for your own good, you shouldn't do anything that might change my disposition."

"You murdered my father. You think I'm going to forget about that?"

"If you want to live, it is best you do. I don't blame you for wanting revenge, but what's done is done. Accomplishing your death by rash actions will fail to bring your father back."

"True, but it will bring me a great deal of pleasure to see you dead."

The man smiled at Creed. "Yes, I'm sure it would. However, let's not dwell in the past. Your father didn't die in vain because his death brought *you* on the scene and look where that has led, to the tomb we now all stand in. It's a secret no more."

"Who are you?"

With his gun kept aimed menacingly at Creed's head, the man backed away slowly and then turned his attention to Ben. "Ben Harper, at last we meet. Since your website was brought to my attention, I have followed your progress with interest. I was amazed to find that someone had finally deciphered Saunière's clues; I myself tried for many years, but alas with no success. I'd begun to doubt the priest had left any secrets in his church to unravel. But I'm pleased to say you proved my doubts false. You, Ben, were a second string to my bow, so to speak. If Creed failed to lead us to the tomb, I was certain you would. Your escapades in Rosslyn caused us a few problems in tracking you, and then I was disappointed to be informed you had given the man ordered to watch you the slip and disappeared. He had fallen asleep, but has paid dearly for his mistake and now experiences a sleep from which he will never wake. It was only through luck that I learned of your present whereabouts through a local hunter. I was surprised to find you had returned to France again. Another surprise was that you had teamed up with Creed. I must admit I hadn't seen that coming. Nevertheless, mistakes aside, everything has proved fruitful in the end." He gazed around the chamber and up at the hole in the roof where Ben, with the aid of a video camera on a pole, had revealed to him what had once been lost was now found.

He turned his attention back to Ben. "I recognize many of the artifacts here from your web images, Ben, and I want to thank you for finding them for us."

"I didn't find them for you, whoever you are."

"Are you going to tell us your name or not?" asked Creed.

The man smiled. "I suppose it's only fair. I am Nicolas Pavillon. My distant relation, whose name I carry, was once the head of an organization called the Compagnie du Saint-Sacrament. My two companions, who you might meet later if you behave yourselves, are related to Jean-Jacques Olier, who was the founder of the seminary of…"

"…Saint Sulpice in Paris," finished Ben.

"Correct. I'm surprised you've heard of us?"

"Though I have heard of you, I confess I know little. You keep what you do and who you are a secret, which obviously makes it difficult to find out anything, but if I'm right, you are a breakaway group of the Priory of Sion."

Nicolas scoffed. "The Priory is run by women. Feeble men who lack the determination to take things into their own hands. They sit and talk and wait for something to happen, then they talk some more and wait again. They have been waiting for hundreds of years and will for hundreds more. I have no time for them. We, the Compagnie du Saint-Sacrament, make things happen. We act, we search, we listen, and then we discover…"

"…Don't forget to add torture to that list," Creed spat.

Unperturbed, Nicolas continued, "We do what is necessary to achieve our goals, that is why we are here, and the Priory is not."

"What are you going to do with all this?" Ben asked, indicating the artifacts around him.

"I am going to bring the Christian church to its knees and then start a whole new religion."

"Of which you will be the head."

"Of course." Nicolas smiled. "Once the body of Christ has been brought out into the open it will reveal what a farce the Christian faith is and people will flock to me in their millions."

"And why would they do that?" asked Ben.

Nicolas walked over to the cloth decorated with the Star of David and grabbed hold of the shroud. "They will flock to me because I will have this." He threw back the cloth dramatically. A cloud of disturbed dust rose into the air.

The dust-choked light radiating from the modern lamps glinted off the shiny gold covering the wooden construction. It had survived its thousands of years of existence remarkably well and resembled the magnificent image described in the Bible that had so often been depicted in many books and films.

Nicolas stared in awe at the wondrous object, and for once he was speechless.

Ben and Creed were also at a loss for words as they stared in wonder at the two winged cherubs facing each other atop the mercy seat, even with the dim light they could see the fine detail was still as sharp as the day it was crafted.

The dust floating in the air glowed yellow from the harsh lamplight reflected off the gold as if someone had thrown a handful of fine golden powder into the air.

It was Creed who broke the silence that had settled in the tomb. "Can it really be the Ark of the Covenant?"

"Of course," stated Nicolas confidently. "It can be nothing else."

Ben wasn't so sure. The Bible describes the Ark of the Covenant as two and a half cubits long; a cubit is about eighteen inches so the Ark should be forty-five inches. The golden box before him fell far short of this described length. He kept his doubts to himself and turned his gaze away to direct it at the cloth-covered body, deep in thought.

"It truly is the Holiest Relic of all time," Nicolas stated. "People will flock to join the religion that has the Ark of the Covenant in its possession."

"What makes you think it will let you?" Ben asked.

Nicolas scoffed. "I didn't take you to be of a superstitious nature."

"I'm not as a rule, but since entering this tomb, I'm not so sure. I sense a power here that I find difficult to explain."

"I feel it also," Nicolas agreed, as his excited eyes roamed over the golden casket. "It comes from the Ark. This power belongs to me now, and I plan to yield it with full force to achieve my goals."

"I can't remember the exact words," said Creed, "but doesn't it say in the Bible that the Ark will destroy all who have evil in their hearts or something along those lines? Perhaps you should leave while you still can as you fit that description perfectly."

"Let's put it to the test shall we?" Nicolas motioned with his gun for them to move away.

Ben and Creed were more than glad to distant themselves from the Ark; both had seen the Indiana Jones movie. If Nicolas was going to open the Ark, the farther away they were, the better. They watched in anticipation that something bad might happen when Nicolas slid back the lid. Ben briefly thought about closing his eyes, but they remained firmly fixed on the Ark as it was opened. There was no fire and brimstone. No bolts of lightning. Nothing happened.

Nicolas smiled smugly. "Well, as I have not been struck down by the almighty God, it must be confirmation He wants me to have the Ark."

Creed glared at Nicolas. He would do everything in his power to prevent him from carrying out his plans. A man like him should not be in charge of such a Holy relic.

The two captives, still covered by Nicolas's weapon, watched Nicolas shine a light inside the open casket. A smile played on his lips when he laid eyes on its contents. He motioned Ben over.

"I think you might want to take a look at this." He stepped aside as Ben approached and awaited his reaction.

Unable to prevent himself, Ben peered into the Ark. His eyes picked out lines of writing he recognized as an ancient form of Hebrew. Though he couldn't read them, he knew exactly what they said. The clue was given by what they were written on, slabs of stone. The text inscribed on the stone tablets could only be the Ten Commandments given to Moses by God in the wilderness. It was the reason for the Ark's construction. To house the stone tablets and the words of God emblazoned on them. He stepped back unable to speak, now uncertain of his previous doubts. *Why had Saunière made no mention of this in his confession? Perhaps he was too fearful of opening or approaching the Ark.*

Ben was beginning to think Creed was right when he said the things in this Tomb should remain undisclosed and perhaps the world in its present climate is not ready for such things.

Nicolas had no such doubts.

"Soon the whole world will know what I have in my possession," bragged Nicolas enthusiastically. "Imagine how the world's press will flock to see the body of Jesus Christ and the Ark of the Covenant. Within a few days, the whole world will know of…"

"The body of Christ?" Ben interrupted, halting Nicolas's dialogue. He waved an arm around the tomb. "Where?"

Nicolas looked at Ben. "You know exactly where the body is, right behind you."

"Have you checked?"

"I have no need to check, look around you. The two crosses either side of his body, just like when he was crucified, the Ark, the clues in Saunière's church, it all fits. Besides, Creed's father told me just before he died." Nicolas remembered Pascal's dying words as if they were yesterday. Realizing the man wasn't going to talk, Nicolas had plunged a dagger into Pascal's heart. Just before Pascal died, he had uttered a few last words. *"You will never find…His body. With my…death… the secret is safe… I… destroyed… the Journal… I am the only one… who knows."*

Nicolas had panicked. He had grabbed Pascal roughly by the shoulders, shook him and screamed, *"Your son, you must have told your son. He will lead me to the tomb of Jesus."*

Pascal had smiled, *"You...are...wrong. Only I...know the...location!"* It was the last words he ever spoke.

Nicolas had screamed in frustration. All the years of waiting were now for nothing.

Nicolas looked at Creed. "At first, I thought by killing your father, I had lost the chance of ever finding the tomb However, just in case he was bluffing, I had you watched, and when you bought digging and tunneling equipment, and provisions, which on my journey through the passage I saw you have made good use of, I knew he had confided the secret to you. I had also learned of Ben's success, so I knew it was only a matter of time before one of you led me here and then my waiting would be over. So, to return to your question, Ben, the ancient documents I have in my possession and the little information Creed's father revealed, this is why I am certain the body in this tomb is the body of the biblical Jesus Christ."

"I really think you should take a look as you are in for one hell of a disappointment."

Nicolas stared at Ben and searched his face for signs he had lied, but found none.

Creed glanced at Ben. *What was Ben up to and why is he so sure about the body?*

Nicolas arrived at a decision. "Okay, let's get this charade over with. You two move over to the body and uncover it. Then you will see I have been proven correct."

Ben and Creed moved into position. Each gripped a corner of the cloth either side of the head. Nicolas stared at the outline of the face hinted at in the shroud. Finally, after his long wait, he was only seconds away from staring into the face of Jesus Christ, *the man*. The object he needed to crush the Church. He would have preferred to do this alone so he could dwell on the moment as he pulled back the cover, but circumstances had taken that away from him.

"Are you ready?" Ben asked.

"I am prepared. Uncover Jesus."

Ben and Creed slowly revealed the corpse.

CHAPTER 13

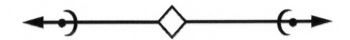

The Magdalene

CREED WAS SURPRISED.

Nicolas was devastated. "It's a woman!"

Ben smiled. Though it wasn't the body he had expected to be revealed, he sensed immediately who it might be and shared his thoughts. "If Jesus was married, as it seems he was, then this woman is most likely his wife, Mary Magdalene."

The stunned, disappointed look on Nicolas's face spoke volumes as he felt his long laid plans begin to unravel. The Ark was not enough on its own to fulfill his Order's ambitions. "It's supposed to be the body of Jesus," he said in disbelief.

"Well, it's definitely not," Creed smiled, pleased with Nicolas's setback.

Nicolas required the body of Jesus to fulfill his plans of destroying the Catholic Church so his new religion could rise from the turmoil to take its place. He was confident *He* would be here. All the evidence he had painstakingly compiled over the years had led him to believe this tomb would contain the mortal remains of the biblical Jesus.

"Uncover it all," Nicolas ordered.

Disturbed dust rose into the air as Ben and Creed pulled back the cover and let it drop to the ground.

All stared at the female form. Scraps of blue cloth remains of the blue dress she once wore, were all that covered her nakedness. The tautly stretched skin had darkened over time.

Ben noticed her fingers were entwined and matched precisely the hands of Mary Magdalene Saunière had placed in his altar bas-relief.

"It seems your plans have fallen to failure," stated Creed, adding a smirk.

Nicolas ignored Creed while he concentrated on the body and wondered if he altered his plans slightly he could use her instead. He soon arrived at the conclusion that it wouldn't work. He needed the body of Jesus. Nothing else would do. When his eyes turned to examine the marble slab she rested upon, he noticed something that gave him hope. "Stand back."

Ben and Creed stepped away when Nicolas approached the body and noticed his gun never diverted from them, an indication the man would be difficult to get the drop on.

Nicolas ran a hand along the top side edge of the marble and discovered he hadn't been mistaken. A thin joint ran along the side of the marble. *It's a lid!* He stepped away and ordered his two captives to see if the top would slide back.

Ben and Creed approached the marble block. Both had been watching Nicolas and the focus of his attention and realized he had discovered the large marble block was hollow, something they had both learned from the journal and knew who Saunière believed was inside the sarcophagus and that Nicolas's plan was about to be fulfilled.

Though Ben knew something the other two didn't, it wouldn't be a secret for much longer. They each placed their palms on the top and pushed. The grating of marble filled the chamber when the top shifted. All glimpsed the black void they had uncovered. They turned the slab until it was at a slight angle to leave a gap wide enough to peer inside.

Eager to discover what was hidden within the darkness, Ben whipped off his headlight and shone it into the sarcophagus.

Nicolas stepped closer so he too could peer inside. Creed stepped aside to give him a better viewing angle. This could be his chance to overpower the man while his attention was focused on the coffin. He sidestepped to maneuver behind Nicolas. The man's gun whipped up to point at his face.

"Just because I'm not looking at you, Creed, don't assume I'm not aware of your every action." He waved the gun towards the head of the sarcophagus. "Stand over there."

Nicolas then turned his attention back to the open coffin to find out if it contained what he thought and hoped it did.

Though they both stared at the person inside, unlike the body that was as expected; flesh and bone, the head on the corpse inside was carved from black glass, so shiny their faces could be seen reflected in its smooth, unblemished surface. An examination of the body revealed the taut skin had survived surprisingly well for two thousand years and still bore evidence of the suffering the man had been forced to endure before finally succumbing to death. There was no mistaking the wounds on his wrists were the result of large nails hammered through them; dark streaks of ancient blood were easily recognizable where it had run down his outstretched arms as he hung from the cross.

Ben had thought if he ever got the chance to enter the tomb, the body inside would turn out to be a Knight Templar. The reason being that the red-cross design on the cloth is an emblem associated with their Order. It would have been far more favorable than the remains of the woman on top or the man his eyes now reflected.

The feet bore similar marks to the wrists. Evidence his feet had been placed one on top of the other and then a large nail hammered through to lock them together. The nail, long enough to pass through both feet and then into a block of wood, had left two tell-tale wounds. Ben thought of the agony this man must have endured, not only from the excruciating pain of his crucifixion but also from the abuse and torture he'd suffered beforehand. This was equally apparent from the many wounds received from the harsh whipping and flaying repeatedly delivered to his body. The resulting shredded and bloodstained skin was still evident.

"Look at the wound in his side," pointed out Nicolas. His recent disappointment banished to be replaced with the exhilaration of the hopeful discovery.

"Where the Roman soldier, Longinus, used his lance to check Jesus was dead before they removed him from the cross," stated Ben in fascination. "Is it actually the body of Christ, though?"

"His name may have been Jesus, but that doesn't mean he was the son of God," Creed said, unhappy with the new discovery and Nicolas's new found pleasure.

"I agree wholeheartedly with you, Creed. The Catholic Church would have us believe his body ascended to heaven, so if this is the same Jesus mentioned in the Bible and by the wounds evident on his body that's difficult to believe otherwise, Son of God or not, it shouldn't be here. Just another of the many lies they cobbled together to form their faith."

Both Ben and Creed found it hard to disagree with the man. The body did seem to be that of the biblical Jesus.

Ben gazed at the glass head. He knew without a doubt the head he found beneath Rosslyn Chapel belonged to this body. "Yes, there can be little doubt this is the body of the biblical Jesus," said Ben, finally convinced. "It seems I owe Saunière an apology."

"Even if it is the mortal remains of Jesus, what good is it to you without a head? It would be like telling everyone you have a long lost Picasso painting but all you show them is the frame," said Creed. "It seems your plans are still doomed to failure."

"I agree the missing head is an unforeseen problem, but it must be somewhere. It will take a while longer than expected, but I will track it down." Nicolas glanced around at the artifacts and the scrolls. "I'm certain I will find a clue concealed amongst the artifacts around me to reveal its whereabouts," he stated confidently. "However, before I can start my search I need to deal with you two. I can't take the risk that you will somehow rob me of all this, so..."

He left the rest unsaid, but all in the chamber knew what was about to happen. The tomb was about to have two new corpses to replace the two Nicolas would shortly remove.

"He aimed the gun at Creed. "Say hello to your father from me when you see him." His finger tightened on the trigger.

"Stop!"

Nicolas glanced at Ben.

"Kill us, and you lose."

Nicolas scoffed. "How can I lose?" He swept an arm around the tomb. "I have all this."

"There's one thing you don't have, something that would make all the difference to your plans and something you need."

"And this thing is?" asked Nicolas, intrigued enough to delay the executions until he'd heard what Ben had to say.

"I know where the missing head is."

Nicolas gazed at Ben. He had already made one mistake by killing Creed's father too soon and was hesitant to repeat the process. "You bluff. How could you possibly know where the head is?"

"Because I found it!"

"Okay Ben, I'll play along. Continue." Nicolas turned to Creed when he attempted to move towards him. A warning glance held him in check.

"I found it in Rosslyn Chapel, or to be precise, in the catacombs beneath."

"Now I know you're lying. The entrance to the underground chambers has been lost for centuries. I know because we have searched."

Ben remembered the story Malloch had told him about the attempt to drill a hole through the floor of the chapel to locate the underground rooms. He wondered if it was the man before him or the group he belonged to who had arranged it. "You also searched for this tomb, but failed to find it, but I did."

"That's true, but I need more convincing to save your lives. How did you gain entry to the catacombs?"

"I entered through a long tunnel from Rosslyn Castle, whose entrance is cleverly concealed. It led to the catacombs under the chapel. There I gazed into the dead eyes of the deceased Sinclair family."

Nicolas stared at Ben. He had heard the rumors about a tunnel leading from the castle to the chapel. It was the reason why they had scoured it but had found nothing. "The castle has been thoroughly searched. No entrance was discovered."

"I didn't say the entrance was *in* the castle. It's in the glen through the lair of the ghost hound."

Nicolas knew the legend of the ghost hound that reportedly dwelled in a cave in the glen, was it this tunnel? There were so many rumors, myths and legends surrounding Rosslyn chapel and the castle, he hadn't taken many of them seriously. With this new information, perhaps he should have. *If Ben is telling the truth and I kill him, I could lose it.*

"Ask Doyle, he'll confirm what I say. His boss, Silas, sent two men in after me to kill me. Instead, I survived, and they died down there."

"Due to certain disagreements concerning an excavation beneath the chapel floor and the deaths that followed, regrettably, for some time I was estranged from that particular group, however, that relationship, with your arrival here in France, has since been renewed." He stared at Ben thoughtfully for a few moments before speaking. "Though I will check out your story, I am inclined to believe you. If you give me the head, I will spare both your lives."

From what he had just been told, Ben assumed Nicolas was the man from Rosslyn whom Malloch had seen when he stole the chest found in the small chamber beneath the floor. "It seems I have no other option but to agree. I don't suppose you would consider us taking a few artifacts as part of the deal?"

"Be content with your lives, Ben. Everything here belongs to me."

"It was worth a try. How are we going to do this? Will you send one of your thugs back to England with me to fetch the head, or shall I just go alone and post it to you."

"I will tell you exactly how this will be done, Harper. First, you two will help me and my men move the artifacts above ground. When that task is completed and the relics stored somewhere safe, I will travel back to England with you while Creed remains in the company of my...*thugs*. If you have lied about the head, then, of course, you both will die. In the unlikely event of you managing to incapacitate me somehow during the journey, and I do not return, Creed will be killed, and you will be hunted down and also killed, is that clear enough for you both?"

"Crystal," said Ben.

"You won't get away with this," Creed stated angrily.

"Calm yourself, Creed, I already have. Learn to live with it. Now, we have wasted enough time, the relics must be crated up as I cannot risk them becoming damaged." Nicolas glanced at Doyle's sprawled body. "Wake him up. I want everyone outside."

Though both knew they had only prolonged the inevitable, the delay had furnished them with much needed extra time to find a way out of their current situation. When Creed had woken an angry Doyle with a few less than gentle slaps around the face, they followed Nicolas back through the tunnel and outside just as David arrived in a large white box van. He parked it beneath the cave entrance and climbed out.

He grinned at Ben and Creed. "Miss me?"

"Like a hole in the head," Creed quipped."

David pointed his gun at Creed's head. "That's something I can soon remedy."

"Kill him, and you'll have to carry half the stuff out the tomb yourself," said Nicolas.

The threat of hard work convinced David to lower the weapon.

Nicolas opened the rear roller-shutter door and looked at the displaced load of jumbled stacks of different sized wooden crates. Amidst the chaos were extra lengths of wood, a box of tools and a large roll of bubble wrap. He turned to David. "How fast did you drive up here? I said take it easy and avoid the bumps, not drive like you're in a fucking rally."

David shrugged. "I went as careful as I could," he argued.

"Which wasn't very careful at all by the look of this mess. Get in there and sort it out."

Creed wagged a finger and tsk-tsked David as he passed. "Naughty, naughty."

David scowled and climbed into the back of the van.

"As you can see, I've come fully prepared," said Nicolas.

"I see that, but how did you know what size to make the crates?" Ben asked.

"From the pictures on your website. I calculated the body to measure no more than six feet tall, so using that as a known size I measured everything in relation to it. I have spare wood, screws, and tools if we need to make any alterations or build new crates. As you can see, I have left nothing to chance."

Ben and Creed knew Nicolas would be a hard man to defeat. His intelligent, watchful eyes rarely left them unattended and were aware as soon as Nicolas had everything he wanted from them he would order their deaths or do it himself. Ben had only delayed that outcome. They had to find a way to turn the tables on their aggressors. While they waited for this opportunity to arise, they did as Nicolas ordered.

They spent the next few hours transporting the objects from the tomb to the van. The smaller and more delicate objects were packed into boxes inside the chamber before being removed. Some of the chests, on closer examination, were too rotten to be moved, so their contents were packed into other crates. Though the shroud had little age, only dating to the time of Saunière, it was carefully folded and placed in a wooden crate for removal. The body of Mary Magdalene was wrapped in bubble wrap, as respectfully as Ben and Creed could manage under the circumstances. A second crate constructed by Doyle ensured she was a perfect fit. After padding around her with more bubble wrap, the lid was screwed on. Its journey through the tunnel had involved a bit of pushing and shoving and, at one point, the removal of two wooden supports so they could maneuver it around a tight corner.

The Ark was nervously emptied of its contents by Ben and Creed. Both were unsure what they thought might happen, but nothing untoward did, and the stone tablets were packed in separate flat crates Nicolas had Doyle build after taking measurements.

The Ark's bulky lid and base were first cocooned in bubble wrap secured with tape before being carefully squeezed through the narrow tunnel and outside where they were then sealed in two wooden crates.

Nicolas oversaw each artifact's removal while David and Doyle kept their guns trained on Ben and Creed. So far there had been no chance to overpower them. David, much to his dismay, had been ordered to remain in the tomb to guard Ben and Creed until they entered the tunnel, while Doyle, still nursing a sore head, stayed at the cave entrance end where Nicolas could keep an eye on him and take over when they crawled out into the cave. Doyle would follow them outside with Nicolas who supervised the loading of the van before sending them back in for another load.

Four hours later, only a few objects remained in the tomb. Ben carefully placed the scrolls that lay on the ground around the base of one of the crosses, in another of the specially prepared crates, which had been divided into sections to prevent damage to the delicate parchments. He was eager to read them, but David, impatient to leave the tomb he imagined was about to collapse, had grown steadily more intolerant of any delay and hurried them along with threats of abuse and occasional prods with his gun.

While Creed and Ben carried the metal chest, David brought the crate of scrolls; these were the last items to be removed. Before Ben left the tomb, he took one last look around the now almost empty chamber. Because they were too big to take, the two large crosses remained where they stood, leaning against the cavern wall. Nicolas was also not interested in them because they showed no sign of ever having been used for the crucifixion of Jesus or anyone else. He assumed they were symbolic and of no worth to him. The marble sarcophagus was also too bulky to fit through the tunnel. Ben yelped in pain when he was again prodded in the back by the barrel of David's gun.

"Get a move on, Harper."

Ben shot him an angry stare and for the last time climbed into the tunnel. As he pushed the heavy chest ahead of him, Creed dragged it from in front as he backed along the passage. A small amount of earth fell from above as the chest knocked into one of the supports in a section where some had been removed so the body could be carried around the corner.

David glanced nervously at the tunnel roof. "Be careful, or you'll bring the whole tunnel down."

It gave Ben an idea. He glanced back at David following a few feet behind, the crate of scrolls tucked under one arm and the gun in the other, moving awkwardly along the tunnel. "You want us to hurry or be careful?"

"I want you to do both, so get a fucking move on."

Ben faced forward and attracted Creed's attention. "I have an idea, get ready to move quickly," he whispered.

Creed shrugged his shoulders and mouthed the word, *why?*

Ben had no time to explain. "Just pull the crate as fast as you can when I give the word, my life will depend on it."

After moving through the tunnel a few more meters, Ben glanced behind. David was exactly where he wanted him if his plan was to be successful. He kicked out at the wooden props supporting the boards holding back the weight of the earth in the shaft which had collapsed on him before. With the mass of soil no longer supported, the boards fell, bringing with them the earth and rocks they no longer held back. Almost instantaneously the tunnel caved in.

"Move!" Shouted Ben, when dirt rained down on his legs. A hurried glance behind revealed earth pouring over David, his mouth open to scream out in horror as his nightmare of becoming buried alive became a reality. Ben never heard the scream as it was quickly silenced by the torrent of earth spewing from the shaft to smother the unfortunate man.

Creed, immediately on hearing Ben's signal, propelled himself along the tunnel dragging the chest and Ben along with him.

Ben kicked out more of the supports as he scrambled along behind the chest, setting a concertina motion of collapsing tunnel to ensure David would never escape. When the loud crack of splintering wood rang out, he glanced back. A wall of earth rushed toward him, snapping any supports still in place. With the chest slowing his progress and too big to allow him to squeeze past, Ben doubted he would make it out in time.

"Faster, Creed, the whole tunnel's collapsing," he warned loud enough to be heard above the noise of falling earth and splintering wood that filled the confined space.

Creed glanced past Ben and recognized the danger his friend was in. He moved even faster along the tunnel.

Ben pushed the metal chest for all he was worth. He could feel the dirt falling onto his legs, then to his horror, the chest stopped moving. He felt the wave of earth move up his body, pinning him down. Suddenly, he shot into the air when he was dragged free of the tunnel. Creed had grabbed his arms and pulled him to safety. The chest had stopped because they had reached the end of the tunnel. They both sat on the cave floor breathing heavily and stared at the entrance when the end of the tunnel collapsed, partially burying the silver chest still sitting in the hole where Creed had left it.

Doyle rushed over and looked at the blocked tunnel. "What happened? Where's David?"

"Cave in," Ben explained between breaths. "He must have...got caught in it. He...didn't stand a...chance."

"I told David we shouldn't remove those boards," said Creed, placing the blame on the man who had ordered them to do it.

"You mean he's dead?" Doyle asked, unable to believe it.

Creed nodded. "No one could have survived that."

"What's going on?" Nicolas asked when he entered the cave.

"David's dead," stated Doyle.

"How?" asked Nicolas, suspicion obvious in his voice. He joined them and stared at the blocked passage.

"Cave in," Ben repeated. "David didn't stand a chance."

Nicolas glanced at the partially buried chest. "What about the scrolls?"

"David had them, they are lost," answered Ben, breathing easier now.

"Damn! That's a loss I could have done without. Who knows what secrets they might have contained?"

Though he showed remorse at losing the scrolls, none was shown for the loss of one of Silas's hired hands.

Nicolas pointed at his two captives. "Haul that chest out and carry it down to the van. It's time we left. Doyle, keep an eye on them."

Ben and Creed manhandled the chest out of the hole.

"But David could still be alive, trapped in the tunnel," argued Doyle, reluctant to leave without attempting a rescue if there was a chance the man was still alive. It could have been him trapped in the tunnel. "We can't just leave him."

"Don't be so damn stupid, Doyle. He's dead, and there's nothing we can do. If you want to stay and dig out his body you can, but you'll get no help from me or these two, they leave with me."

Doyle glanced at the blocked tunnel and then shrugged sadly. There was little he could do on his own.

Closely watched by their captives, Ben and Creed carried the chest out of the cave and down to the van. When everything had been loaded and secured with ratchet straps and rope, including Ben and Creed who had been handcuffed with cable ties and secured to a metal side strut by Doyle with more cable ties, the roller shutter door closed with a loud clang that reverberated around the packed vehicle's interior. The two men listened as Doyle and Nicolas walked along the side and climbed into the cab. Nicolas took control of the van as he didn't trust Doyle to drive with such a valuable cargo along the uneven track that was just wide enough for the large vehicle.

Ben and Creed looked at each other in the semi-darkness.

"We have to do something," Creed whispered.

Ben studied the plastic tie looped around the van strut. "The edge of the strut isn't particularly sharp, but if we slide it back and forth, it might wear through it."

The van lurched forward causing them both to stumble.

"It's worth a try," Creed agreed.

They both slid their restraints back and forth along the edge of metal. The ties bit into their wrists as they pulled on them to keep them taut on the metal edge. The van rocked as it traveled over the rough track and swayed them about, making the process even more difficult. As it bounced over another bump, Creed was thrown off balance. His already-weakened ties broke from the strain. He fell and yelped in pain when his head connected with the corner of the metal chest before falling to the floor where he lay dazed. Though his hands were still bound by cable ties, he was no longer attached to the van. They now had a chance.

The van lurched to a stop.

"Go and see what happened, Doyle. One of the crates may have fallen. I don't want those relics damaged," Nicolas ordered, after hearing a noise from the back of the van. He remembered the state of the empty wooden crates after David's trip up to the cave.

Doyle opened the door to carry out the order.

"And be quick about it. I want this stuff stashed somewhere safe before something happens to it."

Ben and Creed heard the passenger door open and close, then Doyle's footsteps walking alongside to the rear door. His steps halted at the back of the van and the sound of the bar locking the shutter lifting.

Recovered from his fall, Creed climbed to his feet and searched for something to use as a weapon against the gun-toting Doyle who would shortly appear. Amongst a pile of objects laid in a box without a lid, he glimpsed an old friend.

Unaware what was taking place inside the van and the danger that threatened, Doyle unlocked the padlock securing the door, lifted the locking bar and raised the shutter. It had only risen a short distance when he lurched. Blood sprayed from his mouth over the rising shutter. He glimpsed Creed on his knees staring straight at him and something he held. Doyle focused in on the object to discover it was a sword; the weapon from the tomb Creed had knocked him unconscious with. He followed the blade pointed at him to the tip buried in his stomach. As he slowly stumbled backward, he slid off the blade to leave behind a bloody trail on the medieval weapon. He was dead before he hit the ground.

Creed used the sword to slice through the cable tie around Ben's wrists and then freed his own restraints. He jumped silently out of the van and knelt to rummage through the dead man's clothes. Finding what he was looking for, he checked the gun was loaded.

Creed looked at Ben, who was shocked by the man's death and whispered. "Two down, one to go."

While Ben climbed down, Creed peered around the side of the van and observed Nicolas reflected in the wing mirror. He stared out through the screen, unaware that anything was amiss.

Probably dreaming about what he has planned for the artifacts, Creed thought. He glanced down at Doyle and then at Ben. "Quick, put his jacket on and walk around to the passenger door, but try and keep your face hidden. I want Nicolas to think you are Doyle. I'll only need a few seconds."

Ben was doubtful the plan would work. "Nicolas is too sharp. He'll know it's me and he has a gun."

"We don't have much time before he gets suspicious and comes to investigate. You'll just have to trust me. While he's looking at you, I'll nip around to the other door and get the drop on him. Now go."

Ben had no option but to do as Creed asked. He removed the dead man's jacket and slipped it on. It was a reasonable fit and should give Creed the few seconds he required before Nicolas saw through the deception.

"Ready?" Creed asked.

Ben shrugged. "Not really, but let's do it." He kept his face aimed at the ground while he walked towards the passenger door.

Nicolas stared out of the windscreen deep in thought. He could hardly believe that everything was finally working out as he had planned for so long. Yes, there had been a few mistakes and delays, but what did that matter now. Soon he would reveal the Ark and the body of Christ to the unsuspecting public. His picture will be on every newspaper and television screen across the world; soon everyone will know his name. The millions of believers that would flock to him will make him a rich and powerful man. *The Vatican will become obsolete overnight when its followers learn their Christian faith is based on a lie. Of course, some of the Christian diehards won't believe it, but most will. The Catholic Church had experienced a lot of bad press over recent years; this revelation should be the final nail in their coffin.* Footsteps on the stony track turned his head. He looked in the passenger side mirror and watched Doyle approach the door. Nicolas sensed something was wrong. He stared at Doyle's reflection as he attempted to discern what had piqued his suspicion. Though the mirror, dirty and cracked, distorted the image it reflected, he still noticed what was amiss, *the walk was wrong. Doyle walked like a gangly ape.* He gazed behind the walking figure to glimpse something on the ground; an outstretched arm. Something glinted on one of the fingers. He knew it was the ring shaped like a skull that idiot Doyle wore. Something had gone wrong. Doyle had been overpowered again. "Bloody amateurs," he cursed. If Doyle weren't dead already, he would kill him himself. His hand reflectively reached inside his jacket and gripped the weapon.

Creed hadn't taken his eyes from Nicolas's reflection in the mirror when he crept along the opposite side of the van towards the driver's door. He kept pace with the sound of Ben's footsteps so as not to alert Nicolas to his presence. He saw the man's head turn when he heard Ben approach and hoped he'd be fooled long enough for him to act.

Ben took a deep breath and reached for the handle. He hoped Creed was in position as he opened the van door. He stared straight down the barrel of Nicolas's gun. He noticed the gun move to aim at his shoulder. Nicolas intended to wound and not kill. The pain would be intense. In slow motion, Nicolas's finger squeezed the trigger. The gun bucked. The force of the bullet striking him knocked him reeling backward, the sound of the gunshot reached his ears as he fell to the ground.

A split second before Nicolas pulled the trigger, he heard the van door behind him open. Instinct forced him to react to the new threat. He attempted to twist in the seat as the gun fired, but froze when he felt cold metal pressed against the back of his head. He had been tricked. Harper had been a distraction.

"Give me the gun," Creed ordered in a calm but forceful voice.

Nicolas, unable to turn his head due to the gun held tight against it, passed the gun behind and felt it taken from his reluctant grasp. He raised his arms as high as he could in the confines of the van to show Creed they were empty and for the moment posed no threat.

Creed glanced at the open passenger door. "What happened to Ben?" He had heard the gunshot and now feared the worst.

Nicolas shrugged. "You distracted me. If he's dead, it's down to you. I was only aiming to wound him in the arm."

There was a note of regret in his voice. If Ben were dead, gaining possession of the head wouldn't be so easy. Nicolas felt a brief searing pain on the back of his head before blacking out. Knocked unconscious by a blow from the butt of Creed's gun, he slumped onto the seat.

Creed rushed around to the other side of the van. A feeling of dread washed over him when he saw Ben sprawled on the ground. He eyes went to the bullet hole in the borrowed coat directly over Ben's heart. He knelt and pulled the coat open to survey the damage, but was surprised to see no blood and no hole in the clothes beneath it. He ripped Ben's shirt open, and instead of the gaping hole oozing blood he expected to see, there was only an ugly bruise forming on Ben's chest, which rose and fell with Ben's breathing. Creed sighed with relief when Ben groaned and slowly opened his eyes.

Creed sat him up and leaned him against the van.

Ben groaned. "Am I dead yet?"

"No, but you should be."

"I don't understand. I felt the bullet strike."

Creed searched the coat where the bullet had struck. Feeling something hard, he reached into the inside pocket and pulled out the object and held up for Ben to see.

Ben stared at the object in Creed's hand, recognizing it as one of the artifacts from the tomb; a crucifix with four sapphires set into each arm of the cross near the ends. The upright of the cross was about six inches and its cross section just over half that wide. It was not the size of the object that had saved Ben's life, but its inch-thick silver that had stopped the bullet, now embedded dead center in Jesus' chest.

Creed stared at the bullet in the crucifix. "Jesus just saved your life."

"Maybe he did, but I'm not about to convert just yet. Jesus may have stopped the bullet, but it was Doyle's greed that saved my life. He pilfered it from the tomb." A spasm of pain caused Ben to wince. He glanced down at his chest to survey the damage.

Creed let out a surprised whistle. "Will you look at that?"

Ben studied the red mark. It wasn't the actual bruise forming that had surprised Creed, it was its shape. An angry red welt the exact size and shape of the cross imprinted in the flesh directly over his heart. Ben stared at the upside down cross from his point of view and placed the cross on it, it matched perfectly.

"You should keep that as your lucky charm," Creed suggested.

Ben looked at Creed and then at the cross. "You know, I think I will." He slipped it into a pocket.

Creed helped Ben remove the coat and helped him into the passenger side of the van. As Ben climbed in he saw the unconscious form of Nicolas slumped over the seat and guessed that again, Creed's plan, though not exactly as predicted, had proved successful. Creed pulled Nicolas out of the van and after tying him securely with the tow rope he found in the vehicle's toolbox, he tossed him into the back of the van, placed the sword well out of his reach and closed and locked the shutter.

Creed climbed into the driving seat and looked at Ben. "Can you handle a gun?"

Ben remembered his experience with one back in Scotland. "I get by," he grinned.

Creed handed him Nicolas's weapon. "Keep it hidden, it might come in handy."

"Of that, I have no doubt." Ben slipped it into a side pocket.

Creed started the van, steered it slowly down the winding track and then to his house. Now that those who had been watching them no longer posed a threat, they no longer needed to conceal their movements. They carried the still unconscious Nicolas into the house and gagged and bound him to a chair in the living room. Ben slumped into the same chair he'd sat in only a few days before and gratefully accepted the generous glass of whiskey Creed offered. They both sat there for a few moments in silence, reliving the events of the past few days. Everything had happened so quickly, and much had still not sunk in. The discovery of the tomb had been marred by the situation they had found themselves in, preventing them from examining the tomb's contents in detail as they would have liked. They had also killed two people, which though unavoidable, they were each responsible for a man's death.

Ben looked at their prisoner, their roles now reversed. "What's to be done with him?"

Creed gazed emotionlessly at the bound man. "He dies. He killed my father in cold blood and shot you."

"Yes, but he didn't kill me."

"Don't forget, if it weren't for the head you found in Rosslyn, we'd both be dead already."

"Again, you're right, but I'm not like him. I find it difficult to accept the taking of human life as casually as you seem to endure it. It's one thing to kill in self-defense or to save your life, but to kill in cold blood, I'm not sure I can do that."

"You won't have to, I'll gladly do it. He killed my father."

"Then surely you're as bad as him."

Creed shook his head. "I disagree. Nicolas kills for his own gain, whereas I kill to prevent us from being killed. If we let him go, he'll just come back after the tomb stuff and probably kill us in the process."

"Maybe you're right, but there must be some other way that doesn't involve his death."

"Well, if there is, it escapes me." Creed drained his glass. "Another?"

Ben shook his head. "I suppose handing him over to the police would be out of the question."

"It would cause too many problems and too many questions. We would have to tell them about the tomb and what was inside. Also, don't forget we've both killed a man. Explaining it was in self-defense may not be as easy as it seems now we've left the scene. We would probably be arrested on suspicion of murder. God only knows what will happen to the artifacts from the tomb, but I do know one thing, we would never set eyes on them again and neither would anyone else when the Vatican learns of their discovery." Creed replenished his glass and sat down.

"Let Nicolas be my problem. I'll take care of him. Like Pontius Pilot, you can wash your hands of the matter. You needn't know what has happened to him. His blood will be on my hands only," Creed suggested, offering Ben a way out.

Ben thought of everything they had been through together during the last few days. He knew that if it were not for Creed, he would be dead by now. Twice he had saved his life. "No, you're right," stated Ben, finally accepting the inevitable. "We can't let him go free. His personality is not of a forgive and forget nature. If there's no other option, then he'll have to die...but we'll do it together."

"If you're sure?"

"I am."

Creed broke the few moments of silence that followed. "By the way, is it true? Did you really find the head of Jesus beneath Rosslyn Chapel?"

"Yes, amazing at it seems, I found what seems to be the head of Jesus."

"I imagine that's quite a story."

"It is, and one day I'll tell you, but at the moment we have more important matters to attend to. In our haste to escape off the mountain, we left Doyle's body on the track, and our stuff is still in the cave. Now Nicolas has removed the bushes that once camouflaged the entrance, it'll only be a matter of time before someone stumbles across the cave and investigates. Our fingerprints are everywhere. They'll link the dead body to the cave and be sure to try and track us down."

"I was so focused on escaping I didn't even consider anything else. We'll have to go back, collect everything and clean up the scene to hide the excavation. We can push Doyle's body into the ravine so it won't be so easily found, if at all. We can dispose of our friend here at the same time."

"We also have to pick up your car."

"Oh crap! I had forgotten all about that with all that's happened."

"We can go in my car as we can't keep driving that van about." Ben looked over at Nicolas. "The boot's small, but he should fit inside, with a squeeze."

Creed drained his glass and stood. "Let's get going. The sooner everything is cleared up, the sooner we can relax."

Ben sighed. *Here we go again.*

CHAPTER 14

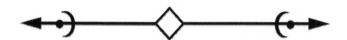

The Boar's Revenge

THOUGH HE FELT the exact opposite, David had been lucky. When the tunnel collapsed, he had reacted quickly, darting back along the narrow passage to escape the falling earth and an extremely unpleasant death. In his mad scramble back along the passage he had lost his gun, but more importantly—and of more use in his current situation—his flashlight.

Forcing himself not to panic, David searched his pockets for the lighter he confiscated from Harper; in his current situation, it was worth more to him than its gold weight. The small flame feebly lit up the tunnel. What he saw filled him with dread. His only exit was solidly blocked. He knew better than to expect a rescue from those above. Now Nicolas had the artifacts, David's life was meaningless to him; the man wouldn't waste time and resources on a rescue and relying on Doyle to save him wasn't even worth contemplating. If he wanted to live, and he did, he would have to dig himself out or die trying.

David crawled into the tomb and searched for something he could dig with. His choices were limited as the tools had been stored in the cave above so as not to provide Ben and Creed with a handy weapon within reach. He searched through the wood that once formed the ancient crates and picked out the most solid piece and returned to the blocked tunnel. Though it would be awkward digging in the dark, he wanted to conserve the lighter's precious fuel and reluctantly returned the lighter to his pocket. He blindly dug, hacked, and scraped at the blockage, pushing the dirt behind him.

The old wood, weakened by age, soon began to disintegrate and snapped when it struck something hard. David flicked on the lighter. The small crate containing the parchments was highlighted in its flame. He tugged it free from the earth's grasp and pried off the lid; he now had a stronger piece of wood to dig with. As he toiled at the pile of dirt, the tunnel behind him rapidly filled with the soil he displaced from in front, but as he planned to keep moving forward, it caused him no concern. He did though ensure a gap remained at the top to allow him access to the stock of life-giving oxygen trapped down here with him.

David, someone who avoided manual labor of any description like the plague, found the work hard and tiring and after an hour he stopped and rested. The darkness was starting to get the better of him, causing him to become disorientated and confused. The lighter again lit up the darkness and the tunnel he hoped wouldn't become his tomb. He placed the lighter on a stone protruding from the tunnel wall and used its comforting flickering light to work by.

It wasn't long before the flame grew weaker as the small amount of fuel it held was consumed. David glanced at the parchment box he'd kept with him as he progressed. He snatched up one of the parchments, rolled it up tightly and with a total disregard for any historical importance or long lost secrets the scroll might contain, he put it to flame. It wouldn't last long, but he had more. He made a small hole in the side of the tunnel with his finger and poked one end of the tightly rolled parchment inside.

As ancient secrets, recorded by those long dead, turned to ash, David dug for his life. By the time he glimpsed light whose source wasn't from inside the tunnel and felt a trickle of fresh cool air on his face, all but one of the parchments had been burnt. Empowered by the discovery, he frantically scraped and dug away at the earth and soon felt the rush of cold fresh air. He dragged down deep breaths of the life-giving substance into his lungs. The air, however, came from an unexpected source, not the tunnel ahead, which was still blocked by tons of earth, but from above. It filtered down through a shaft in the rock. David peered up through the rocky hole that led outside to freedom. Far above was a jagged circle of sunlight. The narrow shaft would be a tight squeeze for his bulk to fit through, but anything was better than remaining trapped below ground. Aware that his clothes would snag on the numerous rocky outcrops, he removed all but his boxer shorts, he wanted some protection, however flimsy, for his most delicate parts. He was about to start on his journey to freedom when he spied the last scroll in the empty crate. He guessed it would fetch a high price from the right buyer and if anyone deserved to make a profit for the many hardships he'd recently endured, it was him. He plucked it from the box and stuck it down the front of his shorts. He carefully climbed into a standing position and squeezed his shoulders into the tight space. He ignored the pain from the rock scraping his skin, rested his hands on the rock either side and pushed and pulled himself upwards until his feet found a foothold. He pushed with his legs, rising a few more inches and grimaced with pain when his back scraped against a sharp piece of rock; warm blood trickled down his skin. By arching his back, he managed to maneuver past it without inflicting more damage.

David kept his progress slow and steady. If he lost his footing and slipped, his skin would be ripped to shreds when he fell. He also lacked the energy to repeat the climb. He paused for a rest and glanced up. Freedom was almost within his grasp. Blades of grass overhung the opening less than a meter away. The day had turned to night, moonlight lit his way now. Not daring to linger too long in fear of diminishing his remaining energy from supporting his bodyweight, he carried on his slow, painful and energy draining journey to freedom.

The wild boar, angry from the constant pain inflicted by the crossbow bolt sticking from its rump, had returned to look for the female. It sniffed the air in an attempt to track the scent of the sow again. Apart from a weak odor of her urine, there was nothing; she wasn't here. Weak from the loss of blood, it settled in the grass and waited. Maybe she would return soon.

The cold breeze David felt on his face when he poked his head out of the shaft was one of the best feelings he'd ever experienced. He had done it. He had escaped certain death. He placed his hands on the grass either side of the hole and with his last reserves of energy, heaved himself out and flopped onto the cool grass. He had only just made it; his arms and legs had all but lost their strength. He lay there recovering, glad to be above ground with stars in the night sky above his head.

The boar watched the man emerge from the earth and fall to the ground. It sniffed the air, the scent was familiar, his brain remembered the last time he had smelt something similar, just before the pain had started. The boar's anger grew as it rose to its feet and charged.

David turned his head toward the sound. Above the tips of the long grass, he saw the largest boar he'd ever seen charging at him. With no time to climb to his feet to defend himself, he took the only option available; he grabbed the animal's tusks and used its momentum he flung the boar over his head and into the bushes.

The boar squealed in pain when the bolt was pushed deeper into its already sore flesh. It recovered quickly and crashed through the undergrowth toward its current source of fury.

David climbed to his feet as the beast leaped out of the bushes and straight at him. The boar struck him in the chest. Its weight and the force of the charge knocked him flat on his back. He frantically grabbed the beast around the head and tried to keep its lethal tusks from gouging his skin. He tried unsuccessfully to break the beast's neck, but either he was too weak, the boar too strong, or maybe it was a combination of the two. For a few moments, they wrestled on the ground. The boar's kicking hooves left red welts wherever they connected with David's already bruised, scraped and cut skin. With his strength already sapped from his recent ordeal, David tired rapidly. If he didn't end it soon, the boar would win the battle. He summoned all of his remaining strength and threw the boar to the ground. He was about to climb to his feet and flee when he spied the crossbow bolt protruding from the boar's side. Before the animal had time to recover, David leaped on the beast. The boar squealed in pain when David yanked out the bolt. The beast's struggling throes were so forceful they almost freed it from David's grip.

David clenched his legs around the writhing animal tightly. It was like sitting atop a rodeo bull. He raised the bolt, aimed for the heart and stabbed it into the boar's chest with his remaining reserves of strength. The boar twitched as it died. David had won. He rolled off the beast and lay on his back beside the dead animal. His tired body, bruised, cut and battered, screamed out for a rest. David duly obliged and fell asleep.

CHAPTER 15

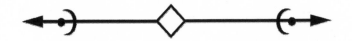

David's Revenge

BEN'S HIRE CAR again struggled over the uneven surface of the foresters' track. Though easier now most of the mud had dried out, the journey was far from comfortable. Because the car lights could be seen for miles on the high open hillside—the last thing they wanted was to attract attention to what they were doing—he drove with them switched off. Luckily, the full moon cast enough light to drive by and avoid driving over the steep cliffs that in places were lined the edge of the track. Ben steered the car around another hairpin corner and saw Doyle's body in the middle of the track where he'd died. Ben stopped the car.

Ben and Creed climbed out and walked over to the body.

"You grab his legs, and I'll grab his shoulders, and we'll toss him over the edge."

Ben did as Creed ordered and grabbed Doyle's ankles.

They carried the body over to the edge of the steep drop, swung it over the side of the cliff and let go. Twigs snapped, and undergrowth rustled when the body hit the ground and rolled down the slope towards the river at its bottom.

"What about Nicolas?" Creed asked, looking back at the car "Shall we do him now?"

Ben glanced over at the small car. "No! Let's do it on the way back. I still have to come to terms with the deed yet, but I will. It needs to be done, unfortunately."

Creed didn't argue. He was willing to give Ben a little more time, but Nicolas would have to be disposed of tonight. "Okay, let's go and empty the cave."

They climbed back into the car and drove on until they arrived at the side track where Creed had concealed his Landrover. Ben waited until Creed had reversed onto the main track and then followed him to the Cave. They turned around on a patch of ground a short distance past the cave and parked directly underneath it to make loading the Landrover easier. They switched off their engines, climbed out of their vehicles and listened to the silence that descended on the hill.

"Seems like we're all alone," Creed said.

"Let's hope it remains that way." Ben gazed up at the entrance. "I'll pass the stuff down, and you can load it."

Ben climbed up to the cave and disappeared inside. After switching on a couple of the battery-powered lamps, he glanced around. Everything was just as they had left it. Working quickly, it wasn't long before the cave was empty. After Ben passed the last item down to Creed, he used a spade to shovel some of the excavated soil into the tunnel entrance until it was full. He spread the remainder over the cave floor but left the wall of rocks by the entrance. He then used a leafy branch gathered from outside to sweep the floor. When he was satisfied all evidence of their excavation and presence had been removed, he switched off the lamps, and after one last look around the cave where so much had happened over the previous few days, he climbed down onto the track. He knew he would never return.

Creed waited for him. "All done?" Creed took the spade and lamps and placed them in the back of his vehicle.

"Yep, I left nothing behind to incriminate us. Even Sherlock Holmes would have trouble finding a clue leading to us now."

"Good, soon we'll be able to relax." Creed closed the rear door of the Landrover. "Follow me, and we'll dispose of our chum in your boot along the track by the drop-off."

Ben nodded, reluctantly. The thought of killing someone in cold blood was something he was still finding hard to come to terms with, even though the man would have killed them and would undoubtedly attempt to again if he was set free. Perhaps Creed would have to carry out the deed himself.

Creed climbed into his vehicle as Ben walked around to the back of his car, took the gun from his pocket just in case their prisoner had managed to untie himself, and opened the boot.

Nicolas was still securely bound, gagged and alive. He hadn't suffocated as Ben had hoped but struggling in an attempt to free his hands. He stared at Ben with pleading eyes, but when his eyes flicked to the side, his expression briefly changed from despair to hope.

Ben turned his head and looked up at the hillside where Nicolas had glanced; there was nothing there. He closed the boot lid, slipped the gun back in his pocket and approached the driver's door.

Creed wound down his window and leaned his head out. "Is everything okay?"

"Yeah, everything's fine. He's still alive."

"Not for much longer." Creed pulled his head back inside the car and started the engine.

A few moments before, David had opened his eyes to see the night sky still above him. He wondered how long he had slept before something had woken him. He lay there and listened. A car door slammed shut. He climbed to his feet to investigate. Though his whole body ached, he felt a little refreshed from the sleep. He moved toward the sound and peered over the edge of the outcrop above the cave, surprised to see Creed's Landrover and Harper's hire car. Confused, he looked both ways along the track for any sign of the van but saw none. *Something must have gone wrong. Where are Doyle and the boss?*

When he instinctively reached for his gun, David remembered he was practically naked and his weapon lost. He continued to watch while he tried to fathom what had happened. He saw Creed in the Landrover and Harper walking over to his car, but instead of getting in he went to the back and opened the boot. David was stunned to see his boss bound and gagged inside. The man's movements indicated he was still alive. When he stared into the boot, Nicolas glanced at him. He dodged out of sight when Harper turned. He remained hidden and listened to Ben and Creed talking.

"Is everything okay?" Creed asked.

"Yeah, everything's fine. He's still alive." Ben replied.

"Not for much longer."

From Creed's words it was obvious they planned to kill his boss. He also knew if he rescued him he would be well rewarded.

The slamming of Harper's car door signaled they were about to leave. He turned away from the edge and ignoring the pain from his cruelly treated body, David ran. He passed the dead boar and sprinted along an all but overgrown track barely visible in the moonlight. Ignoring the brambles and branches ripping at his already torn skin, he continually glanced down at the track as he ran. Creed's Landrover drew level with him and then pulled ahead. David ignored it; the car following was the one that interested him. Harper's car drew level. David looked ahead. The Landrover's brake lights lit up the darkness when Creed slowed to negotiate around a sharp bend in the track. He glanced back at Harper's car and then back at the sharp bend ahead, this was his chance.

When Harper slowed to negotiate the car around the corner, David didn't stay on the path that curved to follow the contour of the track, but veered off and continued in a straight line. Bushes tore at his skin as he crashed through them. The ground suddenly disappeared. He fell onto a steep grassy incline. After sliding down the grassy bank on his back, he arrived on a small rocky outcrop. Using the speed of the fast ride down the slope to his advantage, he rose to his feet and without losing momentum leaped into the air.

The last few days had taken their toll on Ben, and he wasn't looking forward to what was about to occur. He desperately thought of some other way to handle the Nicolas situation, which didn't involve murder, when suddenly, something heavy landed on the bonnet and the windscreen cracked with the impact. Ben swerved and almost drove over the edge of the track. He slammed on his breaks. Whatever it was he had crashed into, slid off the car. He peered out of the cracked screen. His first thought was he had collided with a deer or some other animal, maybe even a wild boar, he knew they lived in this area, though he'd rarely seen one. Whatever it was it had left a large dent in the bonnet. Ben wondered how he would explain the damage to the hire company. Creed's brake lights disappeared around a corner; with no lights on their vehicles, he hadn't noticed Ben had stopped. Reluctant to leave the safety of the car in case it was a wild boar, and was still alive and angry, he was about to reverse so he could get a look at what he had hit when something moved in front of the car. A hand appeared on the bonnet; it wasn't an animal, but a man.

Ben switched on the headlights and was about to get out and help but froze when the figure rose to his feet and stood there bathed in the bright light from the car's twin beams.

"It can't be!" Ben uttered in stunned surprise. He was unable to believe what his eyes were staring at; the nearly naked David, his body battered and bloody.

How the hell did he get out of the tunnel? And where are his clothes?

The smile that appeared on David's face contained no hint of merriment. The message was clear; Ben was in trouble.

Ben wasn't going to wait around to receive whatever sadistic punishment the man intended to inflict upon him. He rammed the car into first gear and slammed his foot down on the gas pedal. The car shot forward.

David reacted quickly. He leaped onto the car, glided across the bonnet and crashed into the windscreen, adding a few more cracks to the already damaged glass, and grabbed hold of a wiper. He made a fist with his free hand and smashed it through the glass, punching out a neat hole.

Ben ignored the glass flying into the car; he was busy trying to avoid the large bloody fingers that groped for his neck while at the same time attempting to prevent the car from plummeting into the ravine alongside the narrow track. He slammed on the brakes in an attempt to throw his attacker off; it had worked last time. The car skidded on a patch of mud and unable to find a purchase on the slippery surface, it skewed towards the edge of the track and the steep slope that ended in a drop almost seventy meters below. The car skidded to a stop with one front wheel hanging over the edge and free of any friction spun freely.

Ignoring the pain from the glass ripping his skin when it dragged over the sharp edges of the hole, David pulled his arm back through the screen.

Ben fumbled with the gears, trying to put it in reverse as he watched his attacker raise both fists and slam them down onto the windscreen. The glass had suffered too much damage to be able to resist this new onslaught and shattered, leaving nothing but air between them.

Operating on rage and adrenalin, David lunged through the empty space and clamped his hands around Ben's throat, their faces only inches apart. Unable to breathe, Ben stared at the madness in the man's eyes as he tried to break the vice-like grip around his throat. When that failed, he tried a different tactic and punched David repeatedly in the face, but his feeble punches had no effect on the enraged madman. David was beyond feeling pain. Only seconds away from death, Ben did the only thing he could, his last slim chance to survive, he knocked the car into gear and pressed down on the gas pedal.

David knew he had won, in a matter of seconds Harper would be dead. He would free his boss, and then they could go and find Doyle and dispose of Creed. It would be good to get back to a normal routine again. He hadn't enjoyed the past few days at all. When the engine revved, David smiled. *Harper's trying to reverse, but it won't save him, I'm not letting go until he's breathed his final breath.*

When the car moved, David sensed something was wrong. A glance to the side at the moving ground revealed precisely what that something was; it was traveling in the wrong direction. He looked back at his victim and saw the grimaced smile on Ben's blue face.

"No!" David shouted in frustration when the car tipped over the edge and at an acute angle sped down the steep slope. Thrown about by the steep, bumpy ride it was all he could do to keep his death grip around Harper's throat, but he was determined to do so. Before they hit the bottom, he would see this man die. To prevent himself from becoming dislodged, he spread his legs across the bonnet to try and get some grip. One of his legs jolted over the edge when the car bounced over a rock. A foot caught under a wheel arch, the friction of the fast revolving tire burnt and peeled away his skin. This time David felt the pain. He screamed in agony, spraying Ben with spittle, but his grip around Ben's throat never slackened. Ben still couldn't breathe.

The car lurched over another bump, freeing David's foot when the front wheels left the ground. He momentarily flailed wildly in the air until the front of the car struck the ground and bounced, slamming him into the bonnet. He slid to the side. A foot caught in-between the spokes of the sporty mag-wheels, snapping his ankle. He screamed in agony and then in frustration when his hands released their grip around Harper's neck when he was yanked off the bonnet and briefly whipped around in circles, matching the revolutions of the wheel his foot was caught in until his leg tore off at the ankle. While his foot remained firmly wedged in the wheel, the rest of David was flung out into space and plummeted into the ravine below. An arc of spraying blood followed his progress.

Ben had been on the verge of blacking out when suddenly he was freed from David's deadly grip and gulped down a lungful of air.

The bottom of the ravine and his imminent death sped ever closer. Ben tried to open the door but found it jammed shut. Instinct took over. He climbed out onto the bonnet and with the wind whistling past him, he clambered onto the car roof, ran across the top and jumped onto the boot that buckled under his weight. Just as the car reached the drop-off and flew out into the void, Ben leaped. He hit solid ground and frantically grabbed out for anything to stop his rapid slide down the steep slope. He snatched hold of a bush flattened by the speeding car. It felt like his arm was being pulled from its socket when his progress suddenly ended with him hanging half over the edge. He twisted his head and watched the car plummet until it struck the bottom of the gorge. The sound of metal twisting and crunching reached him a split second later. *That's one car that would never be hired again.* Now he had definitely lost his damage deposit, whatever Creed might say.

"Ben!" Creed called out.

Ben looked up. Creed was standing on the track far above.

"I'm okay," he shouted. "Can you throw down a rope?"

"Okay, hold on."

Ben dared not move and did precisely that, he held on while he waited for Creed to fetch a rope from his car.

"Here it comes," Creed called out a few moments later.

It swished through the air toward him. Whether it was luck or Creed was a good shot, the rope landed right beside him. Ben grabbed hold and wrapped it around his wrist.

"Okay, pull me up."

Creed took the strain and pulled him over the edge of the drop-off. When his feet touched solid ground, he stood and climbed up the slope while Creed pulled from above. Halfway up, he noticed something and called out, "Stop pulling for a moment."

Creed did as instructed and held the rope tautly. "What's wrong, are you okay?"

"I'm fine, hold for a minute," Ben replied as he maneuvered over to the object he had spied a short distance away. He bent down and picked it up. Not knowing that it had fallen out of David's boxer shorts when the man was spun by the wheel, he stared at the parchment he recognized from the tomb and wondered how it had gotten there. He stiffed it and wrinkled his nose, it smelt old and musty. He placed it under his shirt and called up to Creed. "Pull me up."

When Ben's head appeared above the edge, Creed grabbed his hand and helped him onto the track.

Ben glanced down the slope. For the second time that day he had escaped death.

"What happened?" Creed asked.

"David escaped from the tunnel somehow," Ben explained. "I was following you when he ambushed me. The crazy bastard jumped onto the car. He was mad with fury. He smashed the windscreen with his fists and grabbed me around the throat. He meant to kill me. The only thing I could do to stop him was to drive over the edge."

"You did that deliberately?" Creed glanced dumbfounded down the steep slope.

"It was the only thing I could do."

"Well at least we don't have to worry about disposing of Nicolas anymore, you've already done it."

"I'd forgotten he was in the boot," Ben looked down the slope for any sign of life. "Do you think he could have survived?"

A loud whoosh drifted up from the ravine, and the orange glow of fire reflected off the trees far below when the leaking petrol from the fuel tank connected with the hot engine and exploded.

"I think that answers your question. If he survived the crash, which I very much doubt, he wouldn't survive that. Come on, let's get back to my place, I have a desperate urge for whiskey and a bath."

Ben scanned the slope one more time before climbing into the Landrover. Creed started the engine and drove off along the track.

CHAPTER 16

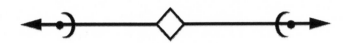

Solomon

BOTH REFRESHED FROM a long hot soak in the bath and dressed in clean clothes, neither Ben nor Creed bore even scant resemblance to the scruffy, dirt-grimed pair that had entered the house two hours before. Ben had taken a couple of painkillers when his chest started to throb again. Creed was busy in the kitchen preparing a meal. The aroma of food drifted into the lounge and made Ben's mouth water. He'd offered to help, but Creed would have none of it, telling him to sit down and rest. He had just come off the phone to the local Gendarme, to report the hire car stolen just in case it was ever found. The French police couldn't have been less interested if they'd tried, and told him to come into the station during the next few days with the details. Tomorrow, when the office opened, he would contact the hire company.

Creed poked his head into the room. "Can you grab a bottle of wine from the cellar? It's through the door under the stairs."

Ben stood. "Red or white?"

"Something to go with the steak, a red I think, but you choose. I'm easy with either."

"Okay, but be warned, I know nothing about wine, so on your head be it," Ben replied.

Creed laughed.

Ben opened the cellar door and turned on the light. The wooden steps creaked when he climbed down. He glanced around at the bottles of wine stacked neatly in the racks stretching from one end of the room to the other. *There must be some sort of system here,* he thought, but he had no idea what it could be.

Would they be stacked by type, age, or just as they were purchased?

He moved along the racks pulling out bottles at random and reading their labels. He ignored the really dusty ones in case they were old and valuable. He also skipped past the white wines, willing to go along with Creed's suggestion of red. When he discovered a rack of bottles that were practically dust free, he assumed they were probably recent additions by Creed. He browsed through them and smiled at one of the labels. He stared at the black and white image of the priest, Saunière. According to the label, the wine was made from local grapes and sold in Rennes-Le-Château; it was a fitting wine for the occasion. Ben had made his choice. He was about to leave when something crashed onto the floor above and startled him. He first thought was Creed had dropped something; he hoped it wasn't the steaks.

"Who the hell are you?" Creed shouted.

Ben had the distinct impression the shouting was for his benefit; a warning. He stared at the underneath of the floorboards when someone ran across them. He followed the sound with his eyes. The old boards bent slightly when weight was placed on them, freeing specks of dust that drifted in the air. The footsteps were pursued by another pair. Ben had no idea which set belonged to Creed, the ones doing the chasing or the ones being chased. The footsteps met in the lounge directly above him, and a struggle ensued. Coming to his senses, Ben rushed for the cellar steps; he had to help his friend.

Something heavy thudded on the floorboards, dislodging years of dust and halted Ben. The sound had been made by a body, but he didn't know whose. He waited to hear Creed's voice, telling him everything was okay, but it never came, evidence that the person who collapsed to the floor must have been his friend. Footsteps on the floorboards approached the fallen body. Ben moved to where the body lay and tried to peer through the gaps between the boards to ascertain what had taken place. Suddenly something banged onto the boards above him; a chair from the corner of the lounge. He turned his head away to avoid the falling dust from entering his eyes and felt a sneeze forming. Unable to prevent it, he tried to muffle the sound with a hand. When he looked back up, blood dripped through the gaps in the boards, but whose blood? He moved his point of view to another board and saw Creed's face turned to the side, his eyes were closed, and blood flowed from a gash on his forehead. Ben stared at his friend, his lips twitched. Creed was still alive.

When a floorboard creaked overhead behind him, Ben took a step back and peered through. He nearly dropped the bottle of wine when he saw a pair of eyes peering through the gap. He froze to the spot, uncertain if he had been seen, and reluctant to move in case the intruder hadn't and noticed movement. The boards creaked when the intruder moved. Ben followed the man's footsteps that walked out of the lounge and headed for the cellar door. The intruder was coming to investigate the cellar.

Ben frantically looked around for somewhere to hide, but there was nowhere to be found amongst the wine racks. He glanced at the cellar steps when the top stair creaked. He moved to the back of the cellar farthest from the stairs. He picked out a possible hiding place on top of one of the wine racks. They were high; not against the walls but standing back to back to create a tall, wide shelf. If he lay on top, there was a chance he might escape detection.

The stairs creaked again, Ben saw a foot appear. As the wine rack was full, he placed the bottle he carried close to its base and quickly removed the light bulb at that end of the cellar, burning his fingers in the process. It left, as he had hoped, the top of the wine rack he planned to hide atop in shadow. The frame wobbled slightly when he climbed up and slid onto the top, transferring years of accumulated dust onto his clothes and hands. Ben laid the hot bulb next to him and pressed his body as flat as possible as he watched the legs of the intruder descend the stairs cautiously until he was fully revealed. The gun gripped steadily in the man's hand followed his eyes as they searched the cellar.

Ben stared at the man's face. Although certain he had never seen him before, there was something vaguely familiar about him. While the armed intruder searched the cellar, Ben held his breath as the man walked out of sight past the rack he hid upon. He daren't turn his head in case he made a noise, or the movement shook the wine rack. He had visions of the man spotting him and raising his weapon to point at the back of his head, sure that any second now he would hear the cocking of the gun followed by a loud bang just before a bullet entered his skull. He felt the urge to jump down and make a dash for the stairs, he could be up and locking the door in a matter of seconds, trapping the man down here. However, Ben remained cowering on top of the wine rack. Any chance he may have had to escape passed when the top of the man's head moved into view. His hiding place had been successful; he hadn't been seen. The intruder paused at the bottom of the stairs, took one last look around the cellar and then, satisfied he had searched everywhere, climbed the stairs.

Ben let out a sigh of relief.

Anxious about Creed's condition, Ben climbed down from his hiding place. The rack swayed slightly, causing the light bulb on top to move. Ben peered through one of the wine rack's compartments at the stairs to check all was clear.

Above him, the light bulb rolled in a circle towards the edge of the wine rack.

Ben pondered his next action. He had to rescue his friend and to achieve that he had to somehow overpower the attacker. For once he wished he had a gun.

The light bulb rolled off the edge and fell. Ben spotted it at the last second, and shot out a hand, catching it just before it smashed on the floor. He let out a sigh of relief and placed it beside a bottle in a slot in the wine rack and then moved forward. His foot hit something; it was the bottle of wine he'd placed on the floor earlier. It shot loudly across the cellar's stone floor and rolled around in a decreasing circle until finally coming to a rest. Ben cursed his clumsiness and stared at the cellar steps. For a few moments, all was silent, but then the steps creaked. Ben knew it would be useless hiding again now it was obvious someone was down here. The intruder reached the bottom of the steps and glanced at Ben, who had picked up the wine bottle.

Ben held up the wine. "Is this good with steak?" He looked at the man's gun, wondering if he was going to use it when he approached the stairs and the armed man.

"Mr. Harper, I presume?" said the intruder.

Ben nodded.

He glanced at the label. A smile formed on his lips. "It's not what I would call a fine wine, but no doubt you thought it appropriate under the circumstances." He stepped away from the steps and pointed up them with his weapon. "Shall we go upstairs where we'll be more comfortable?" Though it wasn't so much a suggestion as an order, the words were spoken in an amicable manner.

Ben walked past the man and up the stairs. The intruder followed at arm's length. Ben thought briefly of slamming the door when he passed through, but as it opened into the stairs, he knew he would probably be shot before it was halfway shut, however cordial the man seemed.

Ben was ushered into the lounge where Creed was sprawled on the floor. A length of rope lay on the seat of the chair next to him. Ben felt reassured by Creed's breathing. The blood from his wounded head was starting to congeal around a nasty cut. Ben guessed it was the result of having been slugged by the man's gun.

The intruder pointed at the sofa with the gun. "Please sit, Ben."

Ben sat down and wondered what was going to happen next.

"Would you like a whiskey?" He asked politely.

Ben nodded and watched the man pour two glasses. "Who are you?"

The man walked over, handed Ben a glass and took the wine away from him.

"Have you heard of the Rex Deus?"

"Yes, I've heard of them. Supposedly they are direct descendants of the priests from the Temple of Solomon, a group of European noble families descended from the Jewish lines of David and Aaron, who escaped from Jerusalem shortly before, or just after, the fall of the Temple."

"Not supposedly, but *are*. Though the bloodline has been watered down drastically after so long, it still exists."

"And you belong to this Order?"

"Yes, I have that honor. In fact, I'm its current leader, Solomon."

"Whatever the reason for you being here, it must be important to have compelled you to come in person."

"Believe me, it is. We've waited centuries for this moment. I wasn't about to entrust it to those unfit or unworthy for the task and see it lost from our grasp again. We have been watching you and those who held you captive, content to let you and them do all the hard work and see how things play out until it was time to make our move. Which as you can see, is now."

"So you know they've already taken the stuff from the tomb, you're too late, it's gone."

"Now, now, Ben, we both know that's a lie, and the artifacts are in the van parked outside."

Ben wasn't surprised his weak ruse had failed. "What do you want from us?"

"Nothing, I already have it. When I leave here the van and all that is inside leaves with me."

"Others have tried to steal it from us and have failed, so I don't expect you to have any more success than them."

"Look around, Ben. Creed is unconscious, and I have you at gunpoint. There's no one here to stop me."

Ben shrugged. "I have no idea how it will happen, but you will be stopped. I can't explain it, but it seems that anyone with bad intentions fails to keep hold of the artifacts."

"Ben the saint," Solomon scoffed. "I don't think so. You've been watching too many movies about good and evil. This isn't an Indiana Jones movie, and God isn't about to strike me down."

"I wouldn't be so certain about that."

When Creed groaned, Solomon went to look at him. "Creed awakes." He stepped back and waved the gun at Ben. "Help him stand."

Ben helped Creed to his feet and led him to the sofa and sat down beside him.

The man poured a whiskey and handed it to Ben. "Give him that, I'm sure he could do with it."

Creed, though still groggy, took the drink and downed it in one gulp. He then stared straight at the intruder. "I'll ask again, who the fuck are you?"

"Now, now Creed, I can understand your anger, but let's keep it civil shall we?"

"What, civil as in you whacking me over the head, civil?"

"I'm afraid you left me no choice, you were struggling. I couldn't let you overpower me, and I was reluctant to kill you unless you left me no other choice. You should count yourself lucky."

Creed tenderly felt the gash on his head. "Yeah, lucky, that's me."

"As I have just explained to Ben, my name is Solomon."

Creed stared at the man. "Rex Deus!"

"Correct. I am here to claim that which is rightfully ours."

"Rightfully yours, on whose say so?" Creed glared.

"That would be the man holding the gun, me. I have no interest in what you believe, it's of no consequence. For many years we have searched for the tomb Ben discovered, and though we investigated the possibility that Saunière may have found it, we were skeptical. We were convinced at one time the objects we sought had been hidden in the area, but they had long since been moved. It was only when you, Ben, posted images of the tomb that we realized our mistake. Since then we have kept an eye on you. I was about to steal the van and the artifacts when you two returned. If you had arrived a few minutes later, I would have been gone, and you two wouldn't be in the situation you are now. Two of my most trusted acquaintances remain outside guarding the artifacts and to take care of any visitors who may call. Now we are all up to speed, are there any questions?"

"What are your plans for the artifacts?"

"To reclaim the Temple Mount from the heathens who have dwelled there for far too long. As soon as the discovery of the Ark is made public, the Muslims will be forced off the Temple Mount. Those who don't go peacefully will be eliminated."

"That will trigger the beginning of a Holy war. There will be bloodshed, perhaps hundreds, or thousands, will die," stated Ben.

"Yes, what you predict is unavoidable if we are to reclaim our heritage. We are God's chosen people. We will reclaim what is rightfully ours, the Temple Mount. The Dome of the Rock will be demolished and turned into dust, so nothing remains. Plans have already been drawn up for the construction of a new Temple of Solomon." A dreamy look appeared briefly on Solomon's face as he envisioned the new Temple. "The Catholic Church will not survive the revelation that the body of Jesus exists, proving him not to be the Son of God, but a mortal man who shits, pisses, and sweats like the rest of us."

Ben shook his head. "Geesh, what is it with destroying the Catholic Church with you so-called secret Orders?"

"Perhaps it's because they deserve it. They've murdered millions of innocent people and stamped out many religions, Catharism for one example, to protect their so-called true faith. It's time for them to pay the price for their years of deceit, murderous tyranny and abuse. All is ready now we have the Ark and the body of Jesus in our possession."

"There's no proof the body from the tomb is Jesus, so what makes you think you'll be believed?"

"Tests will prove us right."

"No test can categorically prove the body is the remains of Jesus Christ, even if the dates work out."

"Perhaps you are right and perhaps not. Faith in the Christian church has been waning over the years; many will believe. Of that I am certain. The seeds of doubt have already been sown."

Solomon fished a hand into his pocket to retrieve the ringing phone. "Yes…okay…how soon can you arrange transport from the port…excellent…and customs?…okay, papers will be with the driver." He hung up, returned the phone to his pocket and aimed his gun at Ben and Creed. "Who wants to be first? Please believe me; it's nothing personal, but you are too much of a threat to remain alive."

"Is that supposed to make us feel better?"

Solomon shrugged. "Sacrifices must be made for the greater good. Well, Ben, your prophecy of doom has failed. I am still alive, and the artifacts are all mine."

"We're not dead yet."

"Something I am about to remedy."

The captives stared at the gun as it roamed menacingly from one to the other. Both prepared to dive to the floor in an attempt to avoid the bullets inscribed with their names. The chances are one of them may avoid getting shot, and though Ben had no idea what do if he managed to escape a bullet, his first thought was to run.

When the gun came to rest on him, Ben knew he would be the first to die.

"Well, Ben, thank you for aiding me in my quest, but now that I have all I need you are no longer an asset."

As his finger slowly squeezed the trigger, Ben prepared to dive to the floor.

Suddenly, the window exploded with a loud crash when something smashed through it. The gun fired. Solomon was knocked to the ground. The bullet whizzed past Ben's ear and embedded itself in the wall behind.

Ben was in shock, but Creed wasn't. He grabbed Ben's arm and dragged him from the room.

"What just happened?" Ben asked.

"I'm not sure, but someone just crashed through the window. Whether voluntary or thrown, I don't know, but I did glimpse a gun so whoever it is—if they survived—they're armed." Creed rushed into the kitchen and over to a cupboard fixed to the wall. He opened it and swept the packets and cans of neatly stacked food to the floor, and then ripped out the shelves.

Brought to his senses by Creed's strange behavior, Ben stared at his friend who had gone mad. "What are you doing? Shouldn't we be making our escape?"

Creed paused and looked at Ben. "Yes, that would be the sensible thing to do."

Ben noticed the determined look in his friend's eyes. "But we'll not be taking the sensible option, will we?"

When Creed pushed the panel at the back of the cupboard, it clicked and sprung open. "I've had enough of people pointing guns at me and looking over my shoulder. It's time we ended this once and for all."

Ben stepped nearer and peered at the secret, shallow compartment Creed had just opened, just deep enough to allow the concealment of a sawn-off shotgun and a selection of three pistols.

Creed glanced at Ben. "I told you I'd taken precautions. I have weapons concealed on all floors."

Ben wished he'd shared this information with him earlier. If Creed had weapons hidden in the cellar, he could have used one on Solomon.

"You can leave if you want, I wouldn't blame you."

"No, Creed, I'm with you, we'll face them together. Besides, Solomon said two of his men were outside. It's a safe bet both are armed."

Creed thrust the shotgun into Ben's hands. "Be careful, it's loaded." Creed grabbed a weapon for himself and turned to Ben. "You ready?"

"I think so," he replied, unconvincingly.

"Aim for the chest as you're less likely to miss. If both men have recovered when we enter, I'll handle the one on the left, and you aim at the one on the right. That way we won't shoot the same target." Before Ben could say anything, Creed had rushed from the kitchen.

Ben sighed and rushed after him.

CHAPTER 17

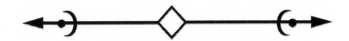

A Surprise Return

SOLOMON, KNOCKED TO the floor by the madman who had crashed through the window, and who now lay beside him, recovered quickly. His eyes roamed over the shards of glass and pieces of window frame littering the floor for the gun knocked from his grasp when he fell. He spied it a short distance away and lunged for it. As the man who had crashed through the window staggered to his knees, he saw Soloman on the floor reaching for something and aimed his gun at him just as Solomon snatched up his own, whipped it around and directed it at the party crasher. Neither made a move; it was a stalemate.

Solomon noticed the gun the man held; it belonged to one of the men he'd left outside to guard the van.

"I assume, as you're in possession of that weapon, you have killed my men outside.

The man's eyes flicked to the gun and back at Solomon. "They were already dead, I just took the weapon."

"Already dead?" he questioned in surprise. "You're joking?"

The man scowled. "I've been bundled in a car boot the size of a suitcase and driven over a long bumpy track that felt like I was in a tumble dryer. Then the car, with me still in the boot, tumbled over a cliff and crashed into a deep ravine. Then, just as I was dragging my bruised and battered body from the car, the fucking thing exploded and shot me twenty meters into the air. I can assure you the landing wasn't a soft one. I then had to drag my aching, tormented and burnt body out of the ravine and walk many kilometers to get here so I could have my revenge on that fucking Harper. So believe me, the last thing I am in is a joking mood."

"Okay, so you've not had a good day. Shit happens." Solomon glanced out through the broken window. "But if you didn't kill my men, who did?"

One of the men guarding the van outside Creed's house had fallen before he knew of the danger.

The second man, who had just stepped into the small group of trees for a piss, had seen his attacker. As he relieved himself, the muffled pop of a silenced weapon alerted him to the attack. As he hastily fumbled his penis back inside his pants, he felt something warm press against his forehead and smelt the unmistakable odor of cordite from the freshly fired weapon. He glanced past the arm holding the silenced gun at the face of a beautiful woman. It wasn't the least pleasant thing to see before he died. A loud *pfft* signaled the weapon's second shot. The man's head shot back, and he collapsed to the ground.

Raven turned away, emerged from the shadows shrouding the trees and paused by the fountain. She observed Ben, Creed, and another man with his back to her through the large window. She lifted the weapon until she had Ben focused in her gun sight. She would not miss. Her finger applied pressure to the trigger but halted a fraction away from firing the bullet waiting patiently in the chamber.

"Damn!" Raven cursed. She relaxed her finger and lowered the weapon, confused why she was reluctant to kill the man responsible for her brothers' deaths. She glared at Ben, turned away and disappeared into the night.

"I neither know nor fucking care who killed your men. When I arrived there were two dead men outside, and I took one of their weapons. Who are you and what's your purpose here?"

"The same as you, I expect," Solomon replied. "I want what's in the van."

"The artifacts are mine, and I mean to take them after I've killed Harper. I have no quarrel with you, so if you want to leave, you may do so."

"Not going to happen," stated Solomon, firmly. "We've spent years waiting for those artifacts to come into our possession and I'm not going to let them slip out of my grasp."

"Then we both have a problem."

"May I stand?"

Nicolas nodded his permission.

Solomon kept his gun trained on the man as he climbed to his feet. "There may be a solution to our quandary. Am I correct in saying we are both seeking the same outcome, the destruction of the Catholic Church?"

"Go on," prompted Nicolas.

"I see no reason why we shouldn't join forces to achieve this goal?"

"We do not seek, need, or require a partner."

"Fair enough." Solomon thought for a few moments as to how he could gain the upper hand in this tricky situation. His sharp mind quickly formulated a plan. "You know the Ark was found in the tomb?"

"Of course, it was the main reason we were so eager to gain entry."

"Then, I may have a solution. We split the spoils. I'll take Jesus' body to set in motion the destruction of the church, along with a few other artifacts, and you take the Ark to do with what you will. This way we both have what we most require," he lied. Solomon had no intention of sharing anything. As soon as Harper and Creed were disposed of the man would die.

He continued, "If I kill you, no doubt your group will hunt me down and vice versa I die by your hands. By both taking what we want the most, we can part amicably. I had no idea the Ark was in the tomb until Harper mentioned it, so it has never been part of our strategy."

Nicolas thought about the suggestion for a few moments before answering. Though he guessed the man was lying and had no intention of giving him anything except a bullet fired from his gun as soon as he had the chance, he played along.

"Though I can see the merit in your proposal, I have one stipulation. I must end Harper's life."

"I have no problem with that. So we have a deal?"

Nicolas nodded. "We do."

"What happens now?"

"We find and kill Harper and Creed."

Solomon pointed at Nicolas's shoulder with his gun before lowering it cautiously. "You might want to remove that first," he suggested.

Nicolas glanced at the large sliver of glass protruding from his shoulder, grasped it and pulled it free. When he let it drop to the floor, someone burst into the room. The two men turned with their weapons raised towards the sound.

When Creed burst through the door, followed closely by Ben, his weapon focused on one of the men by the broken window.

Because his experience was seriously lacking in the weapon department, Ben was unsure how to hold the shotgun and also worried about the recoil. Thus he entered the room with it held out in front of him. As always when in charge of a weapon, he hoped for the best and aimed it at his target. A surprised look appeared on his face at seeing Nicolas, who was no longer the calm, well-groomed man he'd first encountered. His clothes were ragged, singed, and stained with blood. His grimy face and hands were covered in cuts, grazes, and blood.

Nicolas snarled on seeing Harper and trained his gun on him.

Four shots from four different weapons simultaneously echoed around the room.

Three bodies crashed to the floor.

CHAPTER 18

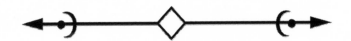

A Bad Shot

SOLOMON AIMED HIS gun at Creed's chest and pulled the trigger.

Nicolas fired his gun at Ben, satisfied that Harper would die by his hands for all the trouble and pain he had caused him.

Creed chose Solomon as his target and fired.

Ben aimed the shotgun in the general direction of Nicolas and pulled the trigger.

Solomon felt the bullet enter his chest and during the seconds before he died, he realized, with much sadness and frustration, his long laid plans would never be fulfilled.

Nicolas never felt the feeling of defeat and died thinking he would be triumphant. The shotgun blast disintegrated most of his face, killing him instantly. He crashed into the wall behind and flopped to the floor.

In his inexperienced hands, the force of the shotgun's recoil shot Ben backward. He crashed into Creed and knocked him to the floor, saving both their lives in the process. The two bullets meant to take their lives buried themselves harmlessly in the wood-paneled walls.

As the room fell to silence, Ben glanced down at his friend. "Are you okay?"

"I'm fine." Creed climbed to his feet and glanced across the room; he saw no sign of the intruders. "Wait here while I check if they're dead."

Creed made to take a step forward, but stopped and turned to Ben. "I think it's best if I take this." He swapped the shotgun for his pistol and loaded fresh cartridges into the chamber before cautiously moving around the couch. He glanced at the neat bullet hole in Solomon's chest, dead center of his heart and smiled. When he shifted his gaze to Ben's victim, he balked at the carnage that greeted him. Over half of the man's face was missing. Blood, brain, and gore littered the wall nearby. He turned to look at Ben. "It's okay. Both are dead."

Ben joined him and looked at the damage his shot had caused to Nicolas's face. The sight made him gag, and he turned away.

Creed shook his head. "I said aim for the chest."

"I did!"

Creed smiled and patted Ben on the shoulder, "Dead is dead, it's just rather a lot of mess to clean up. I need a drink, what about you?"

"Thanks. Whiskey would be most welcome."

Creed poured them both a drink, and they sat together on the sofa.

"How the hell did Nicolas survive the car crash?" Creed pondered.

"Maybe he was thrown clear or just lucky."

"If it was good luck that saved him, it's run out now."

"What about the bodies?" Ben asked. "I assume this incident won't be reported to the police?"

"Correct. I have a big garden with plenty of room to bury those two."

Ben took another sip of whiskey. "What about the artifacts? They won't be safe here now."

"I'd reached the same conclusion. We'll have to find somewhere else to hide them; somewhere safe where they can rest in secret. Whatever my feelings are for the Catholic Church, none of them good, revealing that part of their faith is based on a lie would hurt too many innocent people."

"Also, the Ark is the most sacred artifact there is. If it became known that it has surfaced, there would be bloodshed in Jerusalem. Solomon was right on that score. Plans are already in place to attack the Holy Sepulchre, kill the Muslims, demolish the mosque and reconstruct the Temple of Solomon if the Ark or Menorah ever surfaced. Perhaps with hindsight, it would've been better leaving them where they were after all?"

"You might be right, Ben, but that horse has now bolted. We'll think of something."

Ben thought for a few moments. "I think I already have.

CHAPTER 19

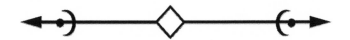

Cardou and Cardo

CREED GRABBED THE large plastic tarpaulin that had covered the stack of provisions from the garage and cut it in half. He laid one piece next to the body of Nicolas and looked at what remained of the man's bloody face. "You can take the head end, or what's left of it," said Creed, and grabbed the dead man's ankles.

Wishing he had taken better aim, Ben grabbed Nicolas under the arms, and together they lifted the corpse onto the tarpaulin and wrapped the body tightly, sealing the edges with duct tape to stop it from unwrapping. They repeated the process with Solomon's body and carried them into the garden.

Creed chose a secluded spot in one corner of the garden, and they set about digging a grave deep for the four corpses; Solomon, Nicolas, and the two guards they'd discovered in the garden. They had assumed, incorrectly, that Nicolas had been responsible. When it was ready, the bodies were placed inside.

As they backfilled the grave, Ben thought about the men he buried. He doubted he would ever become accustomed to being around and sometimes the cause of someone's death, even if it was because of a kill or be killed situation.

After they had spread the excess dirt around to lose it, though it was obvious the ground had been freshly dug, it didn't resemble a grave.

"It will soon become overgrown," said Creed.

Ben leaned on the spade, breathing heavily. "I've done enough digging the past few days to last me a lifetime."

Creed laughed. "Yeah, I know what you mean."

They returned to the house and cleaned up all traces of blood and gore from the walls and floor. Creed removed the bullets from the walls, and while Ben swept up the glass, Creed phoned a local glazier to come and board up the window until a new one could be constructed and fitted.

Realizing they were both famished, while they waited for the glazier to arrive, Creed threw away the food he had prepared earlier and started again. By the time the food had been cooked and eaten, the glazier had come and after taking measurements for the replacement window, boarded up the opening and left. A large cash payment from Creed for the work held the man's curiosity in check.

"That's almost everything back to normal," said Creed. He sighed and sat on the sofa, a glass of red wine in his hand from the bottle brought up from the cellar earlier.

Sitting opposite Creed in the armchair, Ben was pleased the mayhem was over and he could relax.

Creed took a sip of wine. "Now that's finished, what's this idea of yours?"

"Have you heard of the fabled underground Temple rumored to be in the area around Rennes-Le-Château, under or in the mountain, Pech Cardou?"

Creed nodded. Vaguely, why, does it exist?"

"I'm not sure, when I first heard about it I thought it was just another myth cobbled onto the mystery, however, after recent developments and this," he picked up the scroll he found on the hillside and spread it out on the table so Creed could see. "I think it might be."

Creed examined the map as Ben explained.

"This is one of the scrolls from the tomb. David must have had it on him when he attacked me." Ben then remembered the man had been naked except for his underwear and guessed where it had been stored. He wiped the thought from his mind as he continued,

"I found it on my climb out of the ravine." Ben pointed out a diagram. "Though no exact location is mentioned, there's this one word at the top which gives us a clue." Ben pointed at the single word written above the diagram, "Cardo!"

"Pech Cardou?" Creed questioned.

"I think so, though this spelling is slightly different than the name of the local mountain. Cardo was the ancient main road of Jerusalem. It was built in the second century AD by the Roman Emperor, Hadrian the Great, when Jerusalem was renamed, Aelia Capitolina. The Cardo Maximus, as it was named during those times, passed through Jerusalem from north to south to serve as Jerusalem's main road for almost five hundred years. The Cardo is also known as the *'Street of Pillars,'* and the *'Cardo'* of Jerusalem is Latin for heart. The word *'Maximus'* points to its size because it was unusually wide for the era. Located in the Jewish quarter, it was discovered underground after Israel gained control of the old city after the six-day war in 1967."

"So this drawing could depict a temple located in the heart of the mountain known as Cardou," Creed summarized.

Ben nodded. "Yes, I believe it does."

"But how do we find it and get inside?"

"I know someone who might be able to help us find the entrance if he doesn't already know. A researcher once emailed me to say he knew where the temple was, but I was busy at the time and ignored him."

Creed smiled. "Another crank."

Ben shrugged. "I thought so at the time, but now I think it's worth meeting with him to find out. I know where he lives, and it's nearby, so we pay him a visit tomorrow."

Absent any ideas of his own, Creed agreed with Ben's proposal.

THE TEMPLE

CHAPTER 20

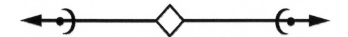

The German

CREED DROVE THE Landrover up the familiar winding road leading to Rennes-le-Château. When Ben pointed out a track leading off to the left, Creed steered onto the grassy path, and a short distance later stopped the vehicle beside a ramshackle construction. The small stone building that was little more than a ruin had been repaired in places with sheets of corrugated iron, blue tarpaulins and anything else it seems its owner could find to block up the many gaps in the roof and walls. The single glassless window revealed nothing of its dark interior. A lean-to construction to the left of the ruin; its roof another tarpaulin stretched across a wooden skeleton, housed the cooking area. This consisted of a double gas-ring and shelves acting as storage for the many cans and packets of food. A small fridge that may have been removed from the rusty campervan parked along the track was fuelled by one of the two gas cylinders on the floor beneath the shelves, the other connected to the gas ring burner. Cardboard boxes and bags of items sat next to a pile of cut logs, presumably fuel for the wood burning stove, whose metal stove-pipe chimney poked out through the hut's roof.

"Not exactly what I would call cozy," Creed stated.

"Obviously, he's a man of simple needs." Ben saw no sign of activity. "I wonder if anyone's home." He climbed out of the Landover and went to find out.

When he walked around the front of the vehicle, Ben had his answer. A man walked along the track pulling a small trolley holding a container filled with water. When he drew near, Ben stepped forward to introduce himself and held out his hand. "Hello, my name is Ben, I'm looking for Pat. Is that you?"

The water in the container sloshed when the man halted the trolley and shook Ben's hand. He gazed past Ben when Creed climbed out of the Landover and joined them.

"Hi, I'm Creed."

The two men shook hands.

"So, are you Pat?" Ben repeated.

The man shrugged and carried the water container over to the lean-to. "That depends on what you want," he said suspiciously, his words shrouded in a strong German accent.

The two men stood beside the lean-to entrance as the German fixed a plastic tap connector to a small piece of hose joined to the water container's outlet and placed it on a shelf with the tap at the bottom. The shelf bowed and creaked with its weight.

"If you are Pat, as I believe you are, we need your help," Ben said.

The man picked up a blackened kettle and filled it from the tap on the freshly filled water container. "What sort of help would you need from the likes of me?" he said, as he placed the filled kettle on one of the gas rings and lit it with a match.

"We need to find an entrance, and we believe you know where it is."

The man grabbed a coffee mug from a shelf and stared at Ben for a few seconds. A look of recognition appeared on his face. "Ben Harper, that's who you are," he returned to the task of coffee making. "Yes, I'm the man you seek." Pat held up a jar of coffee granules. "You two want one?"

Ben and Creed declined.

"What entrance are you talking about?" giving the impression he knew of more than one.

Ben glanced at Creed, not sure how much he should reveal.

Creed shrugged. "There's no point in beating about the bush if we want his help."

Ben agreed. "We seek the entrance to the Cardou Temple."

The kettle's whistle filled the silence. Pat gazed at the two men while he considered his reply before finally switching off the gas to silence its scream. In silence, he poured the boiled water into the mug and stirred it briskly. He walked over to the lone chair beside a table made from a pile of plastic beer crates with a piece of plywood on top, sat down and sipped his coffee before answering. "What Temple?"

"Look, Pat, I appreciate your reluctance to talk to us, two strangers, but in an attempt to gain your trust we're willing to lay our cards on the table. We have recently come into possession of an old Templar parchment that reveals the Temple's location, but not the entrance. We know where it is, but not how to get inside. We could find the entrance without your help. However, this would take time, which is something we don't have. Our intention is not to plunder the Temple, but to put something back!" Ben paused to let the German consider what he'd been told.

Pat placed his mug on the table, took a roll-up cigarette from a tin on the table, lit it, took a long drag and exhaled the smoke.

"Okay. I assume this *thing* you want to put in the Temple is from the tomb you found."

Ben nodded.

"This thing is the body from the tomb, correct?"

Ben nodded again. "Correct."

Pat took another long drag of his cigarette. "Do you have the parchment with you?"

Ben pulled the old parchment from his pocket and handed it to the German. Pat looked at it and then put it to his nose and sniffed. "Musty," he stated, before carefully unrolling the delicate document to examine its details. A flicker of excitement spread across his face briefly. "This is from the tomb?"

"Yes, there were others, but they were destroyed, unfortunately. As you can see, it gives the location of the Temple but not details of an entrance. I assume this information was on another scroll that we don't have."

The German flipped the scroll over, again becoming excited by what he saw. "Have you worked out what the group of symbols mean?"

Ben shook his head. "We haven't had time to examine them in any detail. We only came into possession of the scroll yesterday."

Pat held up the parchment, pointing to the series of small images. "I've seen these symbols before."

"You have? Where?" asked Ben, eagerly; it might be the breakthrough they desperately needed.

The German smiled. "On a door!"

"What door?" asked Ben and Creed together, both surprised by the unexpected revelation.

"The door to the Temple you seek. I think these symbols are the key to unlock it."

"You've already found it! Have you been inside?" asked Creed in amazement.

Pat shook his head and held up the parchment, "I couldn't. I didn't have this."

"I'd be very interested if you could tell us how you found the Temple, Pat, which by the way is an amazing feat of deductive research I would imagine."

"In a way, yes, but probably in the same manner you found the tomb, it wasn't so hard." Pat nipped into the small building and returned with a brown cardboard file crammed with papers. He flipped through, pulled out a photograph and handed it to Ben. "You will recognize this of course."

Ben and Creed examined the photograph.

Ben nodded. "It's the *Shepherds of Arcadia* painting by Nicolas Poussin."

"You'll also be aware of the tomb in Pontils that looked similar to the tomb in the Shepherds painting." He passed Ben another photo depicting the Pontils tomb before the owner of the land—fed up with tourists trespassing on his property—destroyed it.

"I know of it, but how did this help you?"

"Many people believe the 'shepherds' painting contains clues to a vast cache of treasure, which might be linked to what the priest discovered and made him wealthy. These people then, believing the clues will be revealed by the paintings geometry, angles of the shepherds' staffs, etc. cover the painting in lines from one point to another to create all manner of fantastical geometric shapes. Some draw so many lines the painting beneath is no longer visible."

Creed smiled. "I assume this is not the route you took."

"No. I believed if the painting did hold a clue, it would be visual. The shepherds stand before the tomb with the landscape behind. That, though similar to the landscape around Rennes-Le-Château, is not exact. I had the idea that if I explored the landscape behind the Pontils tomb, I might discover something, and I did. Incidentally, there are two rock formations either side of the entrance to the Bezis valley, the one on the left looks like a skull when viewed from Pontils. Though I may be clutching at straws here, I thought this might be a clue linked to the tomb. Anyway, I went to the entrance of the Bezis valley and looked back towards the Pontils tomb and lo and behold I saw the exact shape of the hill from the painting in front of me. It was the reverse view of Les Toustounes. Excited by the discovery, I climbed onto the hill and, looking towards Pech Cardou, I saw a small cave in the rock on the far side of the valley. What was interesting about this cave was that it was almost an exact match for a small crack in one of the stone blocks used to construct the tomb in the painting, below the shadow of a shepherds elbow, as if he points at the cave to indicate its importance."

"Obviously you explored this cave," said Ben, intrigued.

"Of course, but it was bloody hard to get to. Unfortunately, if there was anything of worth inside, it was long gone. However, I did find a small arrow carved into the rock pointing at Cardou. Before I forget, are you aware that if you take all the letters from the inscription to the right of the line one of the shepherd's points out, and pick out the letters not covered in shadow, they can be rearranged to make the word CARDO?"

"No way!" exclaimed Ben. "I've examined that painting many times but never noticed that. Creed and I were talking about the Cardo Maximus earlier, that it might be hinting at Pech Cardou."

Creed was eager to hear the rest of Pat's story. "I take it there's more, Pat."

Pat nodded. "Believing with my discovery of the arrow in the cave I was on the right track, I looked again at the painting. I finally solved the last stage by using the staff held by the only shepherd not looking at the tomb and who also points at a line running straight to the small cave. I transferred the staff's length onto an old map and draw a line starting from the top of the

Toustounes rock formation in the Bezis valley, through the cave and marked where it ended."

"On Pech Cardou," Ben stated.

"Yes, though it wasn't easy to find, because of its location, it led me straight to a cave. Inside I discovered the Temple entrance."

"Well done, Pat. That's an amazing feat of deduction."

"I agree," Creed said. "Obviously Poussin must have known about this cave if he included clues in his painting to lead to it."

Ben nodded. "In fact, Poussin himself hinted that his paintings might conceal something within his talented brush marks other than the scene depicted when he said, "...*these things* (the meaning or message he embedded in his paintings) *I believe, will not displease those people who know how to read them.*"

"There's also something else," Pat added. "Another piece of evidence that Poussin may have concealed a secret in his Shepherds of Arcadia painting. In a letter the priest, Louis Fouquet, sent his brother, Nicolas Fouquet, King Louis XIV's superintendent of finances in 1656, directly after meeting with Poussin in Rome:

'He (Poussin) and I discussed certain things, which I shall with ease be able to explain to you in detail – things which will give you, through Monsieur Poussin, advantages which even kings would have great pains to draw from him, and which, according to him, it is possible that nobody else will ever discover in the centuries to come. And what is more, these are things so difficult to discover that nothing now on this earth can prove of better fortune nor be their equal.'

"Shortly after receiving this information, Nicolas Fouquet was arrested, imprisoned, and held *incommunicado* for the rest of his life. The letter was confiscated by Louis XIV, who later went to great efforts to obtain The Shepherds of Arcadia, which he hung at his private apartments in Versailles."

Ben added, "It's said that Nicolas Fouquet was the man in the iron mask."

"Whatever the meaning of the letter," said Creed, "I believe we all agree if we manage to gain entry to the temple beneath Cardou, we will find something amazing within."

"Amen to that," said Pat.

"So, will you help us, Pat?" Ben asked, hopefully. "If you take us to this door we can use the symbol code to open it and together we will discover Poussin's secret."

"Before I decide, I need you to answer a couple of questions. First, why the urgency?"

"Because we don't want what we have to fall into the wrong hands. Certain secret Orders have already tried and might do again. We must prevent them from doing so."

Pat handed back the parchment. "What makes you so sure it'll be safe in the Temple?"

"Because we plan to seal the entrance once the bodies are inside," said Creed. "It's the only way we can be certain they will be secure."

"You said bodies, implying there's more than one."

"Yes, there are two bodies," Ben confessed. "The one you are aware of from the images on my website was lying on top of what we first thought to be a solid block of marble, but which turned out to be a sarcophagus. The other, much to our surprise, was inside."

"So who are they?" Pat asked. "Not Templar Knights like you first thought, I bet."

"Unfortunately not, but I think you already know the identity of one, or who it's most likely to be, given the circumstances of its discovery, the other we believe to be Mary Magdalene, in all probability his wife."

Pat laughed. "The old bugger, so Jesus was married after all. Good for him. What state are they in, skeletons or mummified and are there marks of crucifixion?"

"Mummified and yes, one has crucifixion marks."

Pat whooped and slapped his knee. "Great, wait until the Vatican hears about this, they'll go mental. Can I see them?"

"All in good time, but the Vatican will never know about this, it will be our secret."

"Why not? If it were left up to me, I'd smuggle the body into Rome and parade it in Saint Peter's square, right on the Vatican's doorstep. That'll teach the bastards to lie about their religion, and for all the deaths caused in the name of Christianity."

Ben and Creed smiled.

"I think Ben would have agreed with you at one time, Pat, but it wouldn't only harm the Vatican. The Christianity might crumble if the body of Christ were revealed and believed to be the biblical Jesus, something that according to their religion shouldn't exist, it would also harm and desecrate the faith of many millions of innocent Christians across the world. If it would only harm the Church, we wouldn't hesitate to reveal it. However, this is not the case. The body has to be hidden and kept secret; We now believe it's the right thing to do."

"Okay, obviously you've given your decision considerable thought and given time I'll probably come to the same conclusion, but it would've been so cool to see the Pope's face when he saw it."

"Yes, but if the Vatican learns of what we have in our possession, they will try their hardest to get their hands on it. It would either disappear inside the Vatican secret vaults or more likely be destroyed and us along with it. But I wouldn't worry about it, the way the Catholic Church has behaved over the past few years it won't be long before they shoot themselves in the foot. People are more aware and informed these days, whereas the Vatican dwells in the past because it knows it can't survive in the future. They don't need our help to destroy themselves. The truth will always out."

"Now you understand how important it is to place the bodies somewhere safe to prevent His body from being exploited by those wishing to cause harm to others."

Pat nodded. "Like you both, I'm also not a religious man, the opposite in fact, and yet it seems that I've been waiting for this moment most of my life."

"I know exactly what you mean," Ben said. "I too have felt I'm being manipulated in some way, but how or by whom, or what, I cannot say, but I feel impelled to see it out to the end, whatever end that turns out to be. So, will you help us?"

Pat thought for a few moments before answering. "You're certain the bodies will be safe in the Cardou Temple."

Ben shrugged. "Who can say for certain? But it's our only choice, though obviously, we'll need to check it out first."

"If you want to keep the bodies a secret why not destroy them? Burn or bury them somewhere. Surely that would be the safest and easiest thing to do."

Ben looked at the German. "Maybe you're right, but believe me, it's not that simple. When you're near the bodies, they seem to give off energy, an invisible aura of some kind that's difficult to explain. Neither Creed nor I am of a religious nature, but we've both felt it and maybe you will also when you see them. Over the last few days people have tried to take the bodies from us, and by all accounts, they should have succeeded, but they didn't. I can't explain it, but I think the bodies are protecting themselves, perhaps this is why they have survived for so long. If we try to destroy them, I've got a strong feeling we would fail and, perhaps, suffer from the attempt."

Pat shivered. "You've just given me goose bumps. This is extremely spooky shit."

"Yes, very spooky shit indeed," Creed agreed.

"I'm not into all this spiritual mumbo jumbo," stated Pat, "however, I do feel compelled to help you."

Ben let out a sigh of relief. "That's great news. Thank you, Pat."

"Do you have any equipment with you?" Pat asked. "I have climbing gear and lights for me."

"We brought stuff with us in the hope you'd agree to help," said Ben.

"Then how about we go there now? I'm dying to get through that door to see what secrets it hides."

"Now would be good," Creed replied.

Both he and Ben were eager to get the task ahead over with as soon as possible so they could return back to some sense of normality.

"Okay, give me five minutes to grab my stuff, and we'll head for the Temple."

CHAPTER 21

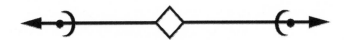

Temple Entrance

PAT HALTED BESIDE the edge of the rocky cliff, sat on a rock, slipped off his rucksack and pulled out three bottles of beer. Ben and Creed arrived a few moments later, finally catching up with the German who had climbed up the side of Pech Cardou with the agility of a mountain goat. Breathing heavily from the climb, they slipped off their rucksacks and chose suitable rocks to sit on for a much-needed rest.

"Ben."

Ben looked at Pat and saw a bottle of beer flying towards him. He caught it moments before it struck him in the face. Creed, better prepared, grabbed the beer Pat flung in his direction more easily.

Ben gazed down at the road far below, no wider than a line drawn on a map. "I can't believe you carried beer up here."

Pat twisted off the lid from his bottle and smiled. "We needed something to celebrate our finding of the Temple. I also packed a few extras to keep us going until we reach it."

Ben shook his head, opened his beer and took a long swig. "I must say, I'm glad you did, it's refreshing after the long climb."

Creed wholeheartedly agreed, thoroughly enjoying the liquid refreshment still cold from Pat's fridge.

Luckily, the cloudy sky held at bay the sun's hot rays and made the climb up the mountain less torturous than it might have been in the intense heat.

Pat reached out, and they all clinked bottles to toast the adventure ahead of them. "Here's to the Temple and the secrets inside."

"The Temple," said Ben and Creed together.

Creed glanced around the top of the mountain but saw no evidence of a cave. "How much farther before we reach the entrance?"

"We're almost there." Pat pointed to the edge of the rocky outcrop. "We climb down to a ledge that leads to the cave."

The two men walked over to investigate. The side of the mountain sloped steeply for about five meters to a meter wide ledge before dropping into the valley below.

Pat noticed their worried expressions. "It's not as bad as it looks."

Neither Ben nor Creed were convinced or reassured.

After they finished their beers, Pat placed the empty bottles in his rucksack and after slipping it back on, crouched at the top of the steep slope. "Copy me, and you'll be okay." He pushed himself over the edge.

It wasn't the slow and steady descent the two men watching had visualized. Pat slid down the steep slope on the soles of his boots. Earth and rocks, disturbed by his passing, followed in his wake. When he was about to slide over the top and plummet to the valley floor far below, he grabbed hold of a small tree growing on the edge and swung around. For a few seconds, his body hung over the void before his feet landed on solid ground again. He smiled up at his two astonished watchers. "It's that easy. Who's next?"

Ben turned to Creed. "After you."

"Cheers." Creed sat at the top of the slope and glanced down.

"It's not as difficult as it looks," said Ben, grinning.

Creed glanced at Ben and pushed himself off. His decent was much slower than the mad German's. He used shrubs and overhanging tree branches to check his speed and arrived on the narrow ledge safely.

Ben opted for Creed's safer method of descent. When he arrived at the bottom, he peered down the long drop and shook his head. A glance along the ledge revealed no sign of Pat. "Where did the crazy German disappear to?"

Creed pointed along the ledge to a rocky outcrop. "He went ahead to secure a climbing rope."

"Witnessing his technique to get down here, I'm surprised he uses a rope."

"That's what worries me," Creed said. "If he's using a rope it must be dangerous."

They went to catch up with Pat to find out.

A short walk along the small ledge took them around the outcrop onto a sloped patch of shrubs and trees nestled between two large outcrops of rock. They headed for the sounds of Pat moving amongst the undergrowth. Ben pushed through the foliage and found his foot treading on thin air. Creed quickly grabbed his arm and stopped him from falling. They both stared at the deep black hole, the surrounding undergrowth almost hiding its existence altogether.

Pat's face appeared through the bushes opposite. "Watch your step, it's a long drop."

Ben shook his head. "I could have done with the warning a little earlier."

They circumnavigated the hole to find Pat had anchored a rope to a thick tree. After testing it was secure, he walked over to the opening and dropped the remaining coil of rope into its depths. All three slipped on a harness and Pat passed around the belay devices to attach to the rope when it was their turn to descend.

Pat handed Ben the belay attachment. "Do you know how to use this?"

Ben nodded.

Bottles clinked together when Pat slipped on his rucksack and backed up to the hole. "I'll go down first as I know what's ahead."

Creed slipped off his rucksack. "Ben can come next, and I'll bring up the rear." He fished out two headband lights and passed one to Ben.

They had brighter torches if needed, but for now, the smaller headlights provided sufficient light and left their hands free.

Pat switched on his headlight and stepped over the edge. His feet searched for footholds in the rough rocky sides of the deep shaft. Within seconds, he had disappeared into the darkness. When he reached the bottom twenty meters below the surface, he released himself from the rope and glanced up the two-meter wide shaft. "Okay, I'm down."

Ben's silhouetted form appeared in the sunlit opening when he began his descent. While he waited for the others to arrive, Pat shone his torch into the long tunnel and walked forward a short distance to check the way hadn't been blocked by a cave-in since his last visit. As far as his light could reach, the passage was clear.

On reaching solid ground once again, Ben released himself from the rope and called up to Creed to let him know he'd reached the bottom. Creed rapidly descended the shaft and joined them.

Pat led the way through the narrow tunnel to the next hole they would have to descend to reach the heart of the mountain. Creed took a rope from his rucksack and handed it to Pat, who pulled a loose rock from the cave wall to reveal an iron ring fixed securely into the rock. Pat secured the rope through the ring and began his descent. Creed and Ben followed him down.

The lower level tunnel was slighter larger than the one above, giving them more room to maneuver as Pat led them deeper into the mountain. After traveling about sixty meters, Pat halted and slipped off his rucksack.

Ben was disappointed to see the tunnel blocked with damp earth and rocks and assumed it was the reason why Pat had stopped. The passage was wet in places, and the walls and floor were covered in mud.

"What do we do now, Pat?"

Pat glanced at Ben, who looked worriedly at the blocked tunnel. "It's okay. The way ahead isn't the way we go."

Ben's eyes searched the tunnel for another opening but found none. "What do you mean?" he asked, confused. "What other way is there?"

"Pass me the shovel, and I'll reveal all." The German grinned, cryptically.

Ben slipped off his rucksack, took out the fold-up shovel and handed it to Pat, curious to see what he would do.

The German moved slowly along the tunnel tapping the damp mud-covered wall with the edge of the shovel's blade. The sound of the metal striking rock echoed along the passage, and then it changed. The shovel no longer struck rock, but damp earth. Pat set about prizing off lumps of mud with the shovel. Ben grabbed a second shovel from his rucksack and copied the German. Chunks of sticky mud were thrown along the tunnel by the rock fall. Unexpectedly, a clang reverberated along the passage when metal struck metal. Excited by what was about to be revealed, Ben and Creed observed Pat clearing a small patch. Three beams of light settled on what had been uncovered; bronze metal etched with symbols. Though some still remained hidden by the mud and a few others only partially revealed, Ben recognized the few visible matched the symbols from the parchment.

"It's the door!" Ben exclaimed.

Creed touched the cold metal and trailed his fingers over the mudded symbols. "It's amazing."

"But why hasn't it been discovered before?" asked Ben. "And how did you know it was here, Pat?"

Pat smiled. "It wasn't easy, but I had help."

A worried frown creased Creed's brow. "Someone else knows about this entrance?"

"Yes and no. Let me explain. You've heard of De Cherisey, yes?"

"Plantard's cohort," Creed answered.

Ben had researched the man and his acquaintances and duly shared the information. "De Cherisey was involved with Pierre Plantard and the supposed Priory of Sion. They released some documents and among them were two parchments they claimed were copies of the messages Saunière discovered in his church," Ben glanced at Creed. "As you know, for years they were thought to be genuine, but most serious researchers now believe them to be a hoax, me included." Even more so since Creed had revealed his father had altered them.

"I wouldn't dismiss them so lightly, Ben," stated Pat. "Although it's likely the documents Plantard possessed were not true to the originals, as it seems certain changes and additions were added, so the true solution could never be found, I believe part of the information is true."

"You have Creed's father to thank for that," Ben told him, "but I'll explain about that later, please continue."

"It's not the parchments that led me here, but something De Cherisey wrote after he had a falling out with Plantard…"

"…*Stone and Paper*," Ben interrupted.

"Correct. He wrote Stone and Paper in an attempt to discredit Plantard by saying it was he who had manufactured the parchments. However, after reading the document, it soon becomes obvious this isn't so. I don't think Plantard and De Cherisey had all the information, or if they did they were unaware of how to use it, which is probably why they included the parchments in Gerard de Sade's book; to see if someone else could solve the puzzle for them, but I'm wandering off track. The important information for now, as it will take too long to explain everything, is the part that helped me, this:

"*The disposition of letters on document 1 represents the section of a mountain where the treasure cave is shown by an almost inaccessible hole. However, the pothole which hangs over the entrance to the cave gives INTROBIT IN DOMUM: he enters into the house. Thus the treasure is both accessible and inaccessible, and this is also what Abbé Saunière signifies by his secret door in the sacristy, a very well arranged and obvious false door, which allows entrance to the secret room.*

"*That simply means that the cavern is damp enough for a mud wall to form continually after one has penetrated it. He who enters the cavern without being warned would think he was in a blind alley and not realize that all he had to do was to get the mud out of the way.*"

"Though I don't claim to understand how he knew this information, it exactly fits the entrance to this tunnel and this mud wall. When I first arrived at the rock fall you see ahead, I knew from Stone and Paper this was a ruse. Anyone who was oblivious to this knowledge would either try to remove the rocks to see if a way through lay behind them, or give up, as I probably would have. However, forewarned, I searched the mud-covered walls and found this doorway. As I said before, I was unable to gain entry because I lacked the information you have in the parchment from the tomb."

"But why didn't you force your way through, cut through the door or something?"

"Good question, Creed, and don't think I hadn't thought about doing just that. What stopped me is that I believe the door is booby-trapped." Pat pointed up at the tunnel roof. "You see the cracks running through the rock?"

The two men examined the long cracks through the rock directly above them and took a step back.

Pat continued with his explanation. "I think if the correct key isn't used to open the door, the tunnel roof will collapse, killing anyone unlucky enough to be standing here and in the process seal the door forever. That's why I decided to wait. As I said before, I had a feeling that someday the key would come to me, and now it has."

"Wow!" exclaimed Ben. "The information was there all the time. It's amazing, and a shame I can't put this in my book."

Pat laughed. "The infamous book by Ben Harper, how many years is it now since you first advertised it?"

"Just over seven now," Ben laughed, "but it's not my fault I keep finding new stuff to include. Come on, let's uncover this door. I want to see what it leads to. I can smell another chapter."

"That will make three, then," Creed quipped.

The three men laughed as they set to clearing away the rest of the mud concealing the metal door. Within thirty minutes the door was revealed. Although still stained with streaks of dirt and covered in blotchy patches of green patina, the symbols etched into the metal were clearly visible. All three stared at the marvelous sight. The outline of the door was easily discerned in its metal frame by the thin joint around its circumference. The twenty-two symbols, each slightly raised on square blocks of metal, were distributed over the door's surface in what seemed to be in no particular order or design. The blocks reminded Ben of the letter blocks he had come across in the catacombs beneath Rosslyn Chapel, so he was careful not to press any when he ran his fingers over their cold metal details, leaving behind finger trails in the mud tarnished surface.

"The Knights Templar must have built this," Ben said, admiring their outstanding ability to create these types of complicated mechanisms.

Pat nodded in agreement. "If my theory's right, what's on the other side was started hundreds of years before the Templars were formed; they just finished it off, and no doubt added their particular brand of improvements, like this door for instance."

Intrigued by his comment, Ben dragged his eyes away from the door and looked at Pat. "Tell me more."

Pat laughed. "One chapter at a time, let's get inside first."

Ben produced the parchment and held it in the light of his headlamp so they could all see. Although the block of symbols on it matched some of the symbols on the door, these ones were set in a 3 x 3 grid, making a group of nine blocks. *The same number as the nine original Templars* thought Ben. The door's twenty-two different symbols, spread out in no order, made it impossible to haphazardly guess the correct sequence. Glancing from the parchment symbols to the door symbols, Ben pointed at the block on the door corresponding to the symbol in the top left corner of the parchment's grid design.

"That's the first symbol to be pressed. We then follow the direction arrows on the parchment to the final symbol and ignore any symbol not mentioned in this parchment."

Creed studied the parchment. "How do you know we have to start with that particular block in the grid, it's blank in the parchment?"

"Good point," Ben agreed. "The clue is the actual design, it's the Alpha symbol. It means the beginning, and the last symbol, bottom right in the grid, also blank, must be the Omega..."

"...The end," Creed interrupted.

"Correct."

Creed looked at the Omega symbol on the door. "Okay, I'm convinced, what about you, Pat?"

"It seems logical to me."

Ben took a deep breath. "Okay, let's open this door. Pat, as you were the one that discovered it, you can do the honors. I'll tell you what symbols to press in the correct order."

Pat positioned himself in front of the door and Creed, and Ben moved a few paces back.

Pat glanced behind at the two men now a short distance back along the tunnel. "You'll have to speak up if I'm going to be able to hear you," Pat quipped. "Any farther and you'll be back on the surface."

Ben and Creed chuckled.

"We don't want to get in your way," Ben explained, with a grin.

"There's no fear of that from that distance, and oh yeah," he glanced up at the cave roof, "you'll probably be safe from any falling rocks if I press the wrong block. I don't suppose you'd thought of that."

Ben couldn't help but smile. "Hadn't even crossed our minds."

Pat muttered something in German, reached out a hand to touch the Alpha block, and glanced at the two men. "You ready?"

"To run, yes. Press the block," Ben answered. He and Creed took another step back, both still chuckling.

Pat smiled. "English humor, very amusing."

Pat applied pressure to the block, and though it resisted at first, it slowly sank into the metal slightly and produced a soft click, and then silence. He looked up at the large hanging rock. "So far so good. What's next?"

"Pentagram," called out Ben, taking a cautious step closer.

Another click filled the passage when Pat pressed the indicated symbol.

Eight clicks later, Pat's hand hovered over the final block, the Omega symbol. His two companions, now confident they had the correct sequence, stood beside him.

"Here goes." Pat pressed the Omega block.

The familiar click was followed by silence. Just as they thought it hadn't worked, a soft rumble gradually increased in volume as whatever mechanism they had set in motion performed the function it had so long ago been designed to carry out. As one, the three men stepped away from the door when the screeching of metal from its other side filled the tunnel. When it stopped, and silence reigned once more, Pat stepped forward and pushed on the door, it didn't budge. He applied more pressure with his shoulder and felt the door give a little. He grinned at the others. Words were not needed. Creed joined him, and together they pushed open the protesting door. Ben, excited about what they were about to discover, placed the parchment in his pocket and waited.

When the door was open wide enough for them to enter, they collected their rucksacks and with Pat leading the way, they stepped through the open doorway to their destiny or their death.

Unbeknown to the three men, their fate lay not through the doorway but would be decided by the person who had followed them into the mountain and had been watching them with interest for the past few minutes.

Raven switched on her torch set to its dim setting and silently approached the doorway. She peered inside to observe the three lights moving away until they disappeared from sight around a bend in the passage. When faint voices drifted from the entrance behind her, she halted her step through the doorway to follow the three men and hesitated for a moment. She turned away from the door and headed back along the passage to investigate the source of the unexpected voices.

Marco gazed into the dark abyss and then at the rope leading into its depths he didn't relish climbing. He briefly pondered waiting above ground until the men they followed reappeared, but the uncertainty that they might leave by another exit caused him to immediately dismiss the thought. Another consideration was he would like to set eyes upon the fabled Temple if it existed and any relics or scrolls secreted there. Marco's orders were clear. If anything he discovered posed a threat to the Church, they were to be destroyed or moved to a secure place — until their fate was decided — the Vatican secret archives. He turned away from the uninviting shaft to look at his twelve companions, who waited patiently for his decision. Each was armed with an identical weapon; an AK-47 assault rifle.

"We climb down," Marco informed them. "The Church needs to know what is below. If the Temple exists all entrances must be sealed."

The men, all members of Inquisition, known today as the Congregation for the Doctrine of the Faith, accepted his decision without emotion or argument. Their mission was to stamp out heresy and protect the Church at any cost. The Church had labeled the three men they pursued as heretics and when they had outlived their usefulness—an event fast approaching—they would suffer the same fate as the millions of heretics before them, annihilation!

"Would you prefer to lead, Marco?" Domenico enquired.

Marco gazed at Domenico, uncertain if he'd detected a hint of mockery in the man's voice. He was well aware Domenico usually ruled the group under his own initiative and obeying orders from a novice such as him, hurt his pride. "No, three of you go down to check it's safe, if it is, I will follow."

Irritated that he wasn't in charge of this mission, Domenico hid his sneer. He would have dynamited the entrance to trap them inside instead of entering to check the place out first. Then, any secrets down there would be buried forever. However, the decision was not his to make. Though Marco was weak and inexperienced in these matters, his own orders were clear. For now, the idiot was in charge, and he would follow his commands.

Domenico hoisted his heavy rucksack effortlessly onto his back, slipped his rifle over a shoulder and approached the long drop into the bowels of Pech Cardou. After ordering two of his men to follow, he grabbed hold of the rope and began his descent.

Raven moved back along the tunnel when the first man climbed down. From the snippets of conversation she had overheard, it seemed the man called Marco was in charge. His mention of the 'Church' was a clue to their employer. She was sure of their purpose; the Vatican wanted whatever had lain hidden for centuries down here spirited away or destroyed. The deaths of Ben and his two companions would also be part of their assignment. With no mention of her, it seemed her stealthy entry had paid off. She stepped through the doorway and went to see what Harper was up to. If anyone were going to kill him, it would be her. She would not show weakness again.

The three beams from Ben's, Creed's and Pat's headlamps revealed the direction of the men's gaze as they walked through the dark passage. The tunnel, hewn from the rock into an arched passage about a meter wide and almost two meters high, gave them plenty of room to walk comfortably. The floor of the tunnel sloped down slightly and in places curved and twisted through the mountain, leaving the impression it was initially formed by nature and whoever had utilized it for their own purpose had enlarged it into the passage. After rounding yet another curve, they stepped into a larger space; a circular chamber about five meters across with a natural rock ceiling four meters above them. An entrance on the far side suggested the tunnel continued into the mountain. A round hole situated in the center became the focus of their attention. When they approached their torches highlighted the top of a circular stone staircase that spiraled down into darkness. The three men looked at each other, their faces bathed in each other's torchlight.

"Well, what are we waiting for?" said Creed. "We go down."

"I think we should check out the other exit first," Pat suggested. "It makes sense to check out each level as we come across them."

"I agree," said Ben. "If we do a systematic sweep of each level we won't miss anything."

Pat led them across the room into the tunnel. After a change of direction, the passage sloped down until it opened into a small natural grotto whose crystal covered walls reflected their flashlights, producing hundreds of tiny light speckles. Stalagmites and stalactites adorned the cavern, some so old they had met to form ancient natural columns.

Pat crossed to the small pool on the far side of the chamber and dipped a hand in the crystal clear water. "It's cold." He scooped some up to drink. "Not as good as beer, but almost as refreshing."

"It probably provided a fresh water source for those who once inhabited this place during its construction," Creed suggested.

The others walked over and peered into its depths. The bottom was only two meters below the surface.

Creed pointed at something below the surface. "Is that a tunnel?"

Pat and Ben joined Creed in looking at the underwater opening, a little less than a meter wide.

"I think it is. It probably leads to the River Sals," Ben said. After all the twists and turns they'd taken, it was difficult to maintain his usually unfailing sense of direction.

"Or maybe another chamber," Pat suggested.

"There's nothing else of interest here, so let's head back to the staircase."

They followed Creed back along the tunnel and down the spiraling steps. During their descent they commented on the staircase, marveling at the effort it must have taken to chisel it out of the solid rock.

When they reached the bottom, the lights from their head torches roamed around the room similar in size and design to the one at the top of the staircase. The difference here was that as well as the steps they had just climbed down, there were three other exits.

"Which one do we enter first?" asked Pat as he crossed over and peered into each tunnel in turn, but gained no insight as to what or where they led. "They're all more-or-less identical."

Ben took out the parchment and examined the map. He ran a finger along the route they had taken to arrive at this point. His finger paused on the room they now stood in with the three tunnels leading off. "We take the middle one, but go slow as there's something ahead that might be a trap."

Pat smiled and motioned for Ben to lead. "You're the one with the directions."

Ben entered the middle tunnel.

They hadn't gone far before they heard the faint sound of rushing water, which grew steadily louder as they progressed. After turning a bend in the tunnel, they entered a large chamber. They edged nearer to the gap in the ground that spanned the width of the cavern and peered down at the source of the noise: a maelstrom of swirling water ten meters below.

Creed stated out loud what they all were thinking "Fall in there and its certain death as you'll never get out."

Ben glanced at the map. "There has to be way across because the map continues past this." He aimed his torch across the chasm that had halted their progress. All three followed the beam of light moved over the object situated on the far side of the gap.

"It's some kind of bridge!" Pat exclaimed.

The metal construction was raised into an upright position. Two lengths of chain fixed to either side of its top, stretched up to disappear into the ceiling and reappear two meters away and angled down to a large, metal wagon-wheel like mechanism at its base that revealed how it was raised and lowered into position. Excess lengths of chain wound around a spindle attached to the wheel's center.

"A bridge it may be, but it's not much use to us unless we can find some way of lowering it to span the abyss," stated Creed.

"There has to be some way of operating it from this side to allow those who built this place a way to get across." Ben examined the walls and floor for any mechanism that would lower the bridge.

Pat lifted the flap on Ben's rucksack, pulled out his small prospectors pick and started tapping the walls. After searching one side, he crossed to the other, and after a few taps, a dull, hollow sound was produced. The area of rock he had struck looked exactly like the surrounding rocky surface and gave no hint there was anything hidden there.

Intrigued, Ben and Creed watched Pat search for the edge of the hollow rock, prise it out and place it on the ground. They all stared at the lever in the space Pat had uncovered.

Ben slapped Pat on the shoulder softly, "Well done my friend, but how did you know?"

"I thought that as the entrance was on this side, there had to be a way of lowering it from this side. If I wanted to hide it, I would have done something similar."

"Okay, give it a pull to see what it does."

Pat tugged down on the lever, moving it from its upright position until it would move no more. They all stared at the bridge in anticipation, expecting to see it lower into place and give them a way across. Nothing happened. Pat tried to raise the lever for another attempt, but it was stuck; firmly locked into position. He shrugged at the others who had been watching. "Maybe it's broken?"

"What do we do now?" Ben approached the chasm. "We need to get across."

Pat joined Ben at the abyss. "We could throw a hook fixed to a rope over the top of the bridge, and then one of us could swing across and lower it manually."

"It's risky, but it could work," said Creed. "However, we don't have a hook with us. We'll have to return above ground to fetch one."

Ben glanced from the bridge to the lever and back again. "We may not have to."

A quick search produced what he required. He picked up a medium-size rock, returned to the edge of the chasm and threw it. It arched through the air towards its target; the top of the bridge. A loud clang echoed around the cavern when it struck. Vibrations rippling along the metal bridge continued along the length of chain that disappeared into the ceiling. Dislodged dust that had settled on the links over the years drifted in the still air. The bridge trembled slightly, and a faint clanking of an unseen chain hidden in the rock above them was heard. Slowly, the bridge moved. The clanking length of chain wound around the spindle gradually fed out, lowering the bridge into position across the chasm.

Pat smiled. "I guess we won't need the hook now. I was trying to be all technical, and you just threw a rock at it."

Ben laughed and patted the German on the back. "It's the British way, Pat. If it doesn't work, we hit it."

Pat shook his head. "And you English won the war, fucking unbelievable."

They all laughed.

As soon as the bridge had settled into position, Ben crossed first. After he reached safety, he waved the others over. By the time they reached the other side, Ben had discovered a stout wooden door fixed into a stone carved arch. A turn of its handle and a hard tug proved it to be stuck fast. Together, they managed to heave the ancient door open, and Ben shone his torch into the revealed passage. It led to an identical door a short distance away.

Before stepping through the doorway, Ben checked the floor for traps but saw nothing suspicious. "Do you think we're safe now we're inside?" he asked. "The bridge wasn't really a trap, so maybe there aren't any now."

Pat poked his head through the doorway and examined the passage. "It looks clear to me. You could be right as it doesn't make sense to riddle the place with traps, the way in, yes, that I understand, but not inside."

"I guess there's only one way to find out." Pat gave Ben a soft push through the entrance.

The two men crowded in the doorway and watched Ben's progress through the short passage until he reached the far door safely before they joined him. Ben turned the handle and with a push and a shove the hinges screeched in protest when it opened. They all stepped through the doorway.

Raven entered the bridge cavern with her eyes fixed on the tunnel the three men had taken in case they returned. Though she could hear the faint sounds of the new intruders behind her, for now, they remained at the bottom of the entrance hole. She guessed they would come when they had all climbed down. As she crossed the bridge, her flashlight picked out the turbulent waters below. She briefly pondered raising it to prevent those following from crossing the chasm but decided against it. The noise would give away her presence, and the operating lever was in plain view. Now it had been lowered, she guessed it would probably perform as intended. Keeping her torch aimed at the ground, she headed for the first door and entered.

The first thing the three men noticed about the vast cavern they had just entered was the warmer temperature. The second was the source of the heat, the steam rising from a channel cut into the floor.

"It must be fed by a hot spring, perhaps from the same source as the thermal waters that feed the nearby hot baths in Rennes-les-Bains," Creed suggested.

They followed the smooth path that led to the warm waters edge and noticed a few steps descended into a three-meter-square pool cut into the channel and lined with rose marble.

"It might have been used as some sort of ritual bathing process before entering the Temple," Ben said.

"So we must be close." Creed knelt and dipped a hand in the water. "It's hot, pleasantly so, like bath water."

Pat pointed at the wall of mist filling the air before them and blocking their view. "The Temple must be through that."

Creed stood and shook his hand dry. "Shall we find out?"

There was no bridge spanning the warm channel, but as the pool was only a meter wide, it was an easy leap across.

All three gazed in awe and fascination at something that until this moment had been thought a myth. Their torch beams roaming the building at the far end of the large chamber confirmed it was real. They had arrived at the Temple.

"It actually exists," stated Ben, in pleased wonderment.

"What a magnificent sight, it's remarkable, unbelievable," Creed stated.

"Ahhh, that's better," Pat uttered.

Ben and Creed turned towards the splashing of water and saw Pat pissing into the warm water.

Ben shook his head in disbelief. "We're standing in front of something spectacular and that no one has seen for centuries, and the first thing you do is have a piss."

Pat smiled. "It'll still be there when I'm done, and I have to make room for another beer."

After zipping up, he rinsed his hands in the warm water upstream from his toilet, took a couple of beers from his rucksack and handed one each to Ben and Creed and grabbed one for himself.

After twisting off the tops, they clashed bottles in celebration of their discovery. As they drank, each admired the construction before them. The huge replica of the Temple of Solomon almost reached the roof of the large, natural cavern that stretched thirty meters above them. Although on a much smaller scale than the original mentioned in the Bible, which suggests the size of Solomon's Temple as 180 feet long, 90 feet wide, and 50 feet high, and at its highest point about 20 stories or about 207 feet, it lost none of its wow-factor. Part of the original Temple had also been overlaid with gold, unlike the Temple here which displayed all its glory in rose marble, probably hewn from the long-abandoned Templar quarry a few kilometers away, where evidence still remained of large stone blocks having been cut from the rock.

With the beers finished, Pat collected up the empty bottles and placed them in his rucksack. Without a word, they approached the Temple to see what secrets lay within.

Though the rising steam obscured them from her sight, their voices gave away their positions and what they'd discovered. Raven could easily shoot them through the wall of mist, but she resisted the temptation. She meant to confront Harper before she killed him. While she waited for them to move away, she knelt to feel the pleasantly warm water and glanced back at the open doorway when she heard approaching footsteps and faint voices. Marco and his men were coming.

Her eyes flicked to the right of the door when she noticed a stack of stout timber, perhaps left over from the Temple's construction. It gave her an idea. She walked back to the door, gently closed it and used a suitable length of timber to wedge the door shut. If they were as determined as she imagined they were, the time weakened wood wouldn't stop them for long, but it would slow them down and warn her of their arrival.

Raven returned to the warm water channel and slipped off her coat. It wasn't only the humid atmosphere that caused her to disrobe, she wanted to make an entrance. In her experience, men rarely shot a woman on first sight, especially a beautiful scantily clad woman, and now she was all three she was confident the men would hesitate when they met and give her the upper hand. It had served her well on many past occasions and had no doubts it would also prove advantageous this time. Men were so weak when faced with the female form. In such instances, their brains switched off, and their cocks took control. After concealing her clothes in the shadows for later retrieval, she leaped through the mist.

Ben, Creed, and Pat climbed the steps side by side. Their eyes roamed over the details of the Temple entrance above them and the two, large circular pillars fashioned from marble that stood either side of the doorway. A row of square pillars supported the roof and the porch that jutted out from the main bulk of the Temple.

The three men paused to admire the large door. Though the layer of silver covering the door had tarnished over the years, it didn't diminish its splendor. An intricately formed image of a seven-branched candlestick adorned the door in bas-relief.

"That's the Menorah," pointed out Ben, unnecessarily, as all had recognized its distinctive form.

"Do you think it's inside," asked Pat eagerly. "It would be priceless."

"Solomon's Temple in Jerusalem was originally built to house the Ark of the Covenant, but if the Ark we found in the tomb was the original, then there may only be a copy inside." Ben reached out, pressed down on the handle and pushed. The door swung open effortlessly without a sound.

The three men directed their lights into the interior. Although the builders had skimped on the gold covering the exterior of the Temple, they hadn't done so on its interior. When they entered through the large doorway, each marveled at the amount of precious metal that adorned the walls and reflected their lights around the room with a golden glow.

"That gold must be worth a fortune," uttered Pat, as he thought of ways to remove it.

"I doubt it's very thick, but, yes, I'm sure it would buy you a few beers," Ben replied, adding a smile.

"A few beers? It would buy him a brewery," Creed quipped.

But gold didn't make up the entire decoration. Green and red stripes adorned the ceiling and the same colors picked out the details on the bases and tops of the many pillars that ran down each side of the room to support the roof. Two rows of large, four-branched candlesticks led from the doorway to a raised platform at the far end of the room. With no daylight to penetrate the small, high glassless openings, these would have been the room's only source of illumination. Nearly all of them still contained thick wax candles of various lengths, extinguished centuries ago by the last person to have abandoned the Temple.

Ben wondered who that would have been, a Knight Templar, a priest, Saunière perhaps?

Each of the men chose a different path when they wandered through the room towards the steps leading up to the raised platform at the far end. Their soft footfalls on the marble floor sounded loud in the silence that shrouded the room. They all felt respect for the place, each sensing its history and its purpose. Pat lit a cigarette and used his lighter to set flame to each candle he passed on his journey through the Temple.

They soon arrived at the steps that rose up to the small elevated platform and a golden door.

Ben pointed his torch at the door. "Whatever the purpose for the Temple's construction, it's behind that door."

They glanced at each other before slowly climbing up to the steps to find out.

"If the Ark from the tomb was a copy, and the original is behind this door, isn't it supposed to have some sort of power?" Pat enquired.

"If you believe what's mentioned in the Bible, then yes, it did have some form of power that supposedly killed some of those that touched it, but we'll just have a look. I'm certain it's not going to be like in the Indiana Jones and the Ark of the Covenant movie. I doubt bolts of fire will shoot out from it to kill us all."

Pat rubbed his chin. "Hmmm, 'doubt' doesn't sound very certain to me. Perhaps you should go first."

Ben smiled. "Thanks."

Ben approached the door, turned the handle and gave it a push. It swung silently open. Ben shot a nervous glance back at his two companions before stepping inside.

Pat was about to follow him through when Ben's scream of agony echoed around the large room, striking terror into the two men.

"Oh my God! Noooooo!"

The two men, who envisioned bolts of energy shooting from the doorway to strike them dead, ran back down the steps.

Laughter halted their escape. They turned to see Ben standing unharmed in the doorway with a grin spread across his face.

"Thanks a lot, you two. Now I know who to count on in a crisis."

"Ha, ha, English humor. Very funny," Pat said, climbing back up the stairs.

"Sorry, I couldn't resist it."

"Yeah whatever," Pat nodded at the entrance when he reached the top of the steps. "Is the Ark in there?"

"Well, sort of," Ben replied vaguely.

Pat stared at him. "What do you mean 'sort of' Either it is, or it isn't."

"It's best you see it for yourself, and then you'll understand. There's also something else." He added cryptically, moving towards the open doorway. "But don't worry, it's safe."

It was not the Ark that first caught their attention when they entered. It was the large golden table with a huge seven-branched candlestick standing on top."

"It's the bloody Menorah!" stated Pat, awestruck. "Is it solid gold?" He stepped forward to try and lift it, but it was too heavy. "Yep, its solid gold. Can we take it?"

"It would look out of place in your old shack, don't you think?" said Creed with a smile.

"Who cares? I'll sell it."

Ben shook his head. "Who to? It's not the sort of thing you can sell on eBay."

"You must realize the significance of the Menorah, Pat," said Creed. "As is the Ark, the Menorah is one of the most sought after Holy relics of all time. If its discovery were revealed, the Jews would claim ownership and demand its return. There would be bloodshed in Jerusalem, and perhaps a war would be fought over it. No, I'm afraid it must remain a secret."

Disappointed, but not surprised, Pat joined the others staring at another object resting on a large raised plinth in the center of the room.

Creed moved nearer and examined it. "I now see what you meant, Ben, but is it the true Ark?"

Ben shrugged. "From its condition, I assume so."

Each shone their lights over the pile of disjointed, collapsed and decayed remains of the Ark of the Covenant. Though some of the wooden pieces still retained its covering of gold, other parts were bare; its gold having peeled off and fallen onto the raised plinth around it.

"Don't forget, it has to be about three thousand years old and never kept in ideal conditions, what with it being carried across the desert and from country to country and to get here probably across the sea as well."

Pat reached out a hand but paused. "Do you think it's okay to touch?"

Ben shrugged. "Perhaps any power it may have once held is no longer present."

"So was that a yes?" Pat questioned, seeking reassurance.

Ben touched one of the cherubs golden wings that still retained its gold covering, with a fingertip. As soon as his finger came into contact with the Ark, he screamed and started shaking.

Pat and Creed shook their heads in dismay.

"Hilarious," said Pat.

Ben smiled, "Sorry I..."

"...Couldn't resist it," finished Pat.

Ben picked up a wing fallen from one of the cherubs. "It's larger than I imagined and the whole thing must have been heavy when it was intact."

"Even heavier with the Ten Commandments stone tablets inside, the purpose it was built for in the first place," Creed offered.

Pat peered amongst the pile of collapsed wood. "Do you think the tablets are under this lot?"

Ben stared at the Ark's remains. "If the tomb ark was a copy, perhaps the tablets it contained were also, and the originals are here. Let's move some of this stuff out of the way."

They carefully cleared away pieces of the collapsed Ark.

When Pat removed one side of the Ark, he exclaimed, "I see them."

Creed and Ben crowded around the inscribed stone tablets.

"It's ancient Hebrew," Ben stated.

None of them needed a translator to decipher the ancient text; they all knew it had to be the Ten Commandments.

"God's law!" Ben said.

Creed cocked a raised eyebrow at Ben. "I thought you didn't believe in God."

"Confronted by this, it's becoming hard not to have doubts."

Pat nodded, "I agree. Maybe there's something to this Bible stuff after all."

Ben smiled. "You're not turning all religious on us, are you?"

"No way, I'd rather stop drinking beer!"

"What do we do now?" Creed asked. Like the others, he was unable to avert his eyes from the stone tablets. "Do we take them with us?"

With a struggle, Ben managed to force his eyes away from the ancient text and shook his head fogged with the faint pangs of a headache. He noticed Pat and Creed, who were slightly nearer, were mesmerized by the stones. He put his hands in front of their eyes to break the spell.

"I couldn't stop looking," Creed exclaimed.

"Me neither," said Pat.

Ben backed away from the plinth. "I think we have discovered the source of the Ark's power."

Pat and Creed joined him by the doorway.

"What do you mean?" Creed asked.

"It's the stones, the tablets. Do you two have a faint headache?"

The two men nodded.

"Me too. I think the stones must soak up something from us, humans I mean. Maybe that's why the Ark was built, to store this energy or whatever it soaks up. Maybe when it reaches a certain level, it can't contain it anymore and has to be released."

"If that's true, and I'm not entirely convinced, it might explain some of the Bible stories about the Ark smiting down people."

"It could also explain why the Ark was always placed in a sealed room," suggested Creed. "No one except the high priest was allowed to go inside, and this was something he rarely did."

Pat shook his head in disbelief. "Look, this is all getting a bit sci-fi. How could a couple of bits of old stone drain energy from humans? It's not possible."

"Before experiencing what we just have, I would have been in total agreement, but we all felt something when we were close to the tablets. I've no idea what, but it was something. All three of us experienced headaches when we were close, that's a fact. Who knows what would happen if we had prolonged contact with them. Maybe the stone is from a meteorite and what we experienced was caused by some form of radiation or something. I just don't know, but I'm not staying to find out."

Creed nodded his agreement.

Pat rubbed his chin while he stared at the Ark's remains. "Radiation you say, now that's something I understand. Maybe you're right. To be safe, we leave the Ark and the tablets alone."

"I propose we leave everything in this room well alone. We leave, shut the door and forget about it. But first, we bring the bodies down here, put them inside and then find a way to seal the pothole we came through, forever!"

"I can get hold of explosives," Creed said.

"That'll do it. Let's go," said Ben. "I'll be glad when this is all over and done with."

Pat and Creed exited the room.

With one final glance at the Ark, Ben followed them through the door and pulled it closed behind him.

Creed and Pat halted at the top of the steps and stared at the figure that had just entered the temple.

Ben sensed trouble. He glanced at the door as he stood beside his two companions. He could just make out the shape of a female figure, "You two are seeing this, right?" he whispered.

The others informed them they were.

"Good, I thought for a second it was an angel."

The figure stepped into the candlelight.

Pat whistled in admiration. "She looks like an angel to me."

Creed drew his weapon.

Pat glanced at Creed's gun enviously as he pulled out a beer, twisted off the top, glugged it down and held the empty bottle like a club. He glanced at Creed, "I don't suppose you want to swap."

Creed ignored him, his attention was focused on the approaching female.

Ben also had his attention focused on the strikingly beautiful woman as she swaggered sexily towards them. It wasn't just her beauty that entirely captivated the three men; the small amount of clothing that hugged the contours of her body was a significant contributor. Her full rounded breasts, which bounced with every step, strained to be free of the shiny, skimpy black bra that matched her knickers in size, color, and material. Her arms and shoulders were also covered in what seemed to be leather. Black straps wound from her waist, down her long legs to her knee-length leather boots. A sheath attached to these straps contained a large bladed knife. Her black hooded cloak fluttered behind her as she walked and one hand held the assault rifle resting casually on one shoulder.

All three men wondered how she had found her way down here and her purpose for doing so.

Raven could see by the men's faces her outfit had produced the desired effect, as she knew it would. She halted a short distance away from the base of the steps and stared at one of them. "Hello, Ben. It's good to finally meet you."

"Likewise I'm sure, and your name is?"

"You can call me, Raven. You killed my brothers, Abe and Isaac."

Hiding his shock at the revelation and the danger it was about to bring, he answered, "I didn't kill them, Rosslyn did. They were reckless and died in traps fashioned by the catacombs builders. If you seek revenge, it's them you should blame."

Creed whispered. "Trouble certainly does follow you around."

"Yeah, I know. I'm like a magnet to it."

Raven briefly considered Ben's words. She knew her brothers sometimes acted recklessly and could easily imagine them blundering into a deadly trap.

"I know it's not much of a comfort, but they died quickly and without pain," Ben lied.

"That might be the case, but if you hadn't gone to Rosslyn, they would still be alive."

"Then perhaps you should blame Silas, the person responsible for sending them into the catacombs after me. I had no knowledge of their presence until after they had died. I nearly perished myself. Only luck saved me. Your brothers were less fortunate. If I could have saved them, I would have. I'm not a cold-blooded killer like they were!"

"All of what you say may or may not be the truth; however, you could be lying in an attempt to save your life."

"Perhaps. But you knew your brothers. Do you think they would have recognized a trap if they encountered one?"

Raven thought about it for a moment before conceding, "No, they probably wouldn't have."

An explosion echoed in the cavern outside.

"It seems we have unexpected visitors," Raven stated, without surprise.

Creed sensed she knew who had caused the explosion. "Who are they?"

"I only know they work for the Vatican. Their intention, I assume, is to dispose of you three and take or destroy whatever's down here."

"They must be after the Ark and the Menorah," Pat blurted.

A look of surprise appeared on Raven's face. "They are here?"

Ben nodded to the door behind him. "In there."

Raven whistled in astonishment. "That explains your reason for coming here. You are treasure hunters."

"We don't want them. We will leave them here as they'll cause too much bloodshed if they're revealed. It's another purpose that guides our hand."

Raven stared at Ben. The man was full of surprises and might not be the greedy treasure hunter she first suspected. He also didn't seem to be armed like Creed.

"It's okay, Creed, if I wanted you dead you would be. Lower your weapon, the enemy isn't in here but out there."

Creed lowered the gun. "How many?"

Raven shrugged. "Though I imagine, unlike us, they will all be armed." She indicated the gun Creed held. "Is that your only weapon?"

Creed glanced at the beer bottle Pat held and nodded.

"Then I suggest we make our move before they arrive and block our only exit." Raven turned and strode for the exit.

"So killing me is off the cards?" Ben inquired.

Raven turned and glanced at him. "I haven't decided yet." She turned away.

Pat and Creed looked at Ben to see his attention focused admiringly on Raven's back view as she walked away.

Creed clicked his fingers in front of his face to grab his attention. "Do we follow her?"

"I see no other choice, and she has the biggest weapon."

"And the cutest arse," quipped Pat, with a grin.

"Amen to that," Ben agreed.

They followed Raven through the door. A shot rang out. A bullet struck the marble pillar by her head. In a blur of movement, Raven slapped the machine gun into the palm of her hand, aimed and fired. The man that had shot at her fell to the ground with a bullet in his heart. More men leaped through the warm mist. Raven fired again. Another man fell. More shots rang out. Bullets peppered the door and frame

A bullet smashed the bottle Pat held as they ducked back into the Temple. Pat glanced at Creed. "It's okay, I have more."

Creed smiled. "I didn't doubt it for a second."

More bullets ricocheted around the entrance, some entered the Temple and left deep gouges in the gold-covered walls.

"Quick, close the door," Raven ordered.

Ben and Pat slammed the door shut.

"Is there another way out?" she demanded.

"I haven't seen one," Ben answered.

"Then now would be a good time to look, don't you think? Creed, hold this." Raven pressed the powerful rifle into his hand and grabbed one of the large candlesticks, dislodging the lit candles, which rolled across the floor. She wedged the candlestick against the door and retrieved her weapon from Creed. "It won't hold them for long, they have explosives."

"Explosives," uttered Pat. He twisted the cap off another bottle. "We're all going to die." He gulped down the beer.

Creed looked at Raven. He admired her quick thinking and weapon expertise. "So, what's the plan?"

Raven shrugged. "We survive and kill them all I suppose. I'm just not sure how to achieve that yet."

Ben returned. "The only other exit is through one of the high windows. We have rope so we could climb out if we can fashion some sort of grappling hook."

A thud against the door made them all turn to face it.

Raven glanced up at the high windows. "Whatever you do, make it soon. They could blow the door at any moment."

Domenico had reached the door first, closely followed by his men. He turned the handle and gave it a push. When it didn't budge, he barged it with his shoulder, but it still refused to open. *Either it's locked, or more likely they've wedged it closed.*

Marco arrived. "One of you shoot the door."

His men glanced at Domenico for confirmation.

Domenico shook his head in dismay. "And exactly what do you think that would accomplish?"

"Punch a hole through it," Marco answered.

"The door's probably a few inches thick. We would do no more than splinter it."

"Blow it open then."

"It's a good job you're here, Marco, I never would've thought of that. Francesco. Set a couple of small charges to blow the hinges."

"But make sure you don't bring the temple down, there may be valuable artifacts inside."

The men ignored Marco's unnecessary comment. Domenico would like to strap a charge in Marco's mouth or better still, up his arse, but he had his orders. However, anything could go wrong in a place like this. He smiled at the thought.

Ben examined one of the large four-branched candelabra and discovered it was in two parts, the stem and legs, and the crown of candle holders. He slipped off the top and felt its weight; the metal was hollow, so not as heavy as it looked and light enough to throw up to the window.

"We can use this as a grappling hook," he informed the others as he bent the four branches back.

Creed took a coil of rope from his rucksack and tied it to the crudely fashioned hook. "Will it be strong enough?"

Ben shrugged. "It's the only option we have." He positioned himself under the farthest window from the door and prepared to swing the improvised grappling hook up through the opening.

"It's going to make one hell of a noise when it strikes the wall?" Pat warned. "Those outside would have to be deaf not to hear it."

"I've got that covered," Raven said, her powerful weapon aimed at the door.

Ben swung the rope and let it fly at the window. When it struck the wall and fell back to the ground, Raven fired a few shots at the door to mask the sounds. On his second attempt, the hook flew through the window. Ben pulled up the slack until two of the candelabra's prongs caught on the outside of the opening and lifted his weight onto the rope to test it. "It seems to be holding."

"Just one more thing," Pat said. "How do we get down? It's just as high outside as in here. We'll break a leg, or worse if we jump."

Creed, who'd been busy tying another rope to the candelabra's stem, passed the other end to Ben, who tied it around his waist.

"Okay, now I know."

Ben glanced up at the window. "I'll go first to test it's okay."

There were no arguments.

Ben found the climb grueling and only just managed it to the top. Grateful it was over, he pulled his exhausted body onto the window ledge and straddled it. He pulled up the stem, and after positioning it across the inside window opening, so it rested against the wall, he secured it to the candlestick hook to stop its weight from pulling it down. When all was ready, he nodded for the next person to climb.

It was decided, as Pat had no weapon, he would go next, and he began climbing. Ben commenced his much easier climb down the outside wall. As his feet touched the ground, an explosion shook the building.

CHAPTER 22

Trapped

THE DOOR BUCKLED when it was blasted from its hinges and shot into the room.

Raven swiftly dropped to one knee when the door flew toward her and skimmed by a hairbreadth above her head. It clattered to the ground and skidded across the floor behind her. To discourage the planned rushed assault she expected to follow from the men outside, she fired a short burst of bullets at the doorway.

Creed arrived and took position beside her, his weapon also aimed at the gaping entrance.

"Dowse the candles and switch off your headlight," Raven ordered, without averting her gaze from the entrance.

Creed went to carry out the order. He extinguished any remaining candles not blown out by the blast and switched off his light. The room was now shrouded in darkness.

Domenico and his men stood back when the small explosive charges positioned on the hinges detonated. The loud boom echoed through the cavern as the force of the explosions blasted the door inside the temple. Shots from inside quickly followed but the bullets whizzed harmlessly into the cavern. Deducing those inside had the entrance covered, Domenico indicated for two of his men to fire through the open doorway.

The two men moved into position, aimed their weapons at the entrance and each emptied a magazine into the Temple and reloaded when Domenico gave the order to enter.

Domenico glanced at Marco still taking refuge behind one of the large pillars. "Are you coming?"

Marco shook his head. "Not yet, let me know when it's safe."

Barely hiding his contempt for the man, Domenico turned and followed his men into the Temple.

Ben moved through the darkness alongside the Temple wall and peeked around the corner as two of the intruders fired into the Temple's interior. With no idea if any of those inside had been hurt or killed, Ben ducked back out of sight. To help his friends he needed a weapon. Though it was dark, his glance around the cavern revealed the two men Raven had shot earlier. Their positions given away by the torches clipped to their chests shining in the darkness. He was about to head for the nearest corpse when someone tapped him on the shoulder. He froze.

Ben turned. The red glow of a cigarette in the darkness.

"You made it okay then," Ben whispered.

"Yeah, nearly fell when the explosions went off, but I made it to the top," he whispered back.

"We need to collect the weapons from the two men Raven shot, but we'll have to make our way through the dark without using our lights. If we move along the edge of the cavern, we should remain undetected, but ensure you keep out of the beams of the dead men's torches."

They quickly reached the dead intruders and collected their weapons. Ben glanced at the AK-47 assault rifle Pat held. "Have you ever fired a weapon?"

"Yeah, many times, I'm a good shot," Pat said confidently. "What about you?"

Ben remembered the last time he had fired a similar weapon. "Yes, unfortunately, they're not easy to control in my limited experience."

Pat grinned and held the weapon across his chest. "I believe the time has come to kick these bad boys' arses."

Ben smiled at his friend's confidence. "Okay, but follow my lead and don't fire until I say so."

That Pat enjoyed the feel of the weapon in his hands, was evident by the big grin on his face. Ben had to admit that, unlike the one he held awkwardly, Pat's did seem to suit him.

Creed and Raven dived for cover when bullets spat through the doorway, striking the stone pillars, the back wall and sending a candlestick to the floor with a loud clatter.

Raven glanced at Creed. "They will enter as soon as the shooting stops."

Creed checked his weapon. "How much ammo do you have left? I'm nearly out."

"A couple of magazines, I wasn't expecting a gunfight."

"Maybe we should retreat to the back room. It will be easier to defend than this large open space."

The shots fell to silence. Raven assumed the men would enter shooting to keep them pinned down while they spread out. Creed's suggestion made sense. "Okay, let's go."

She followed Creed into the Ark chamber and closed the door behind them just as shots rang out from the Temple invaders when they entered. A few bullets struck the solid door harmlessly. Raven shone her torch over the door, but there was no way of securing it. Her light searched the room they were trapped in, letting it briefly linger on the Menorah and then the Ark. "It's not the vision I imagined."

Creed glanced at the sorry looking Ark. "Nor mine."

Raven crossed to the golden table and the large gold Menorah. "Help me move them over to the door."

"That won't stop them."

"I think it will," she replied, cryptically.

Together they strained with the weight of the large gold candelabra. They placed it on the floor, and carried the equally heavy table to the entrance, turned on its end and rested it against the door. They then dragged the Menorah over and leaned it against the table.

"Now the Ark," Raven ordered.

Though Creed was aware the Ark's contribution to blocking the door would be minimal, he assumed Raven had a plan and followed her lead. Together they positioned the larger pieces of the ancient Ark behind the door and stepped back to find out what would happen next.

Domenico entered the Temple. His eyes sought out those inside but found the large room deserted. "Hold your fire," he shouted over the thunderous bombardment. Discharged bullet casings clinked on the stone floor as the gunshot echoes died to be replaced by an eerie silence. A whistle from one of his men attracted Domenico's attention. His glance towards the signal picked out the rope reaching up to a high window highlighted in the man's torchlight.

Domenico ordered three of his men to search outside. "And tell Marco it's safe to come in now," he added.

Domenico focused on the door at the far end of the room as he headed for it. His men spread out and followed.

Domenico halted at the door, raised a fist and knocked. "You're trapped, so you might as well come out. If you don't, we blow the door and likely kill you in the process."

After a few seconds of silence, he received a reply and was surprised it came from a woman.

"I wouldn't do that if I were you. We have placed the Ark of the Covenant and the Menorah against the door. Blow it, and you'll destroy them both. Not something I believe your employer would be very pleased about."

"Nice bluff lady, but it won't work." He turned to Francesco. "Blow the door."

"Cancel that order!"

Domenico sighed and turned to confront Marco. "You can't really believe the Ark and Menorah are on the other side of that door."

"Unlike you, Domenico, I'm not willing to take that risk. Your superiors would be more than a little displeased to find out that *you*, through *your* incompetence, have destroyed two of the holiest relics ever to have existed."

Domenico shrugged. "So how do we get inside?"

"I have no idea, that's your problem, but I do know it won't be achieved by blowing open that door. Have you tried talking to them?"

Domenico stood back and waved Marco forward. "Please, be my guest."

Marco glared at Domenico briefly and stepped forward. "We have you surrounded." He called out, loud enough for those on the other side of the door to hear. "You face superior numbers and firepower and have no way to escape except through this door. If you come out now, I give my word you will not be harmed."

A few seconds of silence passed before he received his reply. "We are not as helpless as you seem to think. Try to enter, and you'll die."

"It's a woman!" exclaimed Marco. He directed a scowl at Domenico. "You are being thwarted by a *woman!*"

"What makes you think she is less of a challenge than a man?"

"Because she's a woman."

"One that is armed and by the sound of it, fearless, which is more than could be said of everyone here."

Marco ignored the comment he knew was aimed at him. "So what do you propose?"

Before Domenico could answer, gunshots from outside side-tracked his thoughts. After ordering two men to guard the door and another two to accompany him, he went to discover its cause.

Ben and Pat watched the three men exit the Temple, walk around the side of the building and after discovering the rope hanging from the window, swept their flashlights through the darkness, searching for escapees.

"Shall we shoot them?" Pat whispered.

"They're too far away. We need to bring them closer." Ben picked up a rock and threw it a short distance away.

Though three beams of light immediately focused on the source of the disturbance, the experienced men weren't about to be caught out by such an obvious trick. They split up and moved in a wide arc out from the center of the sound to seek out who had thrown the rock.

"That didn't work as expected, did it?" Pat stated. "Shall we shoot them now?"

"Wait until they get closer. These weapons are tricky to control unless you're used to them. We stand a better chance of hitting them the nearer they are."

"But won't that work both ways? They'll be able to hit us easier as well."

"We have surprise on our side, and we can see them, but they have no idea where we are."

A single shot rang out. A bullet ricocheted off the wall they were concealed behind next to Ben's head.

"I believe their greater experience is beginning to show," said Pat. "Shall we shoot them now?"

"We can try, but be…"

Before Ben could finish the sentence, Pat had stood, fired three shots in quick succession in three different directions and ducked down again. In the silence that followed, three bodies and their weapons were heard falling to the ground.

Pat grinned. "I thought you said they were hard to control."

Astonished, Ben peeked over the wall. Three beams of light shone on the ground, one aimed back at its owner revealed a neat bullet hole in his forehead.

Ben stared at Pat. "You shot all three with only three bullets."

"Well, from this angle, it would've been an impossible shot to do it with less."

Ben shook his head in amazement. "Where did you learn to shoot like that?"

"Call of Duty."

"You were in the army?"

Pat shook his head. "No, it's a computer game."

"So, when you said you had lots of experience with weapons, it was from playing computer games?"

Pat shrugged. "You've just seen the result of my many hours of first-person shooter mayhem, so what's the problem?"

Ben shook his head. "No problem, none whatsoever." He glanced over at the Temple entrance. "They will have heard the shots inside, so we had better make our move before they come to investigate."

"Shall I take the lead?"

"Yes, my sharpshooting friend, I think that would be an excellent idea."

When Lazzaro, Arrigo, and Domenico stepped through the entrance, a shot rang out. Domenico grabbed the nearest man, Arrigo, by the collar and dragged him back inside as a second shot echoed around the cavern.

Caught off balance by the abrupt change of direction, Arrigo tripped to the ground.

Lazzaro collapsed in a lifeless heap. A hole where his right eye had been revealed the bullets' entry point.

Arrigo put a hand to his ear bloodied ear to find the top half missing. Domenico had saved his life. "Thanks."

Domenic glanced at their dead comrade. "You're welcome, but Lazzaro wasn't so lucky. Whoever they are, they now have weapons; ours by the sound of it. My guess is it's those who escaped through the window." He peered through the doorway but saw no sign of the shooters. "From the shots we heard earlier, I assume the others have suffered the same fate as Lazzaro."

Arrigo climbed to his feet. "Whoever's responsible, they've reduced our numbers to four, plus Marco."

"For all the good he is," spat Domenico. "That's one man I wouldn't mind losing to a bullet. Keep the entrance covered, and I'll send Battista to join you while I work out our next plan of action."

"Did you get them?" called out Marco when Domenico entered.

"No, I didn't get them. They killed Lazzaro and probably the others. Battista, join Arrigo guarding the entrance."

Battista left to carry out the command.

"Do I need to remind you, Domenico, that it's your job to keep me safe and you've already lost over half of your men? I thought you were an expert at this."

Domenico resisted the urge to punch Marco. "I underestimated our quarry, but it won't be a mistake I'll' make again."

"It had better not, because if I don't complete my mission, you will have *his* wrath brought down upon you, and we both know how harsh that can be."

"Your problem, Marco, is that you worry too much." Domenico's glance around the room lingered on the rope hanging from the window before turning to Francesco. "Do you think you can climb that?"

Francesco glanced at the rope and nodded.

"Climb out, come around behind those out there and kill them."

Francesco slipped off his backpack of explosives, looped the strap of his weapon over a shoulder, walked over to the rope and began his climb.

"We still have that woman to deal with, Domenico," Marco reminded.

Domenico handed Marco his weapon and picked up the bag of explosives. "I'm working on it."

"You can't blow up the door, you'll destroy the relics."

"I have no intention of blowing the door." Domenico carried the bag over to the wall dividing the Ark room from the main Temple room, three meters from the door, and knelt. "I plan to make my own entrance."

Ben peered at the Temple doorway scorched from the recent explosion. "They'll have the entrance guarded now, so it will be suicide to try and enter that way."

"I agree. You wait here and be ready to act when I give the signal." Pat rushed off into the darkness.

"What signal?" Ben called out after him.

"You'll know it when you hear it," replied Pat.

What the hell is he up to now? Ben kept his still unfired weapon trained on the Temple entrance and waited.

Francesco wasn't used to such strenuous activity and panted heavily with the exertion of hauling his body up the rope. He glanced up. Two more meters and he'll be at the window. With a grunt, he hoisted his tired body upwards. When he was near enough, he reached out, grabbed the window ledge and climbed into the opening. His look of relief turned to one of surprise when he saw a blond-haired man hanging from the rope below the window outside. Before he could react, the man grabbed his hair and smashed his head against the wall. Hovering on the edge of unconsciousness, Francesco was yanked through the opening. He experienced a falling sensation and then nothing.

Pat watched the man plummet.

Francesco's neck bent at an unnatural angle when his head impacted with the ground before the rest of his body crumpled and then lay still.

Before climbing through the window, Pat listened for any tell-tale signs from inside that the sudden exit of their comrade had been noticed by the other intruders. Confident it hadn't, he peered over the lip of the opening. In the dimly lit room below he spotted two men. One, armed with an assault rifle, stood by the door to the Ark room, the other man, who appeared unarmed, knelt by the wall with his body hiding his purpose. A glance at the entrance revealed the two men guarding it. They would have to be taken care of first. Slowly and silently, he hauled himself into the opening and sat with one leg straddling either side of the wall. He cautiously slipped the weapon from his shoulder and aimed at one of the men by the entrance. Two shots in quick succession echoed around the room. Two corpses fell to the floor.

Marco jumped in fright from the sudden gunshots and directed his eyes at the entrance, thinking it had been Francesco and Battista who had fired their weapons. When he saw the two men collapse to the ground, he realized his assumption had been false. When another shot rang out, he dodged behind a stone pillar and hid.

Domenico didn't look at the door when the shots rang out; his trained hearing told him exactly where the shots had originated from. He rolled to one side a split second before a bullet struck the wall after passing through the space his head had just vacated. He grabbed the gun from its holster as he rolled and in one swift movement aimed it at the man in the window and fired.

The stone chip dislodged from the edge of the opening that struck Pat's cheek, drew blood. Aware he was a sitting duck in his current position, Pat did the only thing he could to save his life; he threw himself out of the window. Three bullets struck the edge of the window in his wake. As he fell he wrapped a leg around the rope and slid headfirst down its length. As he reached the bottom, he placed his hands and the rifle they gripped, on the ground and rolled into a standing position. After a glance around, he cursed, "Damn! That was the coolest move ever and no one around to see it." He ran to the front of the Temple.

Ben heard two shots inside the Temple and glimpsed two flashes from the high window, briefly highlighting Pat's form. Assuming it was the signal he'd been expecting, he ran for the entrance. Trusting that Pat had killed those guarding it, he rushed inside. The two dead sentries inside the doorway proved his faith in Pat hadn't been misplaced. The rifle he held uncomfortably turned to point at a man climbing to his feet at the far end of the room. "Drop your weapon, or I'll shoot."

Domenico realized he had been thwarted. Whoever these people are, they were professionals. He glared at the man by the entrance with the rifle trained on him and dropped his weapon.

Ben sighed in relief when the man's weapon clattered to the floor and cautiously approached. "Put your hands up!"

"Fuck off!" was Domenico's reply.

Ben was more than a little surprised by the man's refusal to obey. "What?"

"I'm not putting my hands up."

"But I have a gun, you have to."

"Or what, you'll shoot me? You're going to anyway. I would if the roles were reversed, so why would I degrade myself even further by sticking my arms in the air like an idiot." *Where the fuck was the spineless Marco and why doesn't he make a move on the man?*

Ben's confidence was fading fast. "Okay, but no sudden moves."

"What like this?" Domenico suddenly reached into a pocket, pulled out a packet of cigarettes and smiled when he lit one and took a long drag.

Ben risked a quick glance up at the window, but Pat was absent from the opening. "Did you kill him?"

Domenico shrugged and smiled. "Hard to tell, though I did try. Hopefully, a bullet or two found its target and Blondie's head."

A hiss, followed by the chink of a bottle top striking the floor, brought a smile to Ben's lips.

"Sorry to disappoint you, but you're a lousy shot. They all missed."

Domenico glanced at Pat, who leaned casually against a pillar by the entrance and shrugged. "Shit happens."

When Pat walked the length of the Temple and stood beside Ben, Marco made his move.

Marco had cowered behind the pillar as he tried to drum up the courage to shoot the man holding Domenico at gunpoint. Though he'd practiced with weapons at a firing range before embarking on this mission, he wasn't a great shot. However, if he could catch the man by surprise, maybe the threat of the rifle would be enough to gain the upper hand until Domenico could kill him. When he was about to enact his plan, the arrival of a second man stayed his hand. Any confidence he had in reserve had quickly disappeared while he waited to see what would happen. As the new arrival walked toward his friend, he knew it had to be now or never. Marco stepped out from behind the pillar, aimed his weapon and fired. There was no explosion of a bullet leaving the barrel, only a dull click.

All turned to look at Marco.

Domenico had not trusted Marco to panic if something happened and, so to avoid being accidentally shot, he had put the safety on before handing him the weapon. It was a wise decision as he was standing in the idiot's direct line of fire. If Marco had sprayed the two men with bullets, he would have been caught in the crossfire.

When Pat instinctively turned his head to look at Marco, he swung out his arm holding the half-drunk bottle of beer and let it fly.

As Marco struggled to find the safety catch, the bottle struck him on the forehead; he collapsed to the floor unconscious. The bottle smashed when it hit the floor beside him.

Domenico took advantage of the distraction, and as he dived behind the nearest stone pillar, he slipped a hand in his pocket and pressed the detonate button.

The explosion shook the building.

Ben and Pat were knocked to the floor by the blast wave and narrowly escaped being hit by pieces of masonry flying through the room.

Domenico hadn't remained unscathed by the explosion he'd set in motion. The blast wave bounced off the sidewall and slammed him against the pillar he had sheltered behind. He did though recover quickly. Ignoring the pain from a nasty gash in his side, compliments of a piece of flying masonry, he picked himself up from the floor, rushed over to the weapon knocked from Ben's hand and quickly brought it to bear on Pat as he stood. Domenico smiled and squeezed the trigger.

A shot rang out.

A body fell to the floor.

Raven, closely followed by Creed, stepped through the jagged hole blown in the wall as the dust settled. She glanced at Pat helping Ben to his feet and then at the large hole in the back of Domenico's head her bullet had caused.

"Are there any more?" Raven asked as she glanced warily around the room for signs of the enemy.

Ben shook his head. "Pat took care of them all."

She glanced at the German in surprise. "Good, then I suggest we leave before anyone else arrives."

As they left the Temple, Creed spied one of the intruder's rucksacks, which had been blown across the room by the explosion. Recognizing the C4 explosive and detonators that had spilled out, he walked over, stuffed them back into the bag and took it with him when he rejoined the others. He noticed Raven, who had paused to watch him, raise her eyebrows questionably. "To seal this place," he explained. "Then the Vatican won't find it so easy to get their greedy hands on the relics."

Raven nodded her approval and walked out of the Temple.

When they arrived at the shaft that led above ground, Raven told the others to wait while she went to check if anyone was up above guarding the entrance. When she had almost arrived at the top, faint voices from above alerted her there were at least two men up there. Her arm was a blur when it reached for her gun and sent a bullet heading for the inquisitive man who peered over the lip of the hole. Projectile and flesh met with expected results, and the dead man fell into the hole.

Raven pressed herself tight to the wall when the body sped by her. "Look out below," she warned.

Ben, Pat, and Creed dodged back as the body crumpled to the ground where they'd been standing.

Raven remained still with her gun aimed at the hole above, but no one else appeared. She glimpsed something out of the corner of her eye; a tiny blinking green light. Her worried gaze around the shaft detected more. The men above ground had rigged it with explosives while the others had investigated the Temple to seal it upon their return. It wouldn't take a rocket scientist to fathom that after hearing gunshots and then the arrival of those their comrades had gone to kill that they were never going to return. They would blow the shaft and seal it forever.

Raven let go of the rope.

She landed surefootedly beside the dead man.

"Run!" she ordered. "They're going to blow the shaft."

They reacted immediately and dashed along the tunnel. When they reached the next shaft, an explosion erupted.

Pat and Creed slid down the rope as the shock blast reached them.

Ben and Raven saw the cloud of dust rolling towards them at the head of the blast wave funneled through the passage. If it caught them, it would slam them against the rock.

Raven pushed Ben towards the hole. "Jump!"

Ben jumped into the shaft.

Raven followed.

The full force of the blast swept across the top of the hole and slammed into the dead end a short distance farther on. Searching for another outlet to expend its force, the blast wave poured into the hole.

Ben and Raven pressed their feet against the side of the shaft in an attempt to slow their descent as they grabbed the rope. They both hit the ground awkwardly as the explosive force swept over them.

By the time the shockwave reached them, Creed and Pat had fled farther along the passage. To escape its full force, they dropped to the ground and pressed their bodies to the floor. Wind, dust and small pieces of debris washed over them.

When the blast had expended its force, and the dust began to settle, silence followed.

Pat and Creed hurried back to the shaft to see how the others had fared. They arrived to see Ben lying on top of Raven, presumably to protect her from the blast.

Creed grinned. "It's okay, Ben, the danger's over. You can get off her now."

Ben glanced at him. "Are you sure, there may be a secondary blast. Maybe its best I remain like this for a while longer." He smiled.

Raven pushed him off and jumped to her feet. "The only secondary blast coming your way will be from my gun. I still haven't decided what to do about you yet."

Ben grinned at her. "I'm confident you'll make the right decision."

"What do we do now?" Creed asked, helping Ben to his feet. "The explosion must have blocked our only exit."

"I'll go take a look at the damage." Pat climbed up the rope and returned a few moments later. "It's totally blocked."

"Then we're trapped," Creed stated.

"What about that water-filled tunnel we came across earlier?" Ben asked. "It might be another way out."

Creed thought it was worth a try. "Well, we all know what the alternative is…"

"The Temple becomes our tomb!" stated Pat, ominously.

CHAPTER 23

Crystal Cave

O N **THEIR** ARRIVAL at the crystal cave, Pat briefly inspected the pool's submerged opening.

"It's definitely a tunnel and wide enough for a person to fit through at this end. I'll go through first to find out if it's a viable way out."

Pat propped his rifle against the wall, slipped off his rucksack and took out a length of rope. He tied one end to a naturally formed column, the other around his waist and handed the slack to Creed. "Feed this out as I go. If I get into trouble, I'll tug the rope a few times so you can pull me out. If I make it through successfully, I'll give the rope two firm pulls as a signal for you to come through."

Pat sat on the edge of the pool and dangled his feet in the water and shivered. "Brrrr! It's bloody freezing. See you all on the other side." He slipped into the water.

The others crowded around the pool as Pat swam into the submerged tunnel and disappeared. Creed fed the rope out to match the German's speed.

Pat used the walls to propel himself through the underwater passage lit by his headlamp. When he turned a bend in the tunnel, he came face to face with another man. Momentarily startled, Pat peered through the goggles of the diver's suit at the corpse's lifeless eyes and the bloated face, an indication he had been a long time dead, and the cold water had preserved his body remarkably well. He turned it to check the gauge on the oxygen tank that kept the corpse buoyant; it read empty. He noticed the disconnected air hose that might explain the reason for the man's demise. It must have pulled free, causing him to panic and drown. Pat pushed the body aside and continued on his way.

A short distance farther , he reached the point of no return. He had almost used up his store of oxygen and would never make it back to the Crystal Cave. He carried on along the tunnel that began to slope up. Enthused by this development, he moved even faster and soon broke surface. He gulped deep breaths of air. It was fresh, evidence it was replaced regularly, and there was an opening to the outside somewhere.

The first thing Pat noticed after climbing out of the water was the dead diver's bag. A quick rummage through it revealed a small amount of old and rotted provisions, a rope, digging tools, a spare flashlight that matched the one hanging from the diver's wrist, and a towel. The batteries of the torch proved to be dead, so he discarded it, but he used the towel to dry his hair and face.

His eyes followed the headlamp beam that searched the dark cavern for an exit. He spied only one, a small opening.

He untied the rope from his waist, secured around a rock for the others to follow and use to pull themselves through the water if he found an exit. Pat headed for the small tunnel and peered inside before entering. The passage was strewn with rubble and large chunks of rock, possible evidence of an unsafe structure. He clambered over a large rock almost blocking the tunnel and noticed the hollow in the ceiling it had dropped from. It was impossible to tell if it had fallen a hundred years ago or longer, or happened yesterday. A short distance farther the tunnel opened up into a small cavern. He switched off his headlamp. A dim glow highlighted a small space below the roof at the top of a rock pile that almost blocked the opening. Pat had the impression the tunnel had once been totally blocked until the diver had discovered its location and cleared it enough for him to crawl through. He scrambled to the top and peered over the rocks. At its end, he saw daylight and green foliage.

Pat smiled. He returned to the water tunnel and signaled on the rope for the others to come through; hopefully, they wouldn't panic at the sight of the dead diver he had no way of warning them about.

CHAPTER 24

Marco

MARCO SLOWLY REGAINED consciousness and opened his eyes, but the view didn't change; total blackness filled his vision. His ears strained to pick out signs of life or danger but heard nothing. As he wondered how long he had been unconscious, his fingers gingerly touched the painful swelling on his forehead.

"Domenico," he called out softly.

Only his weak echo replied.

He sat up and scrabbled around for his flashlight. His fingers brushed over the broken beer bottle, reminding him of the cause of his pain. After a few minutes frantic searching he found the flashlight and switched it on. Its beam stabbed the blackness, bringing Marco a small amount of comfort. When the light that searched the room halted on the still figure of Domenico, Marco realized he was all alone. A short walk across the rubble-strewn floor brought him to the hole blown in the wall. The light he aimed inside reflected off the large Menorah. The magnificent sight almost caused him to stumble in surprise and awe. He stepped through the hole and ran his hand lovingly over the magnificent relic's cold, golden surface. When Marco noticed something on the floor nearby, it took him a few moments before he understood that it was the Ark of the Covenant. He moved nearer, unsure if the explosion had caused the damage to the once wondrous object, or the ravages of time were responsible. What Marco was sure of was the relics in this room were genuine biblical artifacts. He was equally certain of the power and wealth they would bring him. However, first, he had to return above ground and arrange for their removal. There was also Harper and his companions, loose ends that needed taking care of.

Marco retraced his steps back through the Temple, across the bridge and soon arrived at the entrance to find it blocked by tons of earth and rock.

He was trapped.

He fell to his knees, and though the rock blocked his view, he gazed heavenward. "God, why do you test your loyal servant so?" With head hung low, he prayed.

CHAPTER 25

Daylight

MARCO CLIMBED TO his feet, and though he had no idea how he was going to escape, his unwavering trust in his God made him certain a solution would be forthcoming.

When Marco reached the staircase room, the solution manifested itself. Voices, though too faint to identify who spoke or what was said, it could only be Harper and his companions.

Marco sighed with relief. "Thank you, God."

His flashlight flickered and dwindled to a soft glow. He banged the torch with the palm of a hand, but it refused to give him light again. As he stared at the bulb's dim, orange glow, it faded into darkness. Marco sighed and wondered what he'd done to upset his God to be thrown so many obstacles. Did He not understand that all he did was for Him? Well, almost all. Why shouldn't he grab a bit for himself in the process? Those who ruled the Church had been doing the same ever since they came to power; he was only keeping to tradition.

Reluctant to abandon the flashlight in case it miraculously started working again, Marco kept it with him. He used his hands to feel the side of the tunnel to guide his way, and cautiously headed for the voices.

Just as those waiting in the crystal cavern were becoming concerned that something awful had happened to Pat, Creed felt two strong tugs on the rope; the signal Pat had made it through and discovered an exit.

"He's made it," Creed informed the others. "Ben, do you want to go next?"

Ben didn't want to go at all, but to escape from this place, it was his only option. His weak nod indicated his reluctance as he glanced at their rucksacks. "I suppose we'll have to leave all our stuff here?"

"Too risky to take the bags as they could snag on something," Creed advised, as he tied the rope taut. "The dive shouldn't be too bad as you can use the rope to pull yourself along."

Ben climbed into the pool. The shock of the cold water took his breath away. "Bloody hell, that's cold."

Raven smiled. "You've survived worse, I'm sure. Take a few deep breaths to fill your lungs and release your breath slowly as you swim to avoid the uncomfortable feeling of suffocation. But above all, whatever happens, don't panic. If you do, you'll die."

Ben stared at her. "Are you sure you don't want to go first to show me how it's done."

"No, I'll follow behind you."

Ben stared into the water, took a succession of deep breaths and slid beneath the surface.

Creed and Raven watched him orientate himself until he faced the tunnel entrance and pulled himself inside. When he'd gone, Raven climbed into the pool.

Using the rope to propel himself forward, Ben made good process through the submerged passage. Though a thoroughly unpleasant experience, it wasn't as bad as his fear had envisaged, but when he rounded a bend in the tunnel and stared into the face of the bloated diver, he changed his mind. He forced his mouth, which had opened with the shock of the unexpected encounter with the grisly corpse, shut to conserve what was left of his rapidly dwindling air supply. He was startled and almost opened his mouth again when something touched his shoulder. He turned. Raven pointed urgently along the tunnel and pushed him forward. Together they negotiated the rest of the passage, and when they surfaced in the cave, they saw Pat sitting beside the pool drinking the beer he had stuffed down his shirt before entering the water.

Pat smiled at them.

They climbed out of the pool and shivered. Pat threw Raven the towel to dry her long hair.

Ben shivered as he glanced around the cavern. "Did you find an exit, Pat?"

Pat pointed out the entrance. "I did, through that tunnel over there."

"Good. As soon as Creed arrives, we can leave."

Marco paused on spying a flash of light ahead. It was a welcome sight after the total blackness experienced on his nightmare journey through the tunnel. Though the voices had fallen silent, the way the light waved was proof someone was still there. He silently moved forward and peered into the small cavern. He saw only one man; Creed and wondered where the others he'd heard talking had disappeared to. Marco ducked back into hiding when the headlamp turned in his direction. *Had his presence been detected?*

Marco cursed himself for not collecting one of the dead men's weapons when he had the chance, but relaxed when the light turned away. Darkness followed a splash of water. After a few moments of deathly silence, he risked moving and peered into the blackness. He glimpsed diffused light coming from a pool of water and realized where Creed and the others had vanished to. He quickly approached the pool and saw Creed, and his light disappear into an underwater tunnel. Marco smiled. God had shown him the exit.

Marco dropped to the ground and fumbled through the discarded rucksacks he had noticed on first arriving. A sense of relief washed over him when he located the aim of his search and light once again banished the darkness. He roamed the beam around the cave, letting it rest briefly on the rope trailing into the water, before examining the pool. Marco put in his hand and shivered from its coldness. Though it wouldn't be a pleasant experience entering the freezing water, it was his only viable means of escape and something he would have to endure, but not yet. He would wait a while to give time for the others to vacate wherever the submerged tunnel emerged.

He sat down with his back against the wall, closed his eyes and prayed to God, thanking Him for not abandoning him.

Creed's light appeared beneath the clear water of the pool a moment before his head rose above the surface and he gulped down a lungful of air. "I wouldn't like to do that very often," he stated as he climbed out. "Who's the dead diver?"

Pat explained his theory. "I think he's this man I read about a while back. Apparently, a researcher bragged on a Rennes-le-Château internet forum that he'd found an entrance to the fabled Temple in this area. He said he was going inside to check it out and would post his findings on his return. However, that was the last anyone heard from him."

"And now we know why," Creed stated. "He died."

Ben stared into the water "What a horrible way to die. I don't suppose it's possible to report the whereabouts of his body to the police?"

"Not a good idea," Creed answered. "Not if we want the Temple and its artifacts to remain a secret."

"And all the men we killed in there," Pat added. "Also, I assume due to recent developments, the Temple is no longer a safe haven for JC and MM."

Creed shook his head. "Not now. We'd never get the bodies through the tight turns of the submerged tunnel. To safeguard the Ark and Menorah, as soon as I can, I'll ring my contact to obtain enough explosives to collapse the water tunnel and seal this point of entry for good."

"Now the Temple is no longer a viable option, we'll need another location to conceal the bodies," Ben said wearily.

"I think it's time for Plan B."

Ben looked at Creed with a puzzled expression. "There's a plan B?"

"I'll explain later as I first need to make a couple of phone calls."

"Then I suggest we remove ourselves from here," Raven said. "We could all do with a hot shower."

All agreed.

Pat led them through the tunnel and back into daylight.

An hour later, Marco stared into the pool highlighted by the flashlight gripped firmly in his shaking hand. The thought of entering the water-filled tunnel with no knowledge of its length filled him with dread. Not a particularly good swimmer, he knew the chances of drowning were high. Surmising that as the others had gone through, it was a plausible escape route, and the rope he could use to pull himself through so there wouldn't be much swimming involved.

So it wouldn't weigh him down when wet, or snag on some protrusion, he stripped off his jacket. Now all he had to do was gain enough courage to enter the freezing water. He briefly wondered what was worse, to remain entombed under the mountain until he died of hunger, or death by drowning. His conclusion was both were equally as horrifying. Trusting in God to keep him safe, he said a final prayer and entered the pool. The shock of the freezing water almost caused him to climb back out, but he forced himself to persevere. He took a few deep breaths of air and slipped below the surface.

He was in God's hands now.

After travailing only a short distance, his lungs felt fit to burst.

Though aware he had to keep going forward, the urge to go back grew in intensity the farther he traveled. The panic that had threatened to surface since he entered the water began to take a firm hold of his senses. He noticed something picked out by the flashlight; it looked like an opening in the tunnel roof. He pulled himself through the water toward it, but when his face rose above the surface, it slammed against rock. It wasn't the exit he hoped for, only a pocket of stale air, which he gratefully gulped down. As soon as his lungs were refilled with the life-giving substance, he dove below the surface again and continued his hellish progress. Luckily, the rope and the rough tunnel walls provided a relatively easy means of propulsion. He then met the dead researcher. At first, he thought it was one of those that had just left, but this person wore a diving suit. However well-equipped Harper's gang had been, he doubted they would have included a diving suit. When the body turned to face him, he was actually relieved to see the bloated face of the dead man. Unlike those who had just passed through the tunnel, this lifeless form posed no threat. He edged around the floating corpse and quickly pulled away.

Marco swallowed air as soon as he broke the surface. A sense of relief washed over him that he had survived the nightmare journey. After checking he was alone, he climbed out of the pool. His roaming light soon picked out the tunnel entrance and shivering with cold, he headed straight for it.

A few minutes later he discovered the exit.

"Daylight," exclaimed Marco with relief.

He pulled himself into the tight space and ignored the rocks digging painfully into his skin as he squirmed and crawled towards the light.

He pulled back the leafy branch partially covering the entrance and squinted from the bright sunlight invading his pupils. With God's help, he had made it.

He crawled out, fell about a meter to the ground and rolled down a steep grassy bank into the Sals River flowing below the entrance. He swam to the far side and used the trees and bushes growing there to climb the steep bank onto a tarmac road that he recognized and headed left. A walk of a few kilometers brought him to the village of Rennes-les-Bains and his hotel, Maison Christina.

Christina, the hotel's pretty proprietor, was behind the reception bar making a jug of hot chocolate when Marco entered. Unfazed by his soaking wet form dripping water on her tiled floor—she had seen it all in her years of owning the hotel—she cheerily greeted her guest.

Marco returned a weak nod. "There will be a few short for dinner tonight."

"Okay," Christina replied. "How many will there be?"

"Just me." Marco turned away and climbed the stairs to his room. He desperately needed a hot shower and a good meal, and afterward, he would make some phone calls.

Soon there would be no loose ends.

With God on his side, he couldn't fail.

Christina shook her head with a smile as she watched him go. She certainly had her fair share of strange guests. She finished preparing the steaming jug of thick, frothy hot chocolate, placed it on a tray with cups and saucers and carried it outside to her waiting customers.

CHAPTER 26

Plan B

A FEW HOURS later, Ben, Raven, Creed and Pat had all showered, changed into fresh clothes and eaten a much-needed meal.

Raven walked onto the balcony, gazed down at the rooftops spread out below her and then at the ancient walls of the ancient Carcassonne City ringing the fortress. "Impressive."

Ben sat at a table on the balcony sipping wine and staring at Raven's tightly clad body. "Very."

Creed stepped onto the balcony. "I bought this place a couple of years ago to use as a safe house if ever needed, like now," he explained.

They had relocated to Carcassonne as there was a good chance Creed's home was under surveillance. Though they couldn't imagine who else was left to come after them when Marco and his men failed to report they assumed the Vatican wouldn't let the bodies or the artifacts slip from their grasp so easily and might send others to obtain them by whatever means possible.

Pat, a bottle of chilled beer in his hand, joined them and sat opposite Ben. "So, Creed, what's this Plan B of yours?"

Raven chose the seat beside Ben and accepted the glass of red wine he offered.

"First things first," Creed looked at Raven. "We appreciate your help in the Temple, but why are you still here, with us?"

Raven stared back at Creed. "If I could answer that I would, but I've no idea. As you know, I came to France to kill Ben in revenge for my brothers' deaths, but as you can see, he's still alive."

Ben flashed Raven a smile.

"Again, I'm not sure why, because indirectly he is partly to blame for their demise."

"I admit that due to a set of circumstances beyond my control I was involved *indirectly*, however, there are others equally, if not more so, to blame than me," Ben replied defensively. He didn't believe that telling Raven the truth about her brothers' demise would be beneficial for his health or her peace of mind. If her brothers hadn't tried to kill him, they would still be alive.

"You can relax, Ben. If I thought you were the direct cause of their deaths, you'd be dead by now."

"So, are you going to continue helping us?" Pat enquired, hopeful that she would. Not only was she easy on the eye, but also very handy with a gun. He had the feeling her expertise would be invaluable in the coming days.

Raven shrugged. "It seems I am if you want my help."

"I believe we all do and I'm glad to have you on board," said Ben.

"Me too," Pat agreed.

"As am I, however, you may change your mind when you hear my proposition," Creed informed her.

"That's to be seen," she replied.

"I believe I have the ideal place to inter Jesus and Mary."

Even though they'd explained about the two bodies found in the tomb, Raven still found the casual mention of their names in this context a surprise.

"And that would be where," Pat asked.

Ben shook his head. "I have the feeling I'm not going to like the answer."

Ben was right.

Creed glanced at each of them before answering. "When you first hear what I have planned, you'll think me crazy, but consider this, France is no longer viable as a location. I'm certain the Vatican, and perhaps even the surviving members of the Rex Deus, Compagnie du Saint-Sacrament and God knows what other secret sects that haven't made themselves known yet, will want what we have. To this end, I believe we relocate somewhere they would never expect or think of looking. I propose to hide the bodies in Jerusalem! Or to be more precise, the underground chambers beneath the Temple Mount."

Raven smiled.

"Cool," said Pat.

"Jerusalem! And just how are we supposed to manage that?" Ben asked, dismayed.

"Though it won't be easy, I think I have a way it can be achieved. The Temple Mount is riddled with tunnels. Some are discovered when people living in the old city repair or extend their houses, but because of the upheaval it brings the residents, not all are reported to the authorities, and I know of such a tunnel. My father had a good friend he stayed with while visiting the Old City and I remember him telling me the cellar floor had sunk in one place. The owner believed the cause was a tunnel running directly under the house.

Intrigued enough to find out more, my father dug down until he found the tunnel, but it was blocked. Although it was too much work for him to clear the blockage alone, I believe it should pose us no problem. I have just phoned my father's friend who owns the house and told him I wanted to come and finish what my father started, to clear the blockage to find out where it led. Though he was reluctant at first, after I offered an extremely generous fee for renting his house, he agreed to let us stay there for a week while he goes on holiday. All we have to do is enter the tunnel beneath the floor and clear the blockage. If it leads under the Temple Mount, we should be able to find somewhere to place the bodies. As long as we repair the floor when we've completed our mission, no one will ever be the wiser." He glanced around at the skeptical faces staring at him. "You have to admit it would be a fitting location to lay the bodies to rest."

"I agree with you on that point," said Ben, "but I foresee a few problems. For example, how in the hell are we going to transport two bodies to Jerusalem without anyone noticing when we pass through customs or borders."

"Yes, Ben, I know it will be difficult, but I believe it's doable. I also sense it's the right thing to do."

"Sorry to rain on your parade," Raven said, "but you are aware that Jerusalem, thought by some to be the holiest city in the world. To the Muslims, it is their third holiest place and is not only heavily patrolled by armed Israeli soldiers and the ever watchful Temple guards, but you also have the hundreds of Muslims who will attack you if they catch you excavating their sacred site. You also have the Jerusalem police to contend with, the Jewish people, etc. etc."

"Yes I'm aware of the difficulties, but if we follow my plan, we should be okay. We'll be in and out before anyone knows we're there," Creed reassured them.

Ben shook his head in defeat. "Even though I think the plan is utter madness, I do agree France is no longer viable. I also sense it's the right thing to do and even that recent past events have been leading us to this very decision."

Pat nodded enthusiastically. "I agree. Jesus and Mary want to go home."

Raven shrugged. "I think the plan is doomed to fail, but I'm in."

"Then we take Jesus and Mary home." Creed gazed around at their faces. "Agreed?"

They all agreed.

"Now here's the plan, while Pat and I organize things here, which includes our transport, as we'll be driving to Jerusalem, you Ben, accompanied by Raven, will go to England and fetch the head of Jesus."

Raven raised her eyebrows and glanced at Ben.

Ben grinned. "I'll tell you all about it on the way."

"I'll need a few days to prepare things here and seal the Temple entrance, so no need to rush back." Creed smiled. "Relax for a few days and meet me back here Saturday."

"Sounds good to me. I'll go online now and book our flight and hotel as it's probably not wise to stay at my place after all that's happened." Ben looked at Raven. "Shall I book two rooms?"

"Yes Ben, you shall."

CHAPTER 27

Dorset, England.

"WHAT DO YOU think, Raven, is it safe?"

Raven had been studying the house for a few minutes and had seen no sign of anyone suspicious or suspect cars or vans parked along the road that might be concealing anyone keeping an eye on Ben's house. A single silver Ford Corsa car stood in the driveway; Ben had informed her it belonged to his researcher, Alexandra.

"It seems clear, but there could be someone in the house."

"Other than Sandy you mean?" Ben questioned.

Raven left the obvious question unanswered and handed Ben her phone. "Call her to check all is okay."

Ben typed in his house phone number. It was answered after a few rings. "Hi Sandy, how's things?...No, I'm still in France."

Raven nodded her approval at the lie. If there were someone else in the house it would be preferable they believed Ben was still out of the country.

"I'm not sure when I'll be back, perhaps a week or two...Are you okay, is anything wrong?"

Raven saw the worried frown appear on Ben's face. She searched the windows of his house for any sign of an intruder or threatened danger. A crunch of leaves alerted her to a threat much closer. She spun towards the noise and grabbed at the gun purchased from a London contact on the way from the airport from her waist.

"Freeze or die," ordered the man pointing a gun at her head.

Raven froze with the gun half drawn.

Ben turned and looked at the armed man. "I have to go. I'll speak to you soon." Ben ended the call.

The man whistled a signal and shortly another two men appeared through the trees and joined them.

"Now, missy, you pull out that gun nice and slow and throw it into the bushes."

Raven glared at the man and then at his two companions, but she failed to recognize them. She carried out the demand and threw the gun.

"Now, both of you stand, and if you make any sudden moves, it will be your last."

When they had stood, one of the men searched them for concealed weapons. Though Raven could have snapped the man's neck in an instant, the weapons trained on her by the others made her resist the temptation and let the man paw her body.

Raven glanced at the man whose hands squeezed her breasts. "Having fun, are we?"

"You bet," the man replied lecherously.

He groaned when Raven's knee swiftly connected with his crotch and doubled up in pain. "You bitch!" He hissed.

"Serves you right," said Luther, who was obviously in charge. "I said search, not fondle," he snapped.

Luther lunged at Raven and pistol-whipped her around the side of the head. She staggered but kept to her feet.

"You try something like that again, and I'll cut off your tits and give them to Gareth to wank over."

Gareth's wide smirk turned to fear when Luther turned on him. "Same goes for you, yer fucking pervert. Do that again, and I'll cut off your prick and stuff it in your mouth."

"He'd probably enjoy sucking his own dick," Raven said, wiping away the blood dribbling from her mouth.

Luther smiled. "You're probably right. Now both of you, head for the house. You know the rules, so behave, and you'll live."

They entered through the back door and were ushered into the lounge where Alexandra sat on the sofa guarded by another man.

"Ben!" she exclaimed.

"Are you okay?" Ben asked.

Alexandra nodded.

"Enough of the chit-chat," Luther barked. "Pick a seat and keep quiet or I'll have you all gagged."

When Ben and Raven had seated themselves, Luther took out his mobile and punched in a number. When it was answered, he said, "He's here," and hung up.

Though Ben and Raven wondered who he'd called, they both knew they would soon find out.

"Alexandra, can you please make us all a coffee."

Alexandra headed for the kitchen.

"I'll have a tea, please, Sandy."

Luther glared at Ben. "She's making coffee, so that's what you'll have or go without."

Ben glanced at his researcher and thought asking for a cappuccino would be a bad idea. "Coffee's fine, Sandy."

One of the men followed Sandy.

Raven stared at the man in charge. "What happens now?"

"Luther gazed at her. "If I wanted you to know I would have told you already." He turned away.

Realizing her questions wouldn't be answered, she turned to Ben and whispered, "Do you know them?"

Ben shook his head and gathered from her inquiry, neither did she. "What shall we do?"

Raven shrugged. "We wait."

After an hour, the person on the other end of the phone arrived. Luther went out to greet him, and they entered a few moments later.

The new arrival glanced at Raven before focusing on Ben when he sat on the chair opposite.

"Ben, enough time has been wasted, so I will come straight to the point and explain the situation. You have something we want, and we have something you want," he nodded at Alexandra. "You give us what you have, and she goes free."

Ben stared at the man. "And what about us?"

"That depends on your level of cooperation. I have no interest in taking your lives if I gain possession of what I require."

"What is it you want?"

The answer was not the bodies of Jesus or Mary, or the Ark of the Covenant as Ben had expected.

"I want what you found beneath Rosslyn Chapel."

Confusion blanketed Ben's face. He doubted the man meant the few valuable trinkets or the sword. Maybe it was to be the head. "Could you be more specific?"

"Come now, Ben, you know exactly what I mean. We are aware this object was secreted in the catacombs, so give me the Holy Grail, or it won't only be your friends that will suffer an excruciating death."

Ben was still confused. Did he want the head or the bowl he found in the chapel, that he had left there? Though both could be thought of as the fabled Grail, he didn't think it was the head the man was after. "You want the Holy Grail, the bowl that held Christ's blood."

"Now we're making progress." He smiled. "That's exactly what I want."

"Okay, no problem, it's yours…as soon as you let Alexandra go."

Raven glanced at Ben in surprise, not from his demand, but that the so-called Holy Grail is amongst the many things he had discovered.

The man glared at Ben. "There seems to be some confusion, Ben, as you seem to think you are in a position to bargain with me. I assure you that's not the case. Luther, break one of Alexandra's fingers."

Fear spread across Alexandra's face when Luther stepped toward her.

Ben spoke to halt his advance. "Stop, it's yours. I'll tell you where the Grail is."

Luther glanced at his boss to check if he should continue. The man held up a hand to pause the task and gazed at Ben expectantly.

"I hid it in Rosslyn Chapel," Ben told him, telling a half-lie; he'd only replaced it where he found it.

The man's raised eyebrows revealed his surprise. "And why would you do such a thing instead of keeping it?"

Ben shrugged. "It seemed like the right thing to do at the time."

"Obviously you have held it, describe it to me."

Ben described the bowl, the dark stain of ancient blood and the feelings he had when he touched it.

"Do you believe this bowl is the actual vessel that caught the blood of Jesus when he hung on the cross, and thus the Holy Grail?"

Ben stared at him for a few moments and then nodded. "It can be nothing else."

"Where exactly did you hide it?" the man asked. The note of excitement and anticipation in his voice was clear to everyone in the room.

"Before I tell you, what's the deal here? I tell you where it is, and you let us go?"

The man shook his head. "Ben, Ben, Ben. Please don't take me for a fool. No one is going anywhere until I'm certain I have the actual Holy Grail in my hands. It could be a fake or a medieval copy."

"It's not," stated Ben with confidence that surprised all in the room. "There are a series of carvings in a chamber beneath the chapel, and some depict the image of a vessel catching the blood of Jesus from the wound caused by the spear the Roman soldier thrust into his side to check if he was really dead. The image matches exactly the bowl I found. You'll know it's the actual bowl, or the Holy Grail as you like to call it, when you hold it, but you'll need access to the chapel to be able to retrieve it."

"I can assure you, that's not a problem." He stared at Ben for a few moments. "I'm surprised you fail to recognize me."

Ben stared at the man. "Why should I?"

He smiled. "Because we have met before."

"I think I'd remember if we had."

"Let me jog your memory. It was only a few months ago, in Scotland, in Rosslyn Chapel to be precise."

Ben stared at him more closely and then it suddenly dawned on him, they had met, in the Rosslyn Chapel crypt.

Ben backed away from the counter in the Rosslyn Chapel ticket office to give the couple room to purchase tickets for the Chapel tour about to start; the guide and the rest of the group waited impatiently outside for the couple to join them.

Eventually, the man who had disappeared into the back office returned the counter, lifted the access flap and glanced at Ben with a look of disapproval. "Follow me."

Ben was led into a back office, and the man closed the door and left. Ben glanced around the small office, its walls adorned with images of Rosslyn Chapel that included paintings and photographs of its interior and exterior as well as aerial photos and sketches. A bookshelf also followed the same theme and was stacked full of books about Rosslyn. Ben had no doubt the man sitting behind the plain wooden desk with the light from the computer screen reflected in his glasses, had written one or two of them.

A warm smile appeared on the man's face when he walked around the desk to shake his visitor's hand. "Welcome, Mr. Harper."

Ben shook his hand, unaware that this would be the only warm welcome he would receive during his time at Rosslyn. "Please, call me Ben."

"Okay, Ben, and you can call me Robert. Now, I believe you may have discovered a tomb in France which you believe to be Templar in origin?"

"Yes, I'm pretty sure it's Templar due to what's inside."

"And what is that?"

"Would you like to see for yourself?"

"You have photographs?" Robert asked, intrigued.

"No, a video," Ben explained how he had come to film the tomb when his video camera had slid down a hole in the floor of the cave he'd been led to by the clues embedded in a church's decorations. When he retrieved the camera, which had been on record when it fell, the footage he was about to see had been recorded.

"Rennes-le-Château, how I cringe when I hear that name," said Robert. "So many people wasting so much time on a stupid myth. Hasn't it been proved the priest made his money from selling masses and a few trinkets he found buried in his church crypt?"

"Not exactly, but look, I didn't come here to debate how Saunière may have made his money because I already know how he made his fortune. I suggest you watch the video and then decide for yourself." Ben took a compact disc from his pocket and handed it to Robert.

Robert glanced at the disc simply inscribed with a single word, TOMB. He inserted it into his computer and stared at the screen when the film of the tomb played automatically. His look of skepticism changed to fascinated interest. He viewed the short film twice before turning his attention on Ben. "You say you followed the clues in the church at Rennes-le-Château to find this tomb?"

Ben nodded.

"And it's near the village?"

"Within walking distance," Ben replied.

"You haven't been inside, though?"

Ben shook his head. "I couldn't find the entrance."

"Why haven't you reported this to the French authorities?"

"I will in due course when my book is completed."

"Ahhh, a publicity stunt?" As an author, this was something Robert understood.

"If you like."

Robert stared at the paused image of the tomb on his computer screen.

"Do you think it's a Templar tomb?" Ben prompted.

"As you probably realize, I've never seen a Templar tomb, and as far as I know no one else has either, not one like this, so I have no comparison to say for certain. However, with the red Templar cross emblazoned on the shroud I'd hazard a guess that it's possible." He thought for a few moments before continuing, "I know someone who is an authority on this sort of thing and who may be able to tell you more. I'll phone him now to see if he is available." He glanced at Ben. "If you wouldn't mind waiting outside, please?"

Ben held out a hand. "I'll take the CD with me."

Robert continued looking at Ben for a few seconds as if debating whether to keep it. "Of course."

Robert ejected the disc, placed it back in its case and returned it.

As Ben approached the door, Robert spoke. "I'll come and fetch you in a minute."

Ben closed the office door on his way out.

A few minutes later Robert appeared and asked Ben to return the following night at eight o'clock in the evening; this would allow time for the person he had phoned to arrive, which Ben had agreed to do. Robert would not tell him who was coming but did say he was a Mason. Ben got the impression whoever he was going to meet they were high up in the Masonic hierarchy.

Ben returned the following night at the arranged time. When he drove into Rosslyn Chapel's small carpark and killed the car's engine, it began to drizzle. The area looked deserted. There were no other cars there and no lights on in the reception building, though the floodlights around the chapel were on to catch fine rain in their bright beams.

Ben approached the door he had entered before and peered through the glass into the dark room; there was no sign of life. He turned his head at a noise and looked towards the chapel. Robert stood by a small door set in the wall around the grounds. He waved Ben over, ushered him through and led him into the chapel. The church, lit by a few candles, was gloomy and so cold Ben could see his exhaled breath. He followed Robert across the room until the man halted at the steps leading down to the crypt.

"They are waiting for you below," was all Robert said before leaving.

The sound of the chapel door closing echoed through the room.

Ben descended the stone steps. He'd been in the crypt on a previous visit, but when he reached the bottom of the steps the small, ordinarily empty room now contained a table and laptop. The laptop's blue-tinted screen and a candle positioned in a small niche in the wall were the only sources of illumination and left most of the room in shadow. An ideal atmosphere to conceal the three figures, whose shape Ben could just make out, to observe without revealing their identities. The scene caused him to wonder if this had been such a good idea after all. He glanced behind at the worn stone steps rising to the chapel and wondered if he should leave now while he had the chance.

"If you leave, Mr. Harper, you won't find out anything about the tomb," said a man's voice from the shadows, who eerily seemed to have read Ben's thoughts.

Ben stared at the three shadowy figures, whose features remained a mystery in the dimly lit room. "If I leave, neither would you." Ben was determined not to be intimidated.

"Touché," said the voice.

"Who are you and why all the secrecy?"

"Our names…*Mr. Harper*, are not important, but if you like, we could lie and give you false ones. Perhaps in time you'll come to learn who we are, but come, we digress from the reason you sought us out. You want us to view your film of the tomb to see if we can shed any light on it, is that not so?"

"That's why I'm here."

"You have the disc with you?"

Ben fished the CD from his pocket.

"Please place it on the table and retire to the chapel so we can view the film in…secret."

Ben stared at the shadowy figure of the man doing all the talking.

"If you want our help, this is how it must be done."

Ben placed the disc on the table and retired to the chapel. Whispered voices, too hushed for him to hear what was said, drifted up from the room below. He bent low to the floor and peered down the steps to see if he could see anything, but to no avail.

After about half an hour, plenty of time for those below to view the footage a few times, Ben returned to the crypt.

The three men who were examining the pages of an open book on the table dodged back into the shadows on hearing Ben's footsteps on the stairs.

Ben paused at the bottom. "You've seen the film, so what do you think? Is it a Templar tomb?"

The three men whispered.

"Yes, we think it might be a Templar burial, though obviously, we cannot be certain. I understand it is located near Rennes-le-Château?"

"It is," Ben confirmed.

"And you deciphered the clues in the village church, which led you to the Tomb's discovery."

"Yes."

"And there is no access into the tomb?"

"Well obviously there is a way into the tomb as Saunière found a way inside, but I haven't found it yet, and I believe the original entrance has been blocked by modern works. Now it's my turn to ask a question. Do you know *who* is in the tomb?"

More whisperings and then, "No."

Ben got the impression they were lying. "No idea at all?"

The spokesman ignored Ben's question. "Will you reveal the tomb's location to us?"

"I think you already know that answer."

As they held a hushed discussion, Ben looked at the book they'd been reading on the table and attempted to read the title. One of the men noticed the object of his interest and snatched up the book. All Ben could tell was that it was old.

The spokesman stepped into the dim light and glared at Ben. "It would be in your best interest if you told us the tomb's location, Ben."

Ben wasn't about to be intimidated by the man's implied threat. He also knew he could run up the steps and out of the chapel before they reacted, at least he hoped he could. "You already know that I won't."

"You really should reconsider and tell us."

"And why is that?"

"Because it's important to us," the spokesman replied.

"Because you know what's in the tomb?"

"Perhaps some of the objects are known to us, but not all. We think there may be something in the Tomb we have long searched for. It is this that interests us."

Ben took it that the *'we'* in this context, meant whatever secret sect they belonged to, Masonic or otherwise. "Perhaps if you tell me what you know about the tomb, we can come to some arrangement."

His suggestion was ignored. Instead, they began another whispered conference. Then, for the first time, another one of the three spoke, though unlike their spokesman, he remained hidden in the shadows.

"Hello, Ben, you have intrigued us for some time, ever since we first became aware of your discovery. To be honest, at first, we thought it was in all probability a hoax, some kind of publicity stunt to promote your forthcoming book. However, you surprised us when you returned to France, re-filmed the Tomb and posted clearer pictures and revealed more of the tomb's artifacts. Then, to our astonishment, you walked in here yesterday offering to show the film to us. Because we were beginning to doubt our first impressions; what if it wasn't a hoax and you really had found a tomb, it was an offer we couldn't resist. I flew in from abroad, interrupting an important meeting to be here. We are now certain the tomb exists and of its importance to us and us only."

"Why only to you?"

"Because of what we believe is hidden inside?"

"And what is that?"

"I cannot say except it's more important and more dangerous than you could ever realize and you are better off without this knowledge. Informing us of its location and walking away would be a very wise move for you."

"In your opinion."

"Ben, what do you want from all this?"

"I want you, the Masons, if that is who you are, to comment on the tomb footage and any information you can give to shed light on the body and artifacts inside."

"You misunderstood, Ben, not this meeting. What do you want from your discovery? Fame, fortune, recognition, what?"

Ben thought for a few moments before replying. "To be honest, when I first realized what I might have found, I spent time thinking about how much money I might be able to make from my discovery, a book or two, film rights. Even the recognition was tempting at the time, but I see I was naive then. Now, I just want to find out the truth."

"But what if you couldn't handle the truth?"

"I'm a big boy, I'll be okay."

"I very much doubt that, Ben. Have no uncertainties that one way or another we will find the tomb and reclaim what is rightfully ours."

"And how many years have you been telling yourselves that? Your track record seems to be in direct contrast to your statement. If I hadn't found it, you'd still be in the dark."

"True as that may be, for your sake, I hope your brain is as clever as your mouth."

Ben knew by past experience it probably wasn't.

The three men whispered again.

"Thank you for showing us the film, but now it's time for you to leave. Goodbye," he said dismissively.

Their spokesman walked over and laid a hand on Ben's arm to lead him up the stairs. Surprised by his sudden dismissal, Ben shrugged off the man's grip and stared at the man in the shadows. "What about my CD?"

"What about it?" the man replied.

"Come, you must leave," ordered the spokesman forcefully, grabbing his arm again.

Ben pushed him away and slowly walked up the steps with the man following closely behind. About halfway up, he glanced back. One of the men had moved forward to watch Ben leave, his face highlighted by the flickering candle. He ducked back into the shadows, but not before Ben had briefly glimpsed his face.

"We will meet again, Ben, of that you can be certain," were the man's parting words from the darkness.

Ben was ushered out of the chapel, and he headed through the rain to his car. He wasn't unduly worried about the CD; what harm could they do? They were hardly likely to make it public.

Deciding caution would be beneficial to his health, he drove back to his hotel, paid his bill, collected his things and left to find somewhere else to stay for the night.

Ben thought about the man whose face he had briefly glimpsed in the crypt; it was the same man who now sat opposite.

The man noticed Ben's look of realization. "I see you have remembered." He smiled. "I told you we would meet again."

"I assume you work for Silas, who lives in Rosslyn Castle. He also tried to have me killed, but as you can see, he obviously failed."

"Your assumption is incorrect. Silas is quite low in the pecking order and takes his orders from me, and those much higher than I. The attempt on your life was a mistake and something I only became aware of after you had left Scotland. There were those that wanted you tracked down and killed, but I persuaded them your death wouldn't be in our best interest. My presence here proves I was correct, but be assured, Ben, if I ever decide you have become a liability, you will die."

Ben ignored the threat. "I gather, from what you have said, you are not in the Order of the Black Knights; the Templar clean up and assassination squad?"

"No, I am ranked far above them."

"And who exactly are you?"

"I don't see why that matters now, but I am known as Hugh de Champagne."

"Any relation to one of the original Knights Templar who bore the same name? Who was related by marriage to the Saint Clairs at Rosslyn I believe."

"Correct again, but although I have taken his name, I am, alas, no relation. Many of us take the name of a famous Templar as a sign of respect for their courage. But we digress from the matters in hand. It seems we have been looking in the wrong place as we thought the tomb you discovered in France would hold the Grail, but, if you have told the truth, it was at Rosslyn all along and directly beneath our noses, so to speak." He shook his head in dismay. "So much time and effort wasted. But no matter, we have it now, or soon will. The carvings you mentioned also interest me. I would like to see them for myself, so in addition to the Grail, I will need to know how to reach them. You say there is an entrance to the catacombs from the chapel."

"No, there's an exit from the knight's chamber below, but it can only be opened from beneath."

"So the rumor of the knights buried under the chapel is true?"

"It is. There's also a replica of the chapel minus the carvings."

"What an amazing time you must have had down there, Ben."

"It wasn't all fun I assure you. I'm surprised you haven't explored the catacombs yourself as Silas now knows where the entrance."

"I would have, but that damn fool Silas had the tunnel sealed with explosives to prevent anyone else from discovering Rosslyn's secrets. He assumed, incorrectly, that as you made your exit from the catacombs through the chapel, it would be easy to discover it. Alas, this didn't prove to be the case."

"If you want to have a look for yourself, I do know of an easy access point in the graveyard. I discovered it while I was down there."

"Then you shall reveal that information to me also, but first tell me the location of the Grail."

"It's better if I show you as it's hard to describe."

"Now, Ben, you wouldn't be trying to trick me? If that is your intention, I assure you it's doomed to failure and will prove very costly to you and your friends."

"It's not a trick. I know where I hid it, but I need to be in the chapel to locate its hiding place. Anyway, how could I trick you with your men watching me?"

Hugh was silent for a few moments before he spoke. "If you try anything or fail to produce the Grail, your friends will suffer."

"Yes, so you keep saying. When can you get me access to the chapel?"

"I will make the arrangements, and by the time we arrive in Scotland tomorrow, all will be ready. Then I will find out if you are telling the truth." Hugh walked outside to make a phone call.

"I need to know if you're telling the truth," Raven whispered to Ben.

"I am. The Grail is there. I'm sure you already know this, but we can't trust them to keep their word, we have to escape. That's why I played for time."

"You did good. Perhaps an opportunity will present itself during the long drive." Raven glanced at Gareth eyeing her lecherously. She would enjoy killing him.

Hugh entered the room. "All has been arranged. Luther put them in the cars. We drive to Rosslyn."

CHAPTER 28

Rosslyn Chapel, Scotland.

AFTER A NINE hour drive they arrived at Rosslyn. Memories of Ben's last visit flooded back when they approached the chapel, and the driver halted at a temporary barrier stretched across the road. One of the two men manning it approached the driver's window. After a brief conversation with the driver and a glance at the car's occupants, the guard was satisfied with their credentials. He turned away, nodded to the other guard and stepped aside when the barrier rose. The driver drove through and steered the car onto the small track leading around the chapel and down to Rosslyn castle. Silas exited the castle as they parked.

Silas glared at Ben when he climbed from the car. He'd hoped he had seen the last of him. "What happened to David and Doyle?"

"They both had an accident," Ben replied.

Silas cursed the man; another two of his men had fallen at his hands.

Surprise then spread across his face when Raven climbed from the car. "What are you doing here?"

"I enjoyed your company so much. I decided to pay you another visit."

Silas nodded at Ben. "I thought you went to kill him?"

"As you've probably realized, Silas, plans don't always work out as expected when Ben's involved."

Silas glared at Ben again, he knew only too well.

"Everyone inside," Hugh ordered. He turned to Silas. "Are they here?"

"All are present and awaiting your arrival."

"Good. Arrange some refreshments for our guests while I prepare myself."

Silas followed Hugh into the castle.

After a brief rest and light refreshment, Ben was escorted to the chapel while Raven and Alexandra remained under guard in the castle. The two men delegated to watch them had been issued with orders to kill them if they attempted to escape or they received word Ben had lied.

Ben stared up at the starlit sky as he wondered how this night would end. A glance over at the graveyard as their procession passed, picked out the tomb concealing the entrance to the underground chambers lit by moonlight. A plan had begun to form in his mind on how he might be able to turn the table on his captives. The group of men, who had arrived at the castle a couple of hours ago, were now dressed in red monk's habits. The discovery of the grail was to be an occasion only the privileged few had been chosen to witness. Ben noticed Silas watching him, the distrust in his eyes evident.

After they had entered the chapel, the door was locked. There would be no disturbances.

Hugh turned to Ben. "Time to shine. Where is the Grail?"

All eyes focused on Ben when he crossed the chapel. Hugh followed him closely, as did Luther and another armed guard.

Ben halted beneath one of the carved arches and pointed up at the Seven Deadly Sins carvings. "That's where I hid the Grail."

Hugh glanced up at the carved stone disbelievingly. "You do know your friends will suffer if you're lying."

"It's there. Bring me the stepladder, and I'll prove it."

The ladder Hugh had previously arranged, as per Ben's instructions, was brought over and positioned below the arch.

Ben climbed to the top. "I'll need someone to take the stone from me after I remove it."

Hugh, though still skeptical, indicated for the armed guard to help.

The man handed his weapon to Luther and positioned himself beside the ladder. Ben grabbed the carving with both hands and wiggled it as he pulled it free. Surprise was experienced by those gathered when the grinding of stone filled the room, and the carved block slid out from its recess.

Ben glanced down at the man below as he took its full weight. As he stepped down a rung, he pretended to slip and let the stone fall from his grasp to grab at the ladder. "Look out," he warned, too late to for the man below to escape the heavy piece of falling masonry.

The stone struck the man on the side of the head and he crumpled to the floor unconscious, unaware of the large stone smashing his wrist with the crunch of bone before it toppled to the floor.

Luther lunged forward and aimed his gun at Ben's head.

"It was an accident," Ben pleaded.

"Leave it, Luther," Hugh ordered, glancing down at the man sprawled on the floor. His interest lay in what was hidden in the space Ben had revealed, not the injured hired help. "He still lives." He glared at Ben. "Any more accidents like that and you and your friends will not be so fortunate. Where's the Grail?"

Ben climbed to the top and reached into the hole. Before revealing what was inside, he stared down at the sea of expectant faces crowded around the bottom of the ladder and Silas who still glared at him suspiciously.

Silas watched Ben climb the ladder. His experience with the man had taught him to be on his guard. He glanced at Luther—the only armed man in the room now Harper had incapacitated the other, which he suspected wasn't the accident Harper had claimed—to ensure he was observing Harper's actions. Satisfied he was, Silas looked back at Harper, who he suspected was up to something. He was sure the Holy Grail wasn't in the space Harper had reached into and wouldn't be surprised if the man pulled out a grenade. He stared at Harper's hand when as it was slowly withdrawn from the hole. The look of surprise that spread across his face on seeing the object was a testament to his error and disbelief.

Ben held the object aloft ceremoniously for all to see.

Utters of awe and wonderment filled the chapel as Hugh reached up and took the bowl from Ben. A hushed silence then fell as they waited for their leader's judgment of the artifact.

Hugh gazed in wonder at the simple, wooden bowl as he touched a finger reverently on the dark stain inside. *The blood of Christ!* He sensed, without doubt, this was the genuine article, the Holy Grail, the vessel that had caught Jesus' blood as he hung on the cross. He lifted his head, gazed at the expectant faces around him and raised the bowl for all to see. "Behold the Holy Grail!"

After a few moments of stunned stupefaction, someone asked, "Does it contain Christ's blood?"

"There is evidence that it once held the blood of Christ," Hugh answered.

"I've kept my end of the bargain, Hugh, it's your turn now," Ben said.

Luther's gaze had never wandered from him. Not even to glance at the Grail.

"Not quite, first you must show me the entrance into the catacombs beneath us," Hugh reminded him.

"Then we'll be allowed to go free?"

"Yes, then you and your friends will be freed," Hugh answered, impatiently.

Ben glanced at Luther. The thug's cruel expression told a different story. However, for the moment his choices were limited. "Follow me, and I'll show you the entrance."

Hugh handed the Grail to one of the robed men so they could all hold and examine it in turn. He ordered the brethren to remain inside the chapel while he and Luther went with Ben.

Raven glanced at one of the men when he threw another log on the fire burning furiously in the large hearth. She turned her attention to her other captor and was not surprised to see Gareth's lecherous gaze wandering over her body. She didn't need any mind-reading skills to discern his thoughts and decided to give him what he wanted. "It's warm in here, would it be okay if I remove my jacket."

A smile played on Gareth's lips. "Take off as much as you want," he leered.

Raven slipped off her jacket to reveal her ample breasts straining against her tight skimpy top. Gareth's eyes homed in on her cleavage like an eagle on its prey.

Raven stretched to push out her breasts farther to ensure the man had a good look. "Don't suppose I could have a shower? I feel all *dirty*," she asked and looked at Gareth. "I might even let you scrub my back."

Gareth nearly fell off the stool when the image of Raven naked in the shower sprung into his mind. "I can't see a problem with that," he said lustfully.

"She stays where she is," ordered Travis. "Start thinking with your brain and not your prick for once, you moron."

Gareth glanced over at him. "But she said I could scrub her back in the shower, while she's *naked*," he moaned.

Travis shook his head. "You're a bigger fool than I already know you are if you believe that, as I know you do. She only wants to get you alone so she can overpower you."

When Gareth turned back to Raven, she made her move. She leaped from the chair, punched him in the face and threw her jacket at Travis as he aimed his gun at her. It wrapped around his face as the gun barked. The bullet grazed Raven's shoulder before embedding in the wall behind Alexandra, who sat, shocked by what had just happened.

Raven grabbed the stool as Gareth toppled backward and threw it across the room at Travis who pulled the jacket free from around his head. The wooden seat hit him full in the face, breaking his nose. Dazed, he staggered backward. Raven rushed at him, grabbed the gun from his hand and struck him a savage blow on the head. He collapsed unconscious to the floor. Raven turned her attention to Gareth, who reached for his fallen gun. Two strides brought her to him. She stamped hard on his hand. Bones crunched. Gareth squealed in pain. Raven picked up his weapon and aimed it between his eyes.

"You'll never get away with this, you bitch," he spat, nursing his injured hand.

"On the contrary you lecherous piece of shit, I already have, and now I'm going to do something for all the women you've ever set your rapist eyes and hands upon, and I assume there have been many." She pulled the trigger.

The loud blast made Alexandra squeal in fright.

Raven glanced over at Travis's unconscious form and then at Alexandra. "Are you okay?"

Alexandra glanced at the hole in Gareth's forehead and nodded weakly.

Raven glanced around the room for something to tie Travis with. She crossed the room, yanked the electric cord from a floor lamp and bound the man tightly. She slipped off his shoe, pulled off his sock and stuffed it in his mouth. After a quick search through the man's pockets produced the car keys she required, she headed for the door. As she passed Alexandra, she tossed her the keys. "It's time to leave."

Stunned, Alexandra followed Raven from the house.

CHAPTER 29

Saunière's Death

BEN LED THE two men into the graveyard and over to the large tomb decorated with Masonic symbols. "This is it. You'll find the entrance inside."
Hugh studied the tomb skeptically. "Are you certain?"

Ben pictured the tomb entrance on the map he'd found in the chapel on his previous visit and the doorway he discovered in the tunnel. "Yes, I'm certain. I'm not sure what you'll find inside, but it will lead to a large locked door that you'll have to find some way of opening. I saw it from the other side when I was down there. Behind the door, steps lead down to a tunnel partly covered in a fine yellow powder. I have no idea why it's there. I thought it was poisonous and made a suit from black plastic as protection, but I tripped while running through it and ripped the suit," he lied. "I breathed in the powder, and apart from clogging the throat, it's okay, though I'd advise you wear a dust mask of some sort. Turn left at the bottom of the steps until you arrive at a large metal fan." He noticed the puzzled look appear on Hugh's face. "It's what creates the sound of the hound sometimes heard here. I think it's to scare people away," Ben explained. "Step through the fan blades, there's plenty of room, and you'll be in a room with a machine powered by a water wheel that turns the fan at intervals. Enter the water channel and follow it through the wall into another large chamber. Climb the stairs you'll find there and pass through the rooms until you come to a grand staircase. This leads up to the copy of the chapel I told you about. There are two exits from this room. The one on the right leads to the Knights' chamber and the carvings depicting the Holy Grail, the other to the room with the exit to Rosslyn chapel. On a column near the steps, you'll find a wheel to raise a slab in the chapel floor. There were some traps I set off, but as there are no keepers to reset them, you should be safe. Except, that is, for a chest you will find in the room at the top of the first set of stairs, which I advise you to leave well alone or you'll bring the ceiling crashing down. I've also marked a tread on the steps leading down from this room. It's a trap, so don't step on it. That's everything I know."

"Well, Ben, you've been very thorough in your report, but until I discover you're telling the truth, I think I'll hold on to you a while longer so you can be our guide."

"That wasn't the deal," Ben argued, though unsurprised at the outcome. He knew if they forced him into the tunnel, he'd have to reveal the truth about the yellow powder and suffer the consequences. He glanced at Luther. The man watched him intensely in case he tried anything. He had to make his escape somehow.

"Come, Luther, we need to gather some equipment from the castle to open this tomb and discover if Harper tells the truth." Hugh headed for the graveyard exit.

A prod in the back from Luther's gun forced Ben to follow.

Raven glimpsed the men approaching the castle. Though dark, there was enough moonlight to recognize them as Ben, Hugh and Luther. She dodged behind a tall finger of stone beside the bridge that spanned the gorge. Three men, but only one held a weapon, though Hugh might have a gun concealed under his robe, she thought it unlikely. With the element of surprise in her favor, her odds of success were favorable. She would wait for them to pass, shoot Luther and Hugh, grab Ben, meet up with Alexandra, whom she had left sitting in a car parked by the castle, and make their escape. The plan was sound.

As Hugh, Ben, and Luther stepped onto the bridge, the moon, previously concealed behind some dark, moody clouds drifting across the night sky, appeared once again. Luther noticed something strange about a shadow on the ground cast by part of the ruins. As he stared at the shadow anomaly, it moved. Luther stared at the silhouette of a gun held by the person hiding behind the ruin and then at the finger of rock that hid the assassin. He placed a hand on Ben's shoulder to halt him.

Forced to a stop, Ben glanced back at Luther. *Had the plan for him changed?* He was well aware of the long drop the bridge spanned and hoped his body plummeting over the edge wasn't the reason for the unexpected halt.

Utilizing Ben as a human shield, Luther cautiously pushed him forward.

Unaware of her presence, Hugh walked past Raven's concealed position as she prepared to act. Ben and Luther should be close behind. When they failed to appear, Raven sensed danger. She then glimpsed her shadow on the ground and cursed her stupidity. The moon had been shrouded by cloud when she had first hidden here. Having lost the advantage of surprise, she stepped out onto the bridge and faced Luther.

Ben was more than a little surprised to see Raven appear, but her presence revealed why Luther had acted so strangely. As Raven tried to get a clear shot at the man hiding behind him, Luther's gun appeared beside his face and aimed at Raven. He acted swiftly and stamped on Luther's foot, and as he lunged backward to knock him off balance, Ben was temporarily deafened from the close proximity of the loud blast so close to his ear.

Caught off guard, Luther stumbled back into the low wall at the side of the bridge. Ben turned, raised a foot and kicked him in the chest. As Luther tumbled over the wall, he reached out for something to stop his fall. His hand connected with Ben's raised leg and grabbed hold tightly, dragging Ben over the edge when he fell.

Raven rushed forward and dived at the low wall and clasped Ben's wrist and saw Luther held onto Ben's ankle. The strain of supporting the weight of both men felt as if her arm was being torn from its socket. As her hand holding the gun was also gripping the wall for leverage against the heavy burden, she was unable to shoot Luther to lessen the load. If she let go of the wall, they would all fall. She had to do something fast as she couldn't support their weight for much longer.

"Well, well, well, what do we have here?" said Hugh, appearing beside her. He glanced down at Ben and Luther and turned to Raven. "We must cover the details of your escape shortly and punish those who allowed it to take place; but first, I see you are in difficulty."

Raven grimaced with the strain.

Hugh picked up Luther's dropped gun. "Allow me to help my dear." He leaned over the edge, aimed the gun and fired.

Raven assumed he had shot Ben, but it was Luther that fell; his wrist shattered by the bullet. The reduced weight, though still a strain, was slightly more manageable.

Hugh watched Luther strike the ground. For the moment he needed Harper alive, and though Luther had been a loyal and useful asset, he could always hire another to replace him. He also thought it was feasible he might survive the fall, but on spying the pool of blood forming around the man's head, he realized he'd been mistaken.

Hugh turned the gun on Raven. "Pull him up."

Raven stared at Hugh, though he'd not yet noticed the gun in her hand, she was unable to point it in his direction. If she let go of the wall Ben's weight might drag her over. She turned her hand slightly in an attempt to aim it at Hugh's leg. The gun scraped on the brickwork.

Hugh glanced at the sound and noticed the gun. He dodged out of its limited line of fire as Raven pulled the trigger. The bullet grazed his leg.

Hugh pried the gun from her fingers. "I may need Harper my dear, but I don't need you. Now pull him up before I decide you have both outlived your usefulness."

Raven hoisted Ben over the top. The release of the pressure from her arm was a welcome relief. Hugh ordered her to sit on the wall beside Ben. The gun directed at her head convinced her to do so.

"Kill her and I won't help you," Ben stated.

"That choice is yours, Ben, but refuse to aid me, and she dies first. Help me, and perhaps I will let you both go free."

The sound of an engine filled the night before they were all caught in the bright headlights of the car rushing towards the bridge. Blinded by the light, Hugh frantically aimed the gun at the speeding vehicle and fired. Bullets struck the car harmlessly as it sped onto the bridge and struck him. He tumbled over the bonnet and roof then spun to the ground. The car skidded to a halt, reversed onto the bridge and stopped. The window wound down.

"I think it's time we left," said Alexandra, anxiously.

Ben and Raven climbed into the car, and Alexandra sped off.

"Did I kill him?" Alexandra asked, still not quite believing what she had just done.

"We can only hope," Raven replied.

Alexandra steered the car onto the main road, gunned the car and crashed through the barrier. The startled guards fired off shots that peppered the car harmlessly until they had pulled out of range.

Ben glanced back through the rear window. Rosslyn Chapel, bathed in moonlight, receded rapidly behind them. "That's it. I don't care what happens in the future, I'm never coming back here again."

Hugh groaned in agony as he slowly regained consciousness. He sensed bright blue flashing lights through his eyelids and felt himself being lifted. He opened his eyes. The hazy figures of paramedics fussed over him. He was alive. When he caught up with Harper and that bitch Raven again, they wouldn't be so lucky. He drifted into unconsciousness again.

After explaining all that had happened in France to Alexandra on the drive back from Scotland, it was decided she would be safer staying at a friend's house until the course of events Ben found himself embroiled in reached its final conclusion. Alexandra bade Ben and Raven be careful before exiting the car, and Ben waited until she had entered the house before driving away.

Three hours later they were on board a ferry from Dover to Calais, France. They had abandoned the stolen car in Folkestone, nearby the Eurotunnel complex and then caught a train to Dover. If anyone were still after them, they would assume they had taken the shuttle and watch the Coquilles disembarkation point for them, instead of the Calais ferry terminal. The head Ben had collected from his house would have been impossible to get aboard an airplane with the strict security precautions every passenger and piece of luggage had to experience before being allowed onto the plane. The relaxed security of the Dover ferry terminal had presented no such problems. After a cappuccino and a snack of ham salad French bread sandwiches, Ben and Raven settled down on one of the many seats to await their arrival in Calais Port in about ninety minutes.

Ben thought back to Saunière's confession and wondered if he'd experienced as much trouble after his discovery of the tomb. His thoughts wandered back to the final pages of Saunière's confession. It did seem that his death might not have been from natural causes, but perhaps a step taken to silence him forever. Though Saunière hadn't said much about this incident, reading between the lines, Ben could visualize a possible scenario as to what had taken place...

Rennes-Le-Château, France January 14th, 1917

Marie, busy in the kitchen preparing food and drinks for Saunière and his guests, glanced out the open window on hearing footsteps upon the gravel path. She stared at the two strangers, dressed in dark suits when they passed the window. Saunière's guests had arrived. She wondered who they were. Though he usually confided in her, recently Saunière had become withdrawn, secretive. She had questioned him about this, but all he would say was there were some things she was safer not knowing. The identity of the two men and the reason for their visit was another of the secrets he had kept to himself. When he had informed her of the men's expected arrival and asked her to prepare some refreshments, he stressed upon her that she must not show him any affection in their presence, but to act like the housemaid her position decreed she should.

Marie went to greet the visitors.

Saunière sat at a table on the belvedere and stood as Marie led his guests through the garden. After a brief, courteous greeting, he dismissed Marie to fetch the prepared refreshments and led the men to the table and bade them sit.

One of the men remained standing and gazed around at the well-tended garden, the Tour Magdala and the magnificent vista the terrace afforded of the surrounding landscape. "You have made yourself very comfortable, for a priest," he said, making no effort to disguise the disdain in his voice.

"It's a long way from the luxury those in Rome enjoy," Saunière retorted.

The man smiled as he sat. "That is certainly true, but they, as am I, are keen to learn how you can afford such a lavish lifestyle on a priest's meager salary."

"That is why you are here after all," stated Saunière. "From my letter I sent to Rome, which I'm sure you have read, you know I have discovered something that could do irreparable harm to the Church, if not destroy it entirely. The evidence for that which I have found is irrefutable."

The men stared at the priest but revealed no outward emotions to what they had heard.

Saunière continued, "The secret is connected to the Knights Templar, who shortly before their arrest in 1307, secreted their most sacred possessions in an underground chamber. The secrets contained in this cave and its location were entrusted to the Hautpoul family, who once dwelled in the chateau you passed in the village. On her deathbed in 1781, Marie Hautpoul passed on the secret to her priest, Antoine Bigou. Before he fled to Spain in 1789 to escape the wrath of the French Revolution sweeping through France, he left details of this secret in his church. During my renovations of the badly deteriorated church, I found Bigou's message, and it led me to the Templar cave in the surrounding mountains. Inside, I found not only treasure, which provided me with ample resources to construct all you see here, but something shocking, as I soon discovered it wasn't only a cave of treasure, but also a tomb containing the mummified corpses of Mary Magdalene and Jesus Christ."

At first, a look of disbelief appeared on the men's faces, but it was soon surpassed by doubt.

"This cannot be so, the body of Jesus ascended to heaven." The man's voice failed to project the belief of his words.

"Yes, that's what the Bible would have us believe and, if I'd not gazed on the body myself, I would refuse to accept it. However, I have. Not only does the body of the man display evidence of having been flayed, but also bears the marks of the crucifixion and in his side a wound. The Bible informs us that all of these wounds would have been inflicted on Jesus Christ." Saunière glanced at the two men, their faces having returned to their emotionless state.

"What proof do you have for what you say you have found?" asked the taller of the two men.

Saunière pulled a rolled up piece of parchment from under his robe and handed it to the man. "It is a list of the tomb's contents."

Saunière watched as the two men examined the broken wax seal long ago placed on the document by the Knights Templar. After the parchment had been unfurled, both men read the ancient words covering its surface. Both had examined enough similarly-aged parchments to know this one was, in all probability, genuine.

When they finished reading, both men looked at Saunière with the exact same expression, shocked bewilderment.

"Is the Ark of the Covenant really there? You have seen it?"

Saunière nodded. "Yes, it's there. I have gazed upon its wondrous details and even touched it. I only took the smaller, easier to sell items. "

The men glanced at the list again before the taller man rolled it and placed it inside his jacket pocket. "What do you want, priest?"

"If I'm to keep this discovery a secret, I want to be compensated for my silence. I'm not a greedy man so I will leave it up to those back in Rome to decide on an agreeable amount."

"I assume you won't reveal its location to us," said the shorter man.

"You assume correctly. If I reveal its location, I am left with nothing to bargain with."

"Rome will pay you for the discloser of the location, but I fear you already know this."

"I'm certain they would; however, they don't deserve to know at this moment in time. The Church is responsible for many heinous crimes against the innocent, all done to protect their hold over the masses and the great wealth and power it brings. No, I want them to live with the thought that maybe one day the bodies will be discovered and their house will come crashing down around them."

The taller man's eyebrows rose. "You do know who we are?"

Saunière nodded. "The Inquisition."

"Then you know what you have said is blasphemy and labels you a heretic."

Saunière shrugged. "The foundations on which the Catholic Church has been built are a lie. If anyone blasphemes, it's those in Rome responsible for spreading and continuing their false religion. If anyone deserves to die at your murderous hands, it is them."

The three men stared at each other for a few moments.

"Have you informed anyone else of the tomb?" asked the tall man.

Saunière shook his head. "No one knows but me."

"It's plain to see you are set in your course of action and though I won't attempt to sway you from your chosen path, I feel I must warn you that you walk along a perilous road indeed." He fell to silence for a few moments. "Could you give us some privacy to discuss the matter?"

Saunière walked over to the terrace wall while the men conferred in hushed tones. He was well aware of the danger that might result from his attempt to blackmail the Church; however, desperate times leads to desperate measures. His thinking was that those in Rome would want to learn of the tomb's location and so readily accept his demands of payment, which would be a small pittance to them, and hope one day he would have a change of heart and inform them of the tomb's location. Killing him would end all hope of getting their hands on what was inside the tomb. He believed he had handled things correctly and no harm would befall him in the immediate future.

He could not have been more wrong.

While he gazed out at the landscape, he failed to notice one of the men pour a clear liquid into his glass of wine.

"We have reached a decision," said the tall man as they both stood. "We will return to Rome to make our report and show them the list of items from the tomb. You will be notified of the outcome in due course."

The two men picked up their wine.

"Before we leave, let us drink to a successful outcome to this matter where all parties involved receive exactly what they deserve."

Saunière picked up his wine, nodded to the two men and drank.

After saying their farewells, he watched the two men walk away until they disappeared from sight. His life was now well and truly in the hands of fate.

After the men had left, Marie went into the garden to speak to Saunière.

"How was the meeting?"

Saunière stared at her for a few moments as if deliberating his answer. "It went well, Marie." He clasped her hand. "Soon everything will be okay again."

Though Marie wanted to probe further, she held her tongue and cleared the table, leaving the half bottle of red wine and a glass for Saunière. She glanced at her priest, who seemed deep in thought. Without saying more, she left him alone.

It was three hours later when she discovered him. She had been preparing dinner and wondered where he had got to; he usually came and sat in the warm kitchen while she made dinner. The temperature had dropped as the sun began to set and he would be feeling the chill unless he'd lit the fire in the library. She glanced out through the window and at the Tour Magdala tower's chimney but saw no evidence of any smoke. She went to find out what he was doing.

As she climbed the steps up to the terrace, she noticed something on the ground by the tower's entrance. The low light made it difficult to distinguish what it was until she was almost upon it. Her heart skipped a beat when she recognized what it was. She rushed forward, knelt and cradled Saunière's head in her lap. His face was deathly pale. At first, she thought he was dead, but then he opened his eyes and looked at her.

"What is it, my love?" Marie asked, her voice sick with worry.

"Pain in my chest, I think it's my heart."

"I'll go and fetch help." She rushed away and returned a few moments later with two men from the village. They carried him into one of the bedrooms in the villa Bethania and laid him on the bed. Another villager had already gone to fetch the doctor, but it would be a while before he arrived from Couiza at the bottom of the hill. She thanked the men for their help, and they left. She sat on the bed holding Saunière's hand and stroking his brow. She hoped with all her heart it was nothing serious and he would recover. She prayed for his health to return.

Over the next couple of days, the priest's health grew steadily worse and realizing his recovery was doubtful, Father Rivière was sent for to hear Saunière's confession and to perform the last rites.

Rivière had been in the bedroom a little over two hours when he unexpectedly rushed from the bedroom and hurried down the stairs. Marie watched the priest go and knew by the man's stricken features that Saunière had confessed everything. She entered the bedroom and stayed by his side until he died the following day.

Snow fell as Saunière's coffin was carried from the church into the small cemetery and placed into the tomb he'd had constructed for this very purpose many years before. The whole village attended his funeral, and all bowed their heads as a final prayer was said in honor of the deceased priest.

The details of Saunière's will left everything he owned to Marie.

A few days later, Marie exited from the villa and walked over to the fire she had lit a few moments before. One by one, to ensure all were reduced to ashes, she dropped each piece of paper covered in Saunière's neat handwriting into the flames. It was Saunière's last request that these all be destroyed so the secrets they contained died with him.

The only clues to the location of the secret he had discovered now lay embedded in the decorations of his church.

CHAPTER 30

Carcassonne, France.

CREED OPENED THE small door set in the larger steel sliding shutter of the rented lock-up and stepped inside. Ben, Raven, and Pat followed him through. Setting eyes on it for the first time, Ben and Raven stared in surprise at the large motorhome that filled much of the workshop's space.

"Nice," exclaimed Ben. He placed the package he carried on a bench and walked around the vehicle. "So, where is it then?"

When they had arrived back in Carcassonne the day before, Creed had explained the plan to transport the bodies to Jerusalem. They would drive in a motorhome, acting like tourists. While they had been away a secret compartment had been constructed to conceal the bodies. It was this compartment Ben searched for.

Creed took a small remote control from his pocket, aimed it at the vehicle and pressed a button. The hum of an electric motor activated beneath the van drew Ben's attention, and he watched in fascination as the steel box fashioned to imitate the bottom of the motorhome lowered down and slid out. Creed released the concealed catches and dropped the side of the box. Ben peered inside. The compartment was lined with foam with enough room for the two bodies.

"What do you think?" Creed asked.

Ben smiled. "I think your plan might work after all."

"I told you it would. Come on, let's reunite Jesus with his head and then we can load the bodies." Creed walked over to a table covered with a large sheet and uncovered the two bodies. Mary Magdalene had already been wrapped in a shroud in preparation for the journey. Jesus had been wrapped up to the chest in preparation of Ben returning with the head.

Ben opened the box collected from England and carefully lifted out the head and carried it over to the body. He glanced around at the faces crowded around the table. All sensed something was about to happen when body and head were reunited. Ben positioned the head in place with the neck and removed his hands. Nothing happened.

"Well that was a bit of an anti-climax," said Pat.

"What were you expecting," asked Raven, "that Jesus would miraculously come alive or something?"

"Well, if the Bible is to be believed, there is precedence for such a thing."

"He hadn't been dead for two thousand years then," Creed added. "Let's get him wrapped up ready for his return home."

Ben eyes had remained fixed on Jesus. "Wait, something's happening."

They watched in fascination and disbelief when the skin around the wound where the head and body had been separated began to quiver. Tendrils reached out to claim what had been parted for so long and the skin melded together. Within a few moments, it was as if they had never been parted. Jesus' lips parted slowly to let out a long sigh before falling to silence again.

"Bloody hell, that was scary," Pat stated.

"I think if there was any doubt that this was the body of Christ, there could be none now," Ben said, still not quite believing what they'd just witnessed.

"Still means the Bible lied when it said his body ascended to heaven," Pat said.

Raven continued staring at the face of Jesus as she tried to understand what they had all just observed.

"Let's not get into a debate about the Bible and its truths and lies," Creed said. "Our concern is to do what is right, and that is to get these two back to the Temple Mount in Jerusalem. Let's wrap Jesus up and get them both on board so we can start our long journey. Like us all, I am eager to see an end to all this craziness and experience some sort of normality again."

"You really think normality is possible after what you have just witnessed," Pat asked. "I'm not saying I'm now a believer, but..." he looked at Jesus, "...it's bloody hard to explain."

"I think we should listen to Creed," Raven said. "We have witnessed something...miraculous, which if I hadn't seen with my own eyes, I wouldn't have believed, but debating the issue will get us nowhere, let's take them to Jerusalem and be done with it."

"Pat and I will finish wrapping him, while you two grab your stuff from the car and load it on board our temporary home," Creed said, eager to get started.

An hour later they exited the lock-up and began their long journey to Jerusalem.

After 2000 years, Mary and Jesus were going home.

THE TREASURE

CHAPTER 31

Jerusalem

FOUR THOUSAND, SEVEN hundred and twenty-two kilometers and fifty-nine hours later, they arrived in Jerusalem. As they approached the City just before dawn, they witnessed the rare and mystical experience of the first rays of the rising sun sweeping over the sand-colored stone buildings and the magnificent walls surrounding the ancient city. Due to the large size of their vehicle, they had no choice but to park outside the city in one of the tourist carparks. After locking the motorhome, they entered the City.

Following Creed's directions, they soon arrived at the Palatin Hotel; one of the oldest in Jerusalem and chosen because of its close proximity to the Old City where they would be working. They booked in, had an early breakfast and then wandered around the hauntingly beautiful city until they arrived at Creed's father's friend's house; an ancient stone dwelling that, like many of the buildings in the vicinity, had suffered the ravages of time and neglect. Creed searched an open joint in the stonework beside the entrance and fished out a key. He unlocked the rusty padlock securing the door and after leading them inside, slid the heavy bolt into place to prevent them from being disturbed. He led them across the sparsely furnished and dust covered room to another door, which creaked loudly when he pulled it open. They descended the stone steps into the dark cellar, and all welcomed the cooler temperature of the room. Even though it was still early morning, the temperature outside was already becoming uncomfortably hot. When Creed pulled a cord hanging from the ceiling, light flooded the small space. The only objects in the room were the tools Creed had arranged with the owner; an electric lead-light, a large pry bar, a pickaxe, and two shovels beside a pile of excavated earth and rock and the spoils from Creed's father's digging.

Creed pointed to the sunken hollow in the old paved floor. "That's the place. All we have to do is lift the slab, and we should see the tunnel." He grabbed the pry bar and with Pat's help lifted one of the large slabs and propped it against the wall.

All gazed at the small dark hole excavated by Creed's father.

Creed lay on the floor beside the opening, turned on a flashlight and poked it and his head inside. After a few moments, he explained what he had seen. "Well it's definitely a tunnel, but as my father said, it's blocked after a few meters, though nothing we can't clear."

Creed plugged the lead-light into a socket crammed with a pyramid of plugs, whose leads led off to various rooms of the house, placed it beside the hole and dropped down. The tunnel, a little over a meter wide, wasn't high enough for him to stand up in. He grabbed the light and walked bent over away from the hole. Ben, Pat, and Raven dropped into the tunnel behind him.

Though the tunnel was blocked in both directions, they would only clear the blockage heading towards the Temple Mount. To avoid the extra effort of lifting the rocks out of the tunnel, they decided to stack them in front of the blockage that would remain. They formed a chain and passed the rocks from one blockage to the other. Before long they glimpsed a clear space on the other side; the pile was only two meters deep.

Creed shone his torch through the gap. A tunnel stretched for as far as the light beam could reach. "Seems clear for as far as I can see," he informed the others and moved out of the way so they could all have a peek.

It took another hour before they had cleared enough rubble to allow them passage past the blockage. They switched on their headlamps and climbed over the remaining rocks. The tunnel this side gradually became higher and allowed them to stand upright.

"There are houses above us so keep your voices low," Creed warned.

The tunnel stretched straight almost fifty meters before it turned to the right and revealed a large rock that seemed to defy gravity and hung from the ceiling. Whoever had originally dug the passage had been worried enough to place two thick wooden props under the rock to support its weight.

Creed examined the ancient props and was surprised to find them stable and still performing the job they'd been placed there for.

"It's the dry air," explained Ben. "It's kept them from rotting, though we should be careful not to disturb them."

They carefully crawled under the overhanging rock and after a few more turns arrived at a dead end. A smooth block of stone that stretched the full height and width of the tunnel prevented them from progressing. It seemed whoever had dug the shaft, for some reason, had stopped here and chiseled the rock flat and smooth.

Creed rapped a knuckle on the stone. "It's solid, so I guess this is the end."

Ben laid a hand on the stone and began examining its edges. "Something's wrong. Why stop the tunnel here and spend so much effort smoothing the rock?"

"Whatever the reason, this is as far as we can go," reasoned Creed. "We'll have to put the bodies here. It's not ideal, but what other choice do we have?"

Reluctant to be defeated so easily, Ben searched with his fingers along the edges of the slab where it met the sides of the tunnel. His fingers detected a groove. "Does anyone have a knife or something thin?"

Pat moved closer to see what had caught Ben's interest. "What have you found?"

"I'm not sure."

Raven held out a large, sharp bladed knife. "Will this do?"

Ben glanced at the wicked looking blade. "Yes, thanks." He took the knife and began scraping at the edge of the slab.

Raven winced with each scrape of metal on stone that signaled the destruction of the finely honed blade.

After a few moments, Ben had cleared a joint down one side of the slab. "I don't think it's solid, but a door of some kind."

"How can it be a door," stated Pat. "There's no handle."

Ben scraped out the joint on the other side, and at the bottom he found a square piece of rock protruding from the joint. He cleared around it with the tip of the blade and then gripped it with one hand. After some effort, he managed to wiggle it free. He held up the wedge-shaped piece of stone for the others to see.

Creed took it from him. "What is it?"

"It's the lock!" Ben moved to the opposite side and pressed his weight against the slab. "Pat, give me a hand. Push the slab near the wall."

Pat did as requested, but it was only when Creed applied his force also that the slab moved and turned on a hidden pivot set in its center. A whoosh of stale air poured through the gap with a low screech, as if glad to be free. The door pushed a wave of sandy earth from the floor when it opened.

"Well I'll be damned," said Pat, when he peered through the newly revealed opening. "It's a room."

They all stared at the wooden door highlighted by their torches a couple of meters away.

Pat patted Ben on the back. "Well done, Englishman."

Ben picked up the knife he had placed on the floor and handed it back to Raven, "Thanks."

Raven studied the scratched and blunted blade and grimaced, she'd be lucky to burst a balloon with it now. "You're welcome." She slid the knife into its sheaf.

Ben led the way into the small room and crossed to the door. Accompanied by the tune of screeching hinges, he pushed it open and stepped through. The others followed.

They found themselves in a circular room with walls of rough-hewn stone and three exits. They crossed to the nearest two openings that were side-by-side and discovered each led to a stairway chiseled from the rock; one flight led up, the other down. The third exit was an arched opening that could be barred by a portcullis, which was now in the raised position. The mechanism to operate it stood to one side of the room. Ben walked over and glanced up at the portcullis, noticing it had a single bent prong.

"I wonder why they needed a portcullis," questioned Pat, when he joined Ben and shone his torch along the passage.

Ben shrugged. "They're normally used to keep people out, and with the operating mechanism this side, whatever it's protecting must be somewhere back there."

Creed, who had climbed the stairs to explore the higher level, returned to the top of the steps and called down. "Come look at this."

Ben, Pat, and Raven climbed the stairs to see what Creed had found.

"Is it gold?" asked Pat hopefully, who reached the top of the steps first to find Creed waiting for them.

Creed smiled. "No, Pat, it's not gold." After the others had joined them he aimed his flashlight at the floor.

They all stared at the many faint footprints in the sandy floor and scrape marks that hinted something substantial had been dragged along the ground.

"It might be an indication that whatever was once down here is long gone," offered Creed.

"The Romans or the Knights Templar, perhaps," suggested Ben.

Pat shone his light along the tunnel. "Where do they lead?"

"I haven't followed them yet as I wanted you all to see them first before I disturbed them, but let's find out."

They followed the trail to find that though some continued on along the passage, the majority of them ended halfway along the tunnel.

Ben pointed at the drag marks by the wall. "Whatever they were dragging they dragged it out of the wall." He knelt for a closer look and pointed at something. "You see this?"

All looked at the footprint Ben pointed out. The strange thing was that it was only half a footprint, the other half was under the wall."

"Another secret door!" Raven exclaimed.

"It has to be," Ben agreed.

They all stared at the wall, but none could see any evidence of a door as it looked exactly like the rest of the wall. The three men attempted to push what they thought were the edges of the door in case it pivoted open like the previous one but to no avail.

Ben took off his headlamp and used its light to examine the wall inch by inch. After a few minutes, he found a small faint cross etched into the rock a meter from the floor and pointed it out to the others.

"What's it mean?" Pat asked.

Ben ran a finger along the lines of the cross, "I'm not sure."

He tried applying pressure at the same time as pushing on the rock, but nothing happened. He continued with his examination until he found a second identical cross near the floor.

"There's another one here. Let me try something." Ben climbed to his feet.

The others moved back to give him room and watched when he applied pressure on the lower cross with his foot and the higher one with his hand. All heard the soft click and witnessed the rock magically swing aside when Ben applied pressure.

Raven smiled at Ben's knack for such things. She was beginning to understand how he'd survived the perils of Rosslyn Catacombs, and her brothers hadn't.

Ben shone his light around the revealed chamber and gasped in fright at the monster highlighted in the beam.

Concern appeared on Creed's face. "What is it?"

"A demon!" Ben moved farther into the room and stood aside so the others could enter.

"Bloody hell, its Asmodeus!" exclaimed Pat on spying the demon poised near the wall at one side of the room.

"It looks alive," said Creed.

A worried look appeared on Pat's face as he stared at the demon. "It's not, is it?"

Ben smiled, "I think that's unlikely, although, according to the Bible, Asmodeus was tricked by Solomon into helping build his Temple and then magically bound to guard the Temple Treasure, so perhaps it still is."

Raven glanced around at the almost empty chamber. "Not doing very well in that regard is it?" she quipped.

The others surveyed the room. Apart from the demon, a large block of marble and objects covered by a cloth at the far end of the room, the chamber was empty.

Creed pointed at the raised block of marble. "I wonder if that's where Jesus once rested."

Ben shrugged. "Impossible to say for sure, but it's a feasible assumption. If he did then it's likely the Templars took him and probably the reason they were granted so many unique favors by the pope."

Ben strolled over to the demon. Though not an exact match, this one looked far more menacing, he was amazed at the similarities to the demon Saunière had commissioned for his church. Creed was correct; the creature did look real, alive almost. He warily prodded it with a finger. It felt like stone. He stared into the creature's eyes and sensed the uncomfortable sensation that Asmodeus was staring back at him. He shook off the feeling and turned away.

"I wonder why whoever took the rest of the stuff didn't take it all," Creed asked no one in particular, as he paused by objects whose shapes were hinted at by forms in the large cloth draped over them.

"Maybe its worthless junk," suggested Pat. "It would be just my luck if it was."

Creed walked to one side of the covered objects. "I doubt worthless junk would be stored in a secret underground chamber beneath the Temple Mount. Whatever's here will be something special." He grabbed one corner of the cover. "Help me uncover them."

Pat held the corner opposite Creed, and together they dragged back the cloth and let it fall to the floor behind the objects.

No one noticed the demon's eyes move. Too long had he been forced to dwell down here in the dark; he yearned to be free. If any of them touched one of the sacred treasures, he would be.

Asmodeus waited to act.

As the cloud of dust displaced by the uncovering settled, all stared at the wondrous treasure before them.

Raven's eyes roamed over the uncovered objects. "Doesn't look like worthless junk to me."

"Solomon's treasure," Ben exclaimed, awestruck. "Or most of it."

"It's magnificent," Creed exclaimed.

"It must be worth millions," said Pat, rubbing his hands together excitedly.

Even though not everything was fashioned from precious metal, it didn't diminish its worth in monetary or historical terms. They all gazed at each object in turn. Ben, who had carried out research into the Temple treasure, recognized most of the objects and shared his knowledge with the astonished group. The treasure hoard included the table of showbread—a small golden table measuring 3 feet by 1.5 feet and 2 feet 3 inches high—it once stood in the Temple on the right side of the Holy Place across from the Menorah. It would have held bread baked by the priests, only permissible for them to consume and could only be eaten in the Holy Place because it was Holy. *Showbread,* also called *bread of the presence,* because it was to be always in the Lord's presence.

Ben pointed to the golden altar of incense and explained that it would have been positioned in front of the curtain that separated the Holy Place from the Holy of Holies. This altar, which was square with each side measuring 1.5 feet and 3 feet high, was smaller than the Brazen Altar next to it. The Brazen Altar, bronze altar, or altar of sacrifice would have been situated inside the courtyard upon entering the gate to the tabernacle. It measured 7.5 feet on all four sides and 4.5 feet deep with four horns projecting from its top four corners with a bronze grating inside to hold the animal to be sacrificed.

The group listened attentively as Ben continued to describe the Laver, or basin—a large bowl that would have been filled with water and located halfway between the Brazen Altar and the Holy Place.

"Although God didn't give specific measurements for the Laver," Ben explained, "it was to be made entirely of bronze. As a cleansing process, the priests had to wash their hands and feet in it before entering the Holy Place."

Ben turned his attention to the object they had all recognized; the huge solid gold Menorah. Formed with a central branch from which three branches extended from each side to form a total of seven. Seven lamps holding olive oil and wicks would have stood on top of each that the priests would have kept burning. Each branch had been fashioned to resemble branches of an almond tree, containing buds, blossoms, and flowers.

"How many of these things are there," Pat asked.

Ben shrugged. "If this is the real Menorah, as I imagine it to be as it's included with the other Temple Treasure items, the one in the Temple in France must be a copy."

"It would seem so," Creed agreed. "Or maybe there were two originals."

"I've never come across any evidence that more than one existed, but I guess we'll never know for certain." Ben turned his attention to the five garments on the table of the showbread that would have been worn by the Temple priests.

He had to think for a moment until he remembered their names and pointed to one of the garments. "This one's called the Ephod, the outermost garment that resembles an elaborate apron."

The Ephod was made from white linen interwoven with threads of gold that seemed to have weathered the ravages of time surprisingly well. Onyx stones that held the garment together at the shoulders reflected their torchlight.

Ben explained that the stones were inscribed with the names of the twelve tribes of Israel. "The blue robe next to it would have been worn underneath the Ephod. The small gold bells you see sown around its hem were so even when the priest couldn't be seen he could still be heard, though I have no idea why this was necessary."

Some of the bells had detached from their moorings and lay on the table or had fallen to the floor. Laid out beside the blue robe was the white robe that would have been worn beneath the blue one. Once a spotless white robe of woven fabric made of the finest quality, it had yellowed with age and had the impression its delicate cloth might fall to dust if touched.

Ben pointed at another of the garments. "Perhaps the most precious and what seems to be the best preserved of all the garments is the breastplate. This would have been worn by the High Priest in the Holy Temple."

Pat eagerly stared at the precious breastplate that measured nine inches square and folded double with four rows of three precious stones attached at the corners with gold rings and blue cords. He knew all the objects were priceless. Any single one would fetch an incredibly high price to the right buyer, and every museum in the world would sell their souls on being able to exhibit such a collection.

"Each of the twelve precious stones represented one of the tribes of Israel," Ben informed them. "And lastly there is the High Priest's Mitznefet, or Mitre, made from pure gold. The rest of the trinkets would probably have been used in various religious ceremonies."

Their eyes wandered across the many gold and silver cups and goblets, some encrusted with precious gems, the golden bowls, and plates.

"Wondrous as it is, let's not disregard the reason why we're here," said Raven and breaking the spell they had all fallen under without realizing. She felt a sense of unease that she failed to explain and was keen to complete their mission and be free of this place. "The treasure has been here for many hundreds of years, so it will wait a while longer until we are finished with our business."

"Raven is correct," Creed agreed. He turned away from the treasure and looked at the marble block. "This chamber will make an excellent tomb for Jesus and Mary, but I suggest we check there are no other entrances down leading here, and then return to our hotel to work out how to move the bodies from the motorhome to the house."

They followed Creed from the chamber.

Pat, the last to exit the room, turned to look longingly at the treasure once more before stepping through the door.

Asmodeus watched them go.

He knew they would return.

As to be expected, the conversation during the meal in their hotel while they waited for nightfall concerned the Temple Treasure and their, soon to be enacted, clandestine operation. During the day the streets were crowded with tourists wandering from one ancient site to another and locals going about their business. However, at night most of Jerusalem's visitors were wary of treading the Old City's dimly lit streets, darker alleys, uneven steps, and rough pathways, and kept to the safer main thoroughfares. There would still be people about during the night but in significantly reduced numbers. This suited their purpose to avoid as many inquisitive eyes as possible while they moved the bodies to the house. To pass the time they'd visited some of the ancient sites and purchased traditional full-length robes from the market to help them blend in with the local population.

When it was finally time to transport the bodies, they collected the old wooden hand-pulled cart Creed had hired earlier and dragged it to the carpark outside the city. After checking there was no one about, they loaded the bodies, and the two stretchers they had brought with them to maneuver the them through the tunnels, onto the cart and covered them with a tarpaulin.

It took twenty minutes to pull the cart to the house and unload the bodies.

Creed shut and bolted the door with a relieved sigh. "I'm glad that's over with."

They had passed two patrolling Temple guards on their journey through the narrow streets, but luckily they barely gave them a second glance.

From here on it was plain sailing, or so they thought.

CHAPTER 32

Asmodeus

CONCEALED WITHIN THE shadows shrouding the dimly lit alley, the man had watched the four furtively acting people unload the cart of its cargo and enter the house. Even in the weak light, it was obvious they had carried two bodies inside. Though confused by what he had seen, he was sure the three men and a woman were up to no good, and he could profit from it. He pondered his next action as he approached the house and peered through the gap running down the hinge side of the warped door. He glimpsed the woman, carrying one end of a stretcher laden with one of the bodies, disappear through a door. The angle of the stretcher indicated the bodies were being moved down to the cellar. Though disguised as locals, their voices had labeled them as foreigners.

Well aware his reward would be linked with the amount of knowledge he had to confide, he examined the door for a way in. Though he had heard the bolt slid home, to an experienced thief like him it posed no problem. He slipped the curved knife from his robe's waistband, slid it through the gap and used the blade to push the bolt back until the door swung open and cringed at the noise it made. After listening for a few seconds to make sure those within hadn't heard, he slipped inside.

Unaware of the figure watching them from the top of the steps, Ben and Pat dropped into the tunnel with the two stretchers that would have been too awkward to maneuver through the opening with the bodies upon them. Creed and Raven carefully passed down one shrouded body at a time before joining them in the tunnel. After slipping off their robes, Pat and Creed carried Jesus, while Ben and Raven carried Mary.

The intruder descended the steps, crossed to the hole and peered inside. A greedy smile appeared on his lips when he realized his profit had just increased substantially. He would inform the Temple guards of this act of defilement to their sacred mount by westerners, the Jerusalem district police and perhaps the Israeli Antiquities Authority also. He exited the house and went to sell the valuable information. Soon the streets would be filled with people calling out for the westerners' blood.

They soon reached the treasure chamber and placed Mary and Jesus side-by-side on the large slab of marble.

When Pat stepped away, he noticed some gold coins partially covered by the sandy earth covering the floor. By the time his search had finished, he had found twenty-four coins. "That's six each," he beamed.

Their attention then turned to the Temple Treasure.

"Do we take it?" Creed asked.

"Of course. Why wouldn't we?" questioned Pat.

"Whoever looted this place before, probably the Knights Templar, for some reason thought it wiser to leave it here," said Ben. "I've been asking myself 'why'?"

"Does it matter?" asked Pat, confused by their reluctance to take the priceless items.

Ben's glance around the room ended on the demon, whose eyes stared at you wherever you were in there. An optical illusion he supposed. "I think we should leave them. They are too recognizable to be able to sell without questions being asked about how they were obtained, and some are too big to fit through the entrance hole anyway."

"I agree," said Creed. "They'll cause too many problems and are too sacred not to imagine others will want to claim them, which will probably bring more killers after us. Leave them here."

Pat wore a disappointed frown. "I suppose that includes the Menorah?"

Ben nodded. "Especially the Menorah."

"Whatever you decide, I suggest you get a move on as I think we should leave," said Raven. "We've been lucky so far, and it might not last."

"Well I've been through too much not to take something," declared Pat, heading for the treasure he stared longingly at. His fingers hovered over the artifacts as he contemplated which one to take.

Asmodeus watched the human's hand move from one object to another, willing him to touch just one to free him. The human would be dead a few moments later.

Pat glanced behind and noticed the others had left the room. He looked at the shrouded forms of Jesus and Mary and back at the treasure.

He sighed deeply, turned away from the treasure and headed for the door.

If Asmodeus could have moved his lips to scream, it would have echoed through the tunnels and likely be heard by those in the Old City above. His frustration at seeing his chance of freedom slip away was almost more than he could endure. He cursed the human heading for the exit and wondered how many hundreds of years more must he suffer this torment. A flicker of hope appeared in its eyes when the human halted by the exit, turned and gazed back at the treasure.

Asmodeus silently goaded him on.

What the hell, I'll never get this opportunity again. Pat walked briskly over to the treasure. Surely it would be okay to take something small as a keepsake, a memento of their adventure. There were plenty of cups and trinkets that didn't seem to be Holy objects. He picked up a solid gold, jewel-encrusted goblet and exited the chamber.

Asmodeus would have shouted for joy, but his mouth wasn't working. Something was wrong. Why wasn't he free? He attempted to move his limbs, but they refused to budge. His eyes flicked at the door when it closed and sealed him once again inside. His frustration knew no bounds. He screamed. His lips moved slightly. He forced his head to turn. It trembled with the strain. He had been paralyzed for so long it was taking time for his muscles to regain their functions. With all the effort he could muster, he forced his limbs to respond. They moved slightly. Hope replaced his frustration; a feeling he'd not felt in an extremely long time. He leaned forward. The heavy basin of water atop his shoulders pushed him off balance. He tumbled forward and crashed to the floor. The basin rolled across the ground and struck the cave wall with a loud bang that echoed around the room.

Ben paused and looked back along the tunnel. "What was that?" He then noticed the goblet Pat held and knew exactly what had caused the sound. "RUN!"

Though the others were unaware of the reason for Ben's anxiety, they trusted his judgment and ran.

Ben glanced behind when the demon smashed through the rock door and collided with the opposite wall. Dazed by the impact, Asmodeus shook his head, climbed unsteadily to his feet and looked straight at Ben. The demon smiled inhumanly and ran awkwardly towards him as its stiff muscles were forced into action.

Creed led them up the stairs, into the small room and slammed the door shut. Once they were all through the pivot door, they pushed it closed, and Ben forced the wedge back into place to lock it.

"What is it, Ben?" asked Raven, taking deep breaths.

"Asmodeus has awakened, probably when Pat stole part of the Temple Treasure."

Though Raven had difficulty believing what she'd just heard, she didn't doubt it was the truth and another of the long list of extraordinary events she had witnessed lately. She glanced at Pat. "You fool."

"It's not my fault. How could I know this would happen?"

"Let's keep moving as I'm not convinced that door will stop the demon if he realizes where we've gone," Ben warned.

They all rushed along the tunnel.

Asmodeus paused at the top of the steps and sniffed the air as he turned his head until he spied the closed door. He rushed over, ripped it effortlessly from its hinges and threw it across the room. Disappointed to find the room empty, he entered. He followed the scent of his prey to the back wall and ran clawed hands over its surface. The humans had somehow passed through the wall. He slammed a shoulder against the wall and felt it move fractionally. Asmodeus smiled.

A loud crash echoed along the tunnel as Ben crawled under the hanging rock. "Quick, Pat, give me a hand to kick out the supports.

While Ben kicked at one prop, Pat kicked at the other. The thick wood posts wedged tightly under the rock, creaked and groaned.

Asmodeus appeared around a bend in the passage and rushed at them with a cruel smile on his lips.

In desperation, Pat threw the goblet. "You can have it back, now leave us alone," he shouted, and he put all his strength behind his next kick.

The goblet struck Asmodeus on the head without inflicting any damage. When he realized what the humans were attempting, he dived onto the ground and slid towards the space under the rock. With a final kick from each of them, the two supports came free. The rock hung there for a few seconds before it fell. The force of the large rock striking the ground rumbled along the tunnel.

"There's no way he'll be able to shift that, he's trapped," stated Pat, confidently.

Ben was less confident. "I hope you're right."

They fled along the tunnel and caught up with Creed and Raven.

As they were replacing the paving slab to cover the opening in the cellar floor, they heard faint, but unmistakably angry, voices wafting down to them.

"That doesn't sound good," said Raven.

Creed agreed. "Let's go!"

They rushed up the stairs, and when they exited the house, they were greeted by a sight they couldn't have imagined beforehand.

The informant had done his job well. After informing the Temple Mount police, the Jerusalem district police and Israeli Antiquities Authority of the two bodies, that might be locals the strangers had murdered, and the sacred Mount was being defiled, he also told anyone he met in the streets. The news had spread like wildfire through the close-knit community.

The informant smiled at the angry crowd formed from mingled religions and the branches of authority attempting to make their way to the front of the surging mass to take control of the situation. If they didn't bring some sort of order to the chaos, it was likely, if they caught up with the culprits, they would be stoned and probably killed. Though they didn't care about the safety of the westerners, they did care about the bad publicity it would bring and the drop in tourism revenue that might follow.

"Now I know what Frankenstein felt like when faced with an angry mob," said Ben, as he stared at the seemingly unstoppable horde of hate and revenge-fuelled people funneled into the narrow confines of the alley.

Though the many angry, shouted curses were unintelligible to them, their meanings were transparent.

Creed reacted quickly. He grabbed the cart and jammed it sideways across the alley. "It's time we left Jerusalem."

"Amen to that!" Ben replied.

The sound of the crowd chasing them gradually faded when Creed led them on a twisting journey through dark alleys, some no wider than a person, and down steep stone steps worn by the millions of feet that had trod them throughout the City's long history. Ten minutes later they arrived at the city wall. They ran through one of its gateways, relieved to see their vehicle a little over one hundred meters away, they sprinted towards it. Returning to the hotel to collect their belongings was not an option any of them considered. Their only thought was to leave Jerusalem as fast as possible.

Glad to be away from the noisy, rampaging mob he had set into motion, the informant sat on a rock against the city wall. Though he pitied the westerners when they were eventually caught, he felt no guilt. As he proceeded to count the money he'd received for his actions, he looked towards the sound of running footsteps. The four westerners he had informed on rushed over to a large motorhome and scrambled inside. It seemed that for now, they had escaped the angry pack. He smiled greedily as he memorized the number plate. It was proving to be a very profitable night. He stood when the vehicle's engine broke the silence and began to pull away. He was about to head back into the City to sell this fresh snippet of information when the wall beside him exploded, and rocks and dust sprayed out and crashed to the ground. As the wall above the freshly made opening began to collapse, something emerged from the dust cloud.

The informant stared at the monstrosity that appeared, and when the fearsome devil turned and looked at him, he was so terrified he pissed himself.

In two bounds the demon was upon him.

His large hands picked him up, and the informant stared into the face of death.

One of the demon's hands gripped his head, and he briefly experienced excruciating pain as his head was ripped from his neck.

He then felt nothing.

The money he had been holding fell to the ground with metallic tinkles. His body joined them with a soft thud.

Asmodeus stared after the strange, fast-moving wagon and wondered how it moved with no horses or oxen pulling it. He recognized one of its occupants. Only when they were all dead would his freedom truly begin. He smiled at the havoc he would soon wreak upon this world. He threw the head at the fleeing vehicle.

"Well, I don't think we'll be welcome back anytime soon," said Ben, thankful to be heading away from Jerusalem the frenzied mob.

"And the demon is trapped in the tunnels, so that's the last we'll see of him," added Pat, happily.

When something struck the window beside Ben, he glanced in shock at the face splattered on the window before it fell from his sight. He peered out and glimpsed Asmodeus leap down to a lower level and run after them. "I wouldn't be so certain of that, Pat. He's back! Step on it, Creed."

Creed glanced in a side mirror and saw the demon approaching fast. He pressed the gas pedal to the floor. The large heavy vehicle increased its speed slowly. It wouldn't be fast enough.

Something smashed into the side of the vehicle. Ben stared out of the window and into the eyes of the demon.

Asmodeus smiled cruelly and pulled his fist back to strike the window.

Creed glimpsed the demon hanging onto the side of the motorhome in the side mirror; he veered across to the opposite side of the road.

Ben backed away from the window when Asmodeus drove his fist at the glass. Suddenly he was gone, knocked off by the corner of a building that exploded in a cloud of rubble and dust. He rushed to the back window but saw no sign of the demon.

Creed narrowly missed an oncoming car as he overtook a long construction lorry laden with heavy steel beams moving slowly around a curve in the road.

Raven's eyes searched for the demon. "Do you think he's dead?"

"I doubt it," Ben replied. "I'm not even sure demons can die, not by normal means anyway." He remembered something. "But they can be controlled. The ring!" He rushed into his bedroom at the rear of the motorhome and searched through the drawer where he thought he'd placed it earlier.

The van lurched to one side. Asmodeus was back.

Creed fought to control the swaying vehicle as the demon climbed on top. Pat and Raven stared at the roof and followed the dents that appeared with the demon's progress along the flimsy aluminum skin. Pat screamed and dodged to one side when the demon's foot crashed through a plastic skylight. Raven reacted quickly and pulled her knife from its sheaf. Hoping its dulled edge would prevent what was needed of it, she plunged it into to demon's calf.

Asmodeus screamed and yanked his leg back through the skylight, snatching the knife from Raven's grip.

Pat looked at Raven. "Don't you have a gun? You always have a gun."

Raven shook her head as she noticed the drops of blood on the floor and then looked at Pat. "It bleeds."

"Of course it bleeds. You just shoved your bloody great knife into its leg."

Raven smiled. "If it bleeds, it can die."

"Yeah, well, good luck with that, but remember, we also bleed and we're a lot easier to kill."

Raven barged by Pat and fell into the passenger seat when Creed swerved in an attempt to dislodge Asmodeus from the roof.

The demon fell off balance, grabbed hold of a protrusion to stop itself and ripped a hole in the roof when it fell to the ground and rolled along the road in the speeding van's wake. It jumped to its feet, threw the piece of metal away and ran after the vehicle.

Creed glimpsed the demon rushing at them in the wing mirror. "Ben!" he called out, desperately. "Whatever you're planning, I suggest you do it soon before Asmodeus rips this van apart."

Pat glanced at the hole in the roof and then through the rear window. The demon gained on them with surprising speed.

Thrown about by the erratic movements of the van, Ben found it hard to keep his balance while he searched for the ring. He plunged a hand at the back of the drawer and dragged its contents forward. The ring was amongst them. He snatched it up and rushed out of the bedroom.

Creed glanced at Raven. "Any ideas?"

Raven stared at the road ahead. "Maybe? Let's swap places."

Creed glanced at the speedometer; it read ninety-two kilometers an hour. "At this speed?"

"You can always pull over."

A glance in the mirror revealed the demon was almost upon them again. "How do we do this?"

"Move behind me." Raven stood and gripped the wheel while Creed squirmed past her and removed his foot from the accelerator at the last possible moment. Raven quickly took his place in the driver's seat and pressed her foot hard on the throttle as the van began to slow.

Ben glanced out of the window at the demon running level with the van, and they stared at each other briefly. The demon flashed him a cruel smile. Ben smiled back. A look of dread spread over the demon's face when Ben held up the ring. Asmodeus screeched in horror of the remembered torment he'd already endured, and that might soon be thrust upon him again. He watched the human move the ring toward his finger. He mustn't let him slip it on. The demon slammed his weight into the side of the speeding vehicle. The force was so great it lifted the van off one set of its wheels. When it slammed back to the ground, Ben pitched forward, struck his head against the corner of a cupboard and slumped unconscious. The ring rolled along the floor and dropped into the small stairwell by the exit door.

Pat rushed over to help Ben.

Creed had witnessed Ben's fall. "Is he okay, Pat?"

Pat glanced at Creed, "I think so. He took a nasty bang to the head, unconscious, but alive."

Creed glanced out at the demon. "Not a bad state to be in at the moment. Does he have the ring?"

Pat glanced at Ben's ring-less fingers and did a quick search of the immediate area. "I can't see it."

Creed turned to Raven, "Time for plan B. What do you want me to do?"

Raven glanced at the wing mirror as the demon prepared to leap onto the van again. "For now, hold on tight." She spun the wheel to the left.

Everything that wasn't secured shot across the van as it skidded with a squeal of protesting tires into a tight turn and drove off the road.

The demon leaped as the van turned. His clawed fingers scrapped gouges in the thin metal body that veered away from its grasp. He tumbled into a roll, regained his footing and ran after the van. He leaped again. This time landing on target as Raven steered the van out of its turn and sped back the way they had come, but this time over rougher ground. The van lurched and constantly bumped, jolting everyone inside and the unwelcome passenger on the roof.

Creed wondered why they were heading back towards Jerusalem and the angry mob waiting for them, but he trusted Raven's judgment. "What's the plan?"

"We're going to kill it!"

"Okay, I like that, but how?"

The van swayed with the weight of the demon as he clawed his way along the roof towards the front.

"We need the demon at the front."

"It's trying to get in," Pat yelled in fright.

Creed turned. A large fist punched through the roof.

Pat stared at the demon's face framed in the broken skylight and backed away pulling Ben's unconscious form with him when it's clawed hand reached for him.

"Pat, keep him there for the moment," Raven ordered.

"And how the hell am I supposed to do that, invite him in for a beer?"

A rush of warm air entered the van.

Raven glanced at the window Creed had opened and guessed what he was about to do. "Be careful."

"I'm climbing out unarmed onto the top of a speeding motorhome driven over rough ground with a hell-spawned demon on its roof, why the concern?"

Raven smiled.

Creed poked his head and shoulders out through the opening. His body and feet quickly followed, and he disappeared from sight. To lessen the jolting, Raven eased off on the accelerator slightly. She glanced to her left and saw what she hoped to see. She turned as gently as she could towards the road to avoid sending Creed and the Demon tumbling off.

Creed felt the van turn and gripped tighter onto the roof-rack rails. The wind beat at his back, flapping his shirt like a flag. He whistled to catch the demon's attention. Asmodeus turned and was surprised to see one of the humans on the roof. He headed for him. Creed backed away until his feet hung over the front of the van and was almost jolted off when Raven bumped back onto the road. The van swerved and then straightened up. When a glance along the road revealed Raven's plan to Creed, he realized just how crazy this beautiful woman was. However, now committed to the course of action, his only option was to follow it through and hope it proved successful.

The driver of the lorry did a double take when he glanced at the reflection in his wing mirror. Though he found the sight the monster on top of the fast approaching motorhome impossible to believe, he trusted his eyes and pressed his foot fully on the accelerator in the hope of coaxing more speed out of the old engine. The weight of the load it carried held it back, and he mouthed a silent prayer to his God.

Asmodeus leaped at Creed.

As the demon flew through the air, Creed did the only thing he could. He let go. He slipped down the large sloping windscreen as the demon landed in the space he'd just vacated. The roof crumpled. The screen blew out.

Hundreds of pieces of glass shot into the air and into the van.

Raven shielded her eyes.

No longer supported by the glass, Creed fell into the van. He slid off the wide dashboard, and as his feet landed on the floor, he twisted and landed in the passenger seat.

Raven smiled. "Back so soon?"

"Yeah, it's a bit crowded on top." Creed glanced ahead. "You really think this mad plan of yours will work?"

"With luck, it might."

"I'm not convinced we have much left of the good variety, so don't hold your breath."

The demon appeared and landed with its feet on the wide bumper. He peered into the van and lunged for Creed. Raven swerved from side-to-side, forcing Asmodeus to concentrate on holding on.

Ben groaned.

Pat dragged his eyes away from the formidable demon to check on his friend. "Are you okay, buddy?"

Ben sat up and winced from the throbbing pain in his head. He noticed Asmodeus perched on the front of the van and realized it hadn't been a bad dream he'd been experiencing but a living nightmare. He remembered the ring. He scrambled about the floor, desperately searching for it. He eventually spied it in the small stairwell by the door.

The demon regained his balanced and grabbed at Creed again. This time its large hand circled the human's neck. He lifted the choking human out of the van to smash his fragile body onto the ground speeding by.

"Stop!"

The demon froze and peered into the van. One of the humans walked towards him with a fist held out in front. On a finger was *the ring*.

"I order you to be still, Asmodeus."

Asmodeus glared at Ben and yelled in frustration.

"I have the ring that controls you, Asmodeus. You must do as I command. Now put that man safely back inside the vehicle."

Asmodeus was unable to disobey, and though he had no idea what a vehicle was, he placed the human back in the seat but kept his grip around the man's neck as he hadn't been given the order to release it yet. He squeezed tighter. Maybe he would have time to kill one of them.

Ben stepped closer. "Release your hold, Demon."

Reluctantly, Asmodeus did as commanded.

Creed clutched his neck and gasped for breath.

"What now, human? Am I to be banished underground again?"

Ben gazed past the demon and saw what was up ahead and drawing nearer. "Are you sure about this, Raven?"

Raven nodded. "Unless you have a better idea?"

Ben hadn't. Under the current circumstances, returning to Jerusalem to enslave the demon under the Temple Mount again would be suicide. There was also no way to get they could do it without being seen. "No, Demon, you will not be banished. It's time to end your torment."

The demon looked at him in surprise, wondering at the meaning of the human's words. *Was he to be set free?*

"Remain where you are and do not speak again," Ben ordered.

The demon's gaze flicked to the rear view mirror fixed to the cabin roof that had been knocked askew and now pointed forward. Reflected in the mirror, he saw his fate fast approaching. When he looked back at Ben, his eyes pleaded for mercy.

Briefly, Ben felt sorry for the creature, though he knew in his heart that Asmodeus was evil and wouldn't be able to fight his urge to destroy and kill. The demon's death was the best solution.

Raven steered the front of the motorhome to line it up with the back of the fast approaching lorry. "I think you'd better move to the back, Creed."

Creed glanced ahead and before joining Ben and Pat at the rear of the van. At the last possible moment, Raven leaped from her seat and rushed for the back of the van.

The van jolted when it struck.

The lorry driver, unable to avoid what was coming, knew that even if the flimsy motorhome struck him, as seemed to be its intention, the solidly built truck and the heavy load it carried would probably survive unscathed. He glanced between the road ahead and the vehicle speedily drawing closer with every second. He could see the monster perched on the front of the van clearly now and recognized by its horns; it was a demon. When the motorhome increased its speed, he guessed the driver's intention. They were going to kill the it. To help, he kept the lorry in as straight a line as possible and said a prayer for himself and those inside the oncoming vehicle. When the collision happened, he hardly felt it. There was a slight jolt and then it was over. Though unsure if the driver's plan had been successful, he was certain he wasn't going to stop and find out. He kept his foot pressed firmly on the accelerator.

The demon screamed when his chest exploded from the steel I-beam ripping through it. Overhanging the flatbed lorry by three meters, the steel beam continued to speed through the van. Raven dropped to the floor, and the beam passed inches above her. When the motorhome struck the back of the flatbed lorry the front of it crumpled like paper. The force from the van's sudden stop propelled Ben, Creed, and Pat forward. Ben and Creed managed to stop themselves, but Pat shot forward and landed atop the I-beam. When the heavily laden lorry continued on its journey and dragged the I-beam back through the van, Pat rolled off and watched the I-beam slide out of the front and deposit Asmodeus in the crushed cab. The demon slumped to the floor, but amazingly, his eyes were still open and looking straight at them.

"It's still alive," gasped Pat.

Raven climbed to her feet. "Not for long." She hurried forward, pulled the knife from the demon's leg and grabbed one of its horns. She lifted its large head until its neck was exposed and swiped the blade across its throat.

While blood poured from the wound, the demon stared at Ben.

"It's okay, Asmodeus, you can die now." Ben watched its eyes close. A last sigh signaled Asmodeus' death.

The demon had been vanquished!

The motorhome slowly rolled off the road and come to a halt on a rough patch of ground.

All were silent for a few moments.

"Is it all over now?" Pat asked.

Ben nodded. "Yes, I think it is."

Creed took control. "Okay, everyone grab what stuff you want, we're leaving. The police will probably arrive shortly."

As most of their stuff was at the hotel in Jerusalem, there wasn't really anything to collect. Luckily, everyone had been traveling light, and they'd kept their passports on them in case they had to leave in a hurry. Realizing they might have a long walk to the next town or village, they each grabbed some bottles of water. Pat grabbed a few bottles of beer.

When they had all exited the van, Creed stuffed a rag into the petrol tank. As soon as it had soaked up some fuel, he lit it and stood back. As they walked away the flames grabbed hold with a whoosh when the petrol tank caught fire and quickly spread through the van. Soon there would be little left of the motorhome except for its metal shell and, except in myth and the lorry driver's mad ramblings, no evidence the demon had ever existed.

CHAPTER 33

Germany - A few weeks later

PAT TOOK ANOTHER swig of his beer to empty the bottle and looked at the man sat opposite. "After we set fire to the motorhome, we walked to a nearby town, purchased a second-hand car for cash and headed back home. As compensation for my efforts, Creed gave me some money, quite a lot actually, which is how I was able to afford this place."

The man, who had been listening to his story for the past two hours, glanced around at the house and garden whose terrace they now sat on and provided an excellent view of the nearby mountains. "It's very nice, and then what happened?"

Pat reached into the cooler beside him and fished out a fresh beer. "You want another?"

"No thanks."

Pat twisted off the cap, took a long drink and then continued. "Creed thought it best we split up until things died down. Though we weren't worried about anyone coming after us, because as far as we knew any likely to were now dead, the Vatican has a long memory and might send more men after us. Not that it would do them much good now. The bodies are secure, the Cardou Temple entrances are blocked and access to the chambers beneath the Temple Mount, now impossible, well until another tunnel surfaces. But as Creed said, it's better to be safe than sorry. I returned to Germany and bought this house, Creed disappeared, and Ben and Raven returned to England, and that's where it happened. The reason you sought me out."

The interviewer checked the battery level on the digital recording device, the story so far had been fascinating, and he didn't want to miss the ending. He nodded for Pat to continue.

After…the incident, Raven visited me to let me know what had happened and to warn me to be on my guard…

Cornwall, England.

Ben steered the car into the driveway and drove the short distance to the house nestled beside a small forest of oak, birch, and pine. He switched off the engine and glanced at Raven beside him. "Well, what do you think?"

Raven looked at the typical thatched roof English cottage and smiled. "It's lovely."

"As are you," he leaned towards her and kissed her gently on the lips.

They climbed out of the car and entered the home they had rented for a year.

It happened two months, two weeks and four days later.

Ben sat on the shaded patio typing on his laptop. He paused to take a sip of wine and stare at the rugged Devon coast stretched out below him, where the sea lapped gently against the rocky cove. A sense of contentment washed over him. He turned on hearing Raven approach. She wore nothing but white lacy knickers and a seductive smile.

"I see you're admiring the view."

Ben smiled. "I was, but I find this one much more delightful."

She leaned down, and they kissed passionately. She then picked up his glass and took a sip of the red wine. "Have you finished your book yet?"

Ben dragged his eyes away from her beautiful breasts and glanced at the laptop screen. "Almost. I'm just finishing the final chapter."

"Good, then perhaps you'll show *me* some attention." She smiled, playfully.

"Perhaps, or I could start another book, I have this great idea..."

Raven pouted. "You do, and I'll throw you and your laptop off the cliff."

Ben laughed. "Don't worry, I won't be writing another for a while. You and your beautiful body will have my undivided attention."

"That's good to hear. I'm going to take a shower, and then you're all mine."

"Always and forever." Ben watched her beautiful bum wiggle as she entered the house. He sighed with pleasure and turned his attention back to his book. A few moments later he heard the hiss of the shower and smiled as he imagined the water cascading down her naked body. Five more minutes and the book will be finished.

Using the trees as cover, the man crept nearer the house and stared at Harper sitting at a table on the terrace. It was an easy shot, even for an amateur like him. Though tempted to confront him to ensure he knew who would bring about his death, he decided against it. He was safe here. All he had to do was aim and pull the trigger. Why complicate things? Harper was the first loose end to tie up, the others would soon follow. It had taken a while to track him down after their return from Jerusalem. But a check on Ben's bank account revealed the name of a rental agency. A break in of the rental office revealed this address.

He steadied the rifle against a tree like he had been taught and aimed at his target.

Unaware of the danger he was in, Ben continued typing. He had finished quicker than he thought. He re-read the last sentence. Satisfied with what he'd written, he typed the final two words. THE END.

Ben didn't hear the shot ring out. He was dead before the sound reached him. He slumped into his chair and slid onto the deck. A neat hole in his forehead dribbled blood onto the wooden decking.

Raven cocked her head to one side and turned off the shower.

Her senses were on high alert from the sound she'd heard; a gunshot. She climbed out of the shower and still naked entered the living room. She noticed Ben's slumped form on the terrace and the neat hole in his head where the bullet had entered.

Her lover was dead.

She glimpsed movement amongst the trees at the bottom of the garden.

A man.

The assassin was making his escape.

She grabbed a large knife from the rack as she passed through the kitchen, ran onto the terrace and without glancing at Ben—he was dead and beyond her help—she sprinted across the grass that brought her to the edge of the forest. She sighted the fleeing assassin. His direction gave away his destination; the lower road where he must have parked his car. She set off at an angle to intercept him.

She ignored the pain from the twigs, stones, and thorns that dug into, cut and tore at her skin. She had a single purpose. For the moment, nothing else mattered. Fifty meters farther she drew level with the man and recognized him as one of the men who had attacked them in the Temple. She didn't waste time wondering how he'd escaped from the underground complex; his presence here was evidence the Vatican was still on their trail.

When the man saw Raven, he fired off a wild shot. Raven ignored the bullet that flew by off target and veered towards the murderer. As she approached, she detected the panic in his eyes; this was no professional assassin. Two more panicked shots and she was upon him. The knife sliced the back of his gun hand. The cut was deep. She heard and felt the blade scrape bone.

Marco screamed in pain as the rifle fell from his grasp.

Raven walked around him as she waited for him to recover.

Even in pain and in fear of his life, Marco could not help but admire the beautiful woman's naked body.

"I will ask you some questions. If I believe your answers, you'll die a quick death, but if I sense you lie, your end will be slow and excruciatingly painful."

Marco had no illusions she was lying or that here and now he would die. He just had to choose how painful that experience would be. He wished he'd never left the safety of his desk in the bowels of the Vatican.

"Did the Vatican send you?"

Marco answered truthfully. "In a fashion. I was sent on a mission to find the Temple in France and discover what it contained. Ben, as are you, Creed and the German, loose ends that needed tying up."

Raven accepted his answer. "Do *they* know our names?"

Marco shook his head, "Except for Harper, no. I was hoping to conclude the mission myself and gain favor with my superiors."

"Will they or anyone else come after us?"

Marco shrugged. "Who can say, but if they don't know you exist, that hardly seems likely. With the death of Harper, they'll probably continue to watch the Rennes-le-Château area and act on any new information they receive in the future. The passage of time means little to the Church."

"What about the Temple? Have you informed them of its location?"

Again Marco shook his head. "I planned to gain the glory of bringing out the artifacts myself."

Raven stepped forward, plunged the knife into Marco's stomach and twisted.

In agony, Marco slumped to his knees, pulling free of the knife in the process. Raven had lied. His death would not be pain-free.

Raven grabbed his tongue, sliced it off and waved it in front of his eyes. "Speak no evil."

Marco then knew what was coming. He attempted to scream, but all that came from his mouth was a gurgle of blood.

Raven stabbed him in both eyes. "See no evil." His ears were next. She dropped them on the ground in front of him and then crouched to wait for his death. It would take a while. She would then dump his body into the sea.

She glanced toward the distant cottage she could glimpse through the trees. Soon, it would be time to mourn.

Germany

"Neither Creed nor I were aware of Ben's death or his funeral, which Raven said, was a private affair until she informed us of it later. So far no one else has come looking for us, so it seems we are safe, for now, and that is where my story ends."

"Well, Pat, what can I say? Except what an amazing story. So amazing in fact, I'm not sure anyone will believe it."

"Then maybe you should write it up as a novel rather than nonfiction," Pat suggested, as the man collected up his things.

"That's not a bad idea. I could change your names to protect you all."

"I have a good title you may want to use, *The tomb, the temple, the treasure*."

The interviewer stood. "Not bad." He was eager to begin writing up the story. "Thanks for your time and for trusting me with your story. I promise you I'll do it, and Ben, justice."

Pat stood, shook the man's offered hand and led him around the side of the house to the man's car at the front. He waited while the man climbed into his car and started the engine.

"Goodbye, Pat, and thanks again."

Pat watched him drive off along the driveway, turn onto the road and disappear from sight. He returned to the terrace, picked up his bottle of beer and held it up to the sky. "Cheers, Ben." He drained the bottle.

"So it's done," said Raven, exiting from the house with Creed and stood beside him.

"It's done. I think he'll write it as a novel."

"As long as Ben's story is revealed he can write it in any form he likes. What was his name?"

"He has the same name and initials as Ben, Ben Hammott."

"You think it will work?" Pat asked.

"Once the information is out there what further interest could we hold for the Vatican or anyone else?" Creed answered. "It's the artifacts they want so let them spend their time and resources trying to obtain them, but if they do decide to come after us, we'll be ready."

All three stood in silence for a few moments.

"It's been a dangerous wild ride most of the time, hanging out with you lot," said Pat, "but to tell the truth, I kind of miss it."

Raven smiled, "Yeah, I know what you mean. Maybe we can find another mystery to solve together." She gazed up at the few clouds moving across an otherwise clear blue sky. "Wherever Ben is, I'm sure he's having another one of his crazy adventures."

Pat smiled, "I don't doubt it for a second."

EPILOGUE

Rosslyn, Scotland.

GARRET **PLACED THE** tip of the large crowbar between the door and frame above the lock and pushed. With a splintering of wood, the door popped open.

Hugh pushed Garret aside, pulled the door open and shone the bright flashlight into the darkness. Steps led down just as Harper had described. News of his death had reached him two weeks before, shortly before he left the hospital. The damage the car had caused to his body had taken time to heal. Though not completely recovered, he was impatient to explore the catacombs beneath the chapel. He turned to Silas, who waited in the main chamber of the tomb and glanced at the robed men waiting in the graveyard. "Bring them in."

The men filed into the tomb and Hugh ushered them down the steps. After everyone was inside, Silas ordered Garret to guard the entrance and followed the men down the steps.

Hugh stood at the bottom of the steps and joined his light to the others roaming through the tunnel and over the yellow powder that covered the floor and rose into the air from their movements, just as Harper had said it would. Though he wondered at its purpose, his eagerness to explore the rooms below pushed any concerns he had aside. He slipped a hand inside a pocket in his robe, pulled out a simple white, paper dust mask and placed it over his nose and mouth. His followers copied his actions.

Hugh led them through the yellow powder.

By the time Silas reached the bottom of the steps, the yellow powder, disturbed by those who had gone before, swirled like fog. He glanced at the front of the column and stepped into the swirling dust.

Hugh faltered and reached out a hand to steady himself against the wall. He coughed and fell to his knees.

Those directly behind him, believing Hugh's recent injuries were responsible for his fall, stepped forward to help. Two men grabbed Hugh under the arms, but before they could raise him to his feet, they collapsed to the ground beside him.

Slowly, a wave of collapsing bodies rippled down the column of robed men as one by one they succumbed to the poisonous powder.

Silas saw it coming and immediately knew Harper had tricked them.

The yellow powder was death.

He spun and rushed back along the tunnel and up the steps. Halfway up he staggered and fell. He called out Garret's name, hoarsely.

Garret appeared in the doorway at the top of the stairs and stared down at the fallen man.

"The powder…is…poison," Silas croaked. "Help…me."

Garret noticed the yellow powder covering Silas and slowly closed the door.

Silas, helpless to do anything, watched the door seal him in.

He cursed Harper with his last breath.

Garret closed the secret door that formed the back wall of the tomb, repositioned the statue in front and stepped out into the graveyard. He closed and locked the tomb's metal door and slipped the key into his pocket.

He gazed up at the stars peppering the night sky and smiled.

He was the Boss now.

He whistled a happy tune as he strolled towards his newly acquired castle.

THE END

ALTERNATIVE FUN ENDING

Heaven

JESUS GLANCED AT the approaching man and smiled. "Hey, Ben, how's it going?"

Ben sat beside Jesus. "So...this is Heaven?"

"Of course, what did you expect?"

Ben shrugged. "I'm not sure, but it's so white and boring, and the sound of those harps constantly playing is driving me mad."

Jesus laughed. "It's better than the alternative."

Ben shrugged. "I'm not so sure, at least there's a chance to escape from that place."

Jesus stared at Ben, a worried frown upon his face. "If you believe the legends, that is."

"In my experience myths and legends often have an element of truth. I thought Heaven was a myth and yet here I am, talking to Jesus Christ."

"What's on your mind? You are not seriously considering going *down there!*"

"I think I am. Heaven is turning out to be my Hell, so maybe Hell will be my Heaven."

Jesus shook his head in disbelief. "Hell is a terrible prison made of bone, flesh, blood, pain, and fear. A place with agonies you can't even imagine."

"Yeah, I've heard the stories. Heaven was also supposed to be a wonderful place and yet... Have you ever been down there to see these things for yourself?"

"Well no, not personally, though we have groups of specially trained angels who can bypass Hell's defenses, allowing them to enter and retrieve human souls that have suffered long enough or have been sent to Hell by mistake. They confirm what I've said is true."

Ben had become encouraged upon hearing this. "How often do these angels go to Hell?"

Jesus shrugged. "Not my department."

"You said you owed me for reuniting you with your wife and returning your bodies to Jerusalem."

Jesus frowned. "I did. Why?"

"I want to go to Hell with the next group of angels. I'll also need a few things to take with me." Ben explained all to Jesus.

"Are you sure about this?" Jesus asked in disbelief when Ben had outlined his plan. He gazed into Ben's eyes and saw that he was. "Okay, okay, I'll make the arrangements, but you know there's no coming back; this is strictly a one-way ticket."

Ben smiled. "I know the risks."

Jesus shook his head. "No, Ben, I'm not sure you do."

Hell

ASMODEUS WAS CHAINED to a wall and unable to fend off the smaller demons pitchforks stabbing at his flesh. It was a part of his punishment for his failure during his time on earth; there was much worse to come. He closed his eyes against the constant pain and cursed the humans responsible for his torment. There was a swishing sound, then the pain abated. He opened his eyes to see why and was greeted with a sight he could never have imagined. It was not the headless corpses of the seven demons convulsing on the ground pumping green blood that had caused the astonished look to appear on his face, it was the man who stood before him who was responsible.

Ben nodded at Asmodeus. "Hello…Demon."

Recovering from the shock, but still confused, Asmodeus replied, "Hello…Human. Why are you here?"

Ben placed the sword tip on the ground, casually rested his hands on the pommel and smiled. "I need your help."

THE END?

NOTE FROM AUTHOR

Thank you for purchasing and reading my book. I hope you found it an enjoyable experience. If so, could you please spread the word and perhaps consider posting a review on your place of purchase. It is the single most powerful thing you can do for me. It raises my visibility and many more people will learn about my book.

If you would like to send feedback, drop me a line, or be added to my mailing list to receive notifications of my new books, receive limited free advance review copies and occasional free books, please contact me at: benhammott@gmail.com

BOOKS BY AUTHOR

ICE RIFT & ICE RIFT – SALVAGE & ICE RIFT - SIBERIA

In Antarctica everyone can hear you scream!

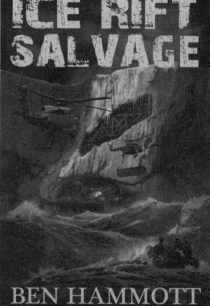

Something ancient dwells beneath the ice...
Humans have always looked to the stars for signs of
Extraterrestrials.
They have been looking in the wrong place.
They are already here. Entombed beneath Antarctic ice for thousands
of years.
The ice is melting and soon they will be free.
Details and concept art at www.benhammottbooks.com

Sarcophagus

Their mistake wasn't finding it, it was bringing it back!

"The Mummy, meets Relic, meets Alien in this scary action driven horror thriller."

Action adventure horror set in the Amazon jungle, on the high seas and London, England.

Concealed in a remote area of the Amazon jungle is something the Mayans thought so dangerous they built a secret prison to entomb it. It remained undiscovered for centuries.

When a maverick archaeologist hears rumours of a mysterious lost city, he heads into the Amazon jungle, determined to find it.

He soon learns that some things are best left unfound. The dangerous past the Mayans tried so hard to bury, is about to become our terrifying future.

Extended book blurb:
When an archaeologist stumbles across a mysterious Mayan city in a remote part of the Amazon jungle, he informs the British museum funding his expedition of the discovery.

When fellow archaeologist, Greyson Bradshaw, receives news of the discovery, he jumps at the chance to travel to the Amazon jungle to collect artifacts for the forthcoming Mayan exhibition he is arranging.

The two archaeologists explore the city's subterranean levels and enter Xibalba, the Mayan underworld. In a secret chamber they discover something hidden away for centuries; a sarcophagus. Realizing its potential as a centerpiece for his exhibition, Greyson transports the sarcophagus and other artifacts back to England. The past is about to come alive.

"Hammott is fast becoming the master of monster horror. Read his Ice Rift books and you'll know what I mean. Fantastic escapism."

"The author has such a creative mind it's scary. The monsters he brings alive in his books are simply terrifying. Add atmospheric locations, characters you root for, racked up tension, a thrilling plot that forbids you to stop reading, and you have Sarcophagus."

HORROR ISLAND
Where All Your Nightmares Come True

Cocooned in rock, the alien organism was propelled into space when the dying planet exploded.
Dormant for many millennia as it travelled through the cosmos, it headed towards a blue planet.
A fiery spectacle announced its arrival when it entered Earth's atmosphere and crashed to the surface.
Trapped on an island it couldn't escape from, it grew, evolved, hunted and spawned.
Time passed. Human's arrived...

Almost sixty years after it was abandoned by the mysterious movie director, Ezra Houghton, successful horror writer Zane Baloc comes into possession of the remote and infamous Horror Island.

Believing it will provide the perfect inspiration for a new horror novel, he wastes no time gathering a small team together to travel to the island to investigate. He plans to spend a few weeks there soaking up the atmosphere and exploring the extravagant horror themed movie sets Ezra spent seven years creating.

Stranded miles from help, the team soon discover they are not alone and the rumours of strange, unearthly creatures inhabiting the island are more than just a myth.

Their mission of exploration and wonderment turns into a bloody fight for survival against the island's monstrous inhabitants.

Stranded on the island filled with fear inspiring buildings and vicious, alien infected monsters, survival will be difficult. Escape unlikely.

The Lost City Book Series

EL DORADO Book 1: Search for the Lost City - An Unexpected
Adventure
EL DORADO - Book 2: Fabled Lost Treasure - The Secret City
**One of the world's most legendary and elusive treasures, sought
after for centuries.**
An ancient mystery
A Lost Treasure
A Hidden City
An impossible location
An unimaginable adventure

Included in Aztec and Mayan legends, Conquistadors had heard
rumours of its existence when exploring the New World, but never
found it.
During World War 2, Nazi inspired archaeologists were convinced
they had pinpointed its location. They packed a U-Boat with supplies
and set a course for the Amazon Jungle. They disappeared!

Many adventurers eager to claim the legendary gold as their own entered one of the most inhospitable places on earth, the Amazon Jungle. Most were never seen again!

And yet the exact location of El Dorado and its fantastic hoard of Mayan, Aztec and Inca treasure so many have dreamed of finding, remains a mystery. Any who may have stumbled upon it never returned to tell the tale. It was as if someone, or something, was protecting it...

Details of the author's books can be found at
www.benhammottbooks.com

Made in the USA
Middletown, DE
01 March 2020